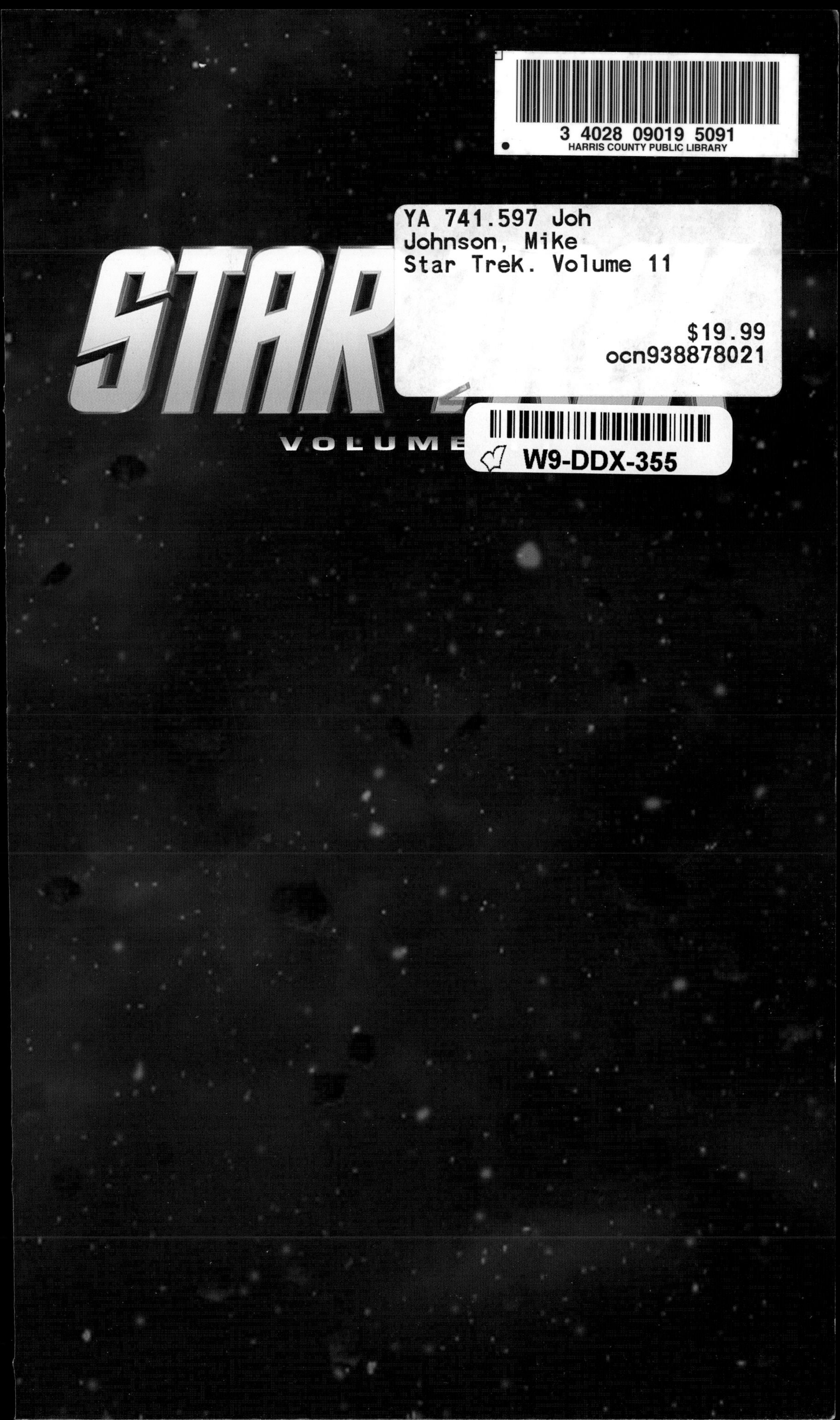
STAR
VOLUME

Story Consultant:

ROBERTO ORCI

Cover by

JOE CORRONEY

Back Cover by

TONY SHASTEEN

Collection Edits by

JUSTIN EISINGER and ALONZO SIMON

Collection Design by

CLAUDIA CHONG

Star Trek created by Gene Roddenberry.
Special thanks to Risa Kessler and John Van Citters of CBS Consumer Products for their invaluable assistance.

For international rights, contact licensing@idwpublishing.co

ISBN: 978-1-63140-521-1

19 18 17 16   1 2 3

Ted Adams, CEO & Publisher
Greg Goldstein, President & COO
Robbie Robbins, EVP/Sr. Graphic Artist
Chris Ryall, Chief Creative Officer/Editor-in-Chief
Matthew Ruzicka, CPA, Chief Financial Officer
Dirk Wood, VP of Marketing
Lorelei Bunjes, VP of Digital Services
Jeff Webber, VP of Licensing, Digital and Subsidiary Rights
Jerry Bennington, VP of New Product Development

www.IDWPUBLISHING.com

Facebook: **facebook.com/idwpublishing**
Twitter: **@idwpublishing**
YouTube: **youtube.com/idwpublishing**
Tumblr: **tumblr.idwpublishing.com**
Instagram: **instagram.com/idwpublishing**

Originally published as STAR TREK issues #46–49 and STAR TREK: FLESH AND STONE.

STAR TREK ®

VOLUME 11

Written by
MIKE JOHNSON

THE THOLIAN WEBS

Art by
RACHEL STOTT

Colors by
DAVIDE MASTROLONARDO

Letters by
NEIL UYETAKE and ROBBIE ROBBINS

DEITY

Art by
TONY SHASTEEN

Colors by
DAVIDE MASTROLONARDO

Letters by
NEIL UYETAKE

FLESH AND STONE

Created for the Qualcomm Tricorder XPRIZE competition. Learn more about XPRIZE at xprize.org!

Written by
SCOTT AND DAVID TIPTON

Art by
SHARP BROTHERS

Colors by
ANDREW ELDER

Letters by
NEIL UYETAKE

Consultants
Rob Hollander and David Zweig

Series Edits by
SARAH GAYDOS

THE THOLIAN WEBS

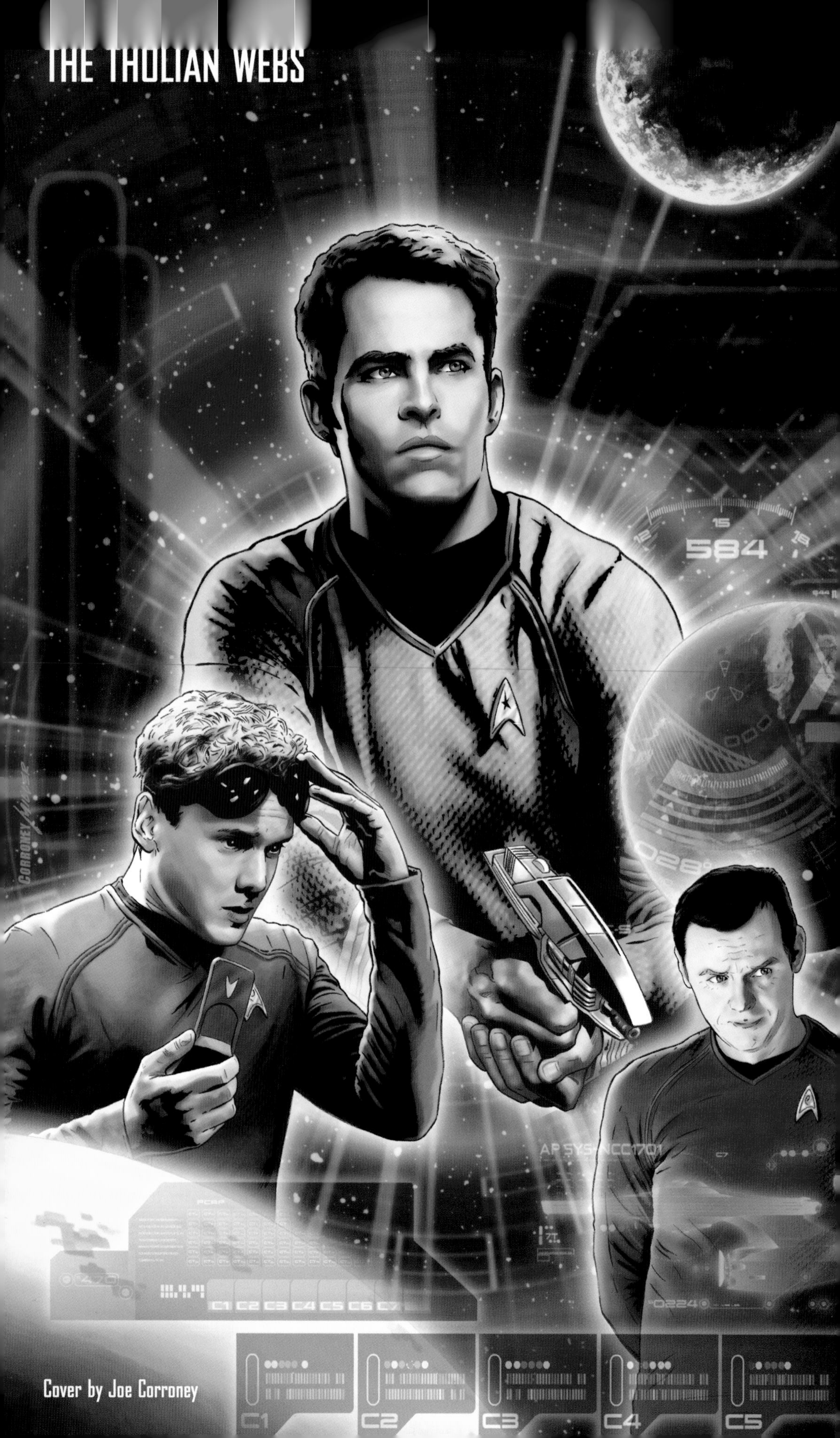
15
584
028°
AP SYS NCC1701
C1 C2 C3 C4 C5 C6 C7
0224
C1
C2
C3
C4
C5

Cover by Joe Corroney

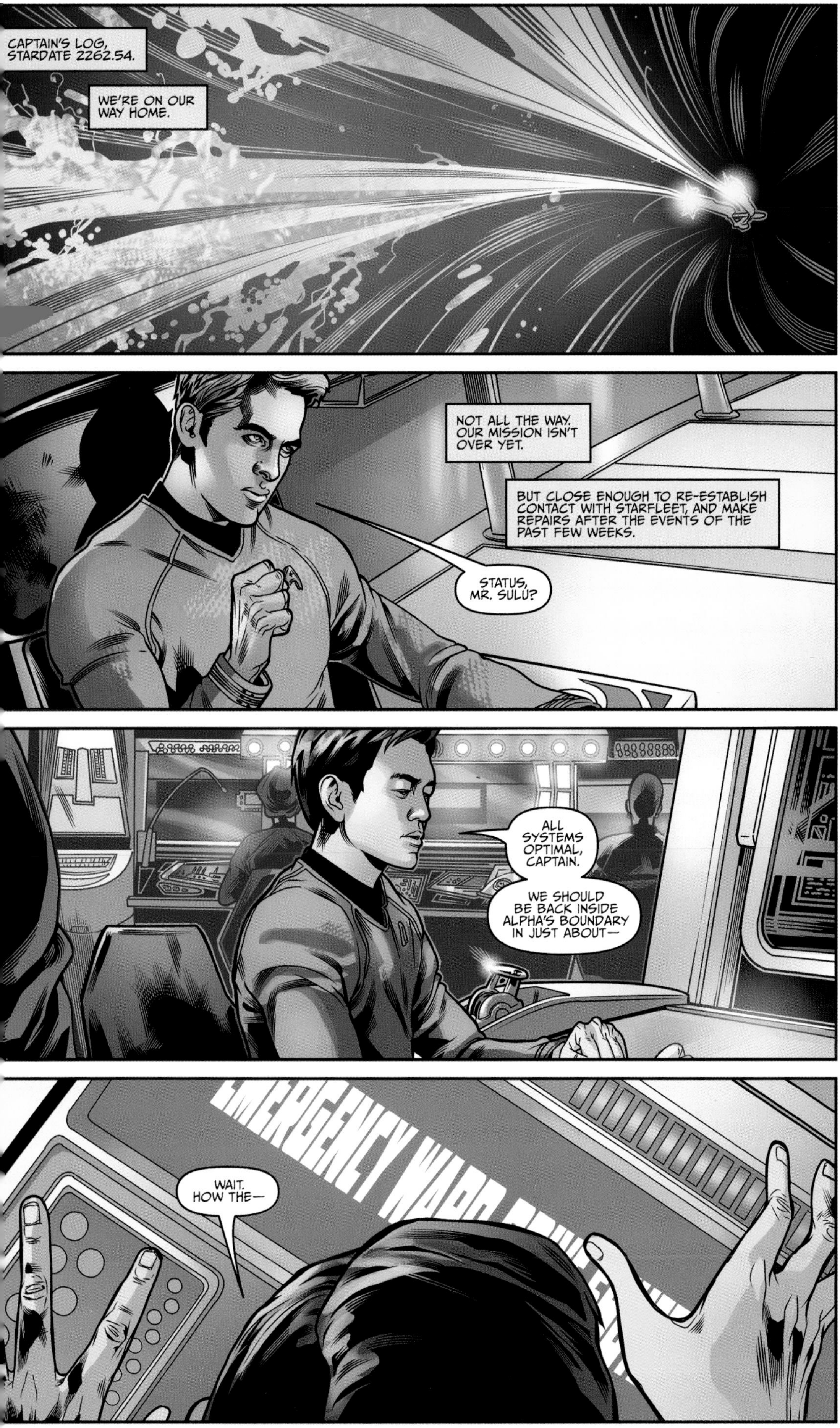
CAPTAIN'S LOG, STARDATE 2262.54.
WE'RE ON OUR WAY HOME.
NOT ALL THE WAY. OUR MISSION ISN'T OVER YET.
BUT CLOSE ENOUGH TO RE-ESTABLISH CONTACT WITH STARFLEET, AND MAKE REPAIRS AFTER THE EVENTS OF THE PAST FEW WEEKS.
STATUS, MR. SULU?
ALL SYSTEMS OPTIMAL, CAPTAIN.
WE SHOULD BE BACK INSIDE ALPHA'S BOUNDARY IN JUST ABOUT—
WAIT. HOW THE—

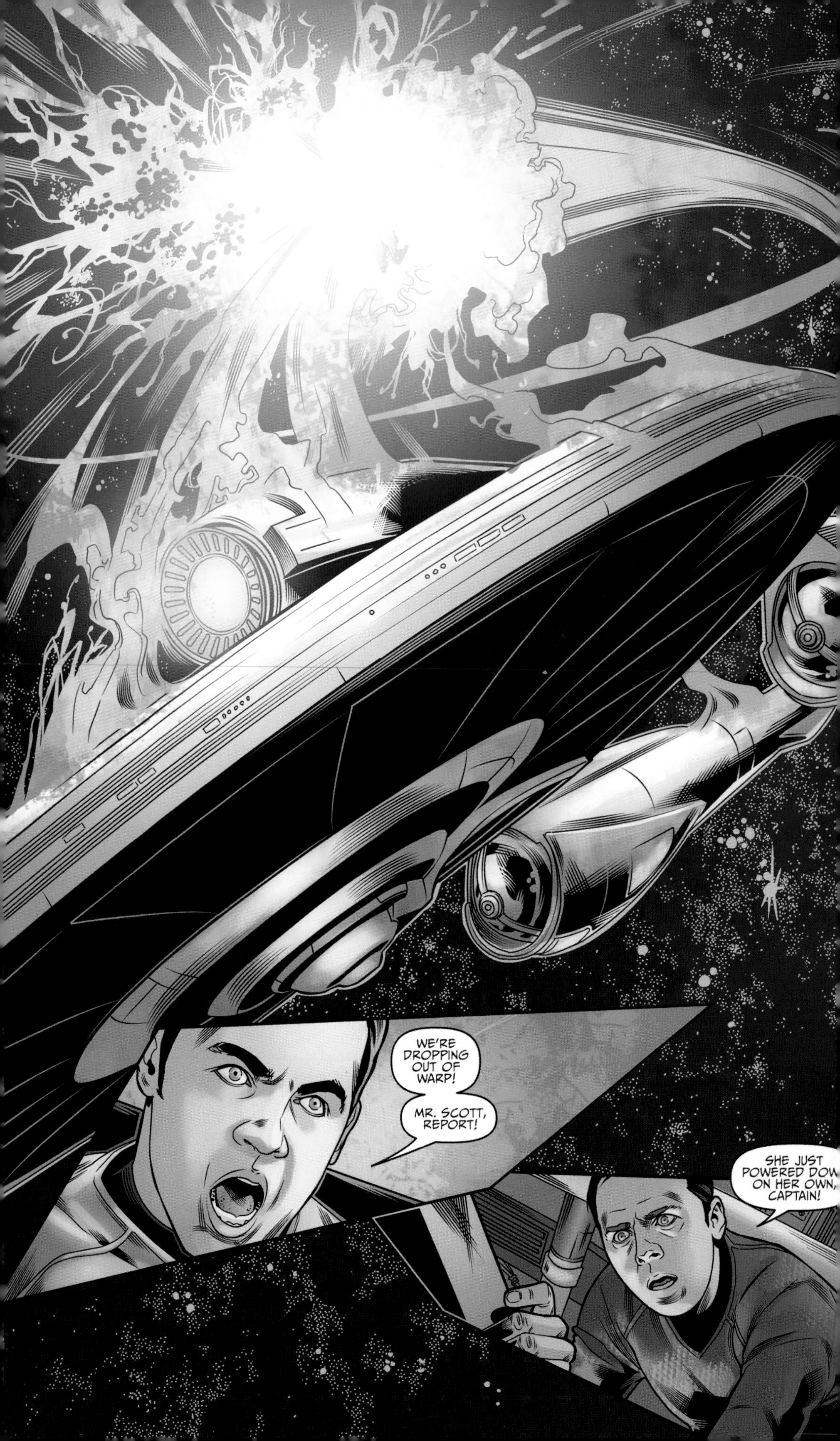
WE'RE DROPPING OUT OF WARP!
MR. SCOTT, REPORT!
SHE JUST POWERED DOW ON HER OWN, CAPTAIN!

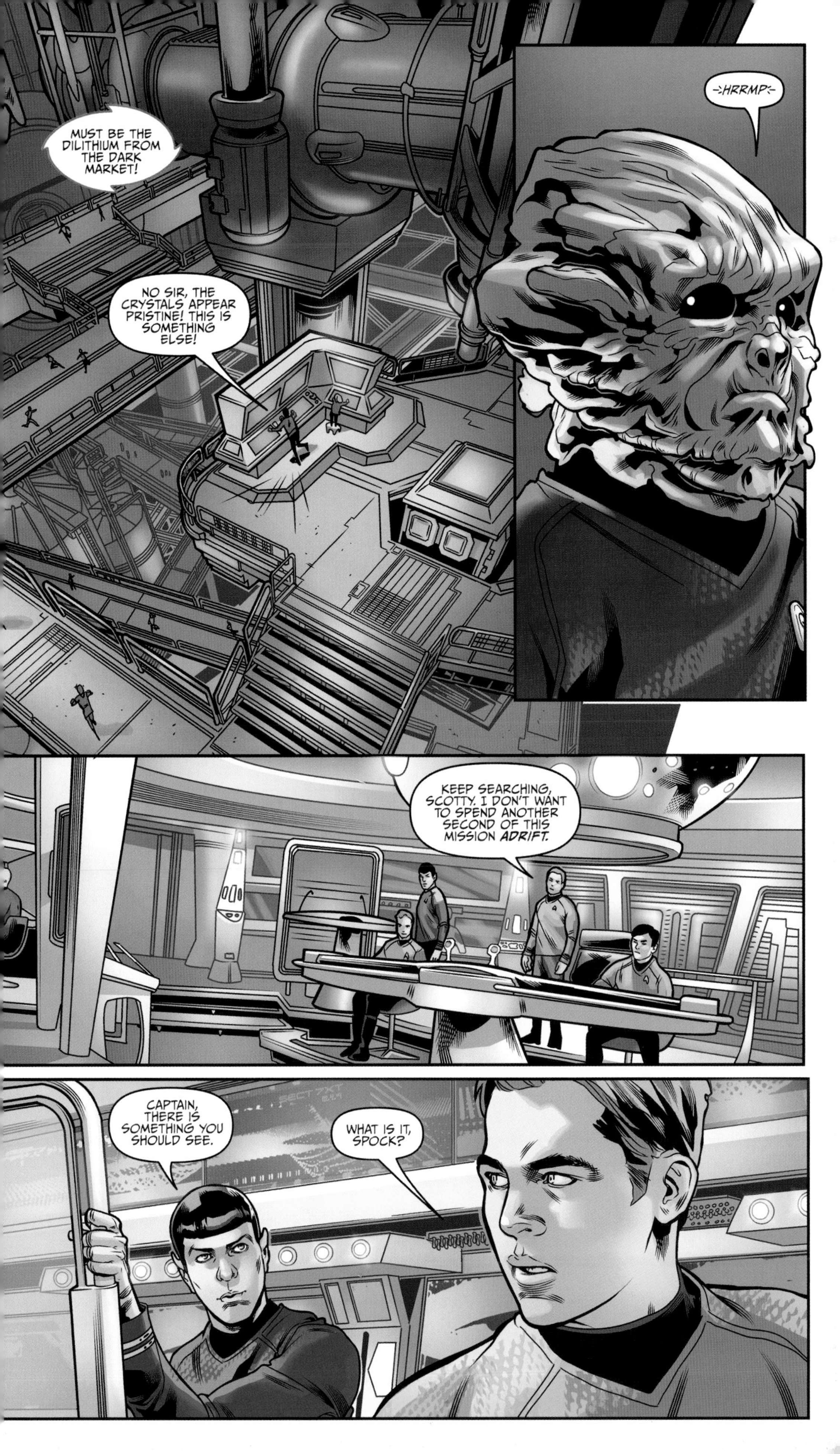
MUST BE THE DILITHIUM FROM THE DARK MARKET!
NO SIR, THE CRYSTALS APPEAR PRISTINE! THIS IS SOMETHING ELSE!
-HRRMP-
KEEP SEARCHING, SCOTTY. I DON'T WANT TO SPEND ANOTHER SECOND OF THIS MISSION *ADRIFT.*
CAPTAIN, THERE IS SOMETHING YOU SHOULD SEE.
WHAT IS IT, SPOCK?

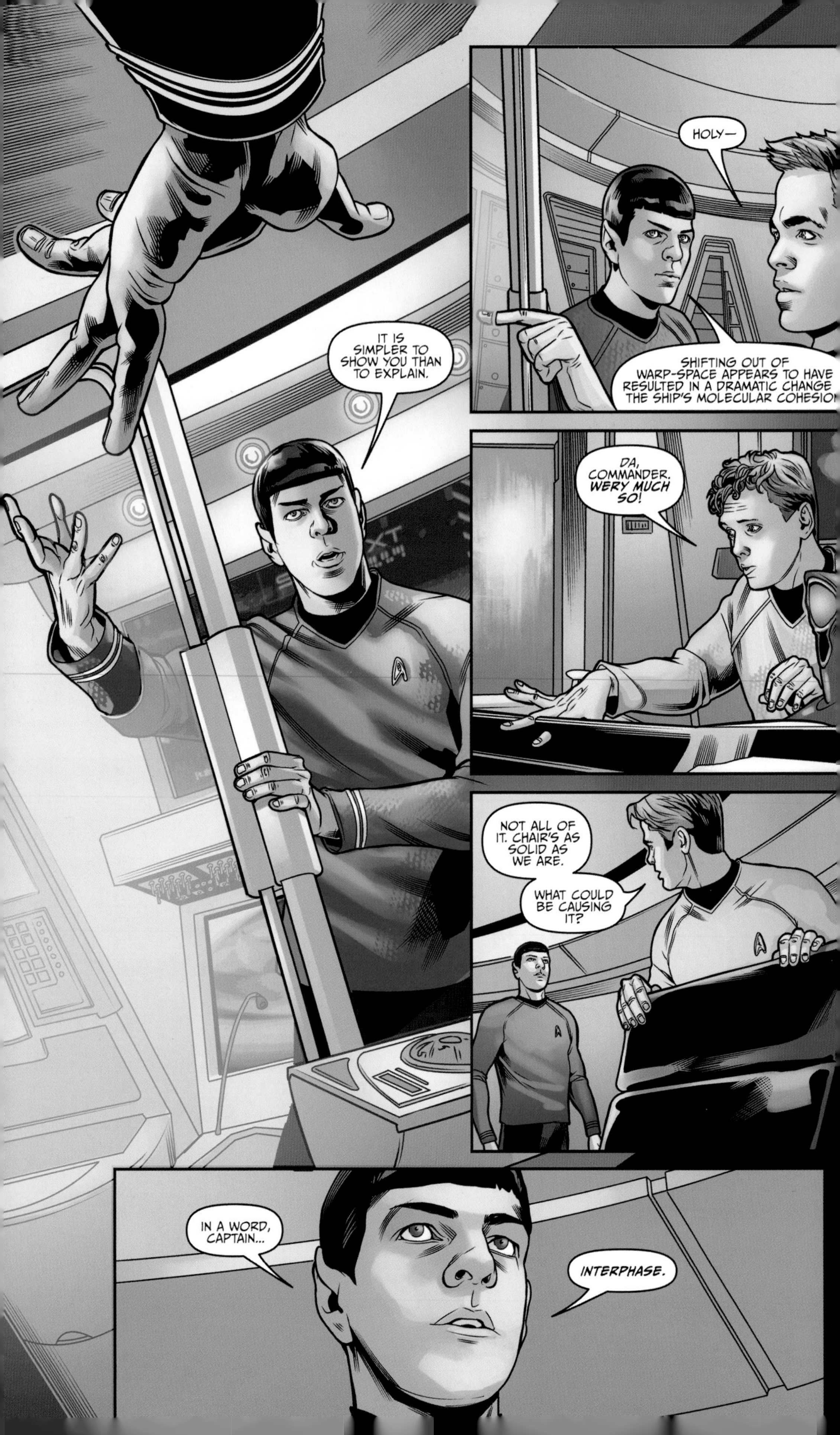
IT IS SIMPLER TO SHOW YOU THAN TO EXPLAIN.
HOLY—
SHIFTING OUT OF WARP-SPACE APPEARS TO HAVE RESULTED IN A DRAMATIC CHANGE THE SHIP'S MOLECULAR COHESIO
DA, COMMANDER. WERY MUCH SO!
NOT ALL OF IT. CHAIR'S AS SOLID AS WE ARE.
WHAT COULD BE CAUSING IT?
IN A WORD, CAPTAIN...
INTERPHASE.

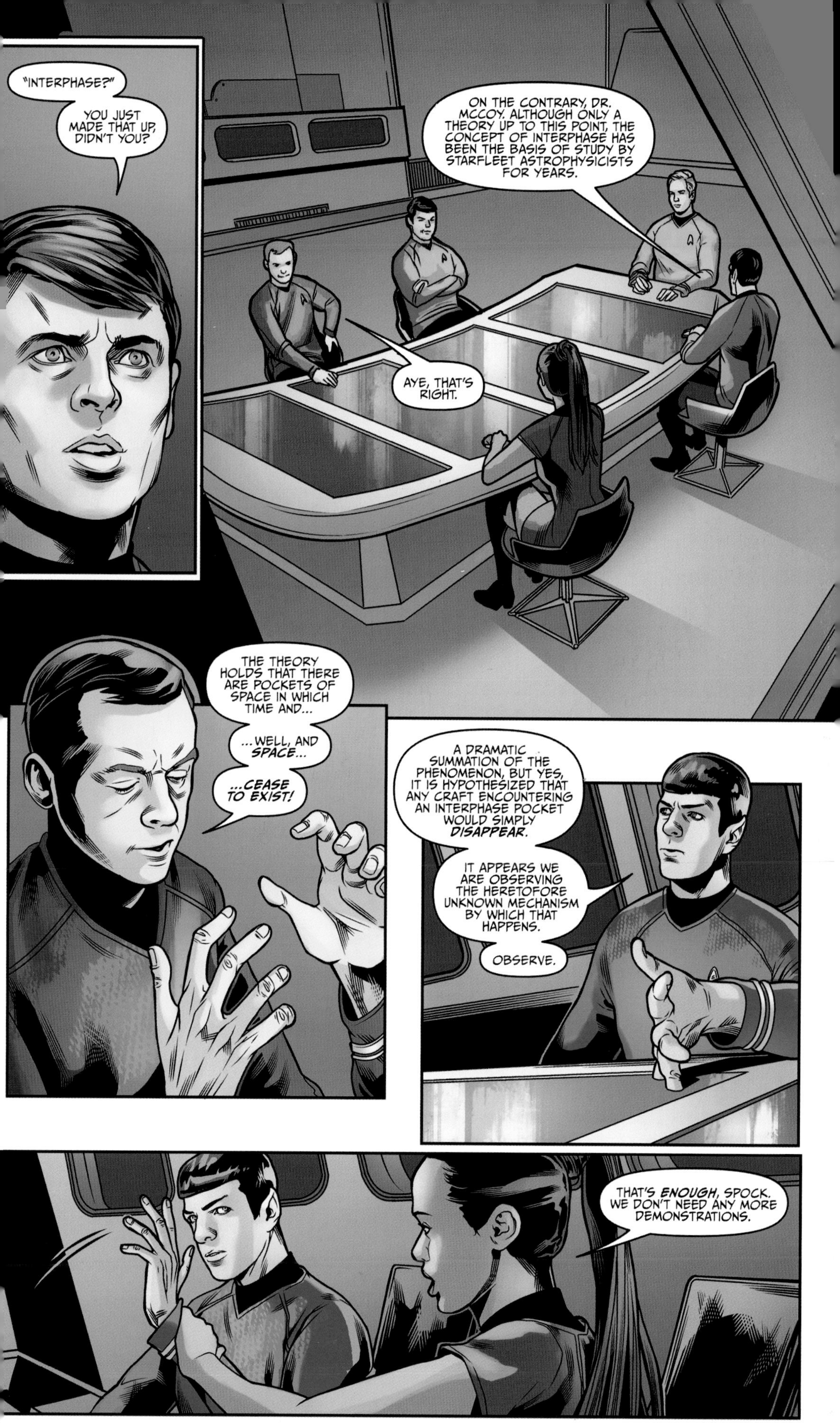
"INTERPHASE?"
YOU JUST MADE THAT UP, DIDN'T YOU?
ON THE CONTRARY, DR. MCCOY. ALTHOUGH ONLY A THEORY UP TO THIS POINT, THE CONCEPT OF INTERPHASE HAS BEEN THE BASIS OF STUDY BY STARFLEET ASTROPHYSICISTS FOR YEARS.
AYE, THAT'S RIGHT.
THE THEORY HOLDS THAT THERE ARE POCKETS OF SPACE IN WHICH TIME AND...
...WELL, AND *SPACE*...
...CEASE TO EXIST!
A DRAMATIC SUMMATION OF THE PHENOMENON, BUT YES, IT IS HYPOTHESIZED THAT ANY CRAFT ENCOUNTERING AN INTERPHASE POCKET WOULD SIMPLY ***DISAPPEAR***.
IT APPEARS WE ARE OBSERVING THE HERETOFORE UNKNOWN MECHANISM BY WHICH THAT HAPPENS.
OBSERVE.
THAT'S ***ENOUGH***, SPOCK. WE DON'T NEED ANY MORE DEMONSTRATIONS.

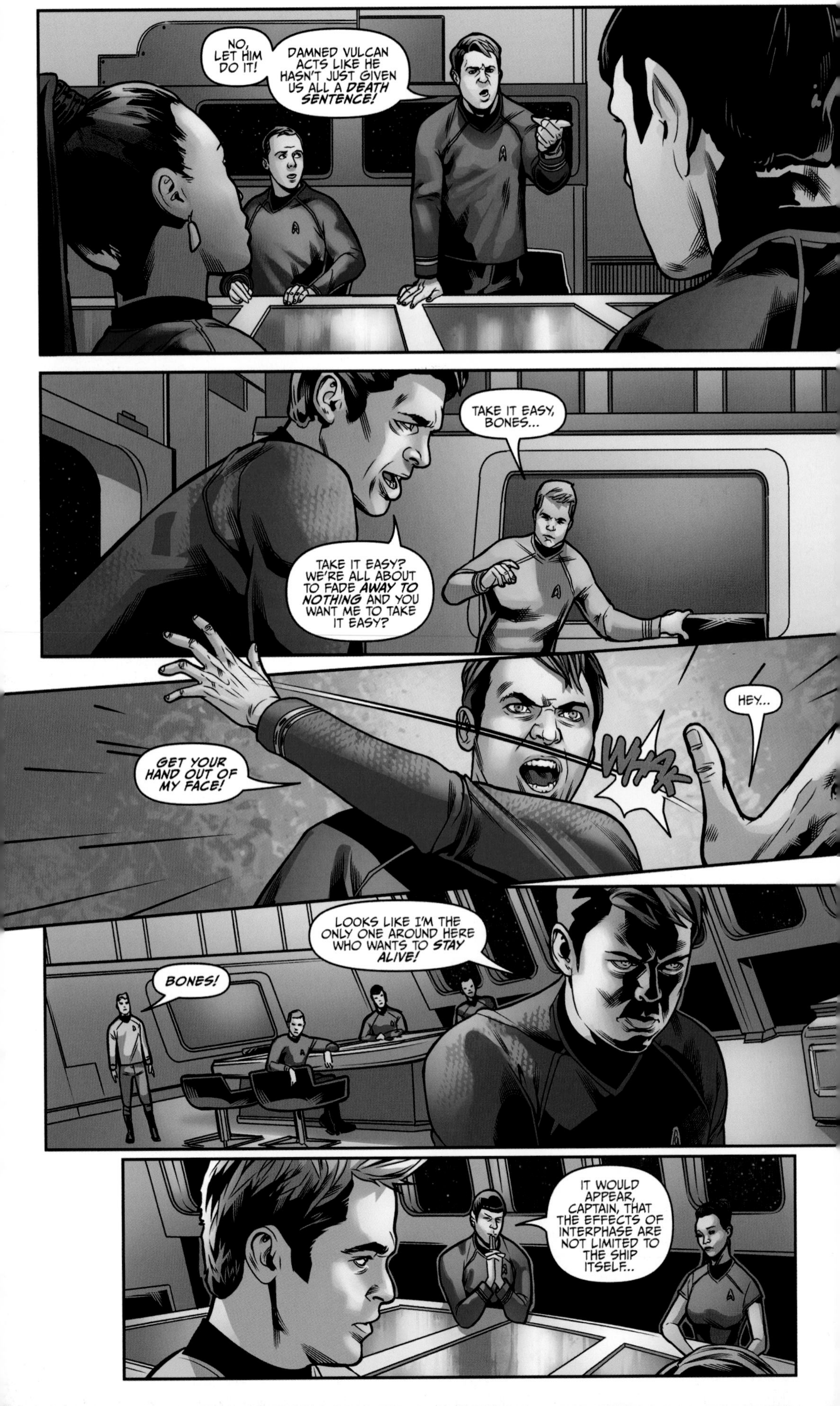
NO, LET HIM DO IT!
DAMNED VULCAN ACTS LIKE HE HASN'T JUST GIVEN US ALL A DEATH SENTENCE!
TAKE IT EASY, BONES...
TAKE IT EASY? WE'RE ALL ABOUT TO FADE AWAY TO NOTHING AND YOU WANT ME TO TAKE IT EASY?
HEY...
GET YOUR HAND OUT OF MY FACE!
WHAK
LOOKS LIKE I'M THE ONLY ONE AROUND HERE WHO WANTS TO STAY ALIVE!
BONES!
IT WOULD APPEAR, CAPTAIN, THAT THE EFFECTS OF INTERPHASE ARE NOT LIMITED TO THE SHIP ITSELF...

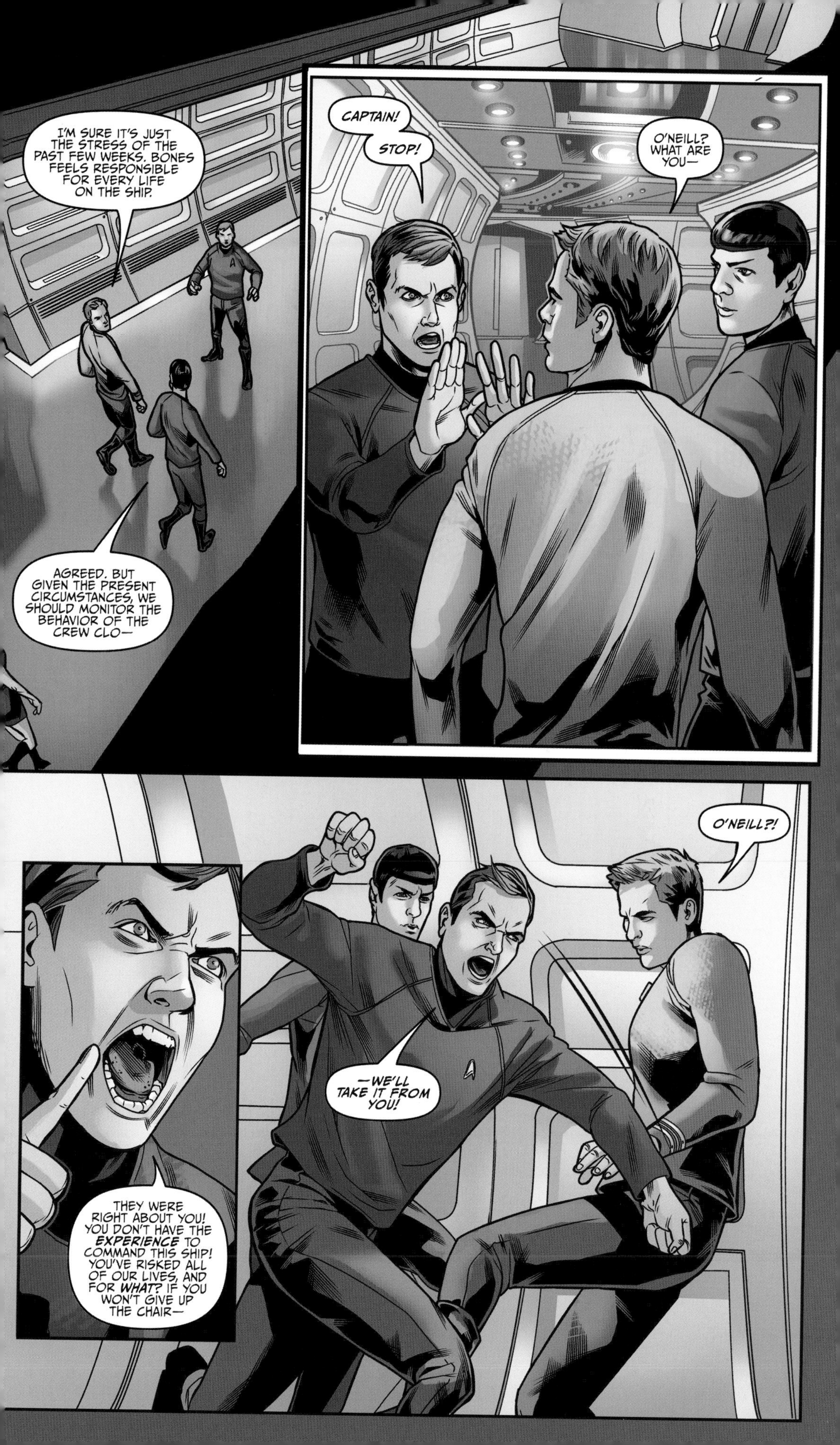
I'M SURE IT'S JUST THE STRESS OF THE PAST FEW WEEKS. BONES FEELS RESPONSIBLE FOR EVERY LIFE ON THE SHIP.
AGREED. BUT GIVEN THE PRESENT CIRCUMSTANCES, WE SHOULD MONITOR THE BEHAVIOR OF THE CREW CLO—
CAPTAIN!
STOP!
O'NEILL? WHAT ARE YOU—
THEY WERE RIGHT ABOUT YOU! YOU DON'T HAVE THE EXPERIENCE TO COMMAND THIS SHIP! YOU'VE RISKED ALL OF OUR LIVES, AND FOR WHAT? IF YOU WON'T GIVE UP THE CHAIR—
—WE'LL TAKE IT FROM YOU!
O'NEILL?!

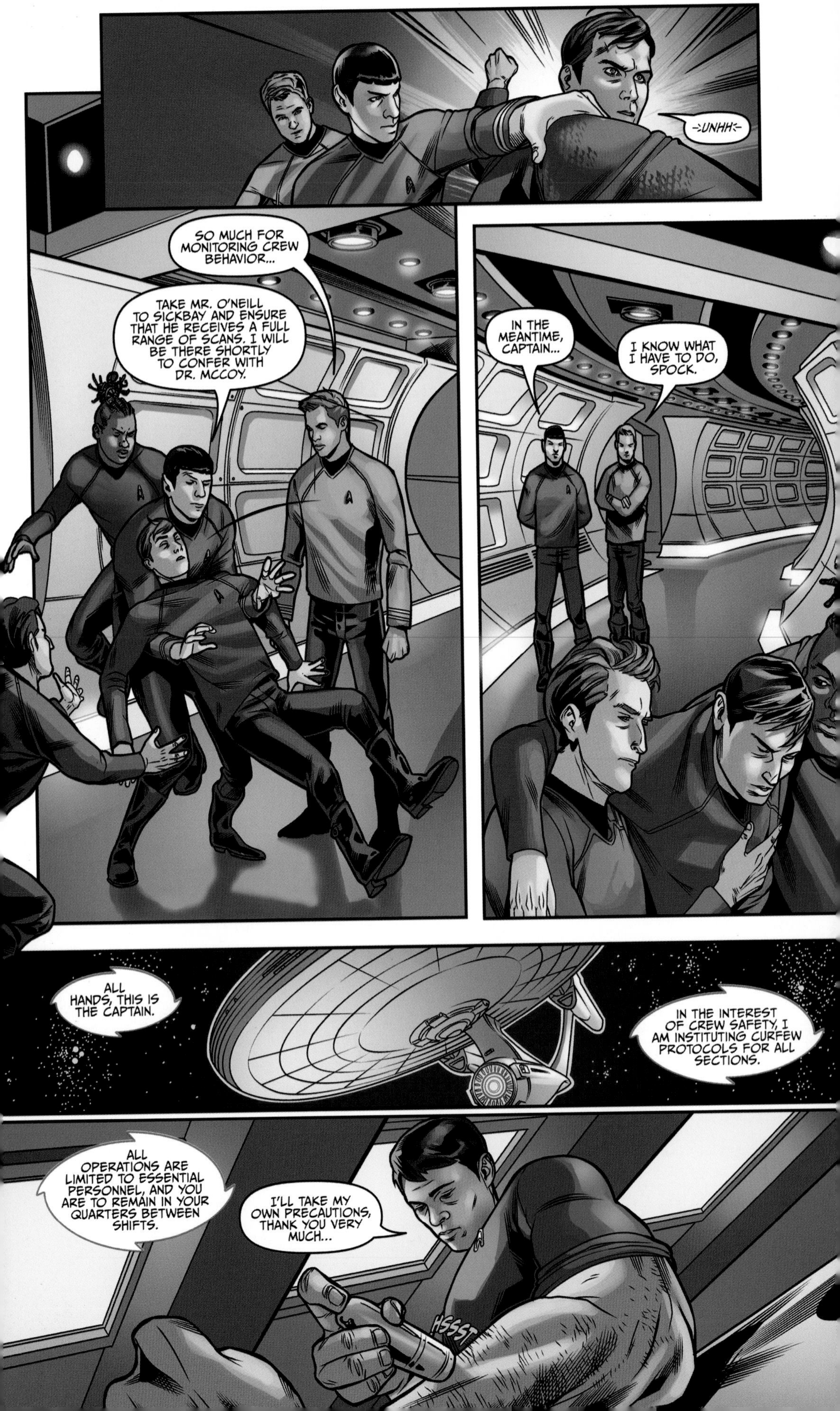
-UNHH-
SO MUCH FOR MONITORING CREW BEHAVIOR...
TAKE MR. O'NEILL TO SICKBAY AND ENSURE THAT HE RECEIVES A FULL RANGE OF SCANS. I WILL BE THERE SHORTLY TO CONFER WITH DR. MCCOY.
IN THE MEANTIME, CAPTAIN...
I KNOW WHAT I HAVE TO DO, SPOCK.
ALL HANDS, THIS IS THE CAPTAIN.
IN THE INTEREST OF CREW SAFETY, I AM INSTITUTING CURFEW PROTOCOLS FOR ALL SECTIONS.
ALL OPERATIONS ARE LIMITED TO ESSENTIAL PERSONNEL, AND YOU ARE TO REMAIN IN YOUR QUARTERS BETWEEN SHIFTS.
I'LL TAKE MY OWN PRECAUTIONS, THANK YOU VERY MUCH...
HSSST

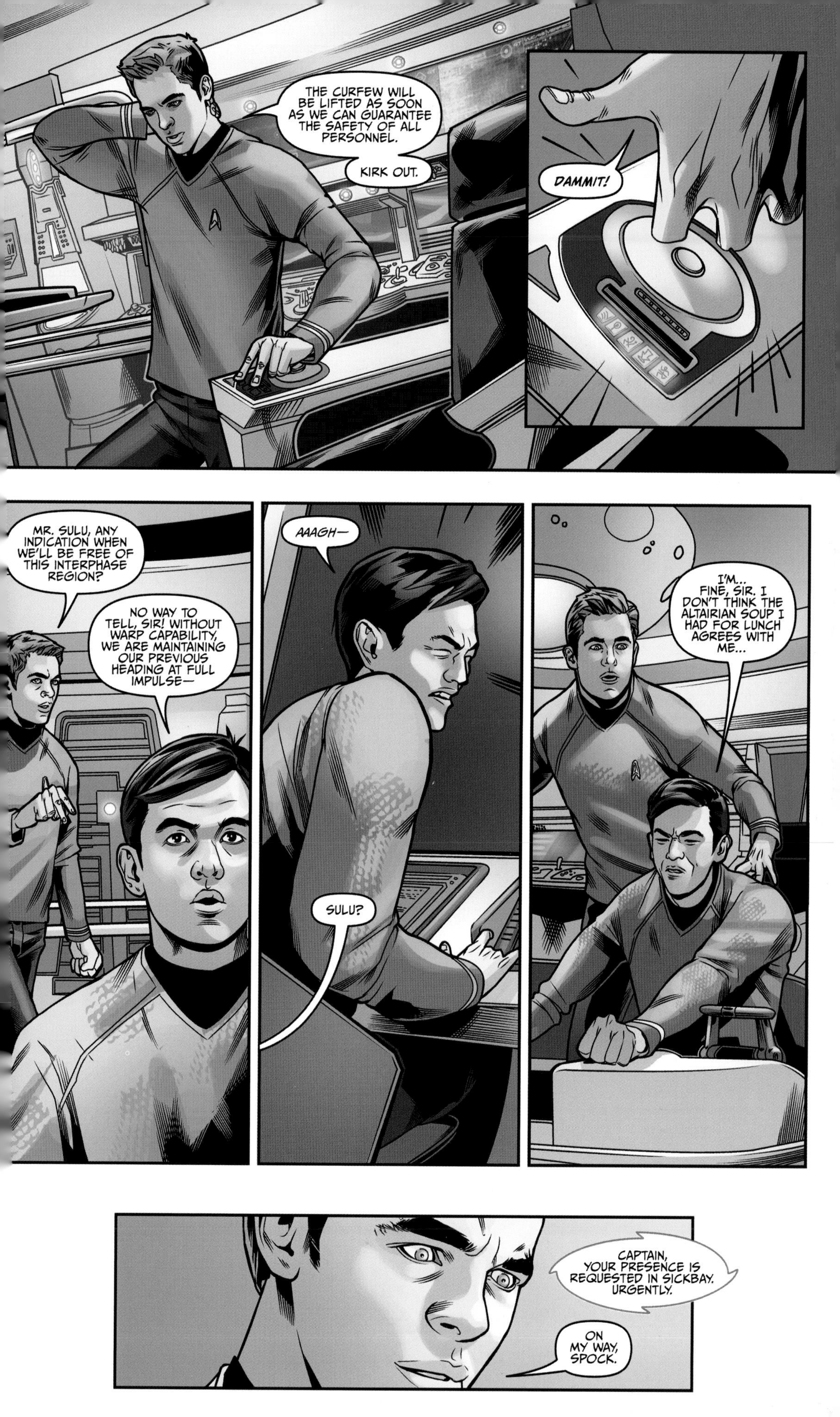
THE CURFEW WILL BE LIFTED AS SOON AS WE CAN GUARANTEE THE SAFETY OF ALL PERSONNEL.
KIRK OUT.
DAMMIT!
MR. SULU, ANY INDICATION WHEN WE'LL BE FREE OF THIS INTERPHASE REGION?
NO WAY TO TELL, SIR! WITHOUT WARP CAPABILITY, WE ARE MAINTAINING OUR PREVIOUS HEADING AT FULL IMPULSE—
AAAGH—
SULU?
I'M... FINE, SIR. I DON'T THINK THE ALTAIRIAN SOUP I HAD FOR LUNCH AGREES WITH ME...
CAPTAIN, YOUR PRESENCE IS REQUESTED IN SICKBAY. URGENTLY.
ON MY WAY, SPOCK.

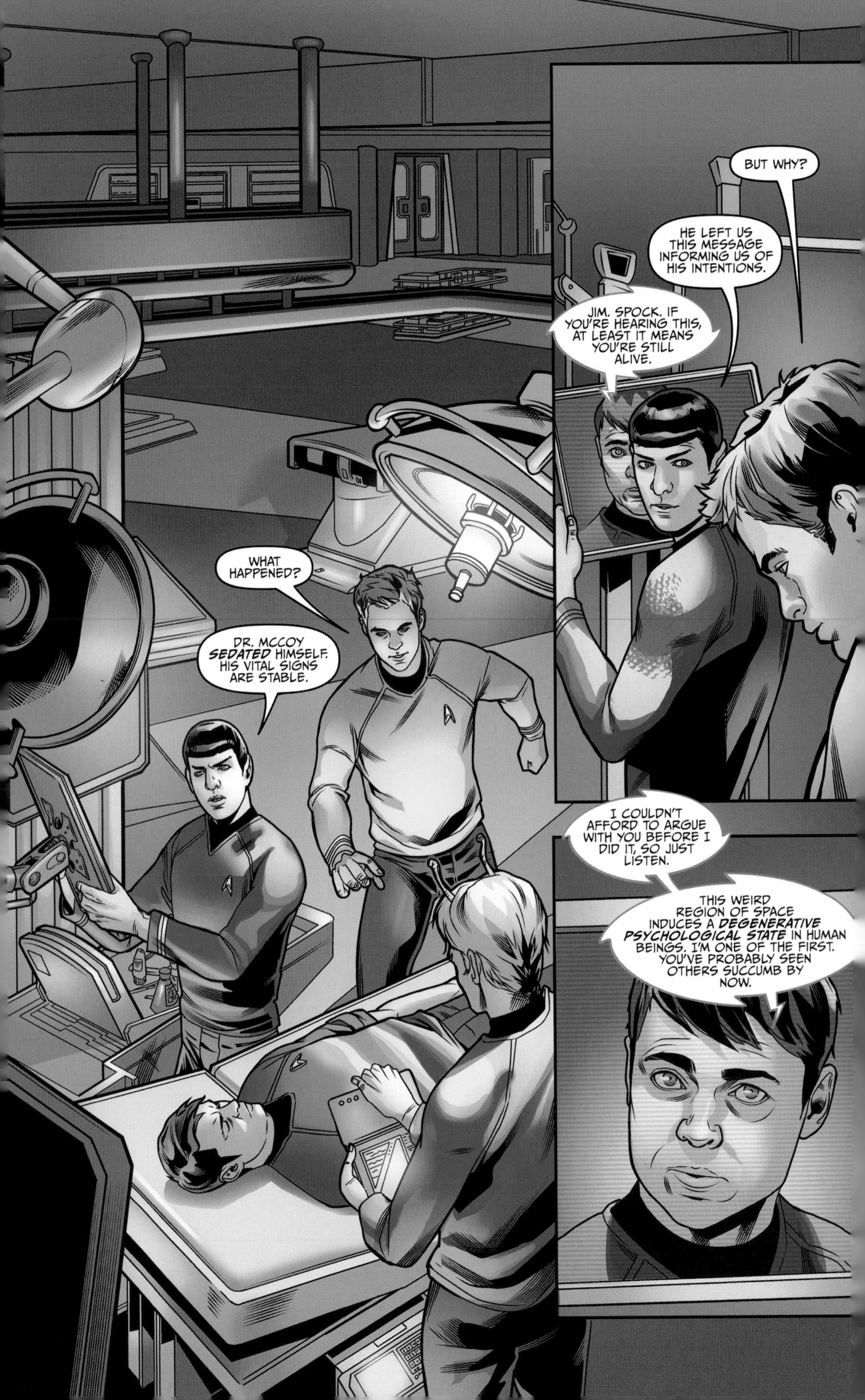
WHAT HAPPENED?
DR. MCCOY *SEDATED* HIMSELF. HIS VITAL SIGNS ARE STABLE.
BUT WHY?
HE LEFT US THIS MESSAGE INFORMING US OF HIS INTENTIONS.
JIM. SPOCK. IF YOU'RE HEARING THIS, AT LEAST IT MEANS YOU'RE STILL ALIVE.
I COULDN'T AFFORD TO ARGUE WITH YOU BEFORE I DID IT, SO JUST LISTEN.
THIS WEIRD REGION OF SPACE INDUCES A *DEGENERATIVE PSYCHOLOGICAL STATE* IN HUMAN BEINGS. I'M ONE OF THE FIRST. YOU'VE PROBABLY SEEN OTHERS SUCCUMB BY NOW.

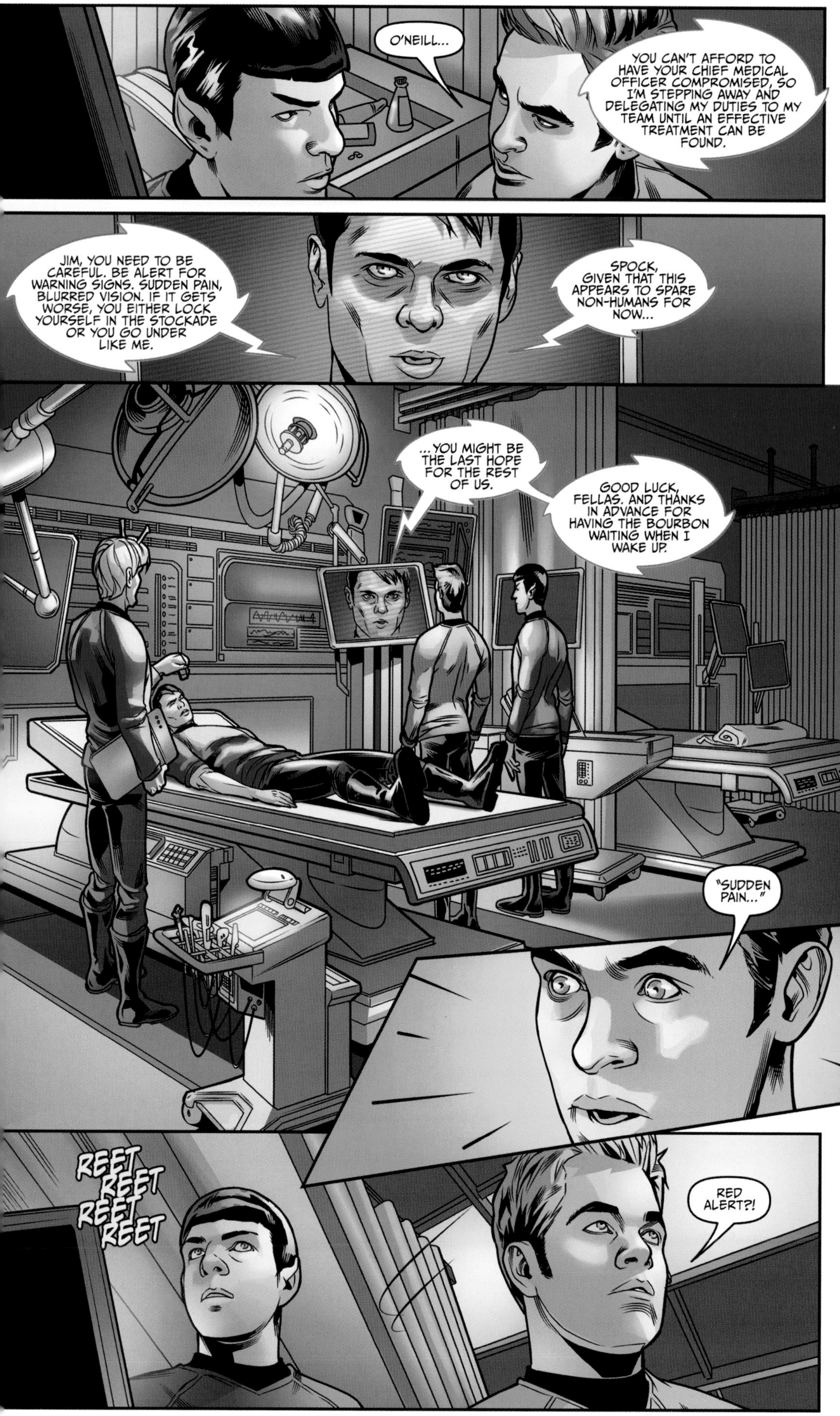
O'NEILL...
YOU CAN'T AFFORD TO HAVE YOUR CHIEF MEDICAL OFFICER COMPROMISED, SO I'M STEPPING AWAY AND DELEGATING MY DUTIES TO MY TEAM UNTIL AN EFFECTIVE TREATMENT CAN BE FOUND.
JIM, YOU NEED TO BE CAREFUL. BE ALERT FOR WARNING SIGNS. SUDDEN PAIN, BLURRED VISION. IF IT GETS WORSE, YOU EITHER LOCK YOURSELF IN THE STOCKADE OR YOU GO UNDER LIKE ME.
SPOCK, GIVEN THAT THIS APPEARS TO SPARE NON-HUMANS FOR NOW...
...YOU MIGHT BE THE LAST HOPE FOR THE REST OF US.
GOOD LUCK, FELLAS. AND THANKS IN ADVANCE FOR HAVING THE BOURBON WAITING WHEN I WAKE UP.
"SUDDEN PAIN..."
REET REET REET REET
RED ALERT?!

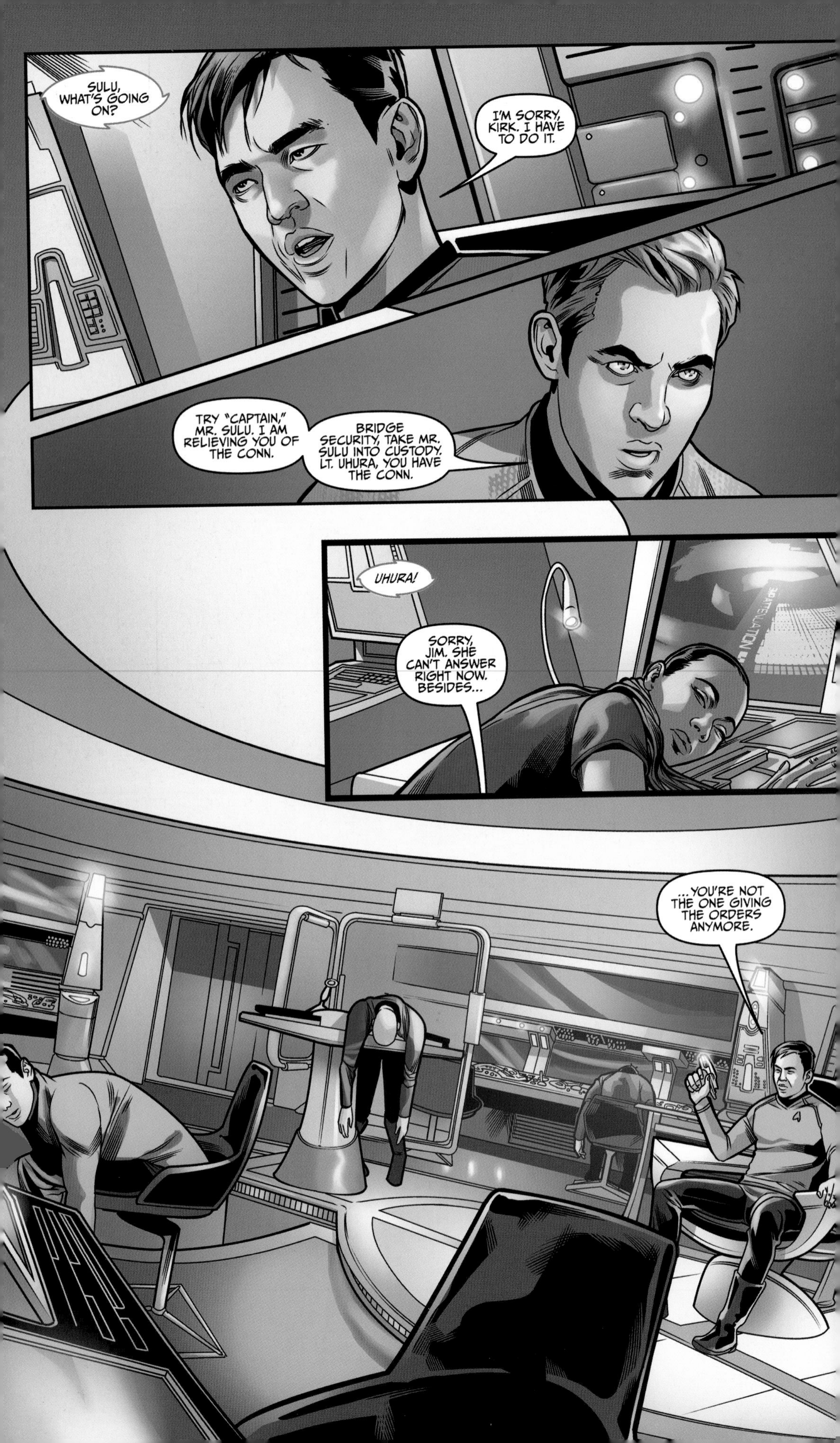
SULU, WHAT'S GOING ON?
I'M SORRY, KIRK. I HAVE TO DO IT.
TRY "CAPTAIN," MR. SULU. I AM RELIEVING YOU OF THE CONN.
BRIDGE SECURITY, TAKE MR. SULU INTO CUSTODY. LT. UHURA, YOU HAVE THE CONN.
UHURA!
SORRY, JIM. SHE CAN'T ANSWER RIGHT NOW. BESIDES...
...YOU'RE NOT THE ONE GIVING THE ORDERS ANYMORE.

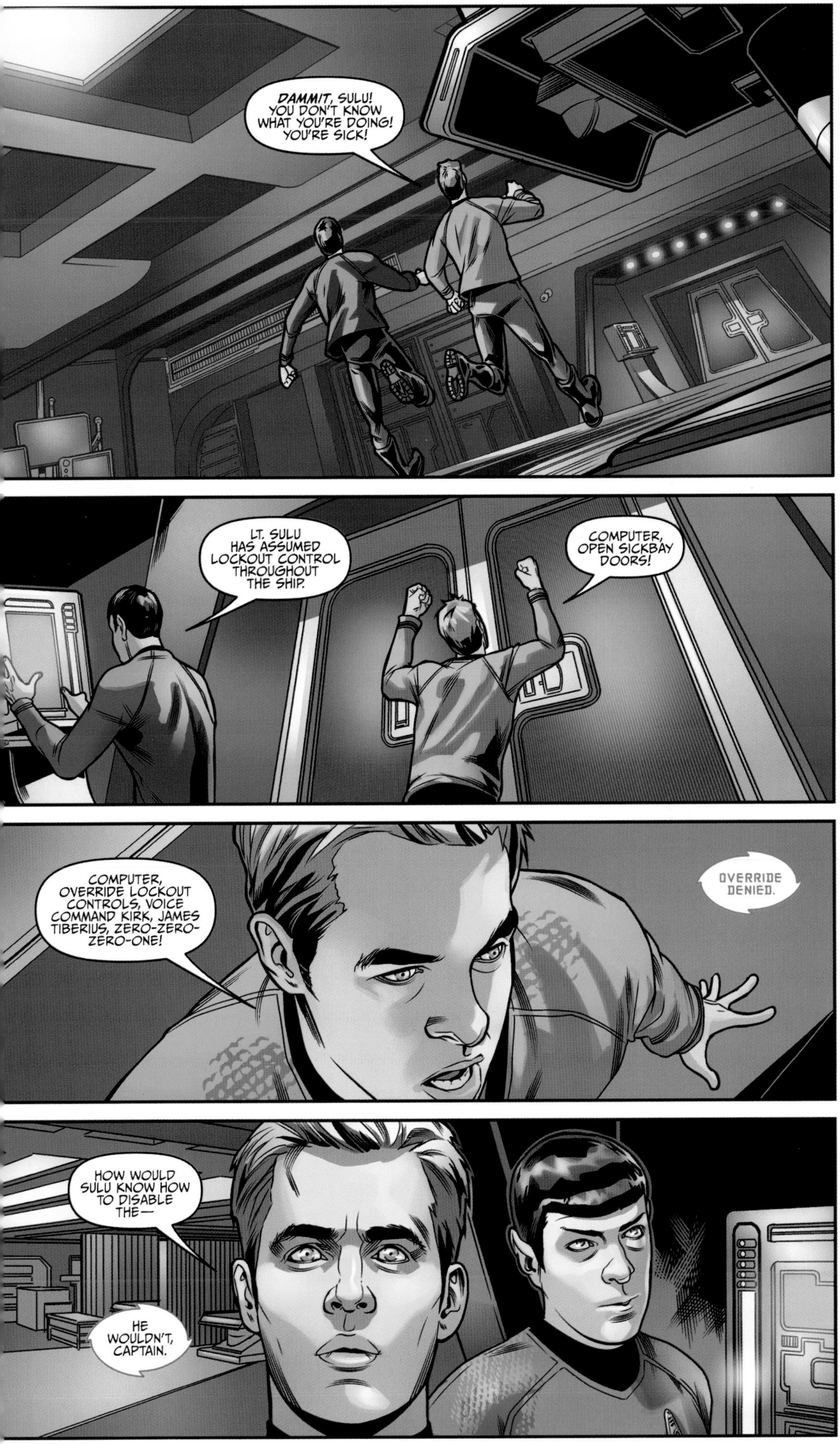
DAMMIT, SULU! YOU DON'T KNOW WHAT YOU'RE DOING! YOU'RE SICK!
LT. SULU HAS ASSUMED LOCKOUT CONTROL THROUGHOUT THE SHIP.
COMPUTER, OPEN SICKBAY DOORS!
COMPUTER, OVERRIDE LOCKOUT CONTROLS, VOICE COMMAND KIRK, JAMES TIBERIUS, ZERO-ZERO-ZERO-ONE!
OVERRIDE DENIED.
HOW WOULD SULU KNOW HOW TO DISABLE THE—
HE WOULDN'T, CAPTAIN.

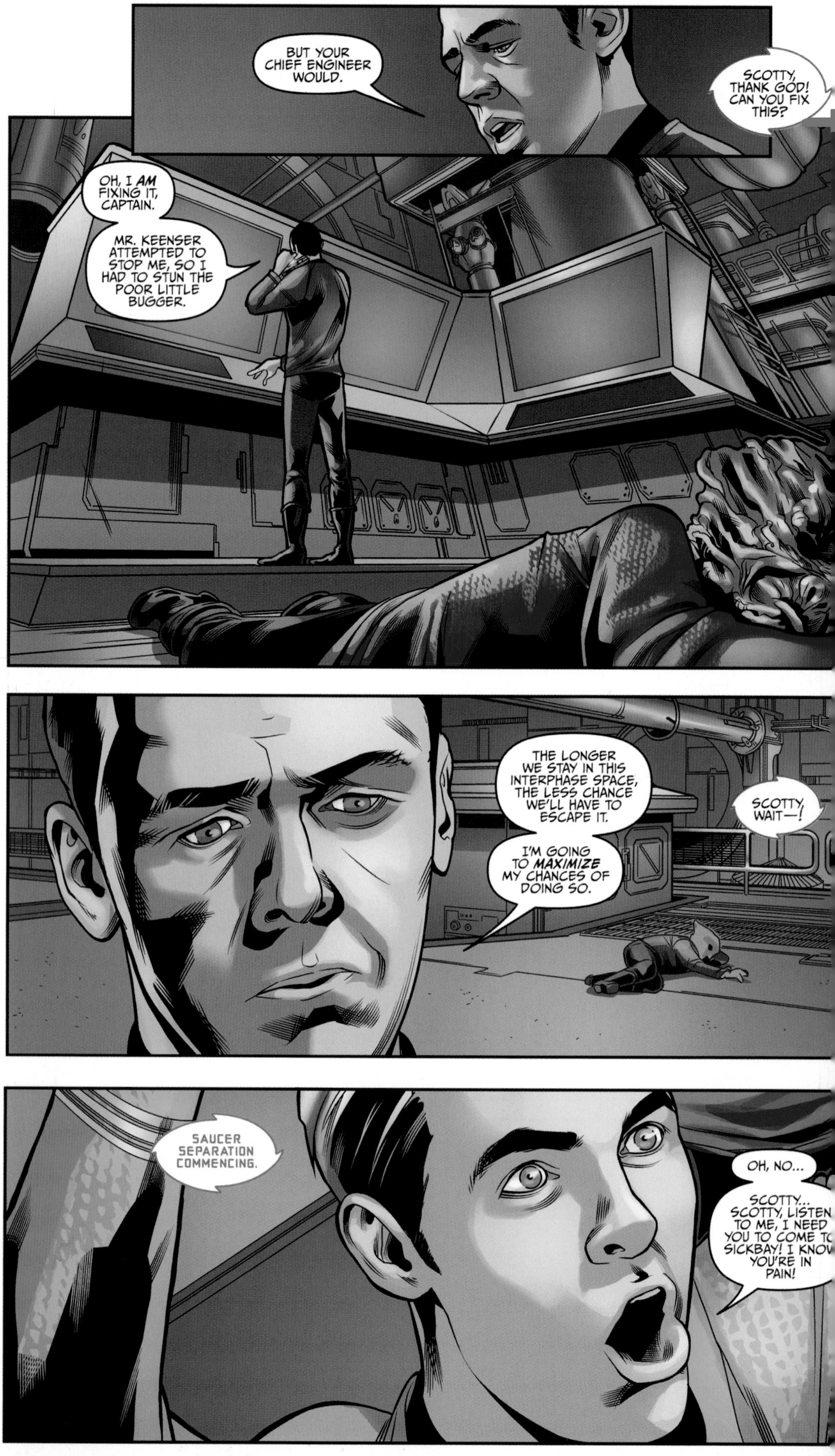
BUT YOUR CHIEF ENGINEER WOULD.
SCOTTY, THANK GOD! CAN YOU FIX THIS?
OH, I AM FIXING IT, CAPTAIN.
MR. KEENSER ATTEMPTED TO STOP ME, SO I HAD TO STUN THE POOR LITTLE BUGGER.
THE LONGER WE STAY IN THIS INTERPHASE SPACE, THE LESS CHANCE WE'LL HAVE TO ESCAPE IT.
I'M GOING TO MAXIMIZE MY CHANCES OF DOING SO.
SCOTTY, WAIT—!
SAUCER SEPARATION COMMENCING.
OH, NO...
SCOTTY... SCOTTY, LISTEN TO ME, I NEED YOU TO COME TO SICKBAY! I KNOW YOU'RE IN PAIN!

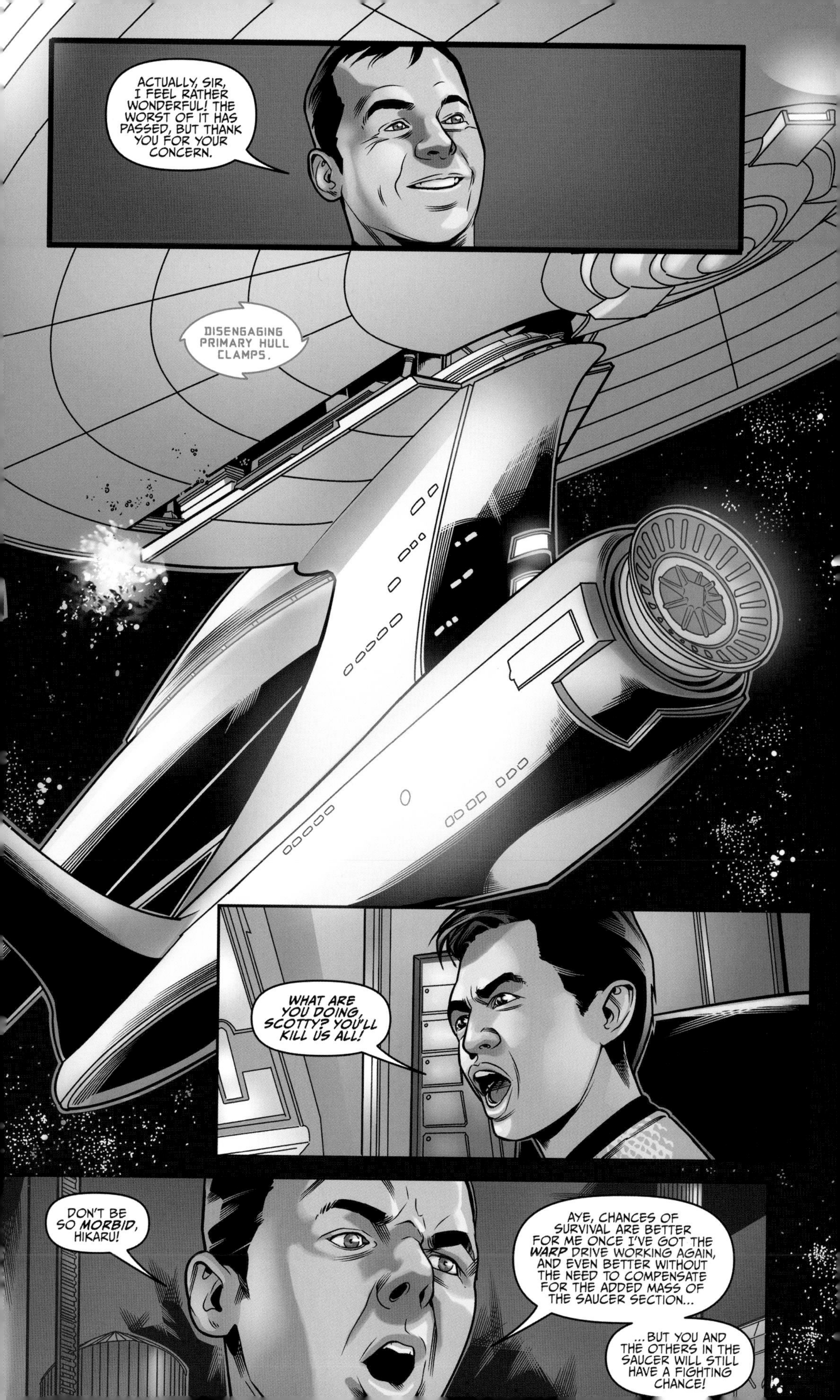
ACTUALLY, SIR, I FEEL RATHER WONDERFUL! THE WORST OF IT HAS PASSED, BUT THANK YOU FOR YOUR CONCERN.
DISENGAGING PRIMARY HULL CLAMPS.
WHAT ARE YOU DOING, SCOTTY? YOU'LL KILL US ALL!
DON'T BE SO MORBID, HIKARU!
AYE, CHANCES OF SURVIVAL ARE BETTER FOR ME ONCE I'VE GOT THE WARP DRIVE WORKING AGAIN, AND EVEN BETTER WITHOUT THE NEED TO COMPENSATE FOR THE ADDED MASS OF THE SAUCER SECTION...
...BUT YOU AND THE OTHERS IN THE SAUCER WILL STILL HAVE A FIGHTING CHANCE!

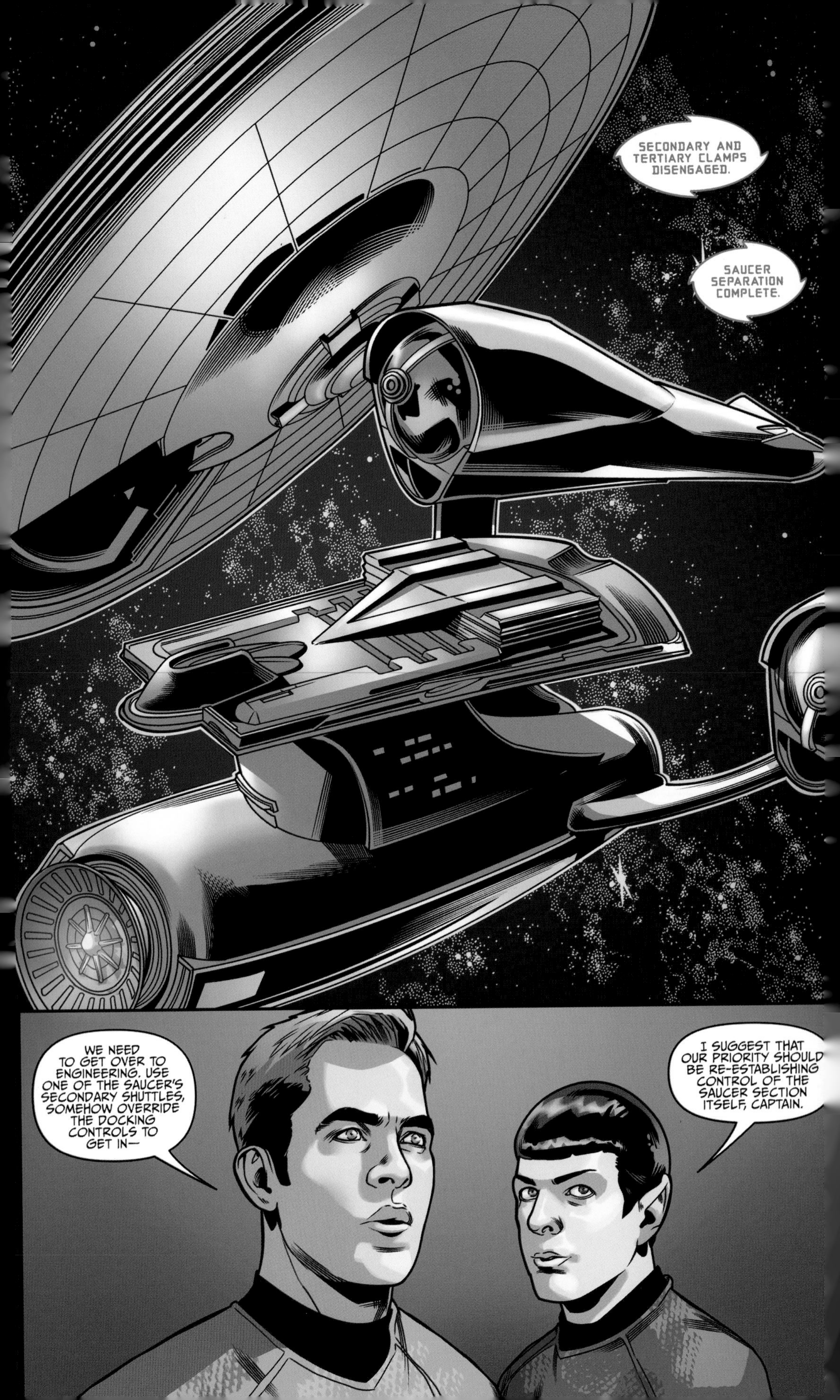
SECONDARY AND TERTIARY CLAMPS DISENGAGED.
SAUCER SEPARATION COMPLETE.
WE NEED TO GET OVER TO ENGINEERING. USE ONE OF THE SAUCER'S SECONDARY SHUTTLES, SOMEHOW OVERRIDE THE DOCKING CONTROLS TO GET IN—
I SUGGEST THAT OUR PRIORITY SHOULD BE RE-ESTABLISHING CONTROL OF THE SAUCER SECTION ITSELF, CAPTAIN.

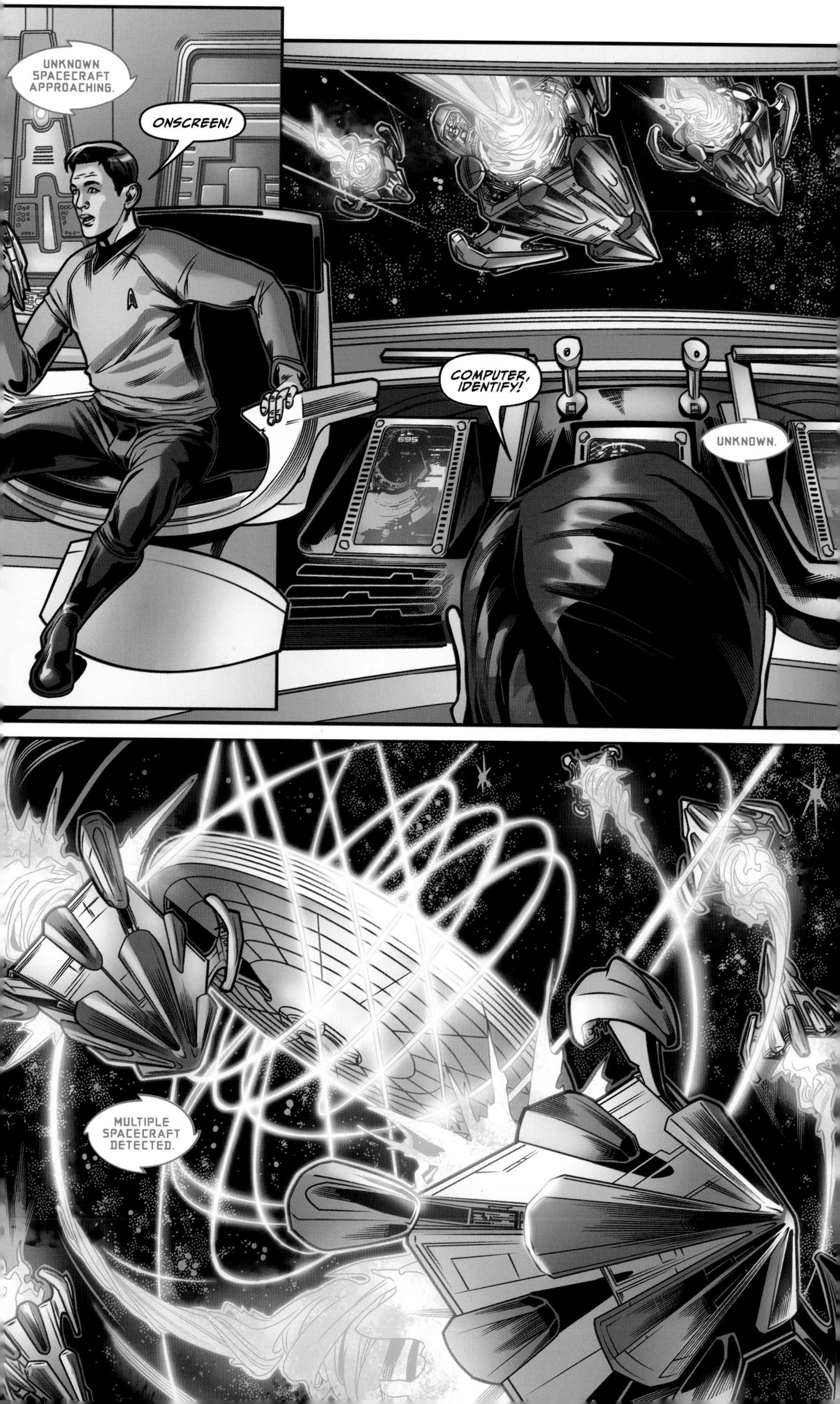
UNKNOWN SPACECRAFT APPROACHING.
ONSCREEN!
COMPUTER, IDENTIFY!
UNKNOWN.
MULTIPLE SPACECRAFT DETECTED.

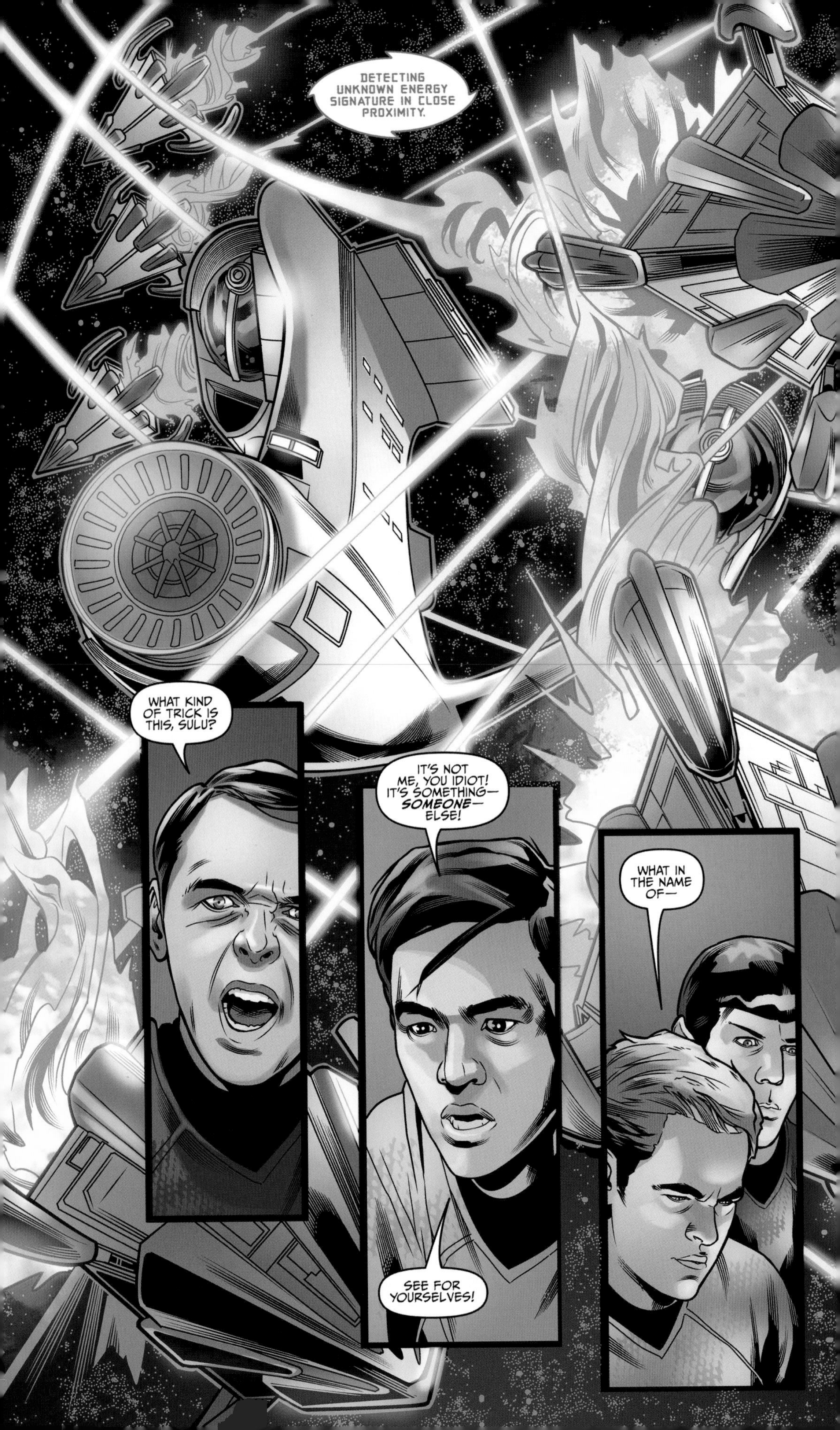
DETECTING UNKNOWN ENERGY SIGNATURE IN CLOSE PROXIMITY.
WHAT KIND OF TRICK IS THIS, SULU?
IT'S NOT ME, YOU IDIOT! IT'S SOMETHING— SOMEONE— ELSE!
SEE FOR YOURSELVES!
WHAT IN THE NAME OF—

WE APPEAR TO BE SURROUNDED BY ENERGY FILAMENTS OF SOME KIND.

LOOK AT THE FILAMENTS. THEY'RE NOT RANDOM.

THEY'RE WEBS.

THINK ABOUT IT, SPOCK. WHY ENGAGE AN OPPONENT IF YOU CAN JUST WAIT UNTIL IT BEATS ITSELF?

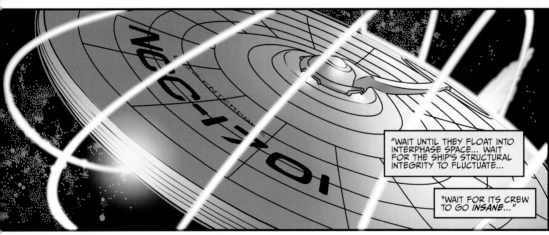

"WAIT UNTIL THEY FLOAT INTO INTERPHASE SPACE... WAIT FOR THE SHIP'S STRUCTURAL INTEGRITY TO FLUCTUATE...

"WAIT FOR ITS CREW TO GO INSANE..."

...AND YOU'VE GOT THEM RIGHT WHERE YOU WANT THEM.

THAT ASSUMES THAT OUR CAPTORS ARE SUFFICIENTLY ADVANCED TO REMAIN UNAFFECTED BY INTERPHASE SPACE THEMSELVES.

I KNOW.

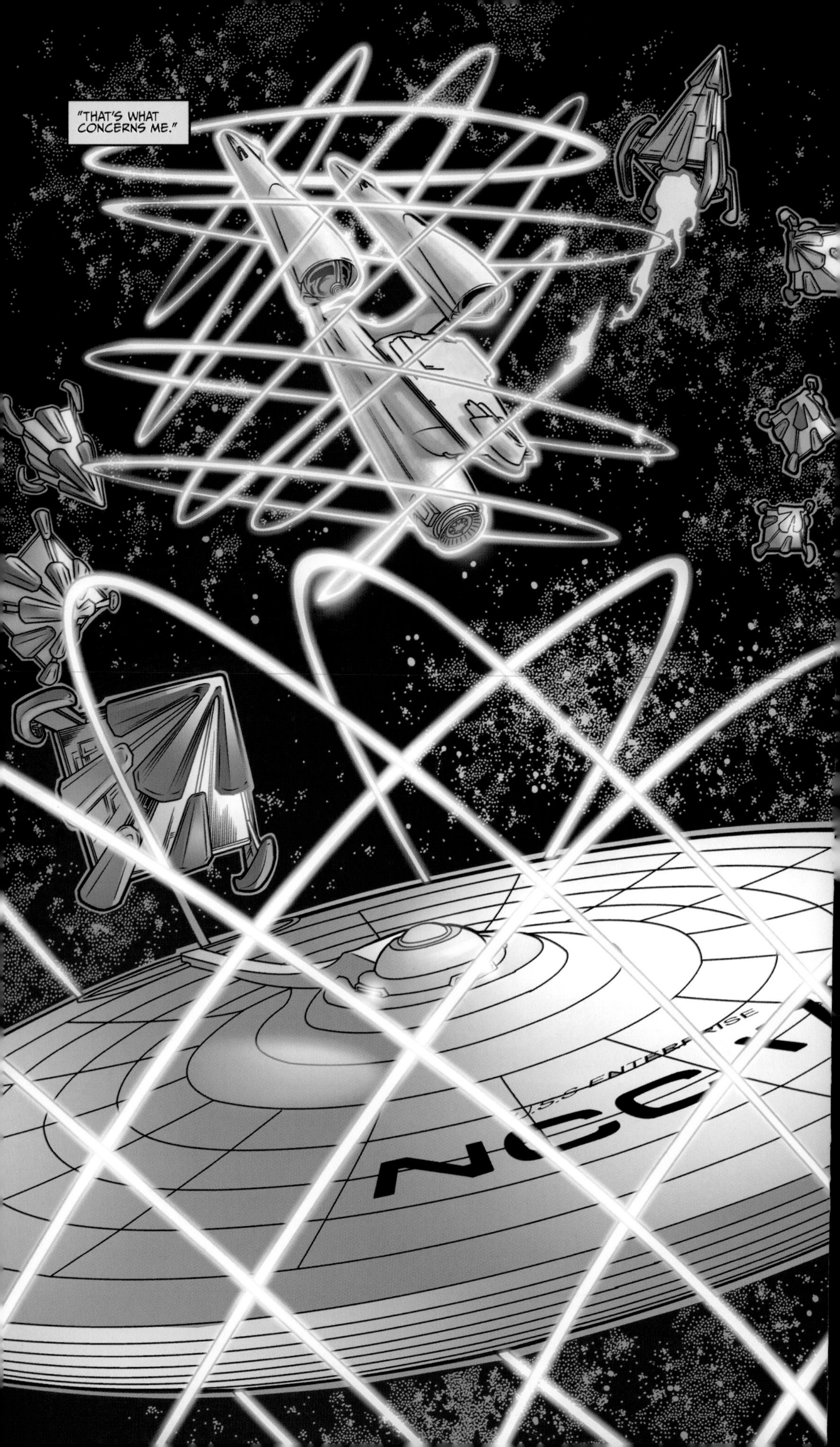
"THAT'S WHAT CONCERNS ME."
U.S.S. ENTERPRISE
NCC-1

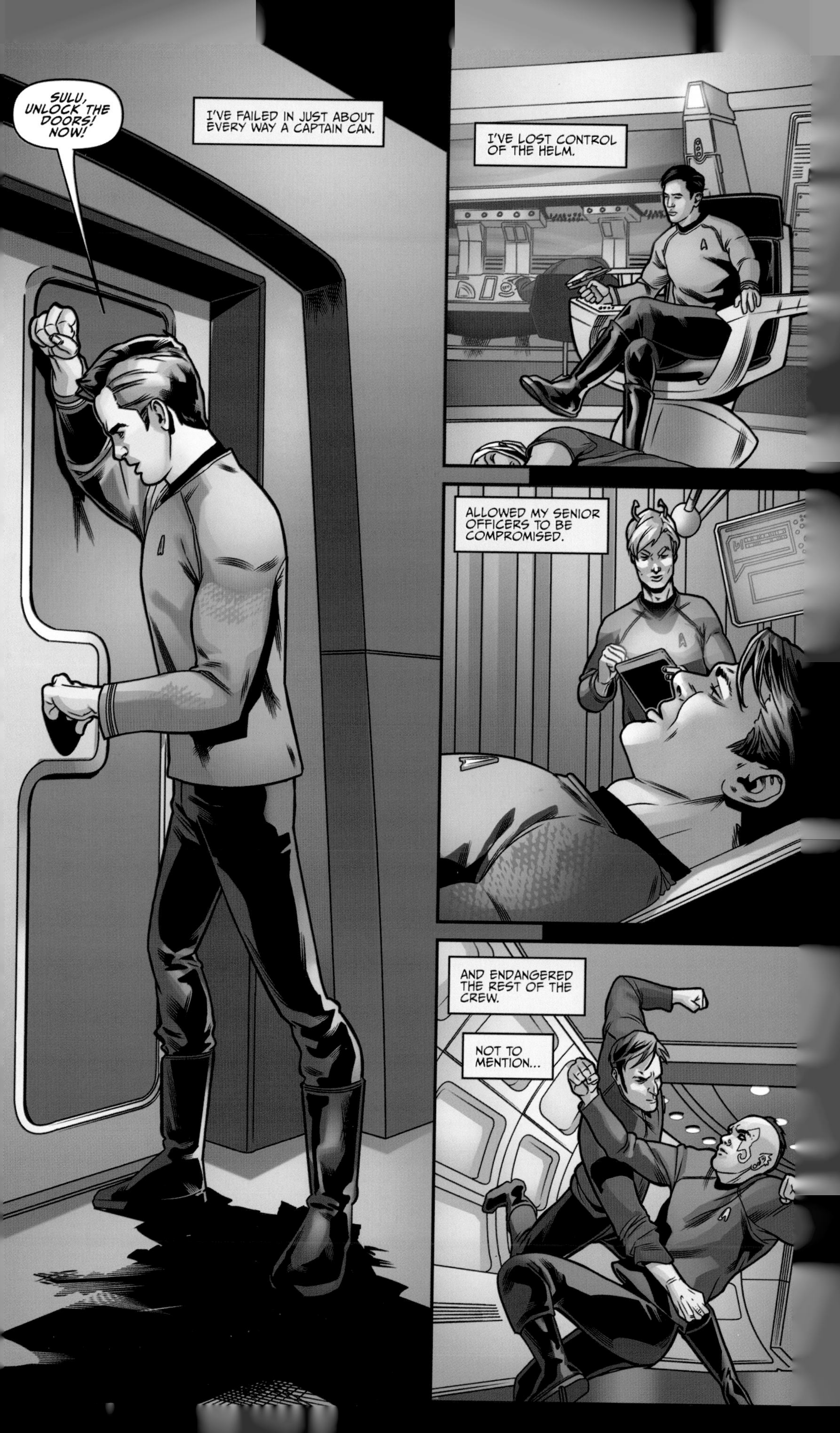
SULU, UNLOCK THE DOORS! NOW!
I'VE FAILED IN JUST ABOUT EVERY WAY A CAPTAIN CAN.
I'VE LOST CONTROL OF THE HELM.
ALLOWED MY SENIOR OFFICERS TO BE COMPROMISED.
AND ENDANGERED THE REST OF THE CREW.
NOT TO MENTION...

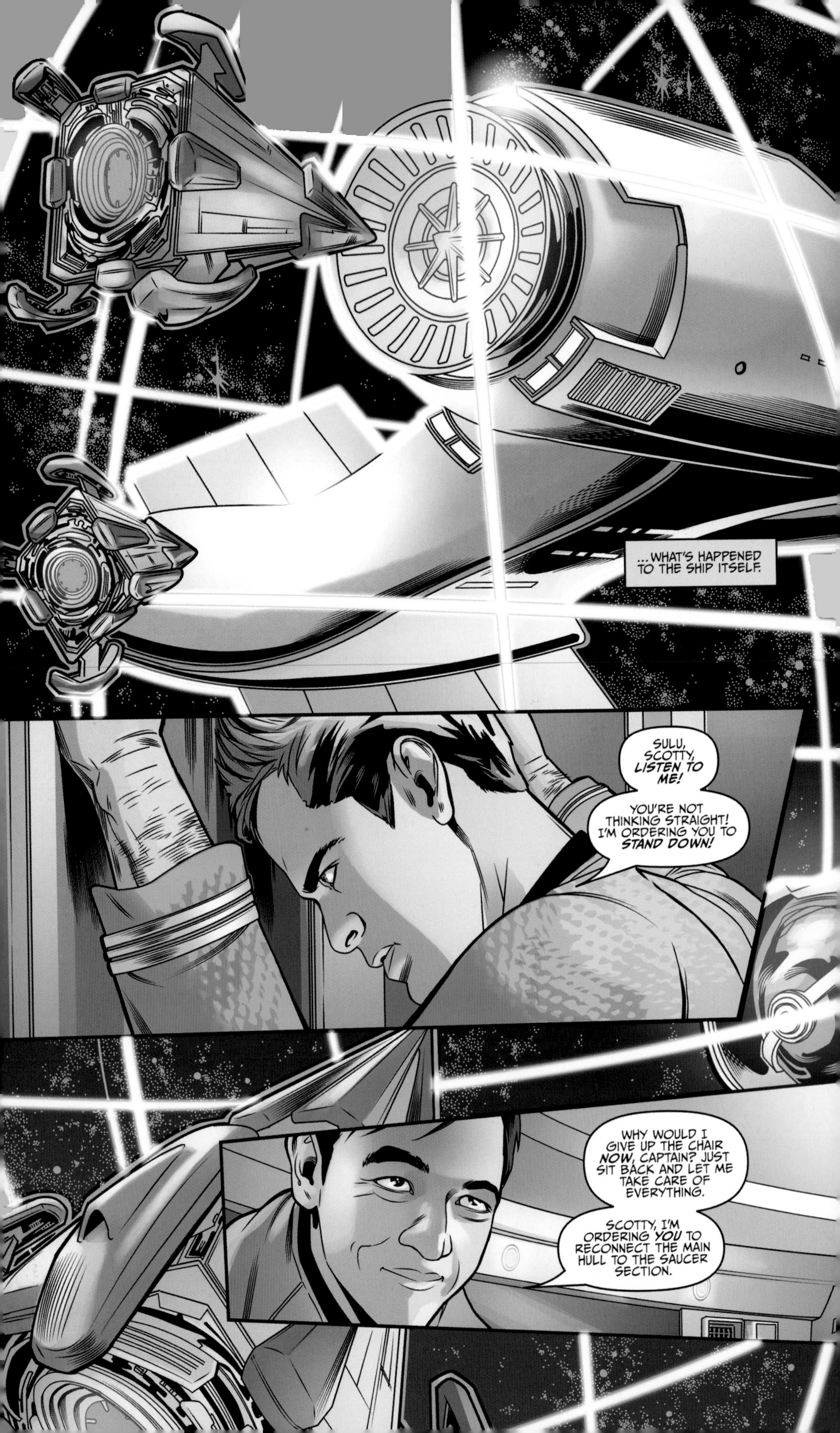
...WHAT'S HAPPENED TO THE SHIP ITSELF.
SULU, SCOTTY, LISTEN TO ME!
YOU'RE NOT THINKING STRAIGHT! I'M ORDERING YOU TO STAND DOWN!
WHY WOULD I GIVE UP THE CHAIR NOW, CAPTAIN? JUST SIT BACK AND LET ME TAKE CARE OF EVERYTHING.
SCOTTY, I'M ORDERING YOU TO RECONNECT THE MAIN HULL TO THE SAUCER SECTION.

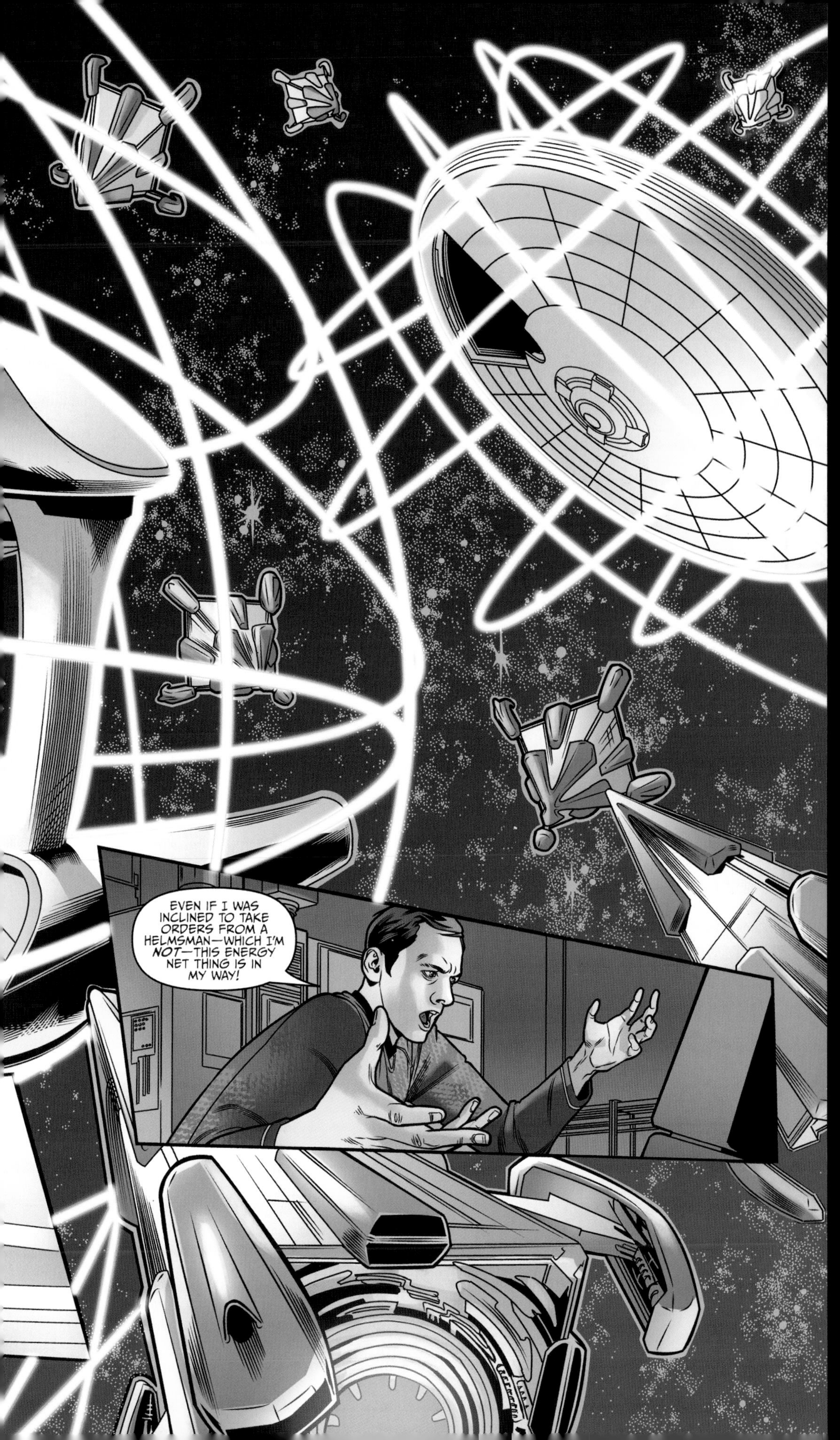
EVEN IF I WAS INCLINED TO TAKE ORDERS FROM A HELMSMAN—WHICH I'M *NOT*—THIS ENERGY NET THING IS IN MY WAY!

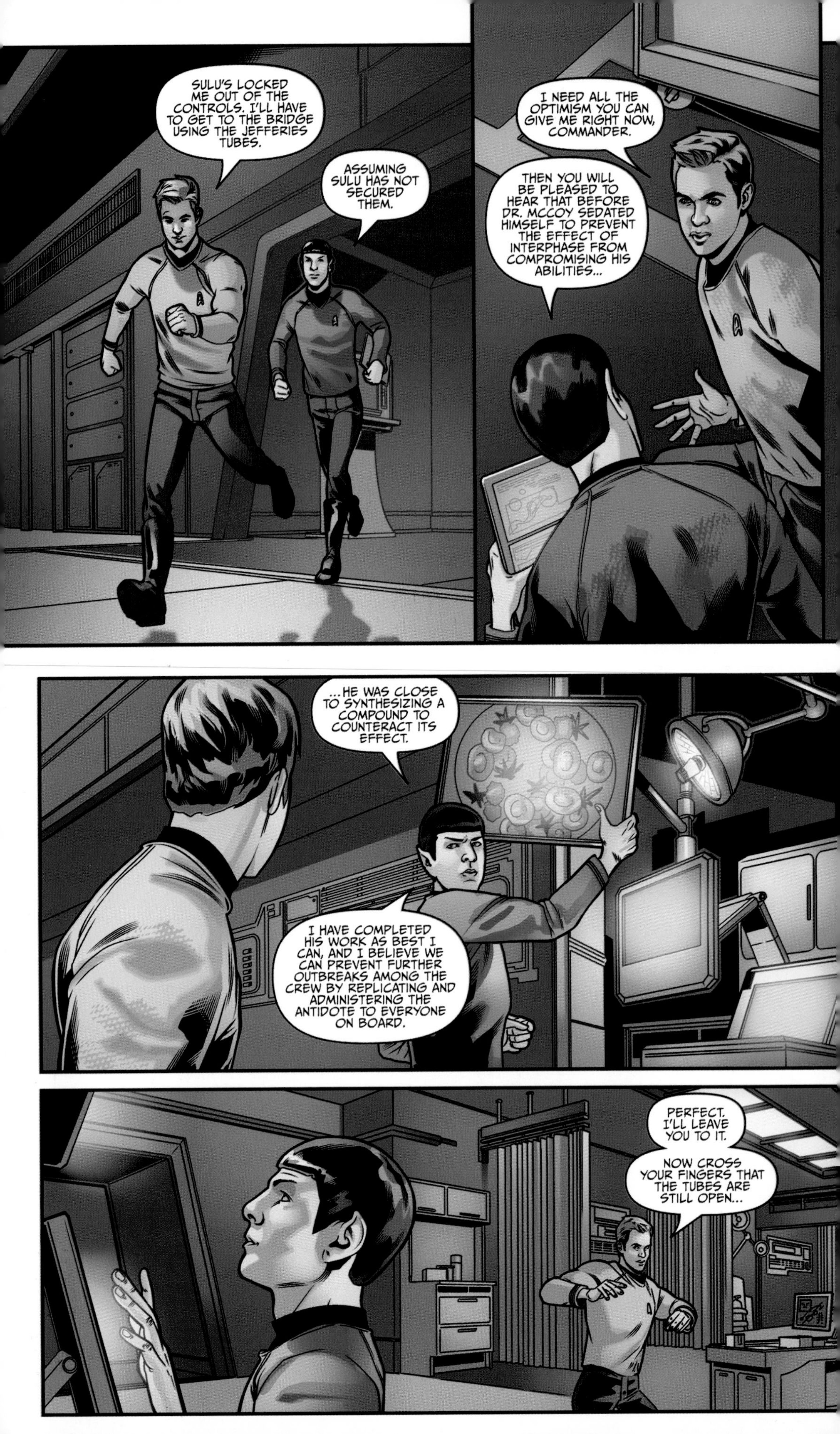
SULU'S LOCKED ME OUT OF THE CONTROLS. I'LL HAVE TO GET TO THE BRIDGE USING THE JEFFERIES TUBES.
ASSUMING SULU HAS NOT SECURED THEM.
I NEED ALL THE OPTIMISM YOU CAN GIVE ME RIGHT NOW, COMMANDER.
THEN YOU WILL BE PLEASED TO HEAR THAT BEFORE DR. McCOY SEDATED HIMSELF TO PREVENT THE EFFECT OF INTERPHASE FROM COMPROMISING HIS ABILITIES...
...HE WAS CLOSE TO SYNTHESIZING A COMPOUND TO COUNTERACT ITS EFFECT.
I HAVE COMPLETED HIS WORK AS BEST I CAN, AND I BELIEVE WE CAN PREVENT FURTHER OUTBREAKS AMONG THE CREW BY REPLICATING AND ADMINISTERING THE ANTIDOTE TO EVERYONE ON BOARD.
PERFECT. I'LL LEAVE YOU TO IT.
NOW CROSS YOUR FINGERS THAT THE TUBES ARE STILL OPEN...

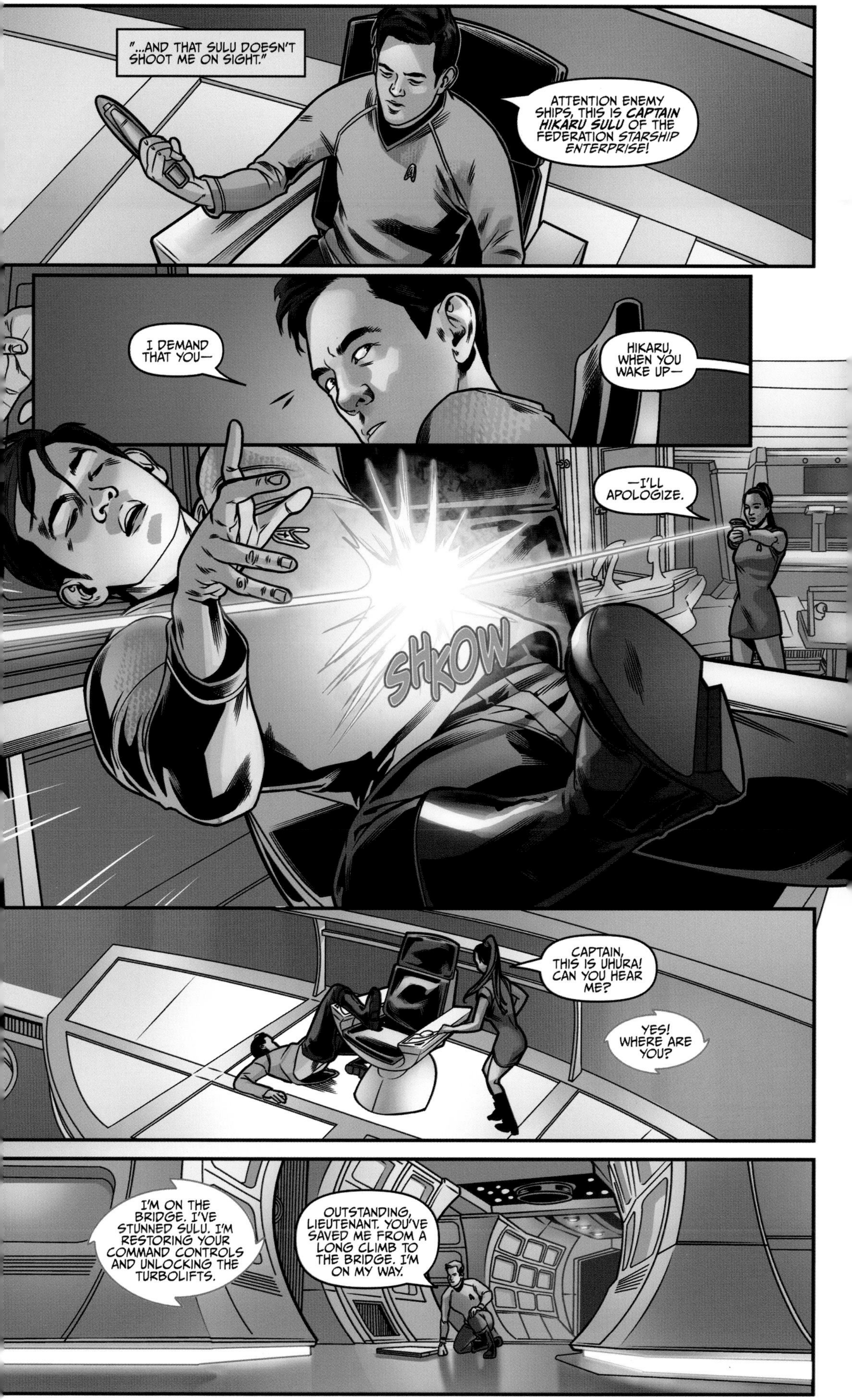
"...AND THAT SULU DOESN'T SHOOT ME ON SIGHT."
ATTENTION ENEMY SHIPS, THIS IS CAPTAIN HIKARU SULU OF THE FEDERATION STARSHIP ENTERPRISE!
I DEMAND THAT YOU—
HIKARU, WHEN YOU WAKE UP—
—I'LL APOLOGIZE.
SHKOW
CAPTAIN, THIS IS UHURA! CAN YOU HEAR ME?
YES! WHERE ARE YOU?
I'M ON THE BRIDGE. I'VE STUNNED SULU. I'M RESTORING YOUR COMMAND CONTROLS AND UNLOCKING THE TURBOLIFTS.
OUTSTANDING, LIEUTENANT. YOU'VE SAVED ME FROM A LONG CLIMB TO THE BRIDGE. I'M ON MY WAY.

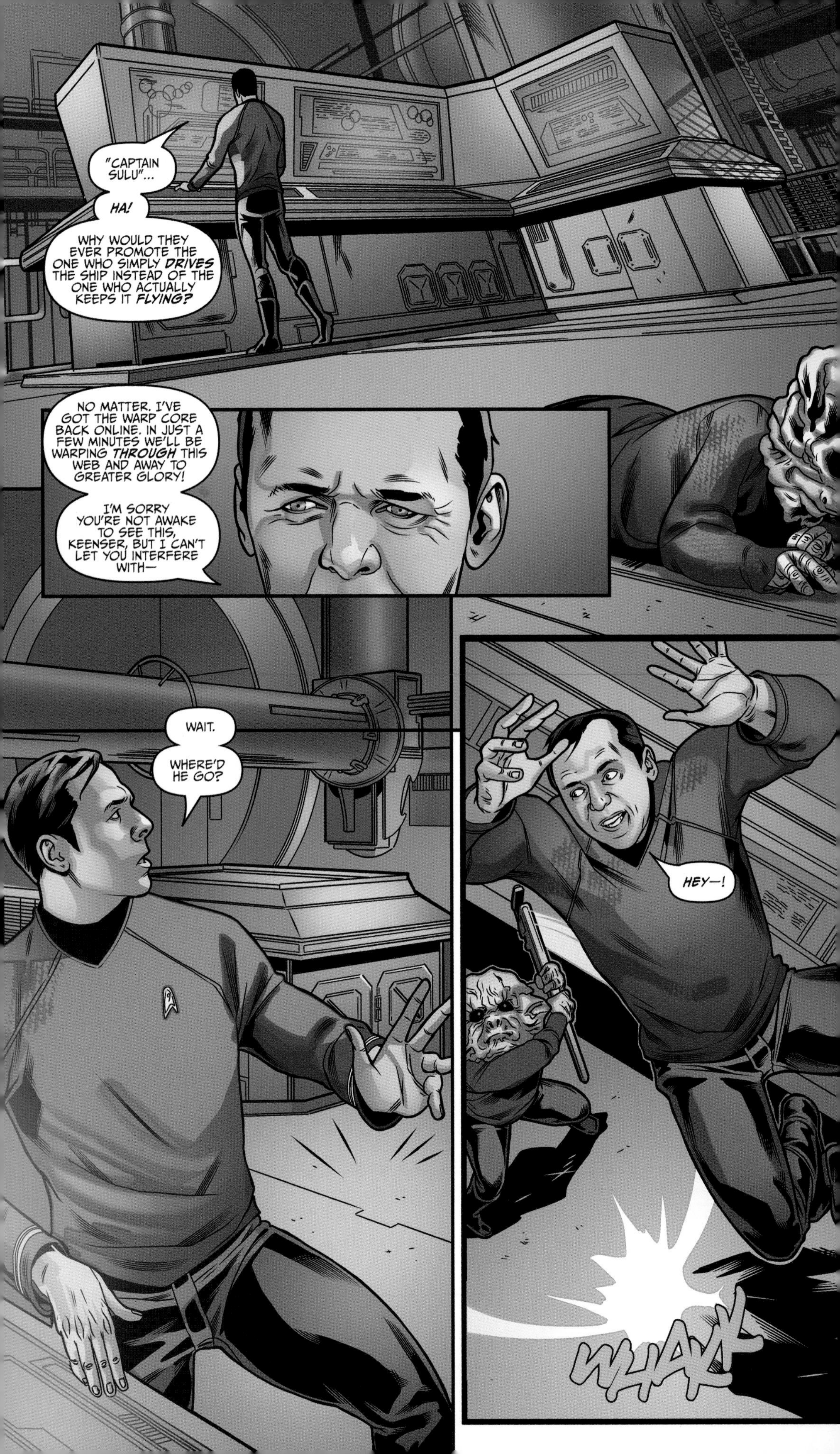
"CAPTAIN SULU"...
HA!
WHY WOULD THEY EVER PROMOTE THE ONE WHO SIMPLY DRIVES THE SHIP INSTEAD OF THE ONE WHO ACTUALLY KEEPS IT FLYING?
NO MATTER. I'VE GOT THE WARP CORE BACK ONLINE. IN JUST A FEW MINUTES WE'LL BE WARPING THROUGH THIS WEB AND AWAY TO GREATER GLORY!
I'M SORRY YOU'RE NOT AWAKE TO SEE THIS, KEENSER, BUT I CAN'T LET YOU INTERFERE WITH—
WAIT.
WHERE'D HE GO?
HEY—!
WHAK

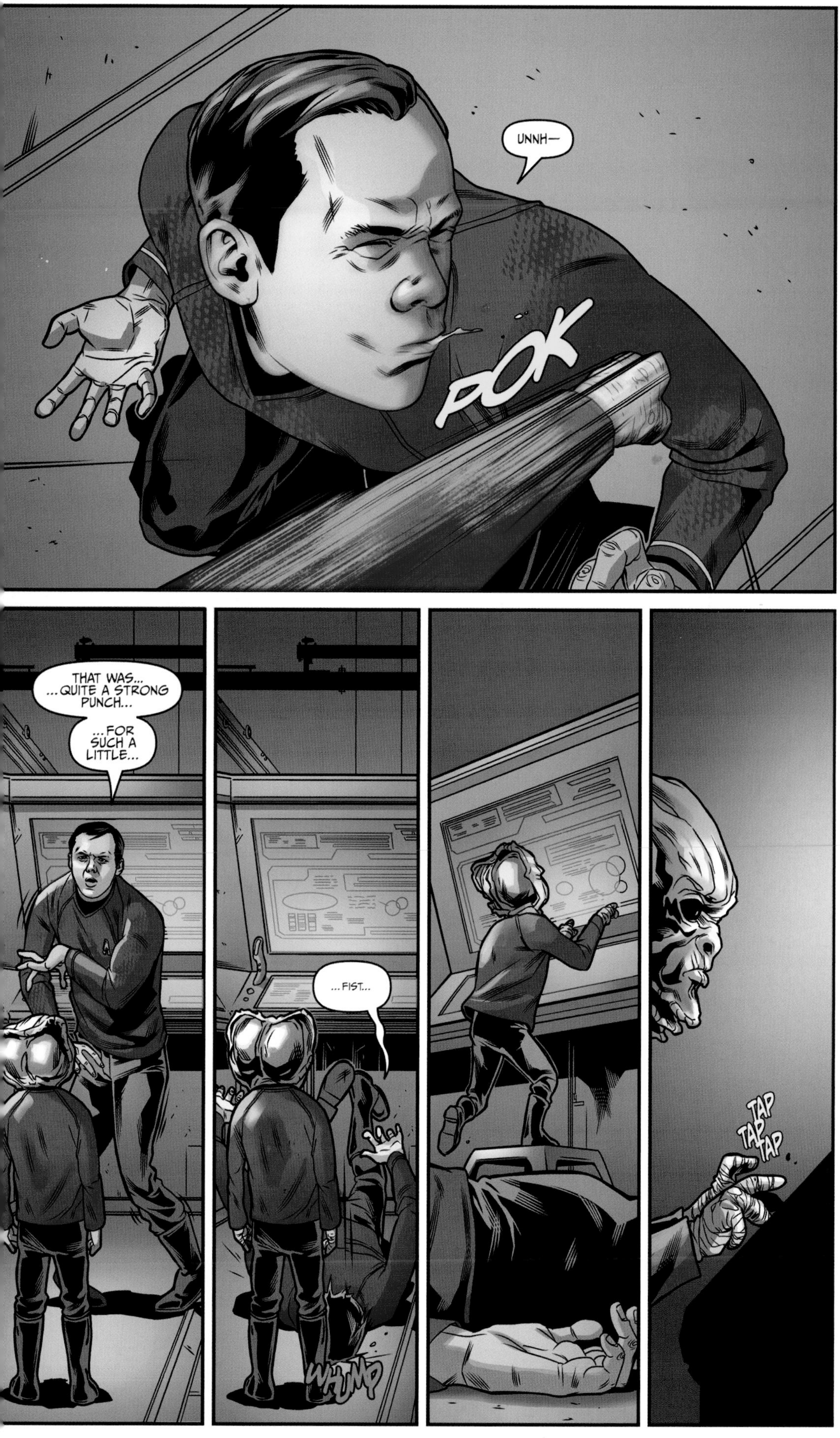
UNNH—
POK
THAT WAS... ...QUITE A STRONG PUNCH...
...FOR SUCH A LITTLE...
...FIST...
WHUMP
TAP TAP TAP

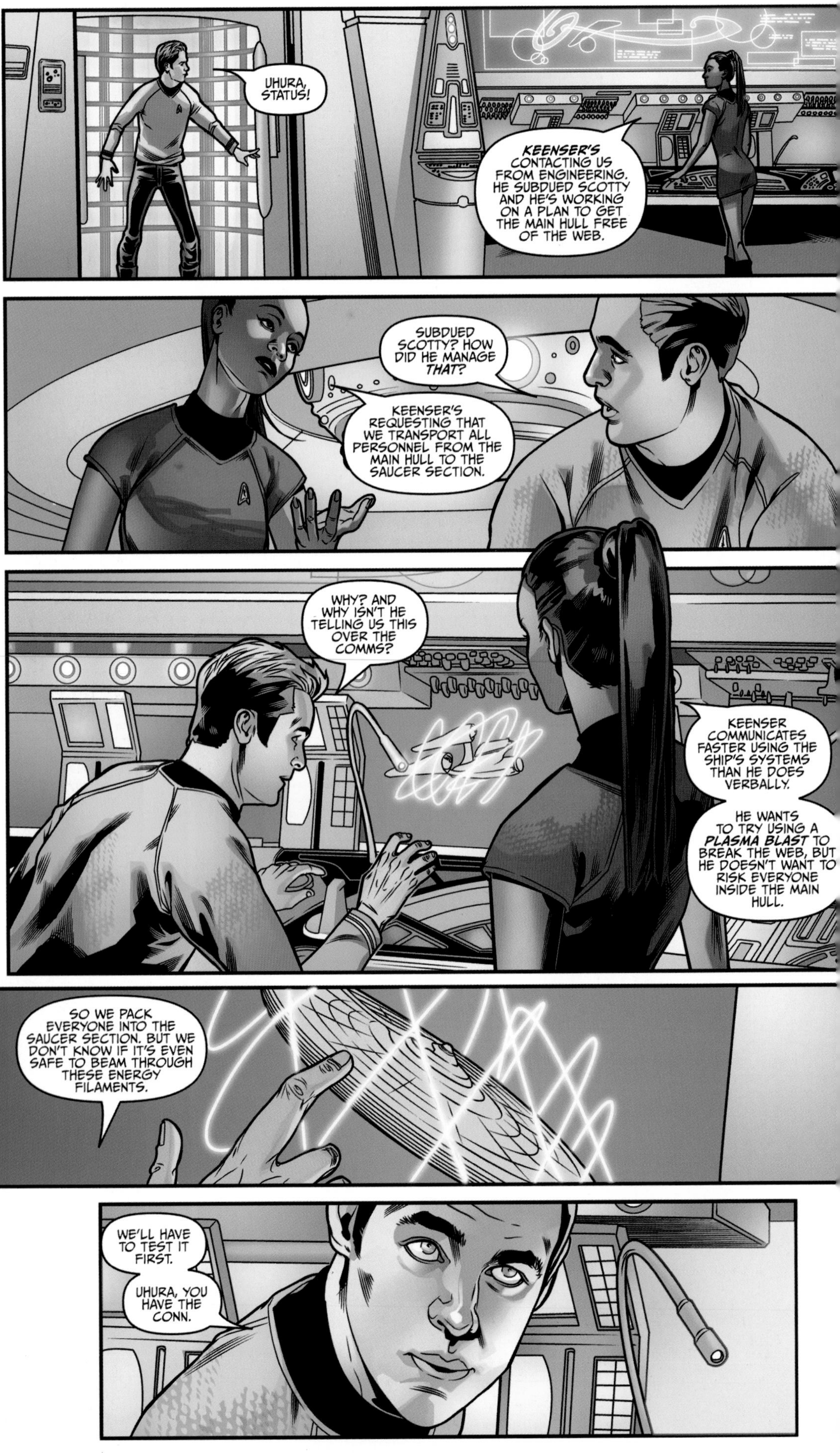
UHURA, STATUS!
KEENSER'S CONTACTING US FROM ENGINEERING. HE SUBDUED SCOTTY AND HE'S WORKING ON A PLAN TO GET THE MAIN HULL FREE OF THE WEB.
SUBDUED SCOTTY? HOW DID HE MANAGE THAT?
KEENSER'S REQUESTING THAT WE TRANSPORT ALL PERSONNEL FROM THE MAIN HULL TO THE SAUCER SECTION.
WHY? AND WHY ISN'T HE TELLING US THIS OVER THE COMMS?
KEENSER COMMUNICATES FASTER USING THE SHIP'S SYSTEMS THAN HE DOES VERBALLY.
HE WANTS TO TRY USING A PLASMA BLAST TO BREAK THE WEB, BUT HE DOESN'T WANT TO RISK EVERYONE INSIDE THE MAIN HULL.
SO WE PACK EVERYONE INTO THE SAUCER SECTION. BUT WE DON'T KNOW IF IT'S EVEN SAFE TO BEAM THROUGH THESE ENERGY FILAMENTS.
WE'LL HAVE TO TEST IT FIRST.
UHURA, YOU HAVE THE CONN.

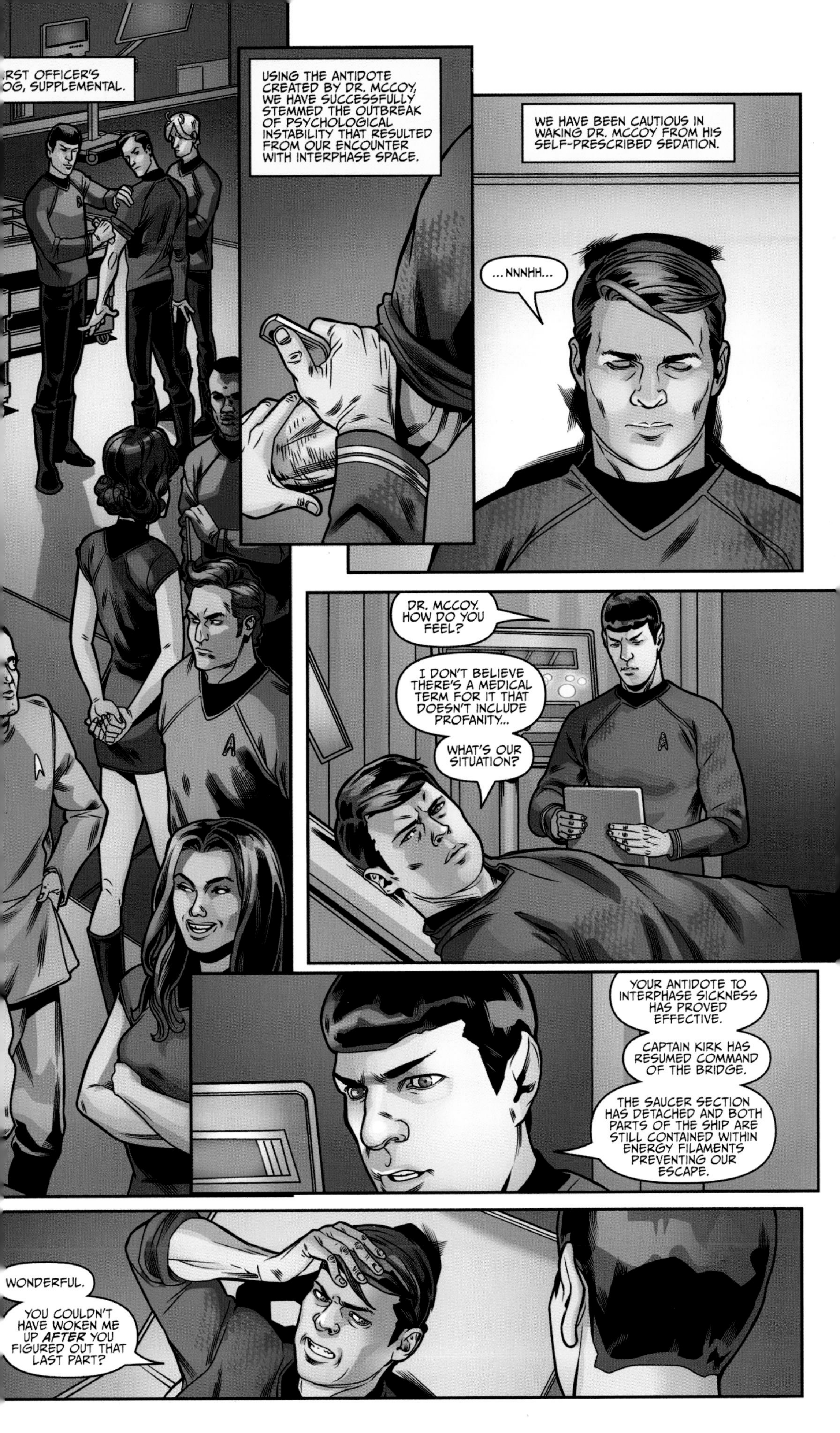

RST OFFICER'S
OG, SUPPLEMENTAL.
USING THE ANTIDOTE CREATED BY DR. MCCOY, WE HAVE SUCCESSFULLY STEMMED THE OUTBREAK OF PSYCHOLOGICAL INSTABILITY THAT RESULTED FROM OUR ENCOUNTER WITH INTERPHASE SPACE.
WE HAVE BEEN CAUTIOUS IN WAKING DR. MCCOY FROM HIS SELF-PRESCRIBED SEDATION.
...NNNHH...
DR. MCCOY. HOW DO YOU FEEL?
I DON'T BELIEVE THERE'S A MEDICAL TERM FOR IT THAT DOESN'T INCLUDE PROFANITY...
WHAT'S OUR SITUATION?
YOUR ANTIDOTE TO INTERPHASE SICKNESS HAS PROVED EFFECTIVE.
CAPTAIN KIRK HAS RESUMED COMMAND OF THE BRIDGE.
THE SAUCER SECTION HAS DETACHED AND BOTH PARTS OF THE SHIP ARE STILL CONTAINED WITHIN ENERGY FILAMENTS PREVENTING OUR ESCAPE.
WONDERFUL.
YOU COULDN'T HAVE WOKEN ME UP *AFTER* YOU FIGURED OUT THAT LAST PART?

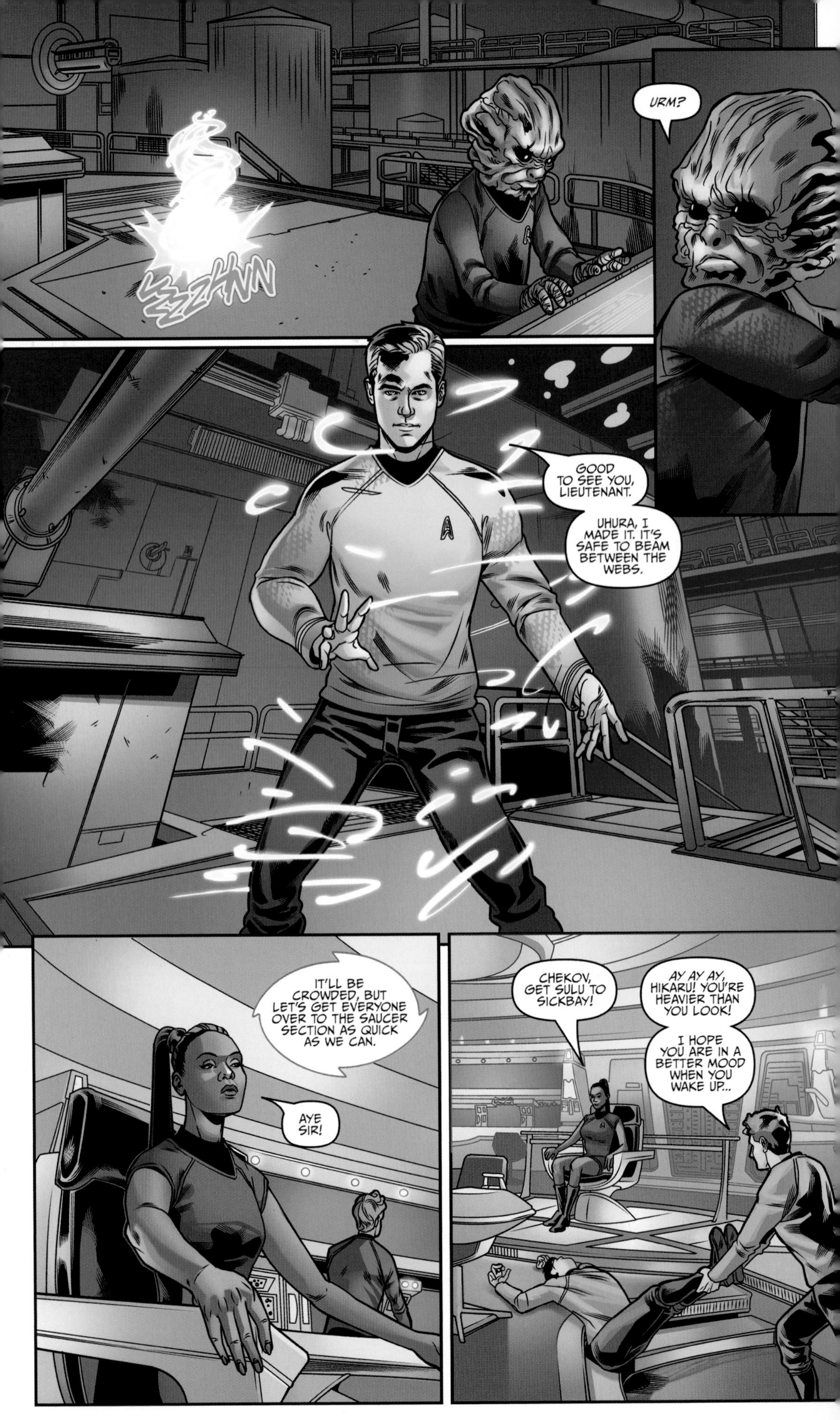
VZZZHNN
URM?
GOOD TO SEE YOU, LIEUTENANT.
UHURA, I MADE IT. IT'S SAFE TO BEAM BETWEEN THE WEBS.
IT'LL BE CROWDED, BUT LET'S GET EVERYONE OVER TO THE SAUCER SECTION AS QUICK AS WE CAN.
AYE SIR!
CHEKOV, GET SULU TO SICKBAY!
AY AY AY, HIKARU! YOU'RE HEAVIER THAN YOU LOOK!
I HOPE YOU ARE IN A BETTER MOOD WHEN YOU WAKE UP...

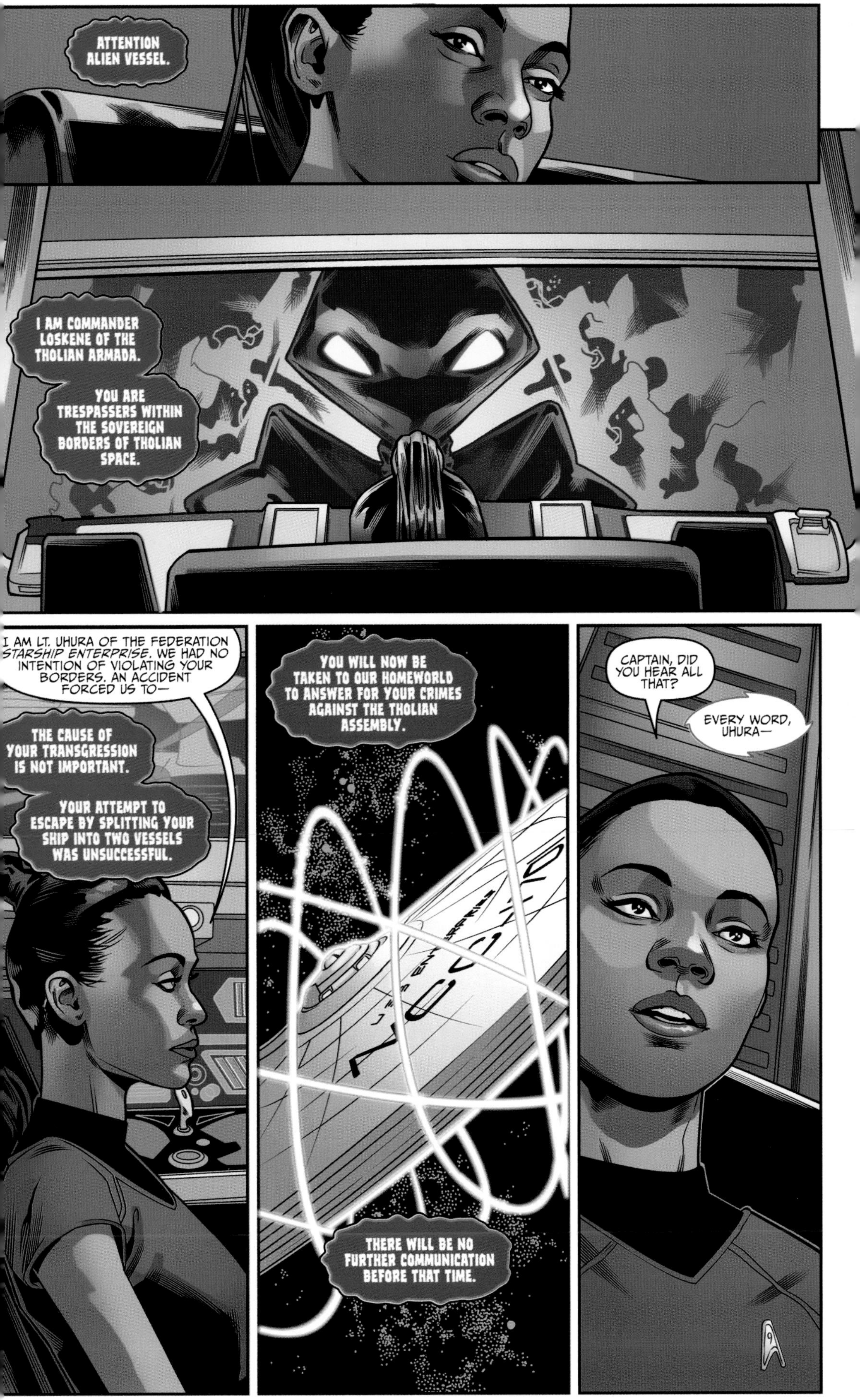

ATTENTION ALIEN VESSEL.
I AM COMMANDER LOSKENE OF THE THOLIAN ARMADA.
YOU ARE TRESPASSERS WITHIN THE SOVEREIGN BORDERS OF THOLIAN SPACE.
I AM LT. UHURA OF THE FEDERATION STARSHIP ENTERPRISE. WE HAD NO INTENTION OF VIOLATING YOUR BORDERS. AN ACCIDENT FORCED US TO—
THE CAUSE OF YOUR TRANSGRESSION IS NOT IMPORTANT.
YOUR ATTEMPT TO ESCAPE BY SPLITTING YOUR SHIP INTO TWO VESSELS WAS UNSUCCESSFUL.
YOU WILL NOW BE TAKEN TO OUR HOMEWORLD TO ANSWER FOR YOUR CRIMES AGAINST THE THOLIAN ASSEMBLY.
THERE WILL BE NO FURTHER COMMUNICATION BEFORE THAT TIME.
CAPTAIN, DID YOU HEAR ALL THAT?
EVERY WORD, UHURA—

—WHICH MEANS THE CLOCK IS TICKING FASTER THAN WE THOUGHT.

WHAT'S THE PROGRESS ON THE CREW RELOCATION TO THE SAUCER?

ALMOST DONE, CAPTAIN.

SPOCK IS MAKING SURE EVERYONE IS INOCULATED AGAINST THE INTERPHASE SICKNESS.

WHAT'S THE PLAN ON YOUR END?

WORKING ON IT.

KEENSER, ARE YOU SURE ABOUT THESE CALCULATIONS? MAYBE WE SHOULD TRY TO WA SCOTTY, SEE IF HE'S REGAINED HIS SENSES

HRRMP

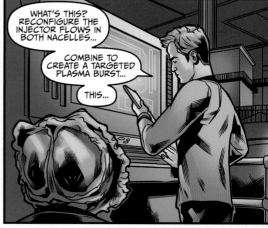

WHAT'S THIS? RECONFIGURE THE INJECTOR FLOWS IN BOTH NACELLES...

COMBINE TO CREATE A TARGETED PLASMA BURST...

THIS...

THIS IS REALLY GOOD.

HRRMP

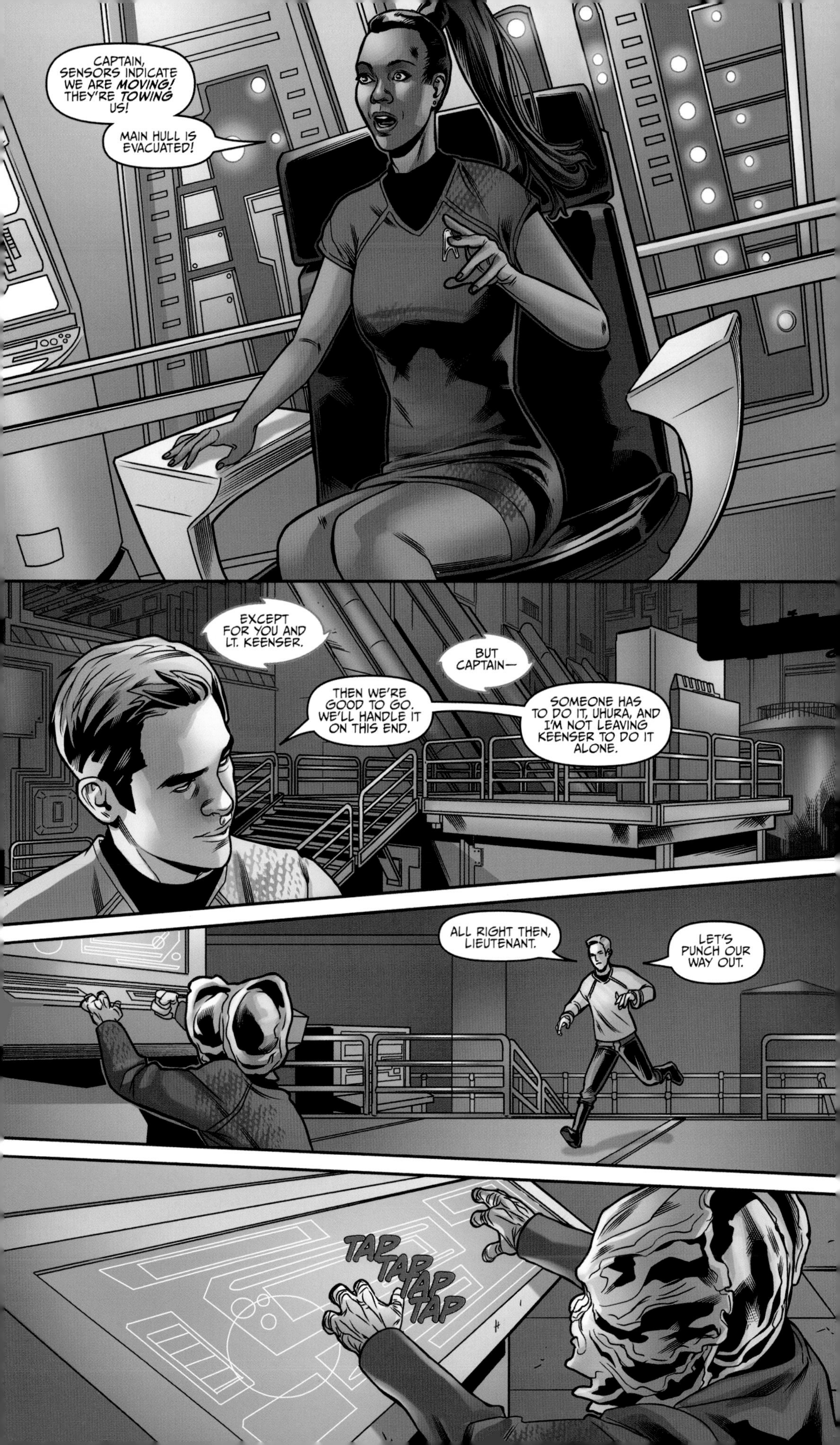
CAPTAIN, SENSORS INDICATE WE ARE *MOVING!* THEY'RE *TOWING* US!
MAIN HULL IS EVACUATED!
EXCEPT FOR YOU AND LT. KEENSER.
THEN WE'RE GOOD TO GO. WE'LL HANDLE IT ON THIS END.
BUT CAPTAIN—
SOMEONE HAS TO DO IT, UHURA, AND I'M NOT LEAVING KEENSER TO DO IT ALONE.
ALL RIGHT THEN, LIEUTENANT.
LET'S PUNCH OUR WAY OUT.
TAP TAP TAP TAP

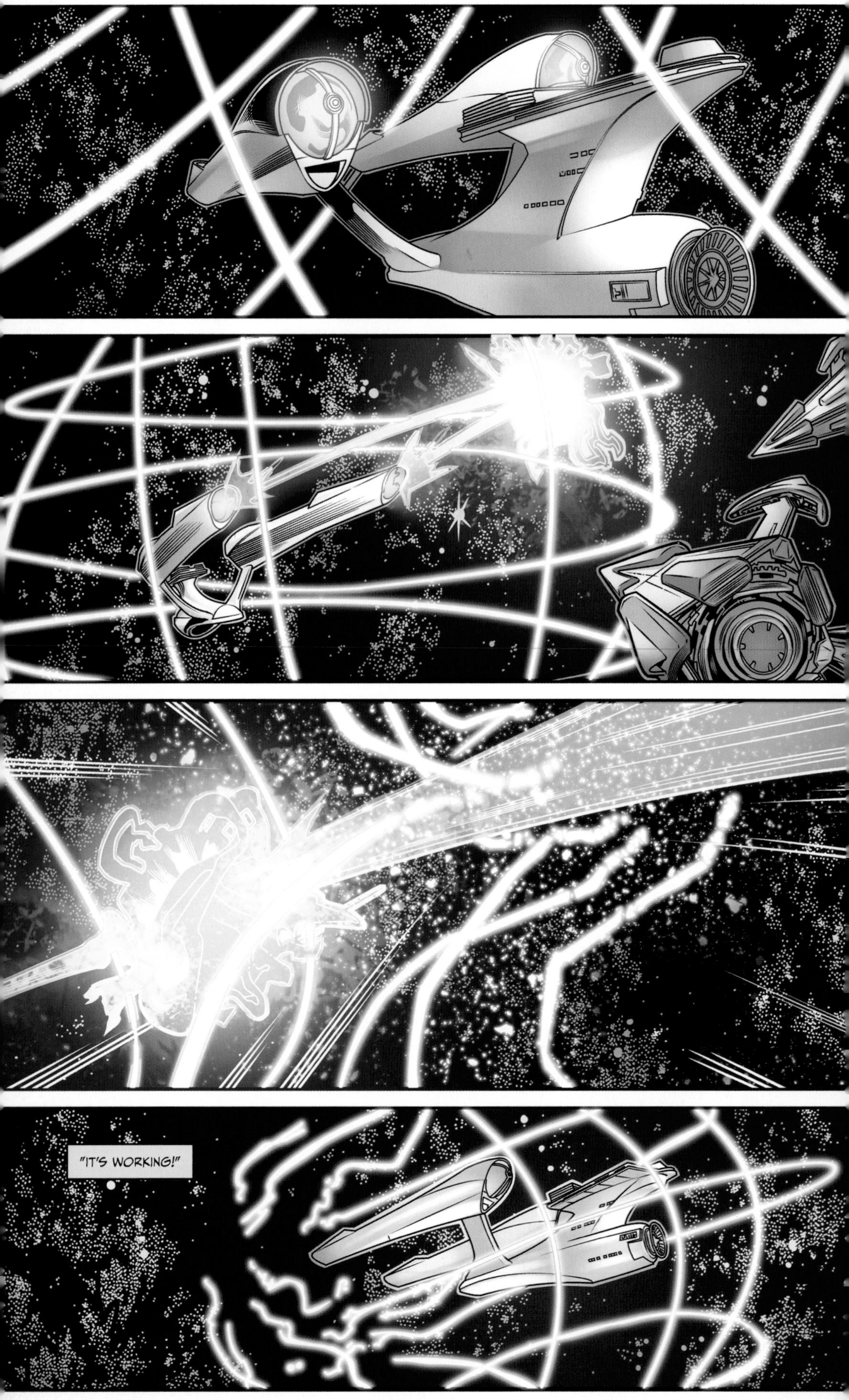
"IT'S WORKING!"

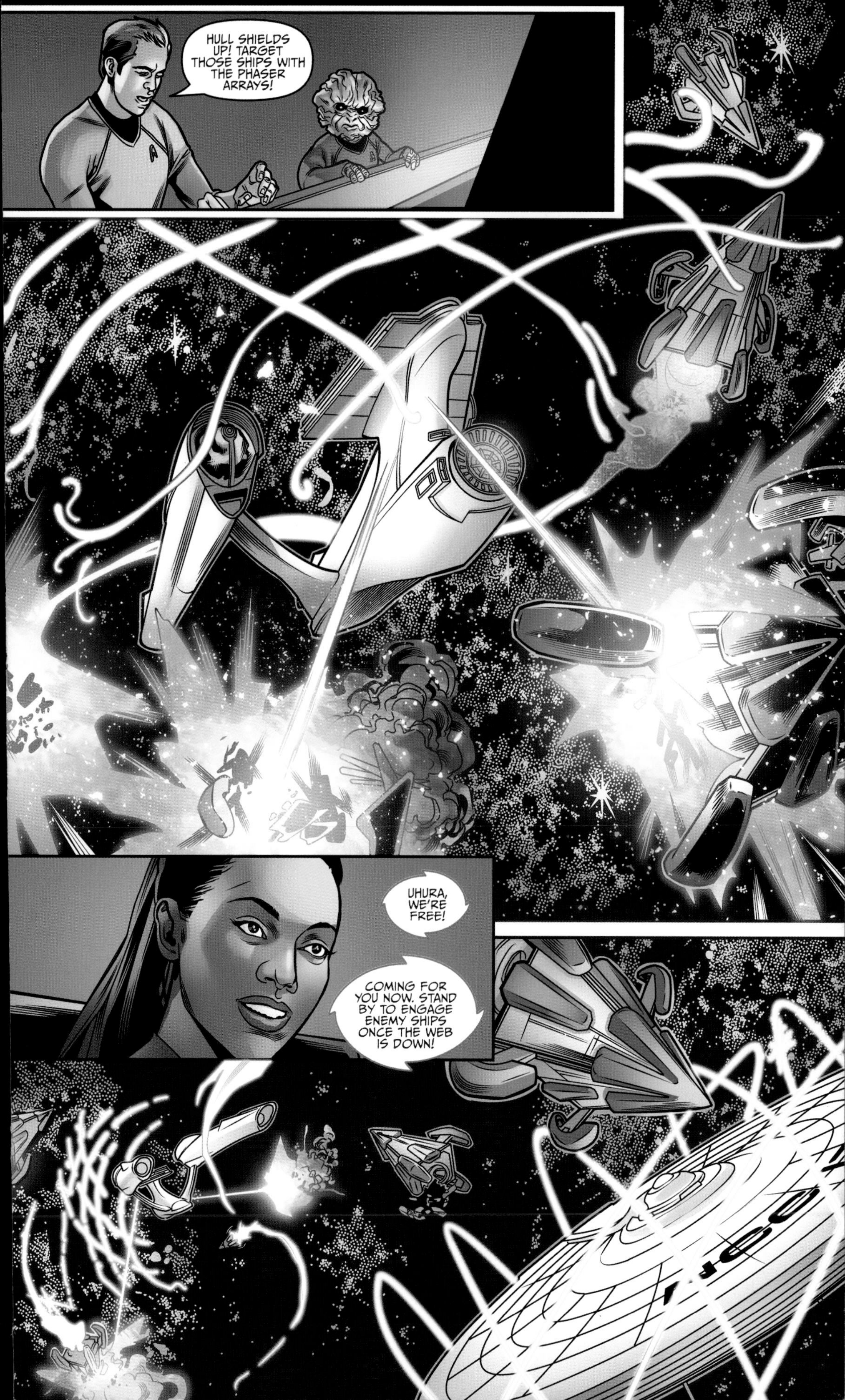
HULL SHIELDS UP! TARGET THOSE SHIPS WITH THE PHASER ARRAYS!
UHURA, WE'RE FREE!
COMING FOR YOU NOW. STAND BY TO ENGAGE ENEMY SHIPS ONCE THE WEB IS DOWN!

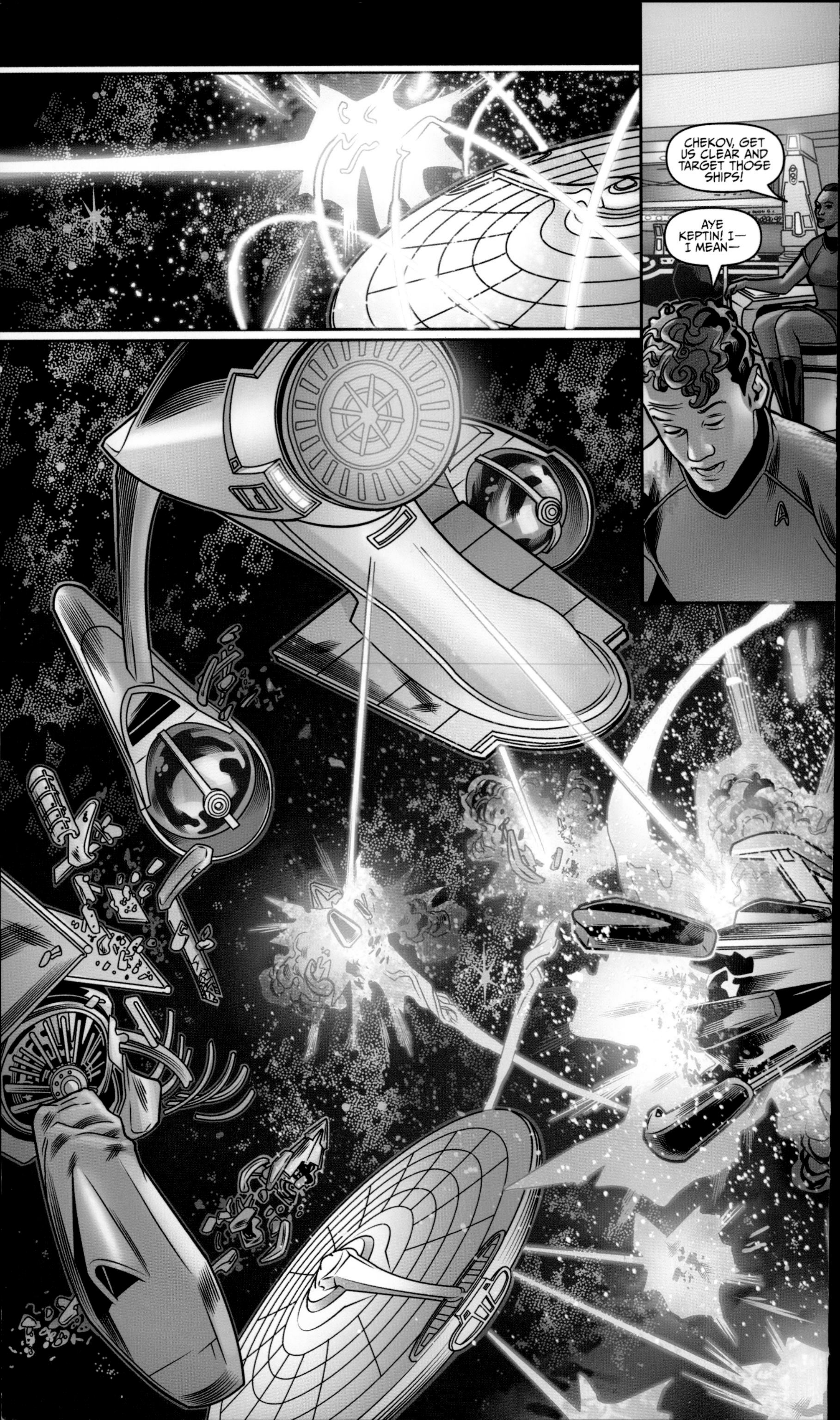
CHEKOV, GET US CLEAR AND TARGET THOSE SHIPS!
AYE KEPTIN! I— I MEAN—

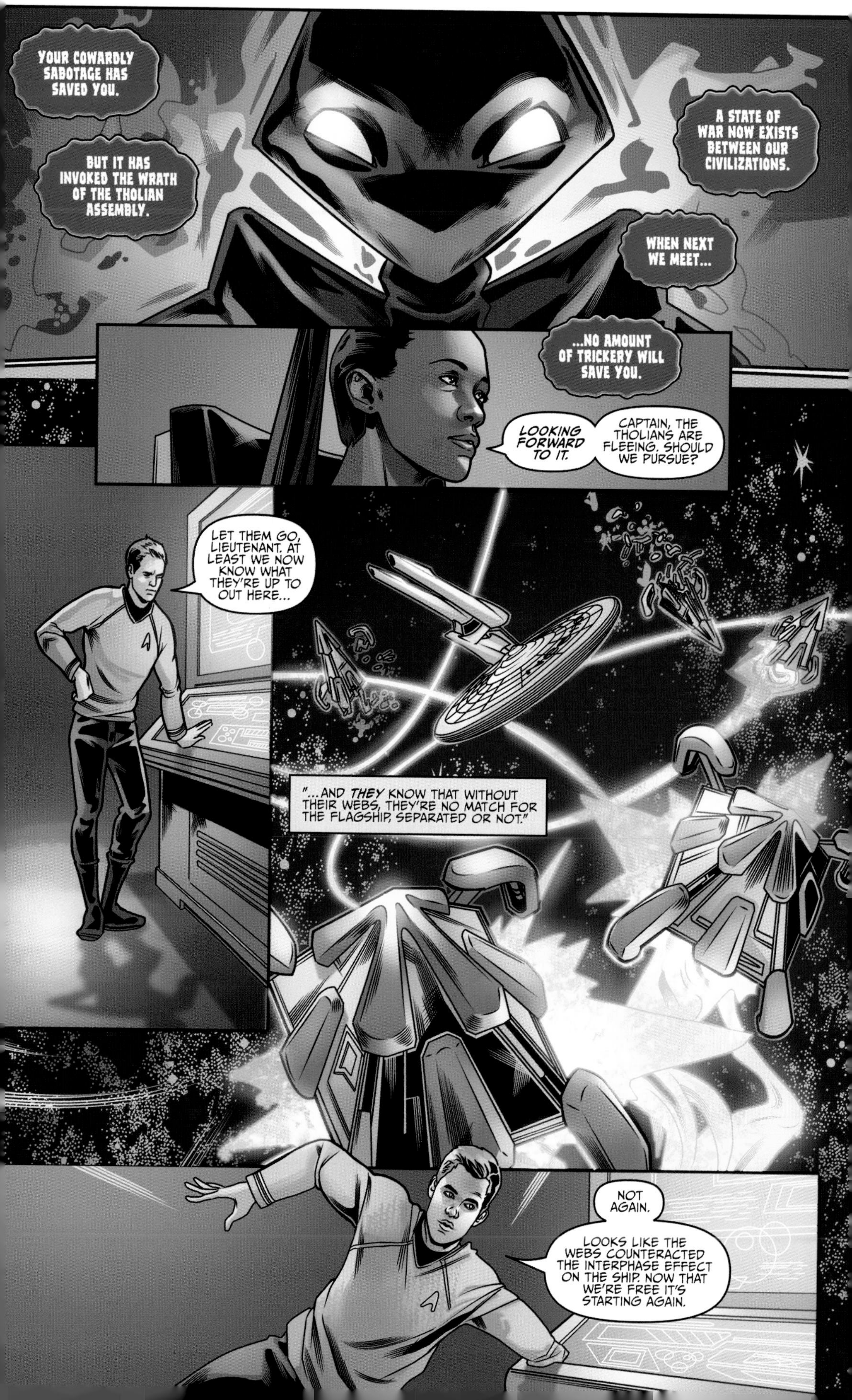
YOUR COWARDLY SABOTAGE HAS SAVED YOU.
BUT IT HAS INVOKED THE WRATH OF THE THOLIAN ASSEMBLY.
A STATE OF WAR NOW EXISTS BETWEEN OUR CIVILIZATIONS.
WHEN NEXT WE MEET...
...NO AMOUNT OF TRICKERY WILL SAVE YOU.
LOOKING FORWARD TO IT.
CAPTAIN, THE THOLIANS ARE FLEEING. SHOULD WE PURSUE?
LET THEM GO, LIEUTENANT. AT LEAST WE NOW KNOW WHAT THEY'RE UP TO OUT HERE...
"...AND THEY KNOW THAT WITHOUT THEIR WEBS, THEY'RE NO MATCH FOR THE FLAGSHIP, SEPARATED OR NOT."
NOT AGAIN.
LOOKS LIKE THE WEBS COUNTERACTED THE INTERPHASE EFFECT ON THE SHIP. NOW THAT WE'RE FREE IT'S STARTING AGAIN.

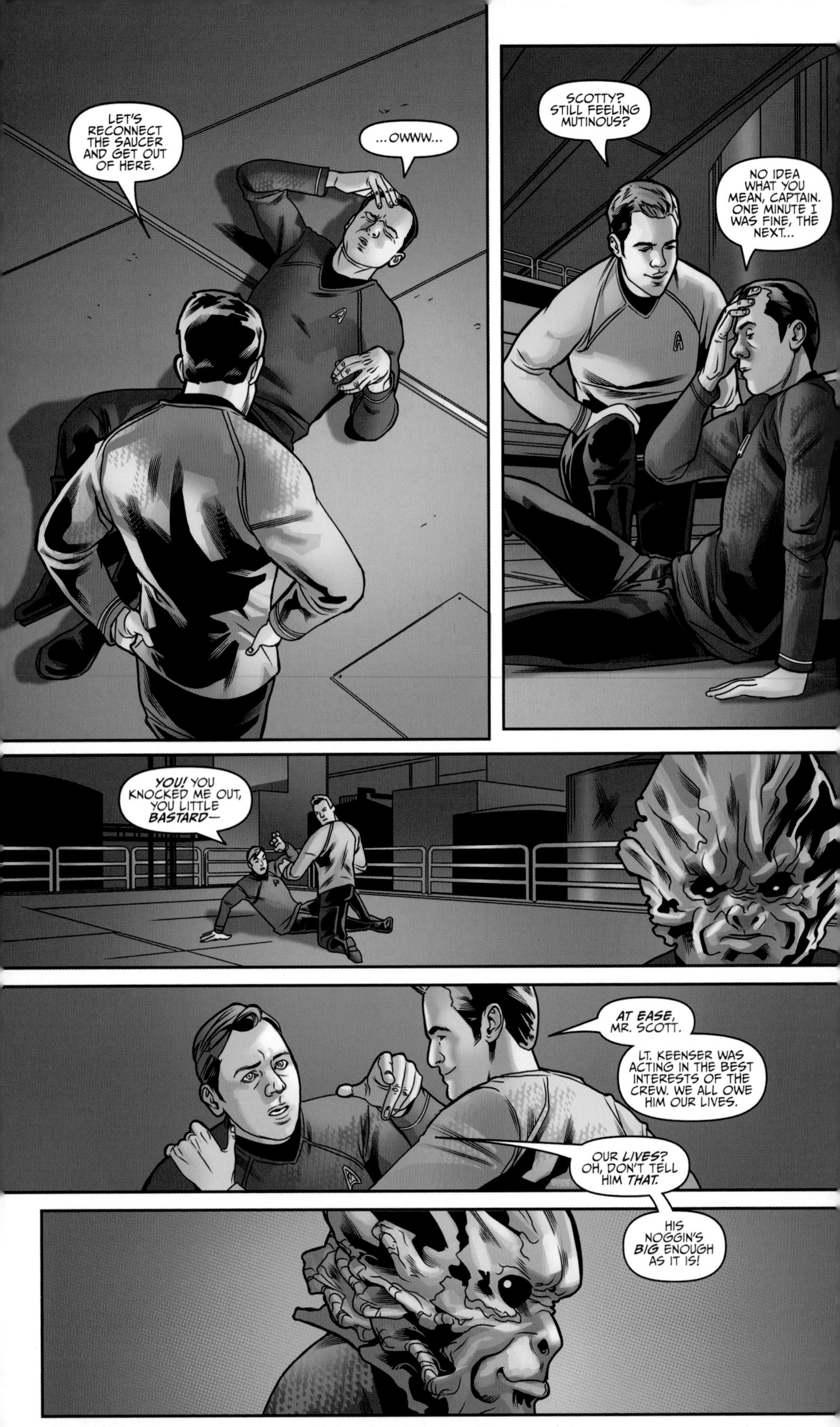
LET'S RECONNECT THE SAUCER AND GET OUT OF HERE.
...OWWW...
SCOTTY? STILL FEELING MUTINOUS?
NO IDEA WHAT YOU MEAN, CAPTAIN. ONE MINUTE I WAS FINE, THE NEXT...
YOU! YOU KNOCKED ME OUT, YOU LITTLE *BASTARD*—
AT EASE, MR. SCOTT.
LT. KEENSER WAS ACTING IN THE BEST INTERESTS OF THE CREW. WE ALL OWE HIM OUR LIVES.
OUR *LIVES?* OH, DON'T TELL HIM *THAT.*
HIS NOGGIN'S *BIG* ENOUGH AS IT IS!

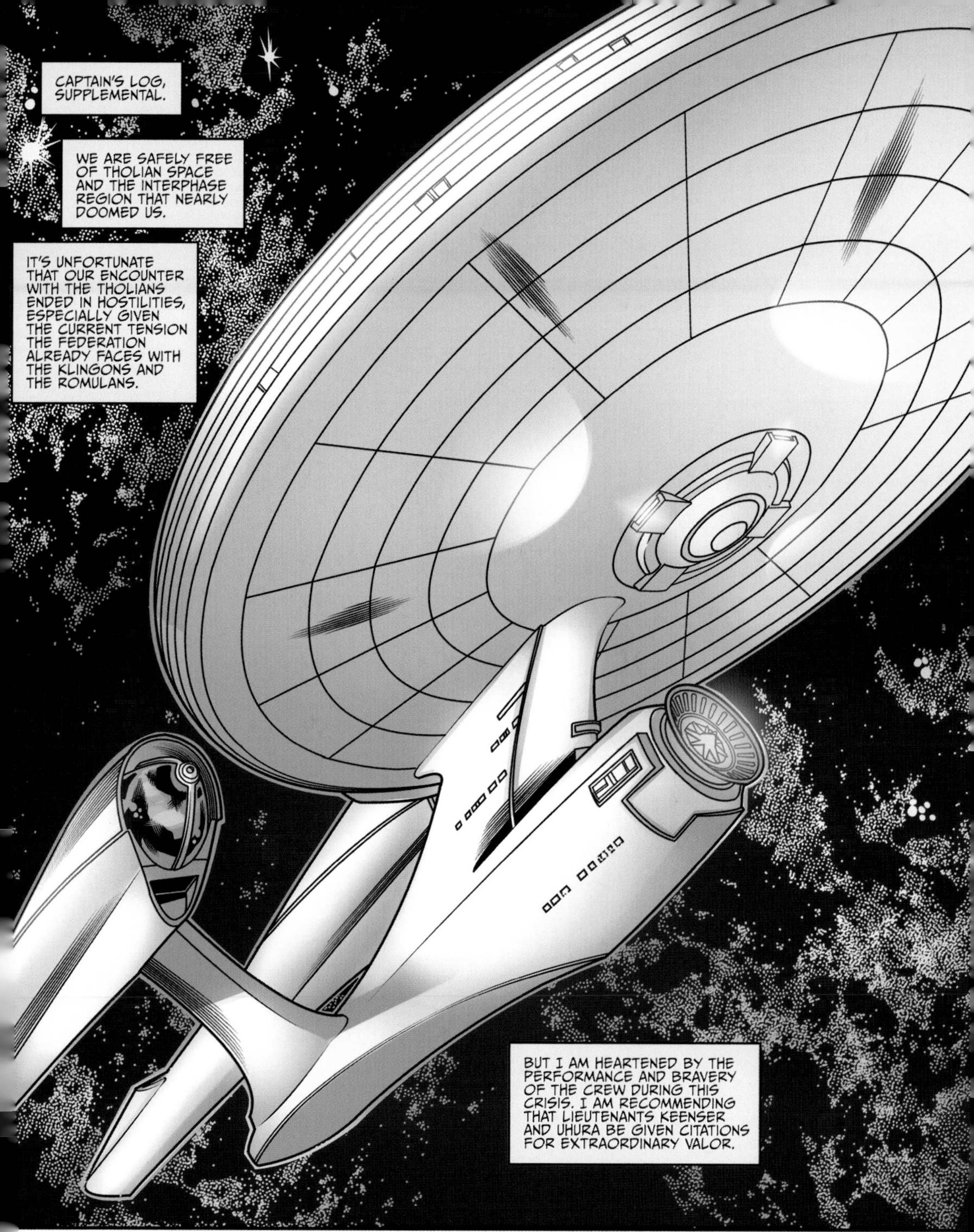
CAPTAIN'S LOG, SUPPLEMENTAL.
WE ARE SAFELY FREE OF THOLIAN SPACE AND THE INTERPHASE REGION THAT NEARLY DOOMED US.
IT'S UNFORTUNATE THAT OUR ENCOUNTER WITH THE THOLIANS ENDED IN HOSTILITIES, ESPECIALLY GIVEN THE CURRENT TENSION THE FEDERATION ALREADY FACES WITH THE KLINGONS AND THE ROMULANS.
BUT I AM HEARTENED BY THE PERFORMANCE AND BRAVERY OF THE CREW DURING THIS CRISIS. I AM RECOMMENDING THAT LIEUTENANTS KEENSER AND UHURA BE GIVEN CITATIONS FOR EXTRAORDINARY VALOR.

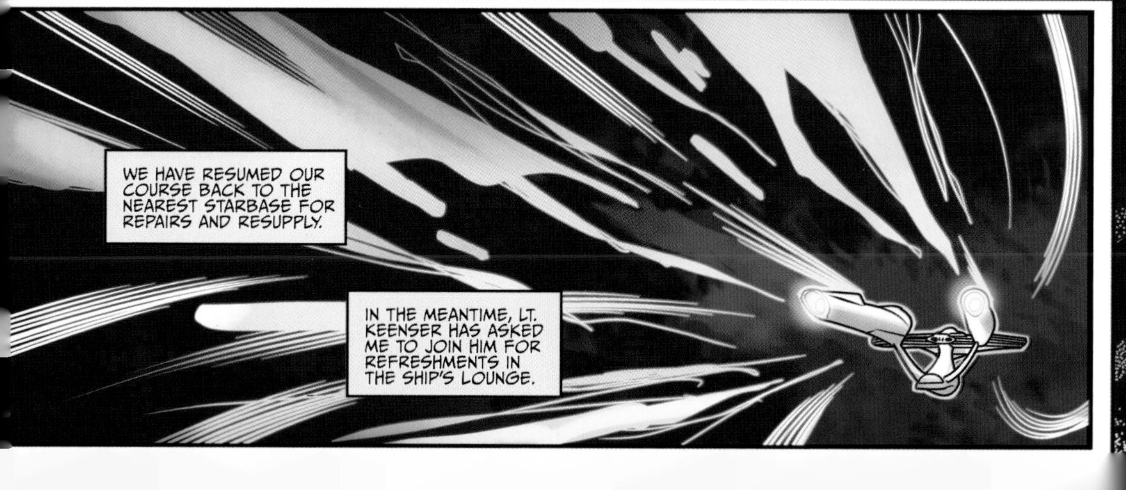
WE HAVE RESUMED OUR COURSE BACK TO THE NEAREST STARBASE FOR REPAIRS AND RESUPPLY.
IN THE MEANTIME, LT. KEENSER HAS ASKED ME TO JOIN HIM FOR REFRESHMENTS IN THE SHIP'S LOUNGE.

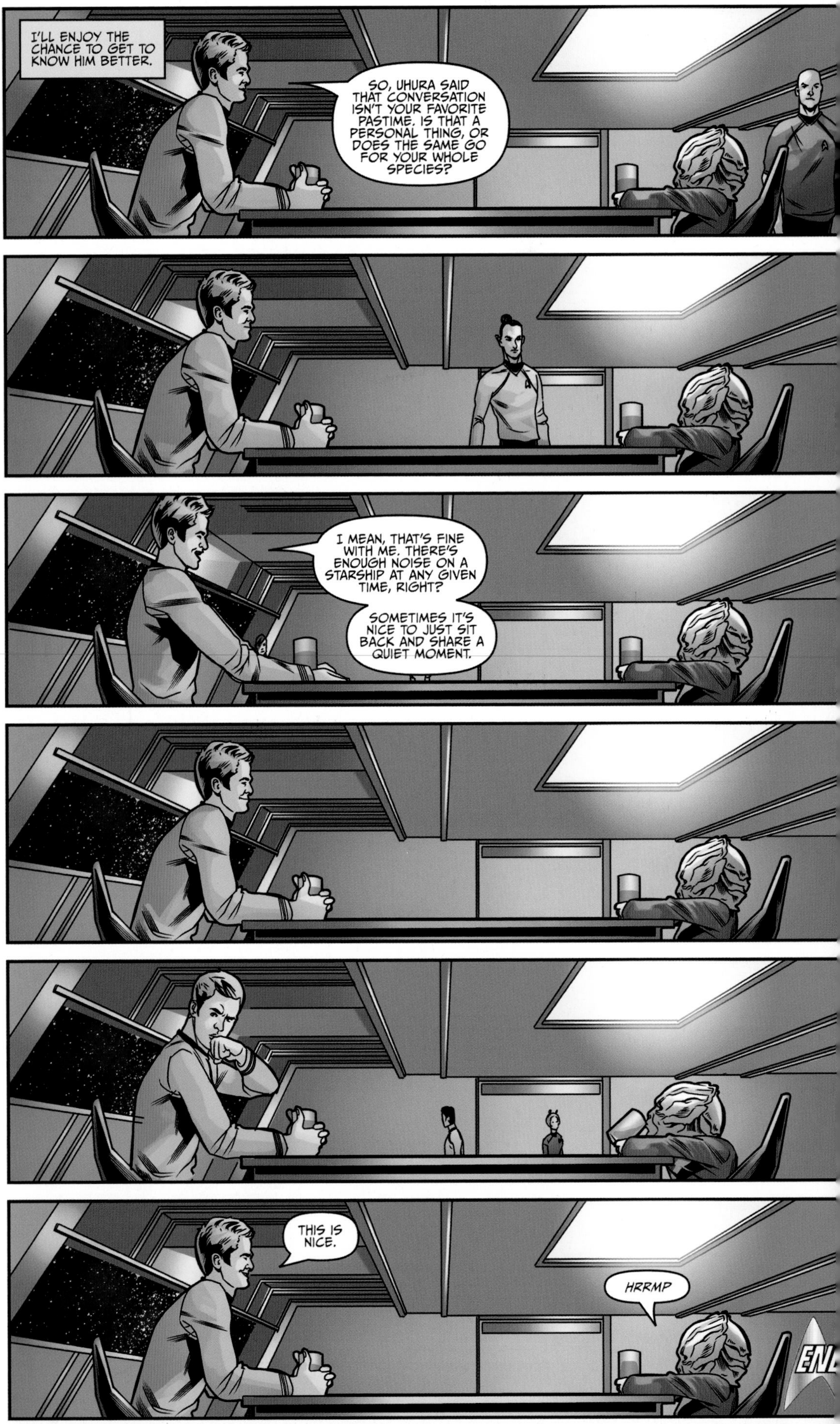
I'LL ENJOY THE CHANCE TO GET TO KNOW HIM BETTER.
SO, UHURA SAID THAT CONVERSATION ISN'T YOUR FAVORITE PASTIME. IS THAT A PERSONAL THING, OR DOES THE SAME GO FOR YOUR WHOLE SPECIES?
I MEAN, THAT'S FINE WITH ME. THERE'S ENOUGH NOISE ON A STARSHIP AT ANY GIVEN TIME, RIGHT?
SOMETIMES IT'S NICE TO JUST SIT BACK AND SHARE A QUIET MOMENT.
THIS IS NICE.
HRRMP

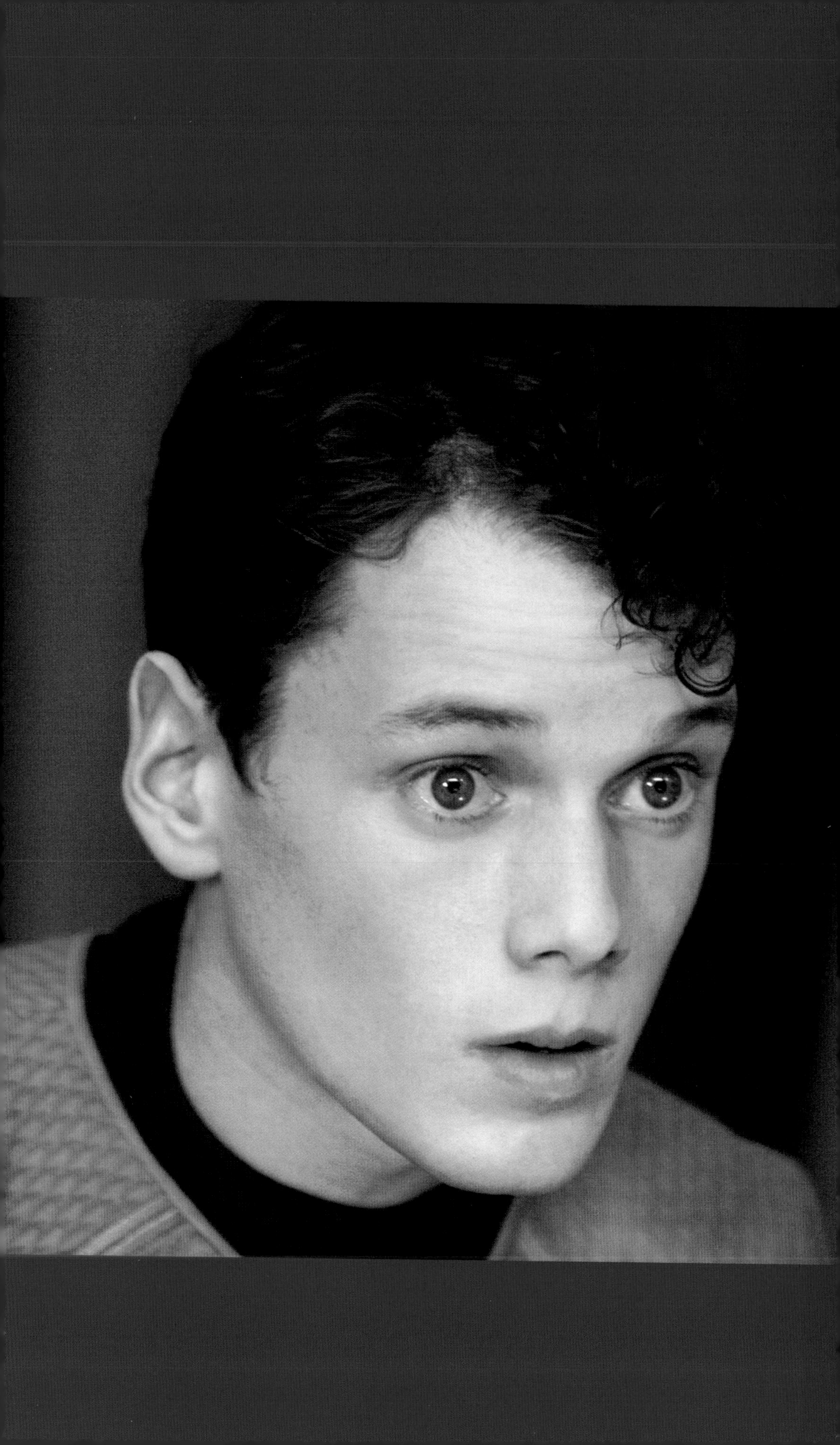

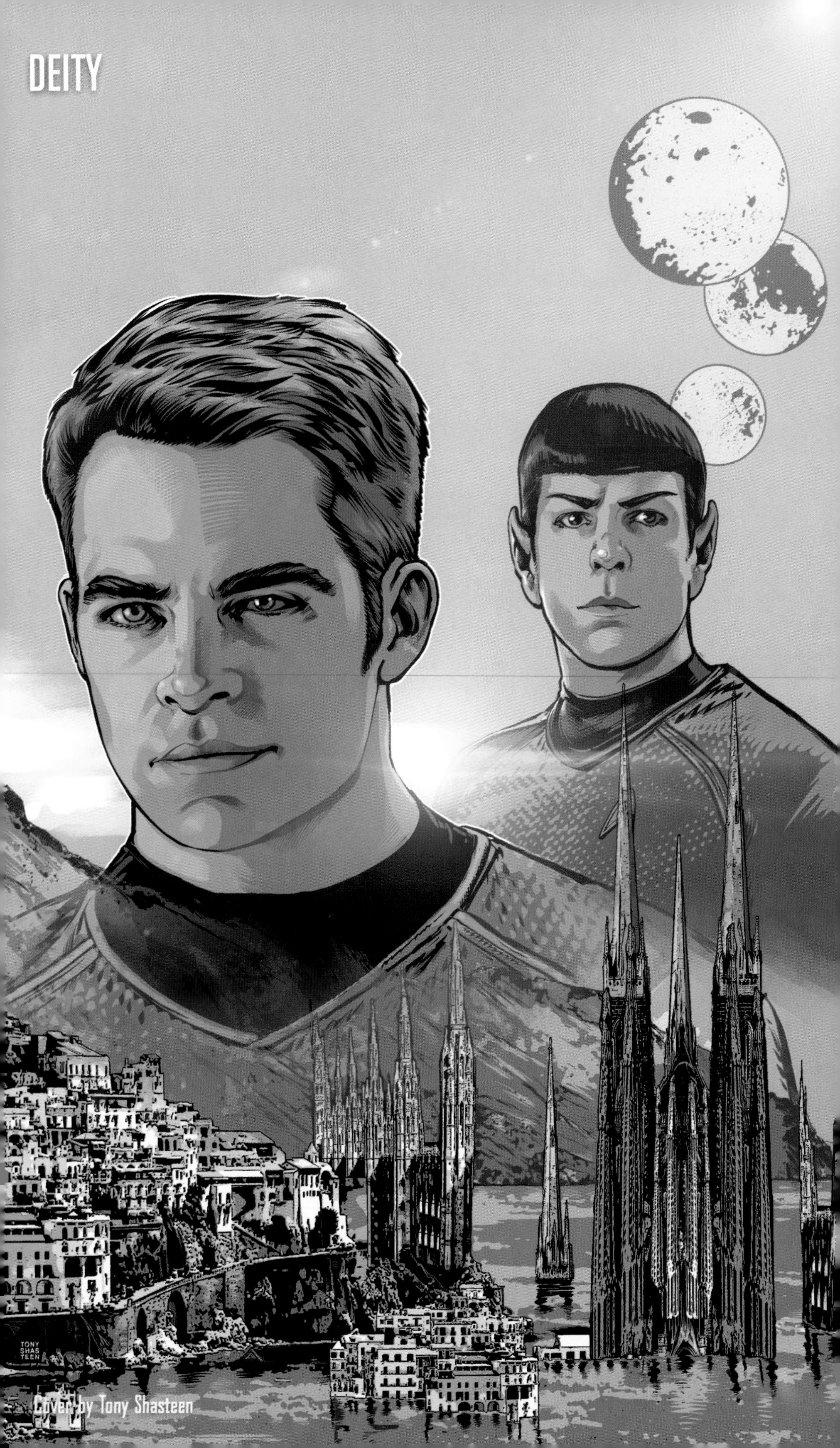
DEITY
TONY
SHAS
TEEN
Cover by Tony Shasteen

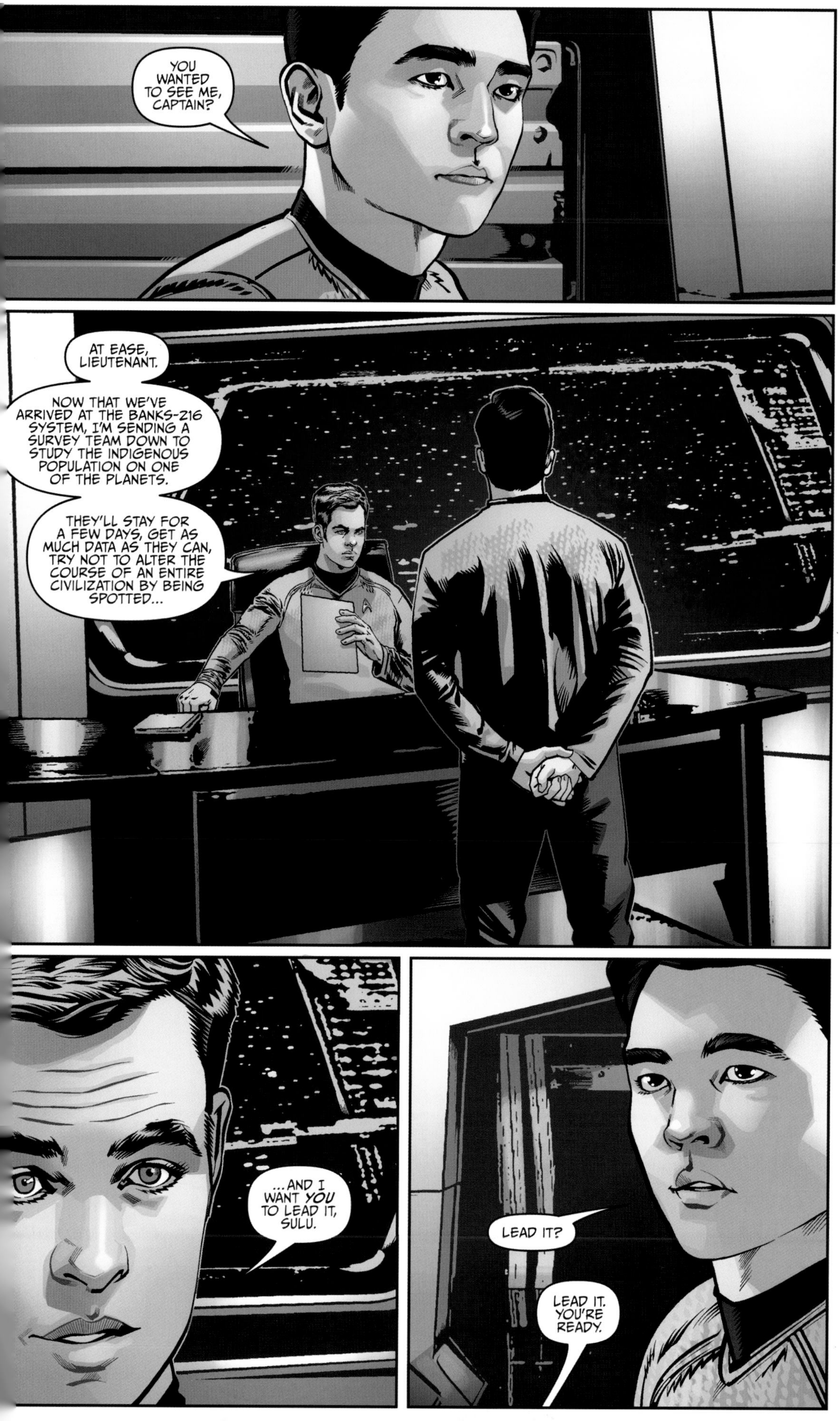
YOU WANTED TO SEE ME, CAPTAIN?
AT EASE, LIEUTENANT.
NOW THAT WE'VE ARRIVED AT THE BANKS-216 SYSTEM, I'M SENDING A SURVEY TEAM DOWN TO STUDY THE INDIGENOUS POPULATION ON ONE OF THE PLANETS.
THEY'LL STAY FOR A FEW DAYS, GET AS MUCH DATA AS THEY CAN, TRY NOT TO ALTER THE COURSE OF AN ENTIRE CIVILIZATION BY BEING SPOTTED...
...AND I WANT *YOU* TO LEAD IT, SULU.
LEAD IT?
LEAD IT. YOU'RE READY.

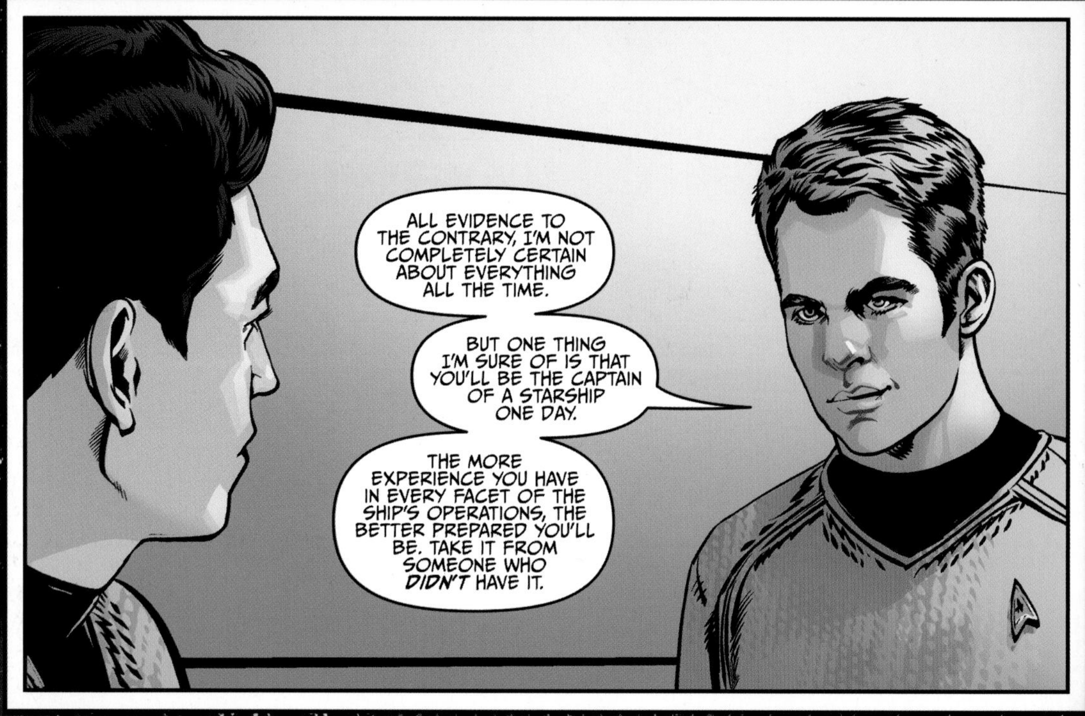
ALL EVIDENCE TO THE CONTRARY, I'M NOT COMPLETELY CERTAIN ABOUT EVERYTHING ALL THE TIME.
BUT ONE THING I'M SURE OF IS THAT YOU'LL BE THE CAPTAIN OF A STARSHIP ONE DAY.
THE MORE EXPERIENCE YOU HAVE IN EVERY FACET OF THE SHIP'S OPERATIONS, THE BETTER PREPARED YOU'LL BE. TAKE IT FROM SOMEONE WHO *DIDN'T* HAVE IT.

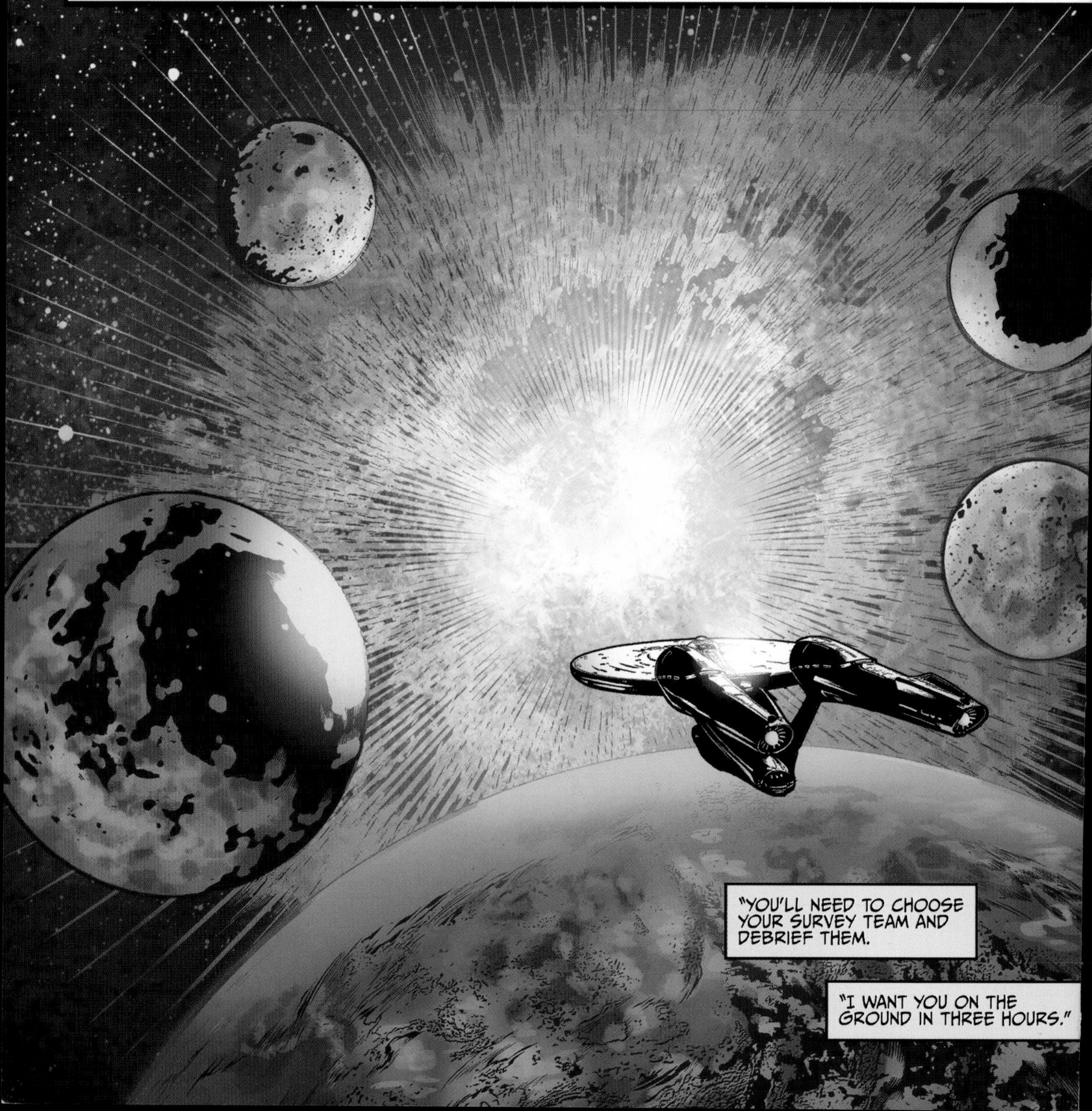
"YOU'LL NEED TO CHOOSE YOUR SURVEY TEAM AND DEBRIEF THEM.
"I WANT YOU ON THE GROUND IN THREE HOURS."

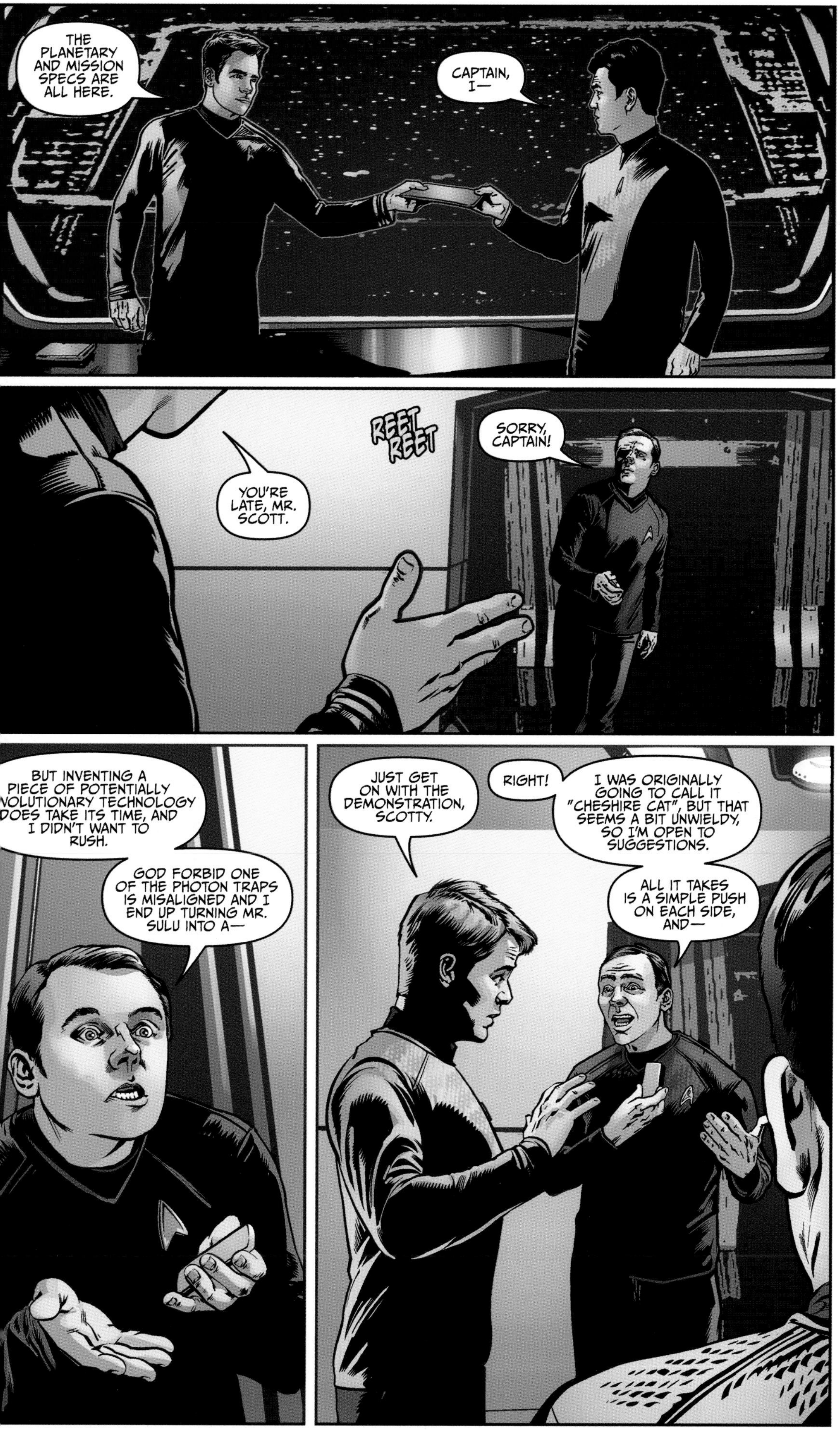
THE PLANETARY AND MISSION SPECS ARE ALL HERE.
CAPTAIN, I—
YOU'RE LATE, MR. SCOTT.
REET REET
SORRY, CAPTAIN!
BUT INVENTING A PIECE OF POTENTIALLY VOLUTIONARY TECHNOLOGY DOES TAKE ITS TIME, AND I DIDN'T WANT TO RUSH.
GOD FORBID ONE OF THE PHOTON TRAPS IS MISALIGNED AND I END UP TURNING MR. SULU INTO A—
JUST GET ON WITH THE DEMONSTRATION, SCOTTY.
RIGHT!
I WAS ORIGINALLY GOING TO CALL IT "CHESHIRE CAT", BUT THAT SEEMS A BIT UNWIELDY, SO I'M OPEN TO SUGGESTIONS.
ALL IT TAKES IS A SIMPLE PUSH ON EACH SIDE, AND—

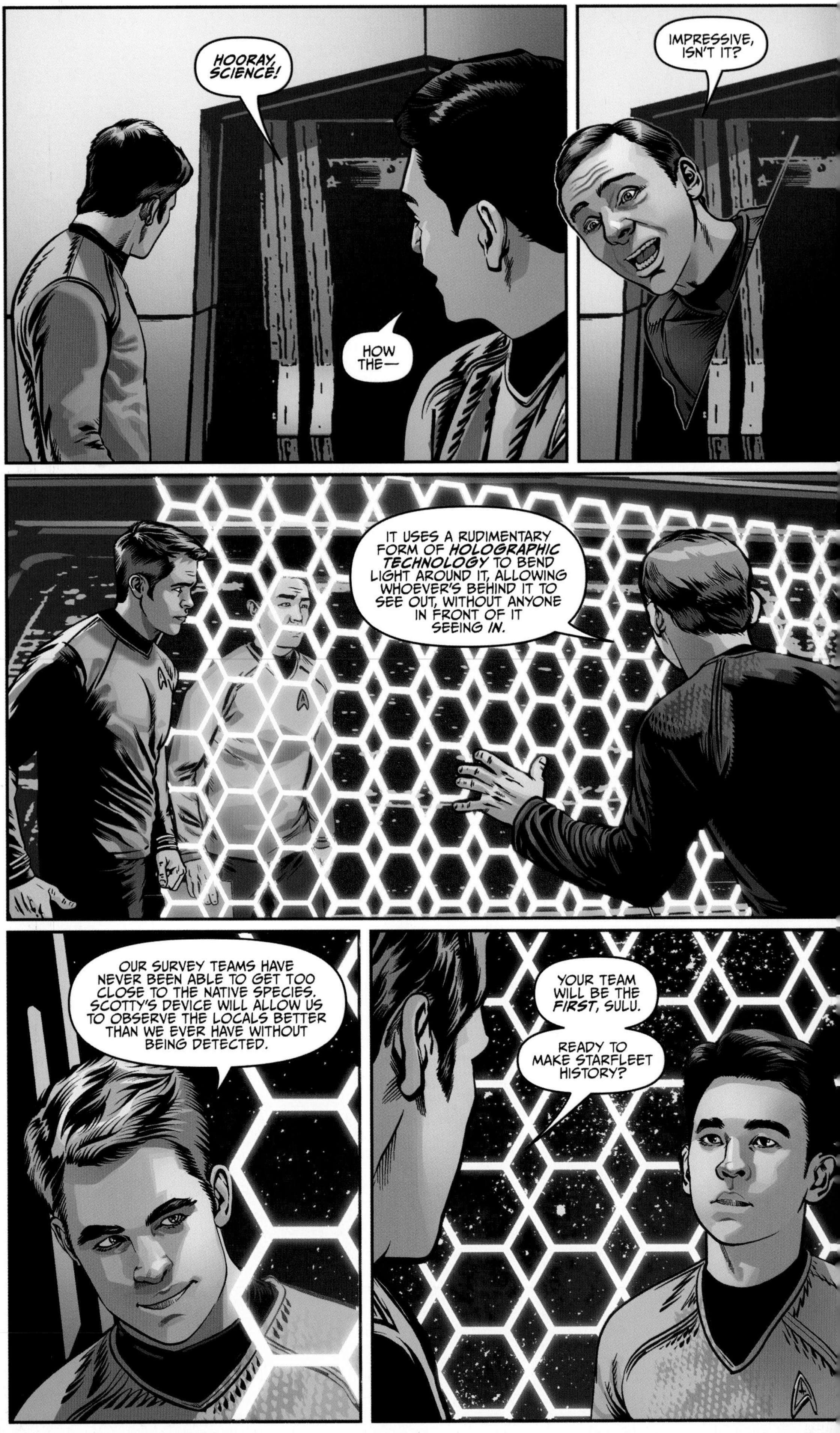
HOORAY, SCIENCE!
HOW THE—
IMPRESSIVE, ISN'T IT?
IT USES A RUDIMENTARY FORM OF HOLOGRAPHIC TECHNOLOGY TO BEND LIGHT AROUND IT, ALLOWING WHOEVER'S BEHIND IT TO SEE OUT, WITHOUT ANYONE IN FRONT OF IT SEEING IN.
OUR SURVEY TEAMS HAVE NEVER BEEN ABLE TO GET TOO CLOSE TO THE NATIVE SPECIES. SCOTTY'S DEVICE WILL ALLOW US TO OBSERVE THE LOCALS BETTER THAN WE EVER HAVE WITHOUT BEING DETECTED.
YOUR TEAM WILL BE THE FIRST, SULU.
READY TO MAKE STARFLEET HISTORY?

HELMSMAN'S LOG, SUPPLEMENTAL.

I'D BE LYING IF I SAID I WASN'T NERVOUS. HOLDING THE CONN ON THE BRIDGE IS ONE THING. YOU'RE SURROUNDED BY SEVERAL HUNDRED EXTREMELY TALENTED PEOPLE AND A STATE-OF-THE-ART FLAGSHIP.

BUT LEADING AN AWAY TEAM DOWN TO AN UNKNOWN PLANET AND TESTING PROTOTYPE TECHNOLOGY? THAT'S SOMETHING ELSE.

SO I SURROUND MYSELF WITH THE BEST.

SCIENCE OFFICER AMOS. RECENT TRANSFER FROM THE *ENDEAVOR*. EXPERT IN XENO-FLORA AND FAUNA.

SCIENCE OFFICER FERDOWSI. ANTHROPOLOGIST. HE'S MADE FIRST CONTACT WITH MORE SPECIES THAN ANYONE IN THE FLEET.

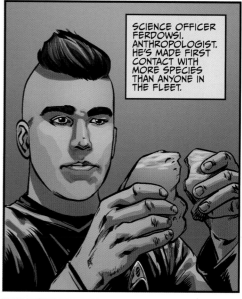

FOR SECURITY, LT. CORDRY. RUMOR IS SHE ONCE TOOK DOWN A FULLY GROWN RABID *SEHLAT* WITH HER BARE HANDS ON A TRIP TO VULCAN.

AND MR. SCOTT INSISTED ON SEEING HIS PROTOTYPE IN ACTION FIRSTHAND, SO THAT MAKES FIVE OF US.

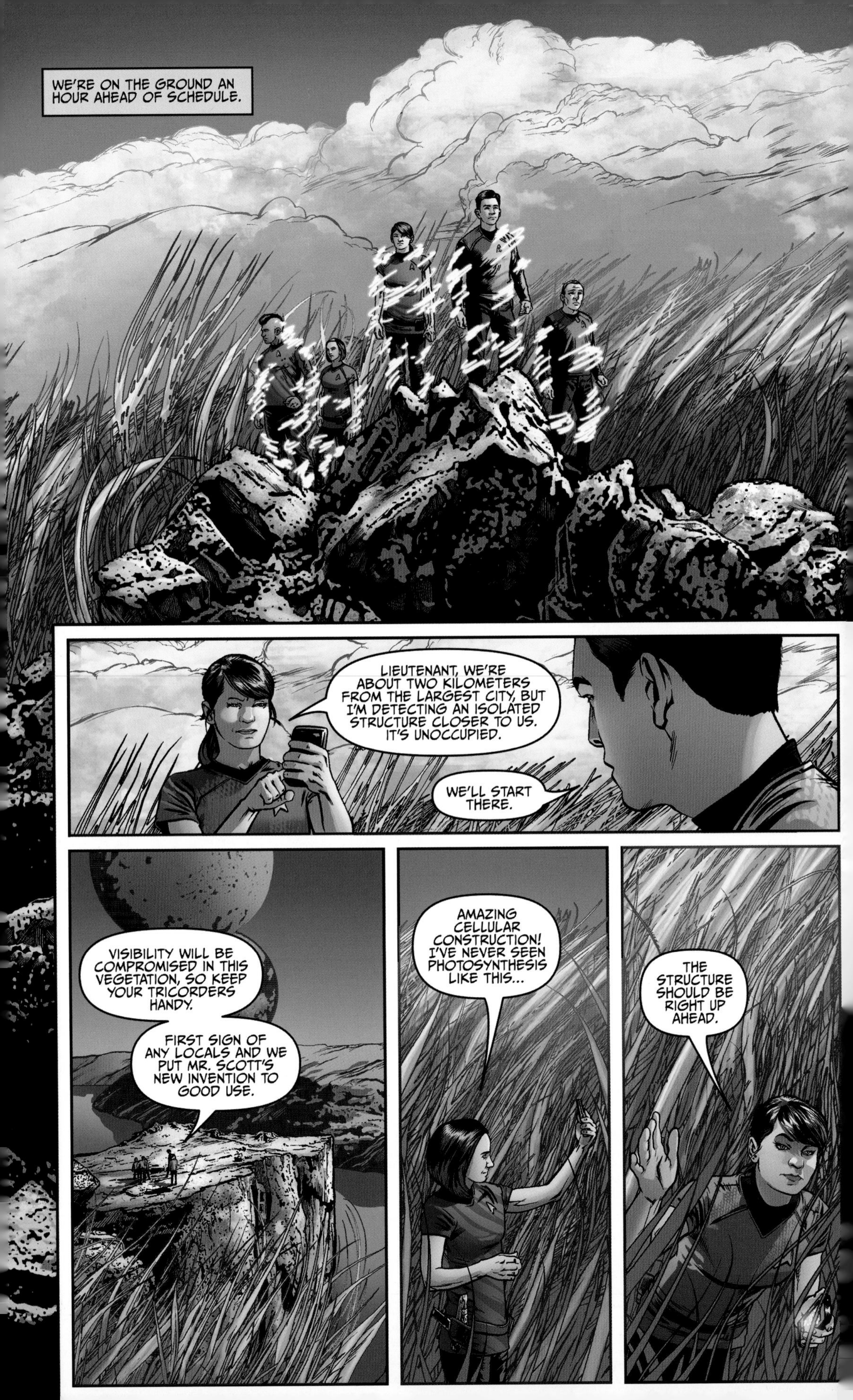
WE'RE ON THE GROUND AN HOUR AHEAD OF SCHEDULE.
LIEUTENANT, WE'RE ABOUT TWO KILOMETERS FROM THE LARGEST CITY, BUT I'M DETECTING AN ISOLATED STRUCTURE CLOSER TO US. IT'S UNOCCUPIED.
WE'LL START THERE.
VISIBILITY WILL BE COMPROMISED IN THIS VEGETATION, SO KEEP YOUR TRICORDERS HANDY.
FIRST SIGN OF ANY LOCALS AND WE PUT MR. SCOTT'S NEW INVENTION TO GOOD USE.
AMAZING CELLULAR CONSTRUCTION! I'VE NEVER SEEN PHOTOSYNTHESIS LIKE THIS...
THE STRUCTURE SHOULD BE RIGHT UP AHEAD.

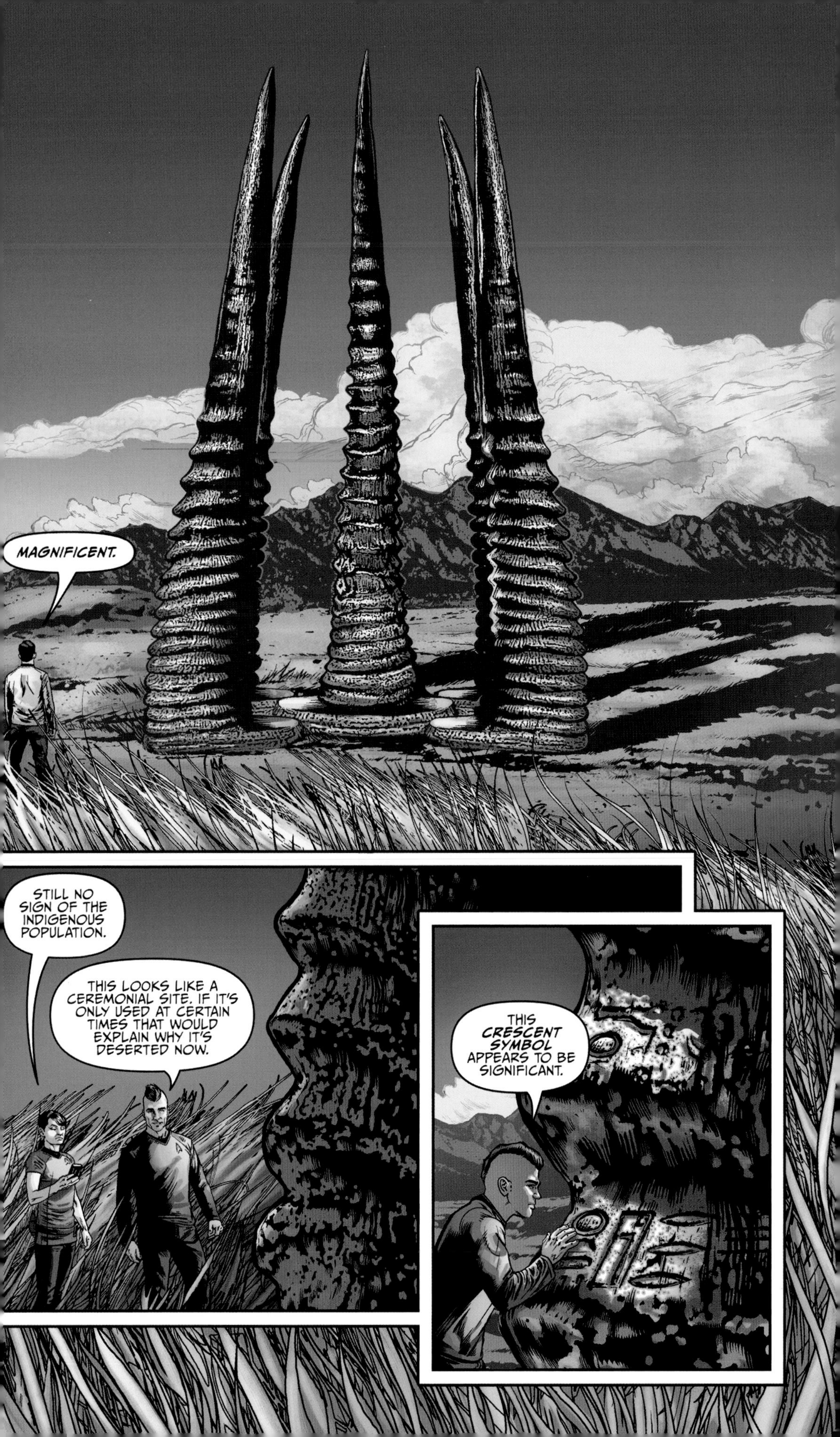
MAGNIFICENT.
STILL NO SIGN OF THE INDIGENOUS POPULATION.
THIS LOOKS LIKE A CEREMONIAL SITE. IF IT'S ONLY USED AT CERTAIN TIMES THAT WOULD EXPLAIN WHY IT'S DESERTED NOW.
THIS CRESCENT SYMBOL APPEARS TO BE SIGNIFICANT.

WRRBOOOM

LOOKS LIKE OUR TIMING COULD HAVE BEEN BETTER.

LIEUTENANT, LOOK AT THIS!

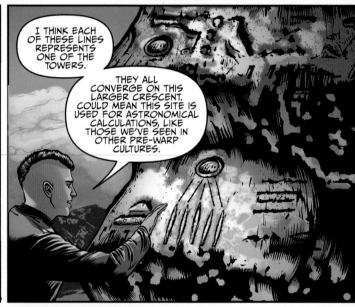

I THINK EACH OF THESE LINES REPRESENTS ONE OF THE TOWERS.

THEY ALL CONVERGE ON THIS LARGER CRESCENT. COULD MEAN THIS SITE IS USED FOR ASTRONOMICAL CALCULATIONS, LIKE THOSE WE'VE SEEN IN OTHER PRE-WARP CULTURES.

WRRBOOOM

LET'S LOOK FOR COVER TO WAIT OUT THE STORM.

LIEUTENANT, I'M PICKING UP MULTIPLE TARGETS HEADING OUR WAY!

FAST!

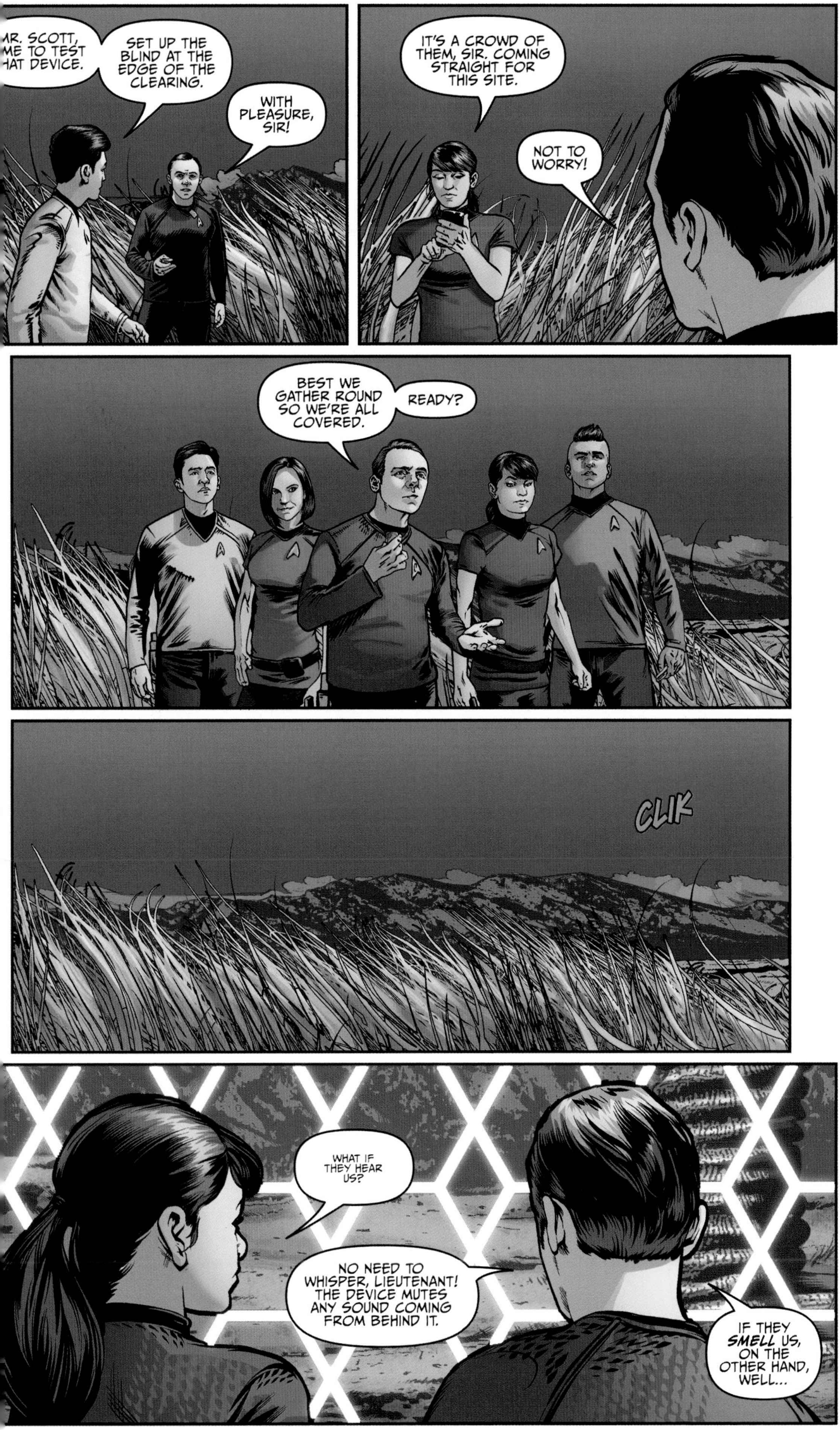
MR. SCOTT, ME TO TEST HAT DEVICE.
SET UP THE BLIND AT THE EDGE OF THE CLEARING.
WITH PLEASURE, SIR!
IT'S A CROWD OF THEM, SIR. COMING STRAIGHT FOR THIS SITE.
NOT TO WORRY!
BEST WE GATHER ROUND SO WE'RE ALL COVERED.
READY?
CLIK
WHAT IF THEY HEAR US?
NO NEED TO WHISPER, LIEUTENANT! THE DEVICE MUTES ANY SOUND COMING FROM BEHIND IT.
IF THEY *SMELL* US, ON THE OTHER HAND, WELL...

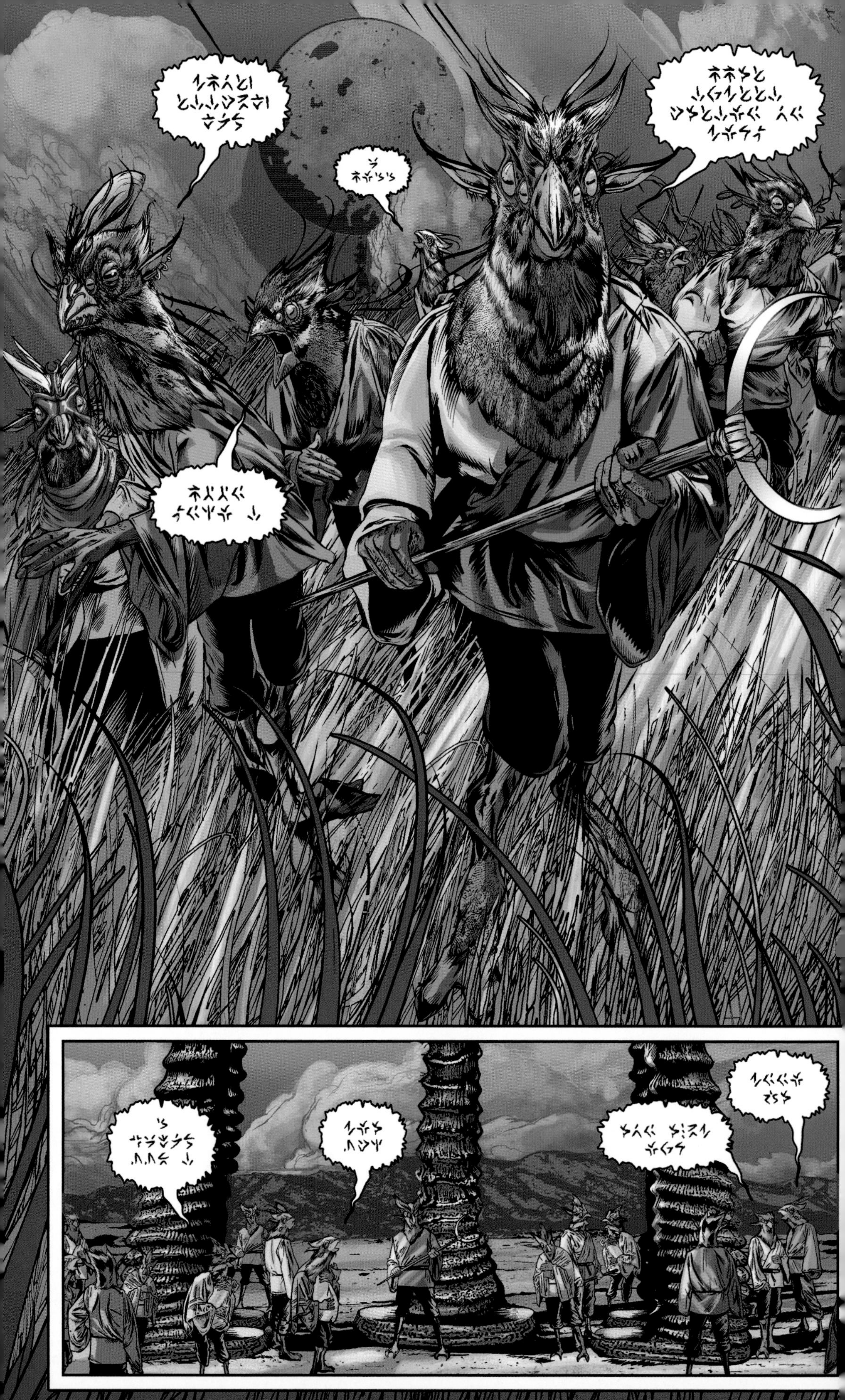

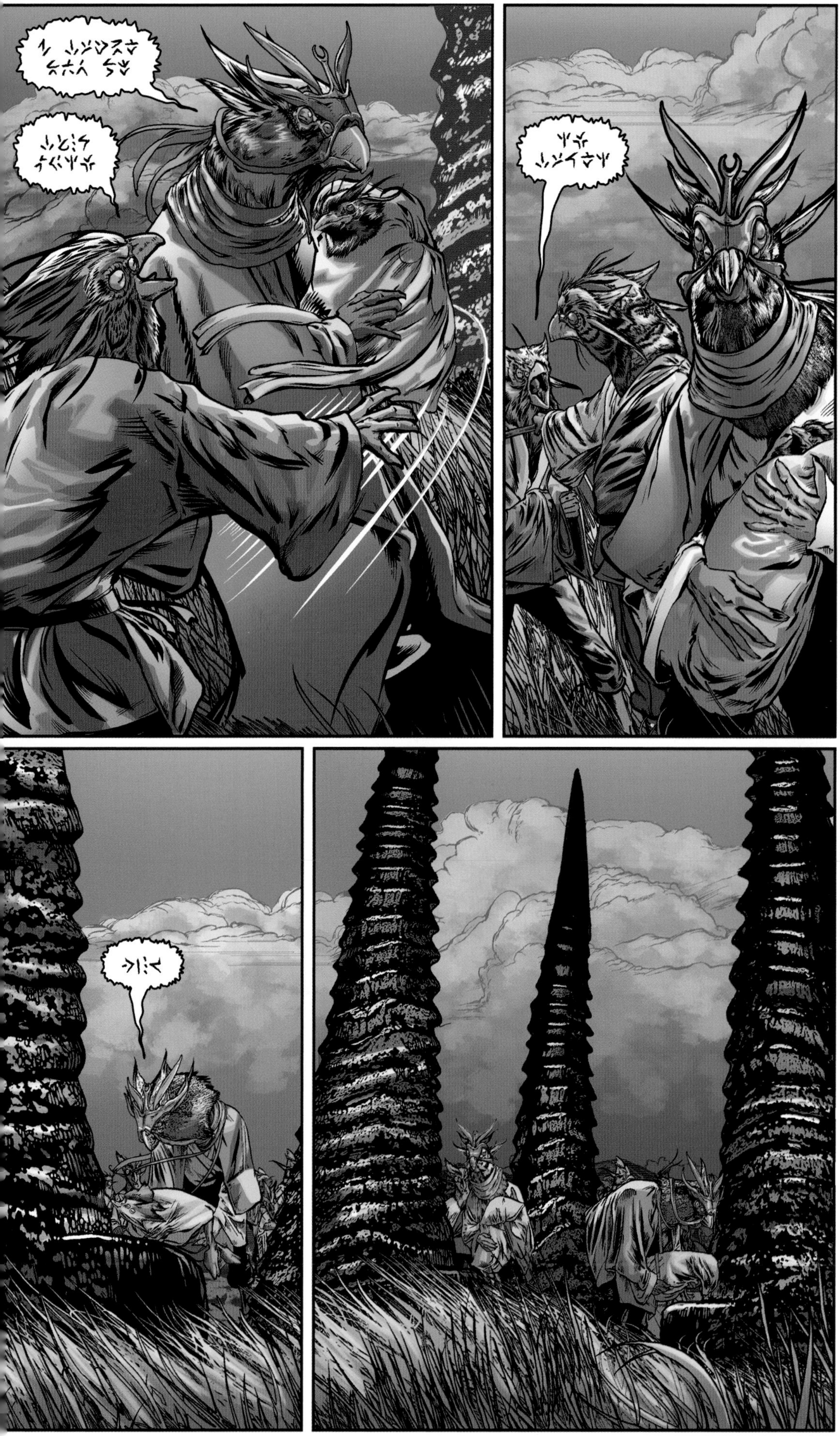

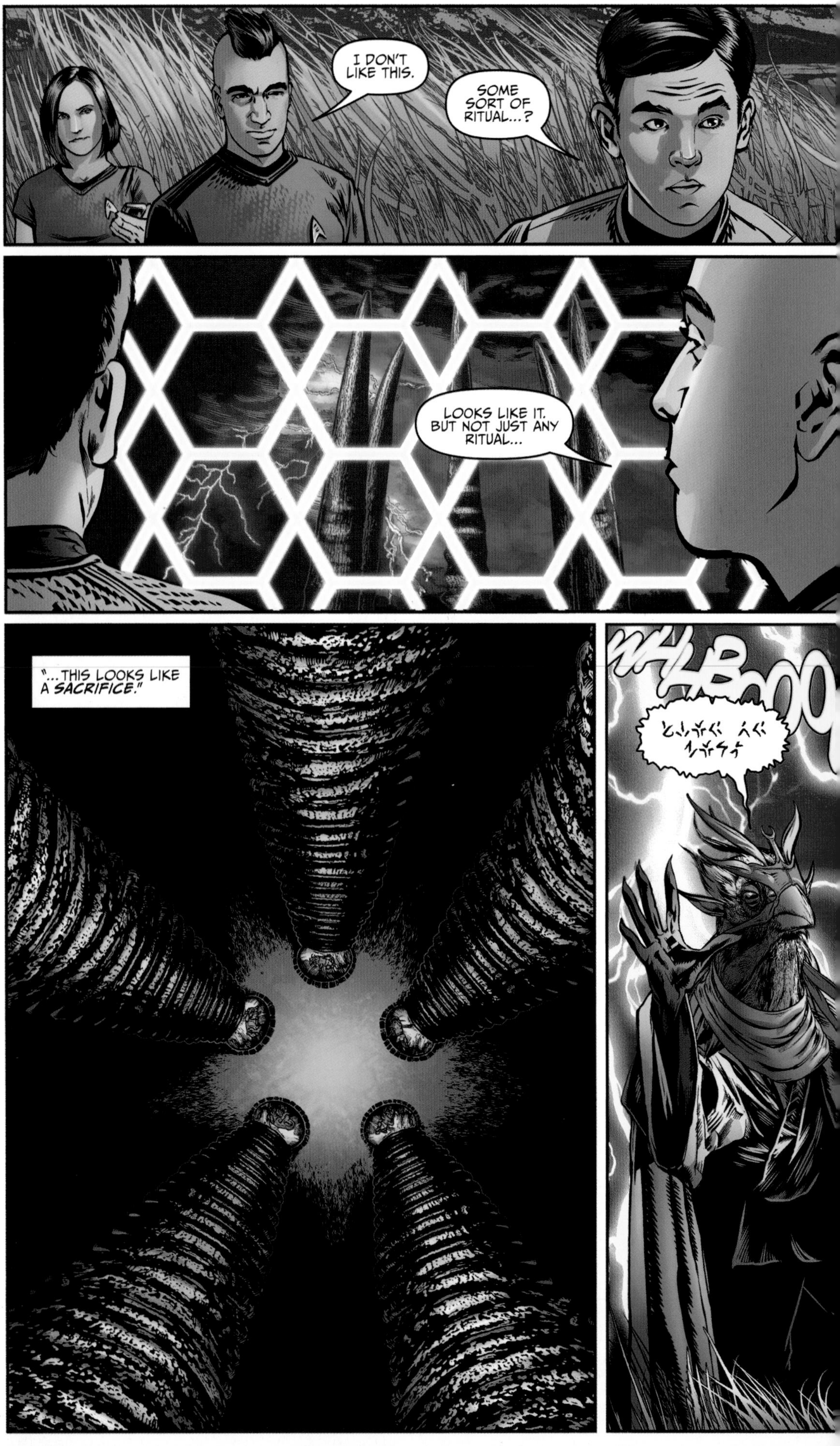
I DON'T LIKE THIS.
SOME SORT OF RITUAL...?
LOOKS LIKE IT. BUT NOT JUST ANY RITUAL...
"...THIS LOOKS LIKE A *SACRIFICE*."

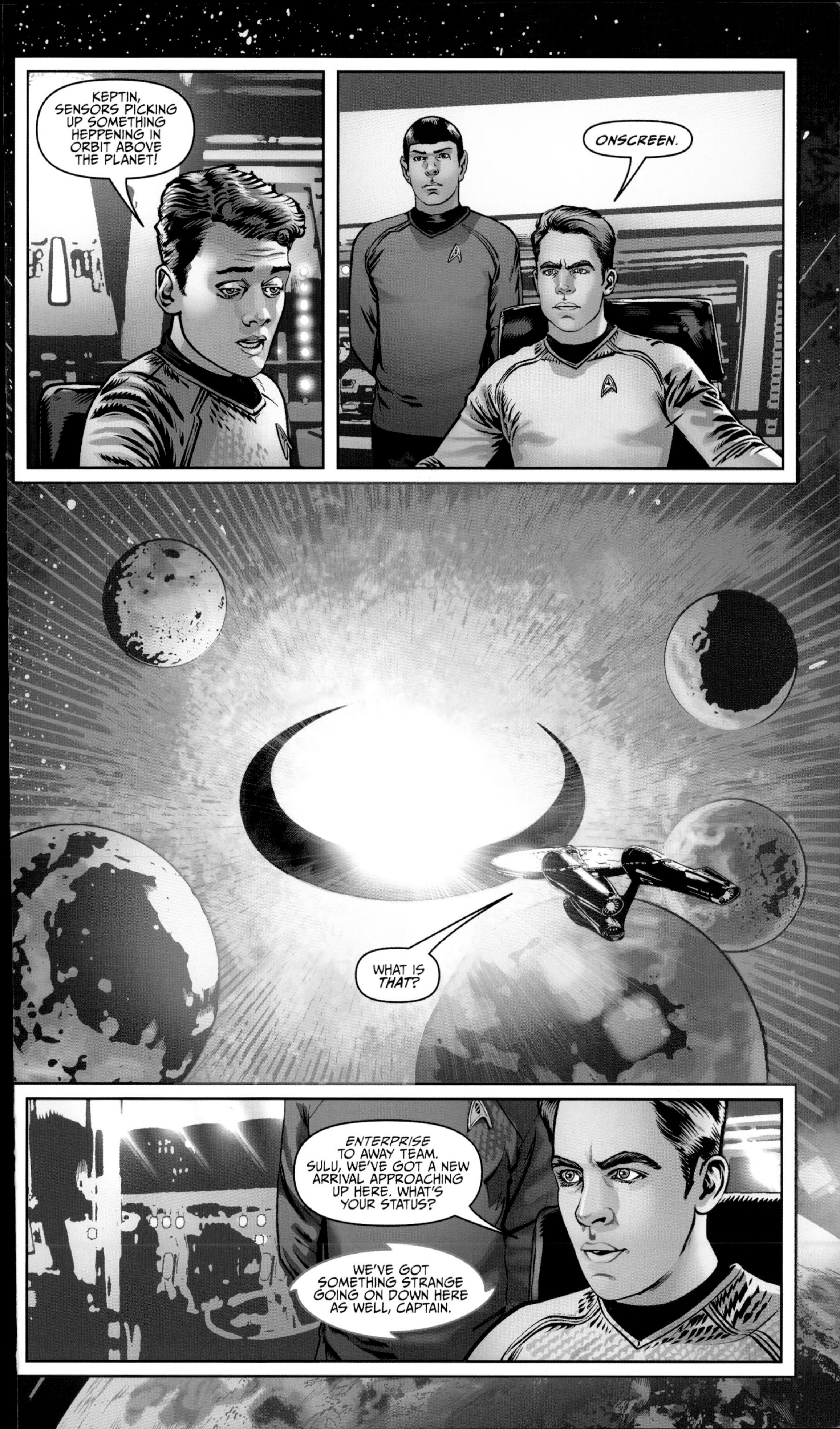
KEPTIN, SENSORS PICKING UP SOMETHING HEPPENING IN ORBIT ABOVE THE PLANET!
ONSCREEN.
WHAT IS *THAT?*
ENTERPRISE TO AWAY TEAM. SULU, WE'VE GOT A NEW ARRIVAL APPROACHING UP HERE. WHAT'S YOUR STATUS?
WE'VE GOT SOMETHING STRANGE GOING ON DOWN HERE AS WELL, CAPTAIN.

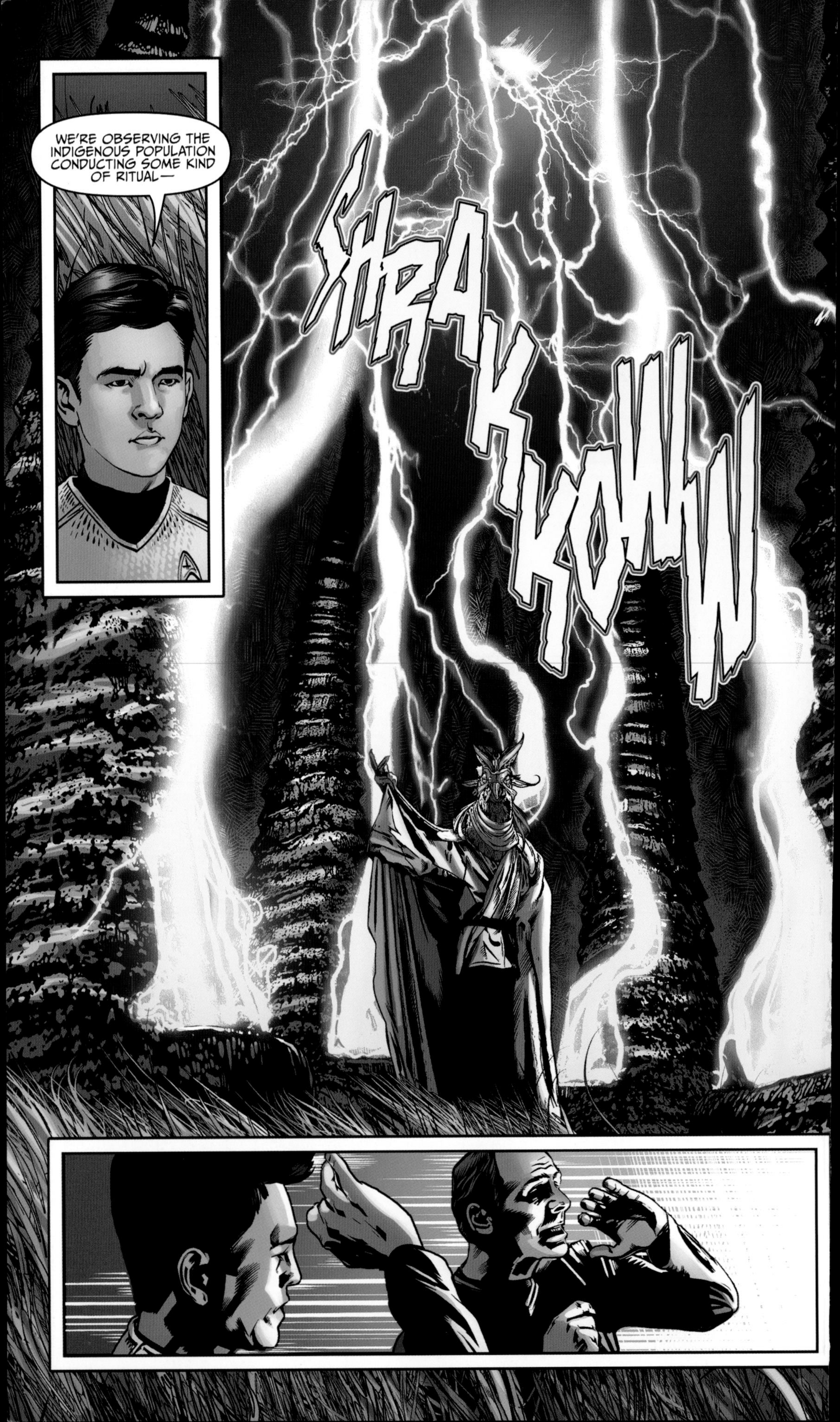
WE'RE OBSERVING THE INDIGENOUS POPULATION CONDUCTING SOME KIND OF RITUAL—
SHRAK KOWW

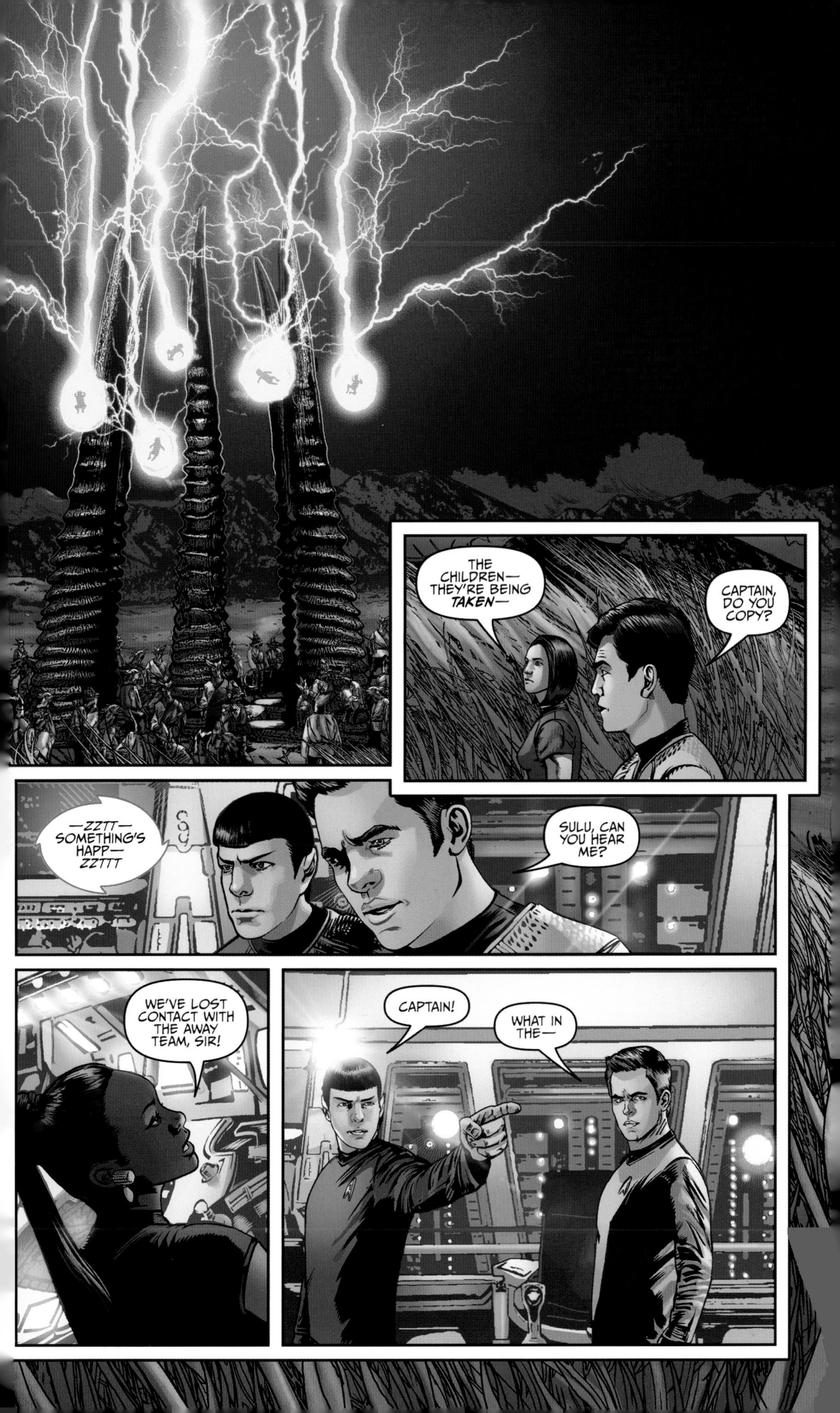
THE CHILDREN— THEY'RE BEING *TAKEN*—
CAPTAIN, DO YOU COPY?
—ZZTT— SOMETHING'S HAPP— ZZTTT
SULU, CAN YOU HEAR ME?
WE'VE LOST CONTACT WITH THE AWAY TEAM, SIR!
CAPTAIN!
WHAT IN THE—

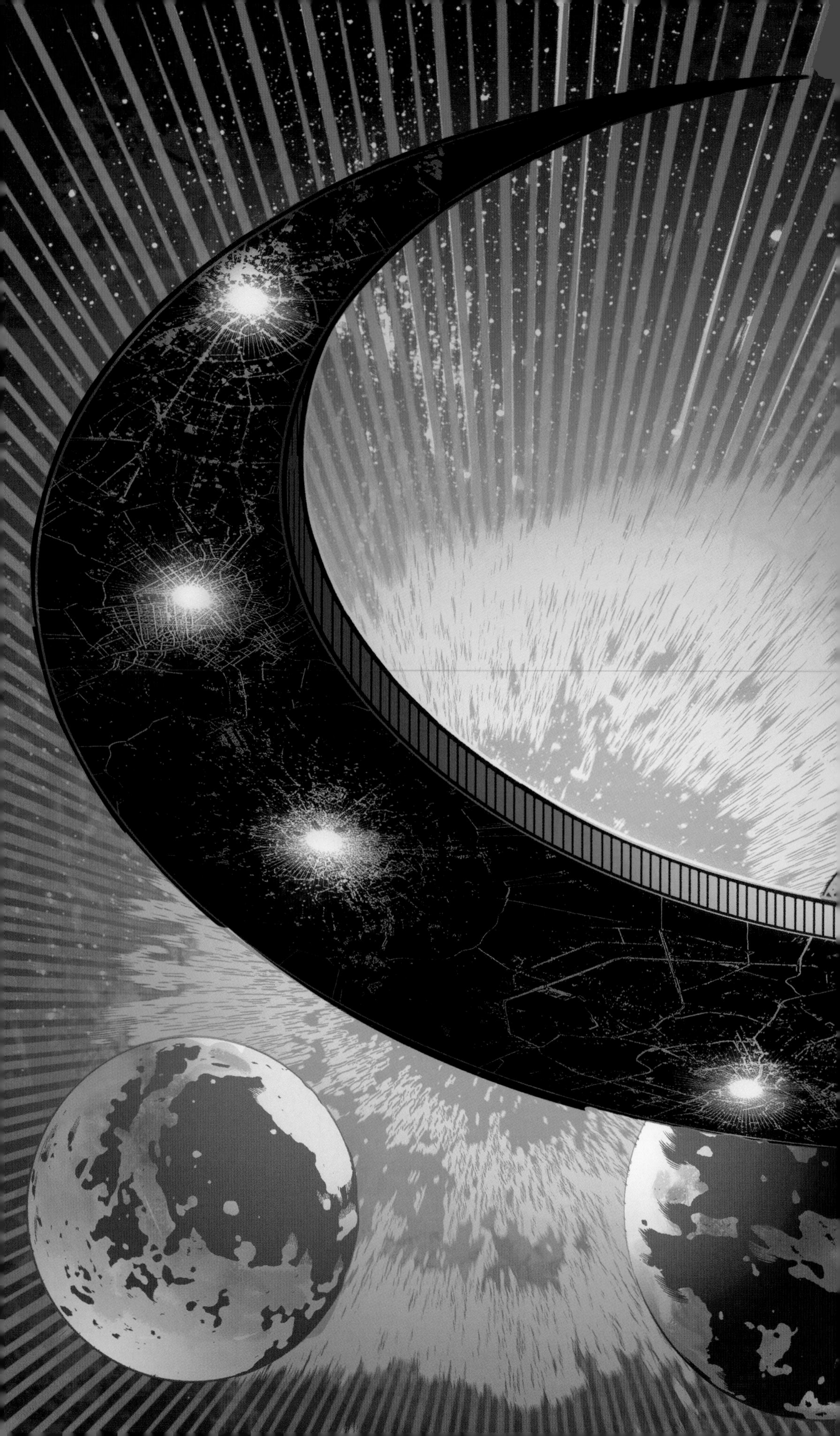

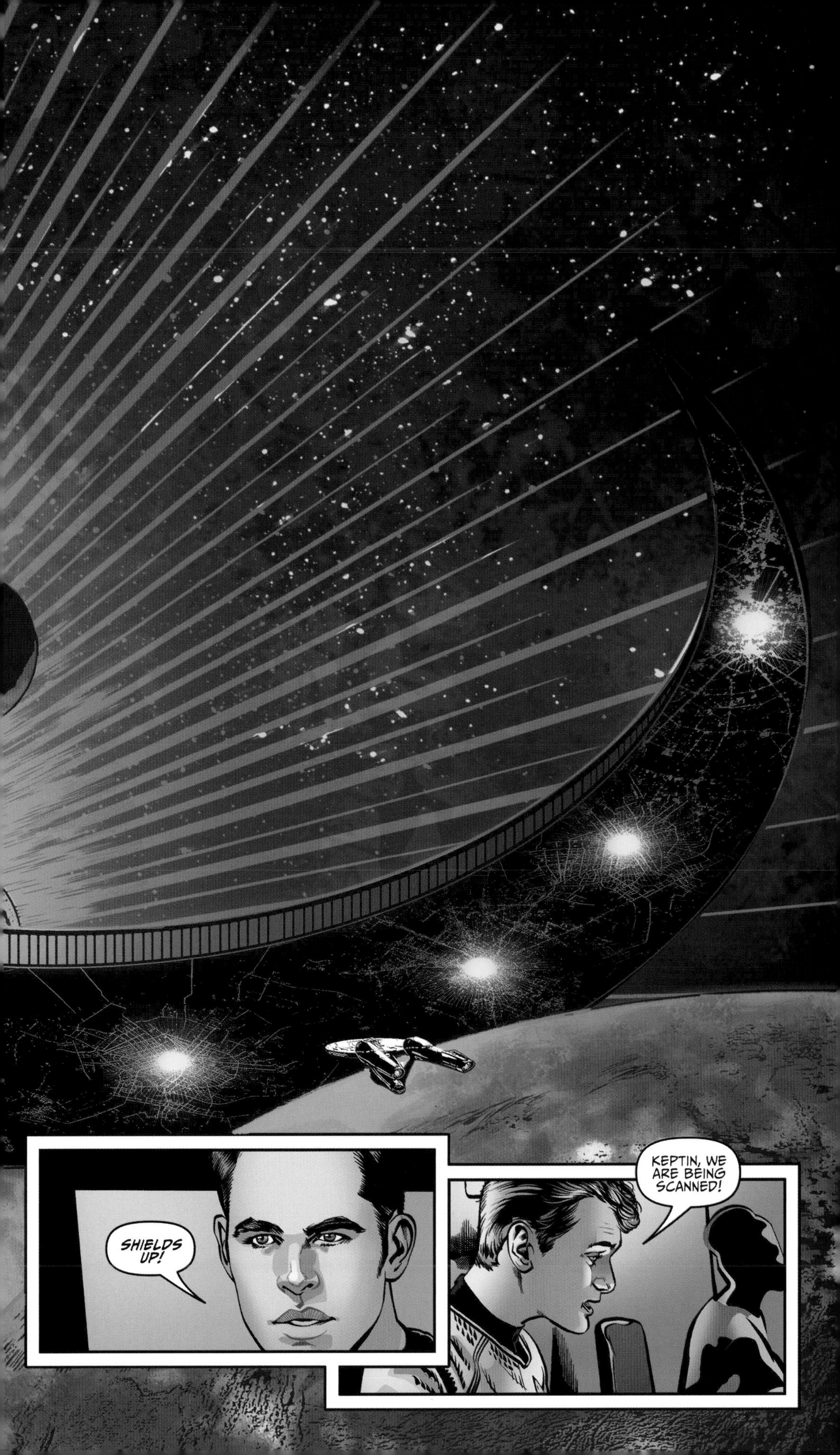
SHIELDS UP!
KEPTIN, WE ARE BEING SCANNED!

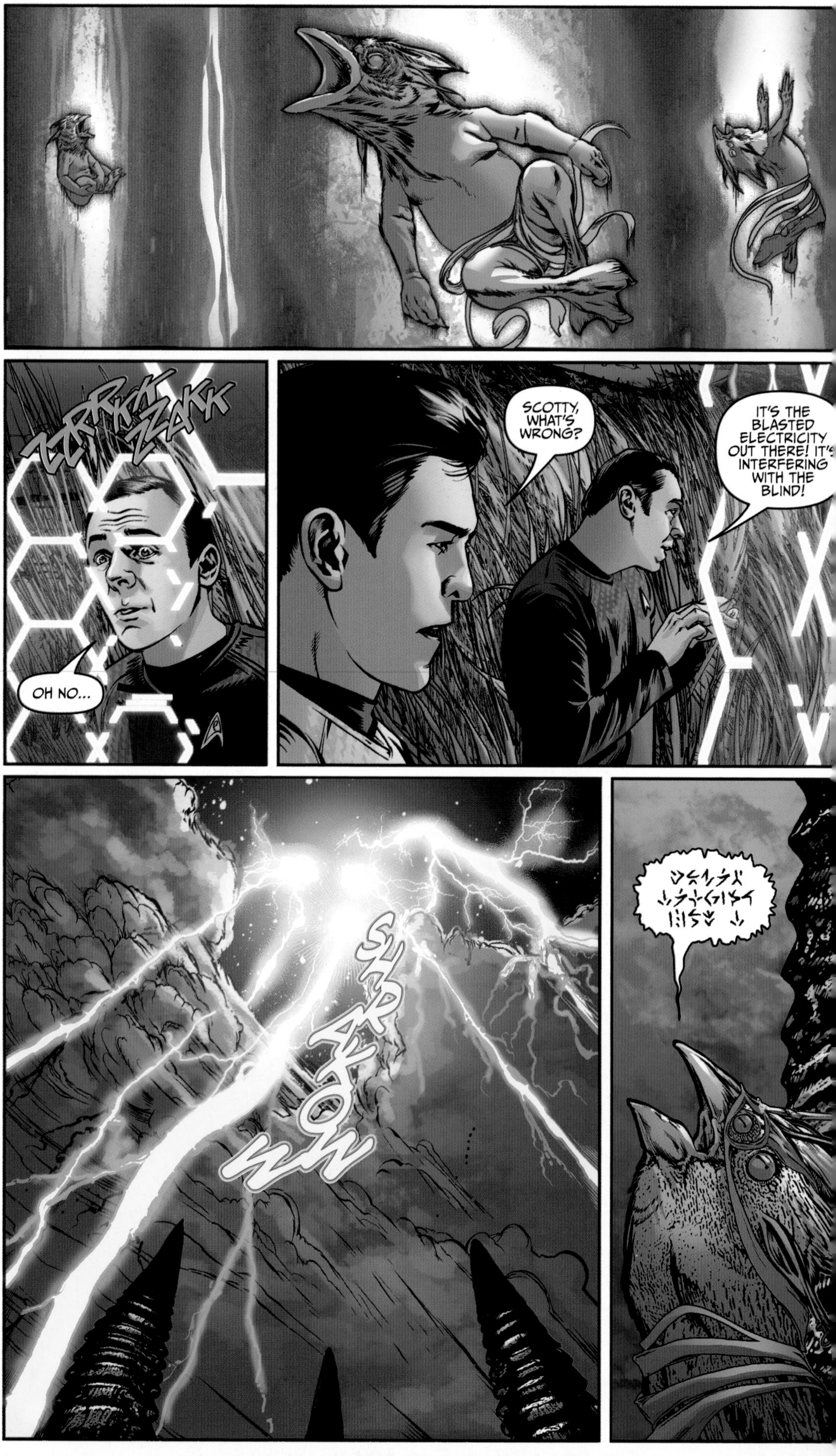
ZZRRKK ZZAKK
OH NO...
SCOTTY, WHAT'S WRONG?
IT'S THE BLASTED ELECTRICITY OUT THERE! IT'S INTERFERING WITH THE BLIND!
SHRAKOW

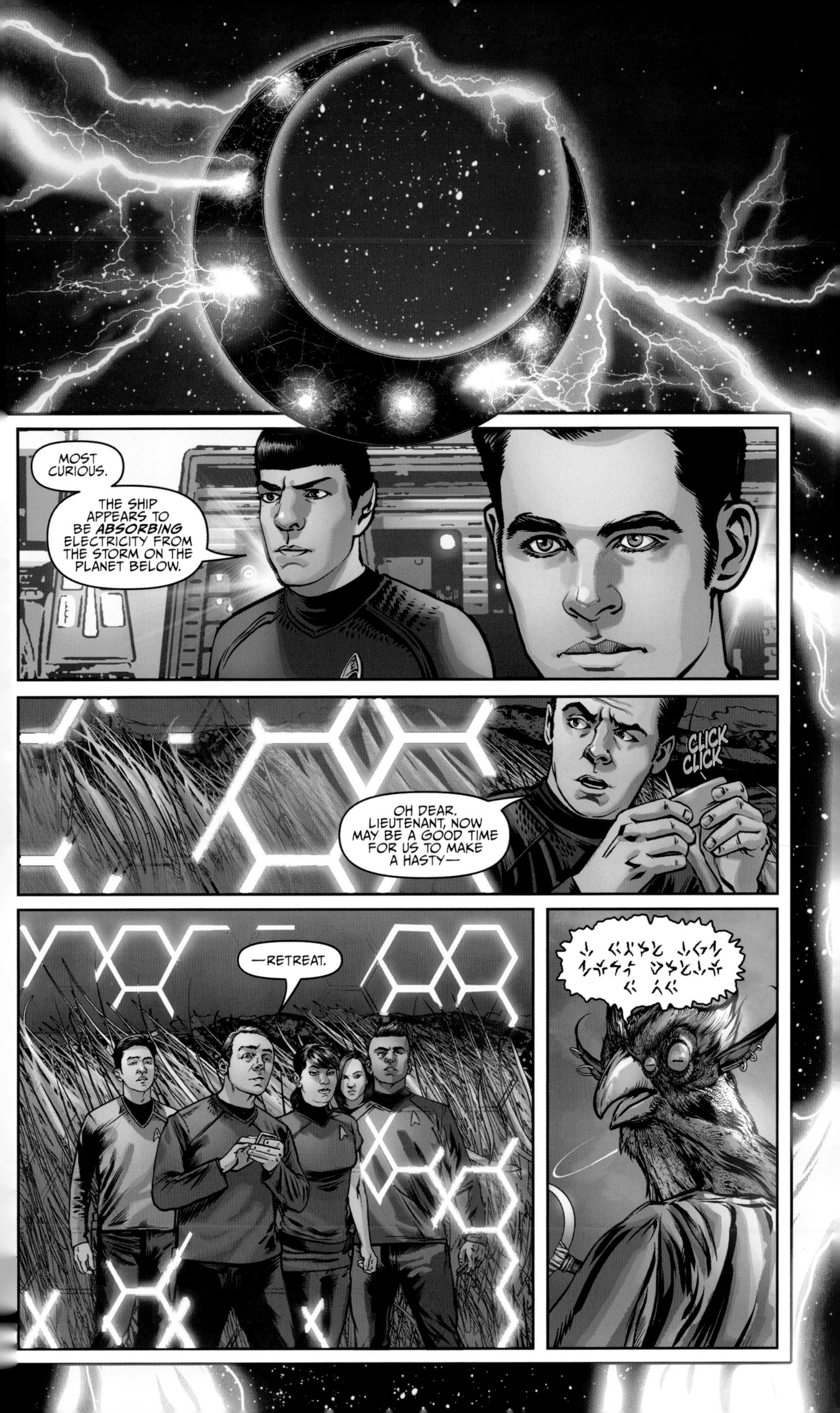
MOST CURIOUS.
THE SHIP APPEARS TO BE ABSORBING ELECTRICITY FROM THE STORM ON THE PLANET BELOW.
CLICK CLICK
OH DEAR. LIEUTENANT, NOW MAY BE A GOOD TIME FOR US TO MAKE A HASTY—
—RETREAT.

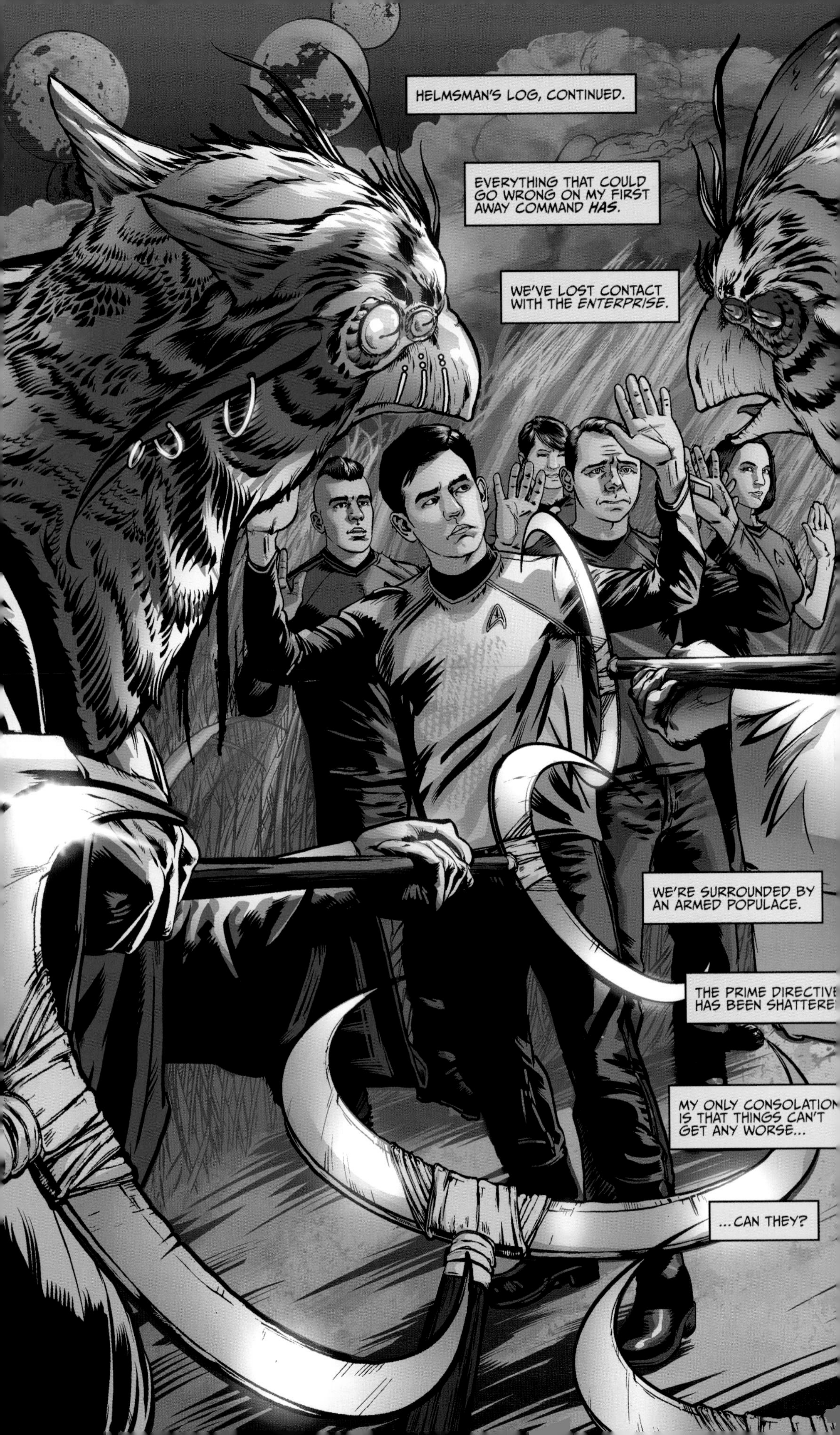
HELMSMAN'S LOG, CONTINUED.
EVERYTHING THAT COULD GO WRONG ON MY FIRST AWAY COMMAND *HAS*.
WE'VE LOST CONTACT WITH THE *ENTERPRISE*.
WE'RE SURROUNDED BY AN ARMED POPULACE.
THE PRIME DIRECTIVE HAS BEEN SHATTERED
MY ONLY CONSOLATION IS THAT THINGS CAN'T GET ANY WORSE...
...CAN THEY?

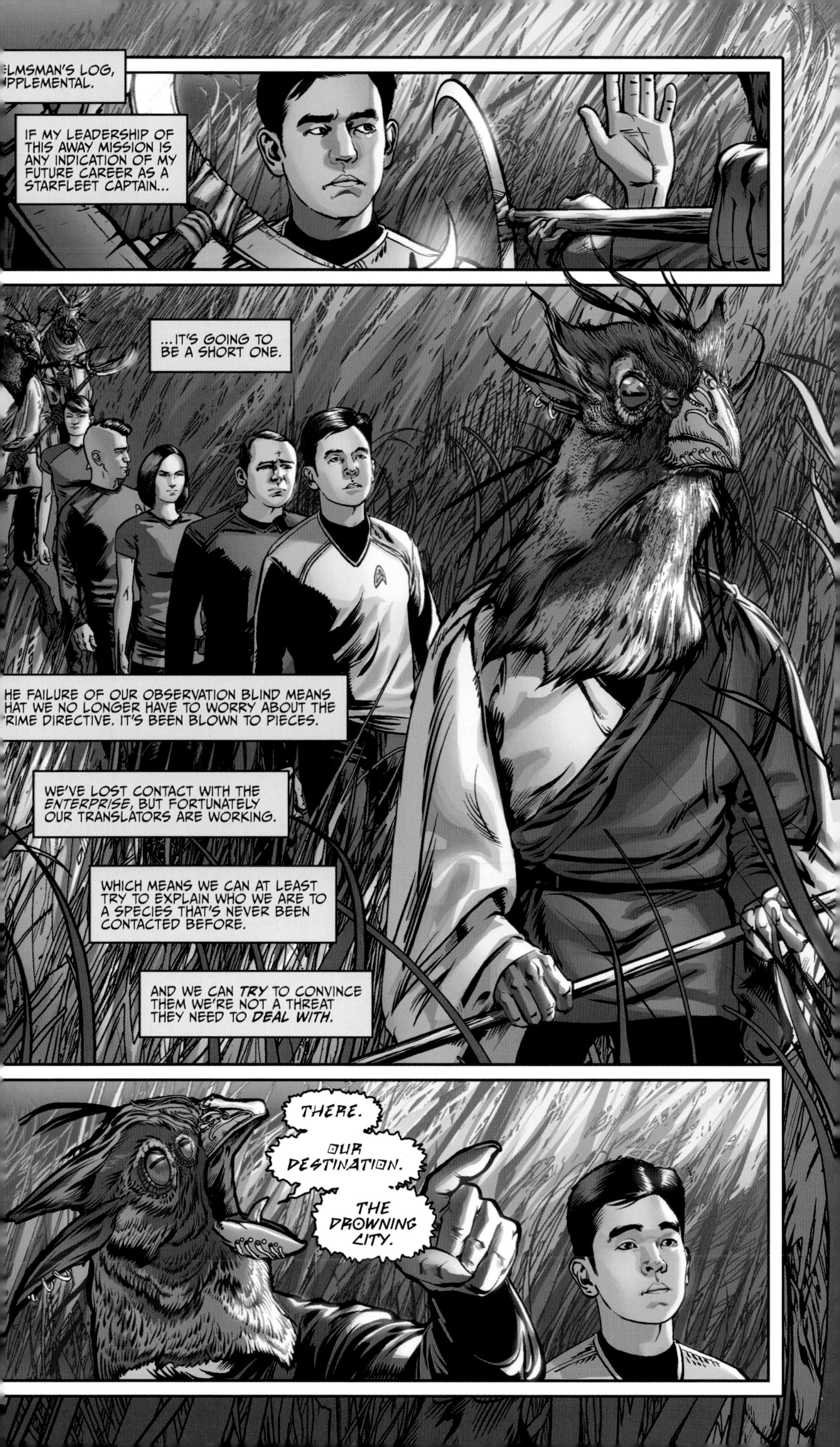
ELMSMAN'S LOG, UPPLEMENTAL.
IF MY LEADERSHIP OF THIS AWAY MISSION IS ANY INDICATION OF MY FUTURE CAREER AS A STARFLEET CAPTAIN...
...IT'S GOING TO BE A SHORT ONE.
HE FAILURE OF OUR OBSERVATION BLIND MEANS HAT WE NO LONGER HAVE TO WORRY ABOUT THE RIME DIRECTIVE. IT'S BEEN BLOWN TO PIECES.
WE'VE LOST CONTACT WITH THE ENTERPRISE, BUT FORTUNATELY OUR TRANSLATORS ARE WORKING.
WHICH MEANS WE CAN AT LEAST TRY TO EXPLAIN WHO WE ARE TO A SPECIES THAT'S NEVER BEEN CONTACTED BEFORE.
AND WE CAN TRY TO CONVINCE THEM WE'RE NOT A THREAT THEY NEED TO DEAL WITH.
THERE.
OUR DESTINATION.
THE DROWNING CITY.

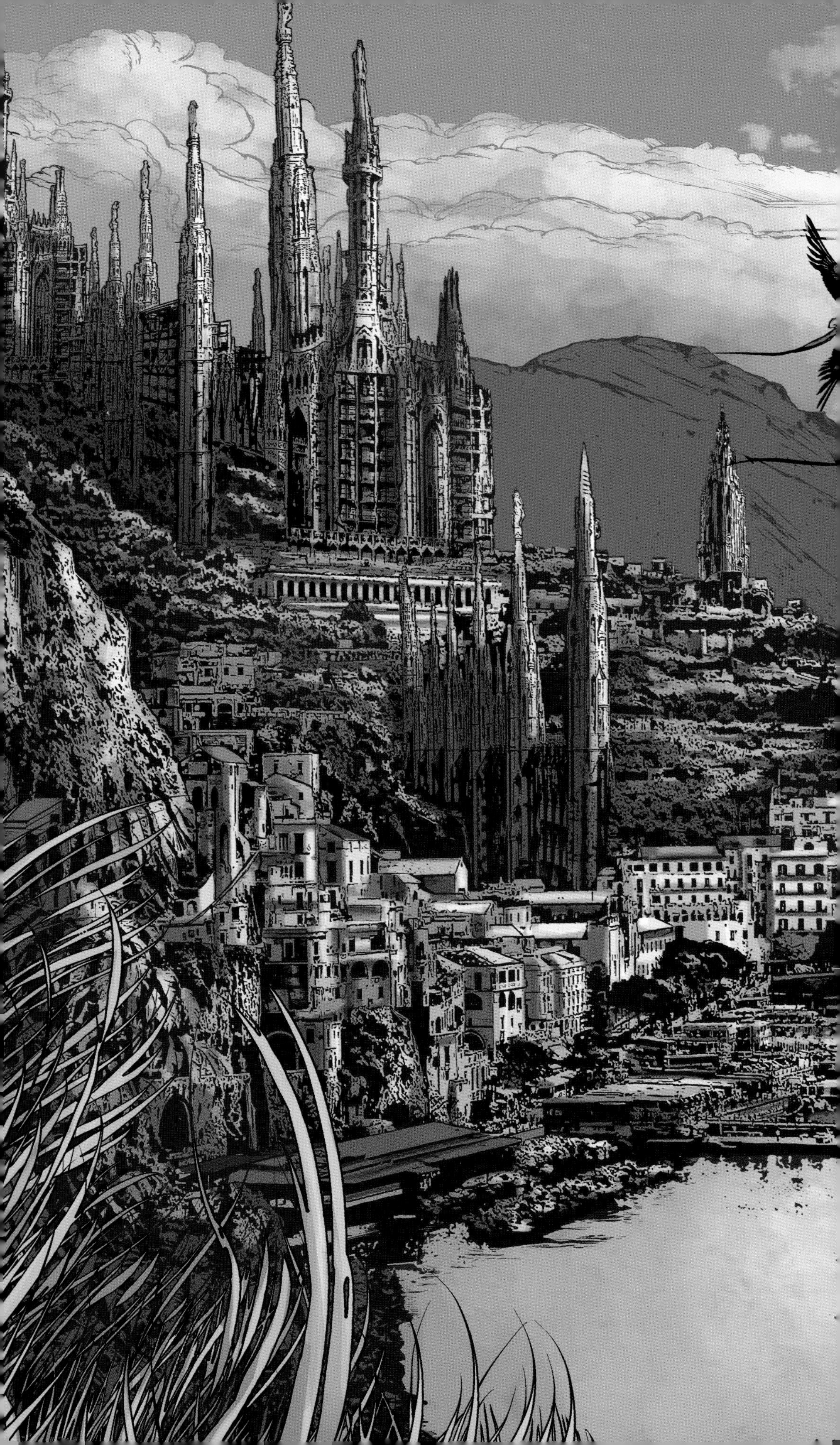

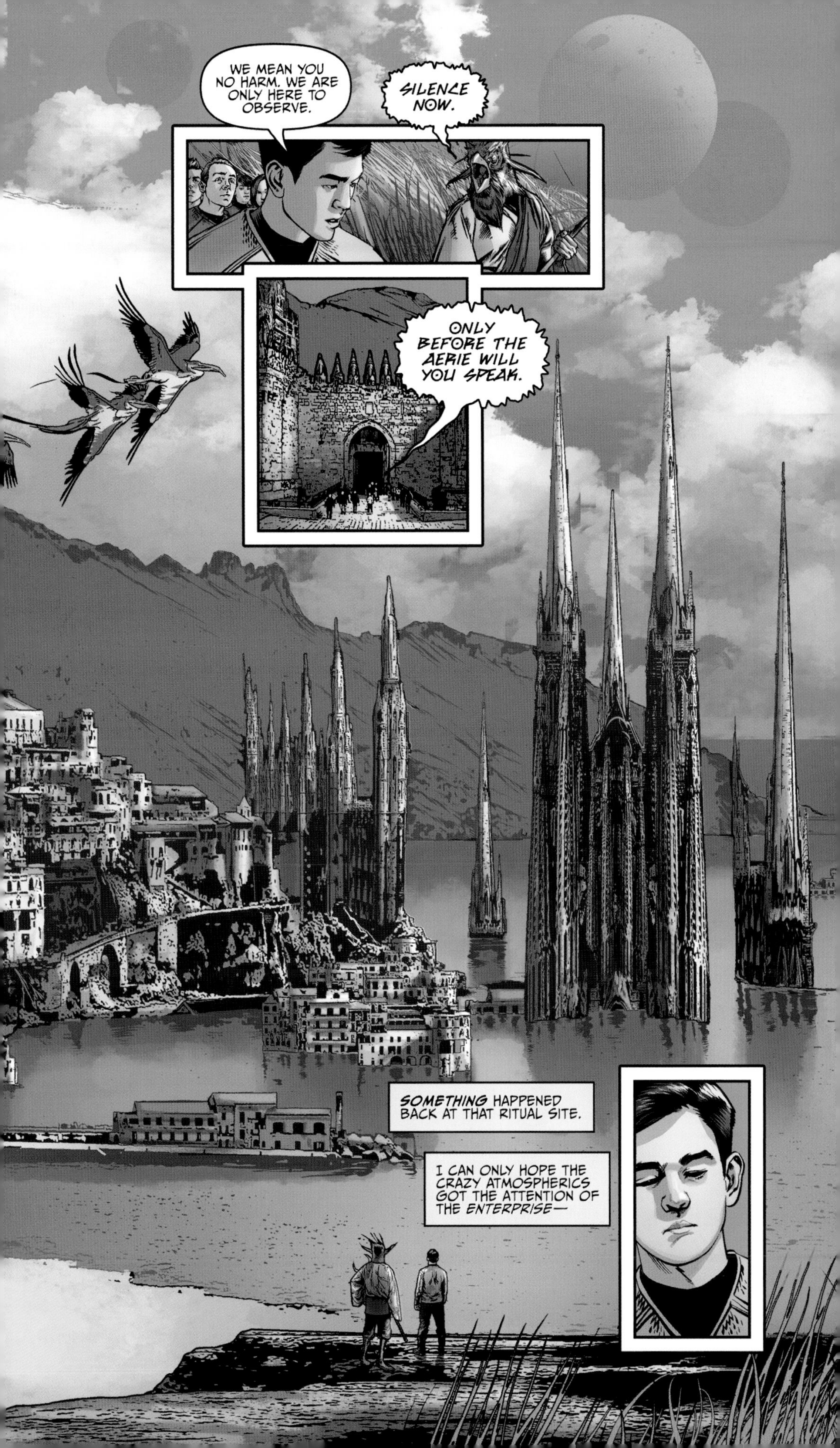
WE MEAN YOU NO HARM. WE ARE ONLY HERE TO OBSERVE.
SILENCE NOW.
ONLY BEFORE THE AERIE WILL YOU SPEAK.
SOMETHING HAPPENED BACK AT THAT RITUAL SITE.
I CAN ONLY HOPE THE CRAZY ATMOSPHERICS GOT THE ATTENTION OF THE ENTERPRISE—

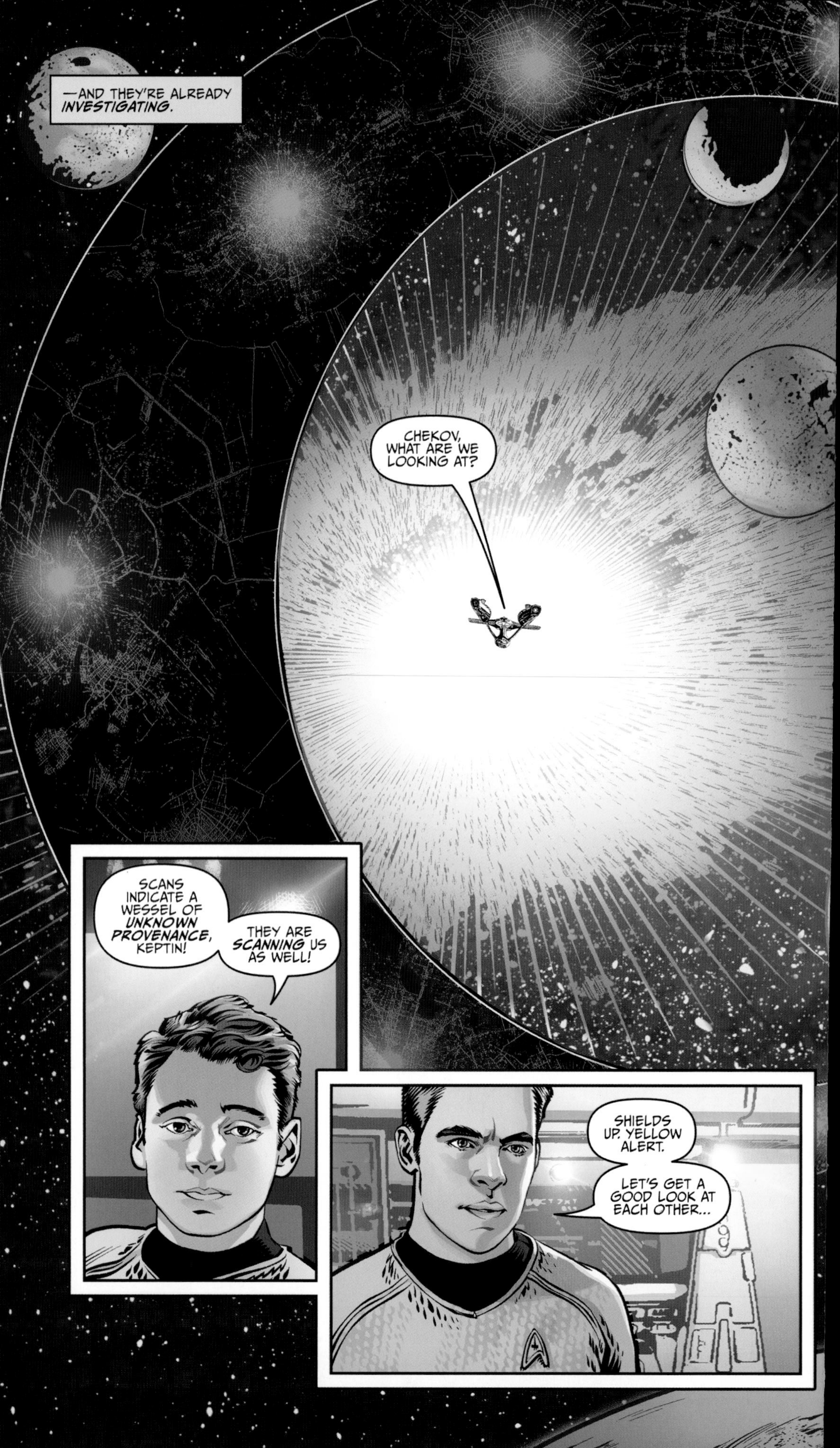
—AND THEY'RE ALREADY *INVESTIGATING.*
CHEKOV, WHAT ARE WE LOOKING AT?
SCANS INDICATE A WESSEL OF *UNKNOWN PROVENANCE,* KEPTIN!
THEY ARE *SCANNING* US AS WELL!
SHIELDS UP. YELLOW ALERT.
LET'S GET A GOOD LOOK AT EACH OTHER...

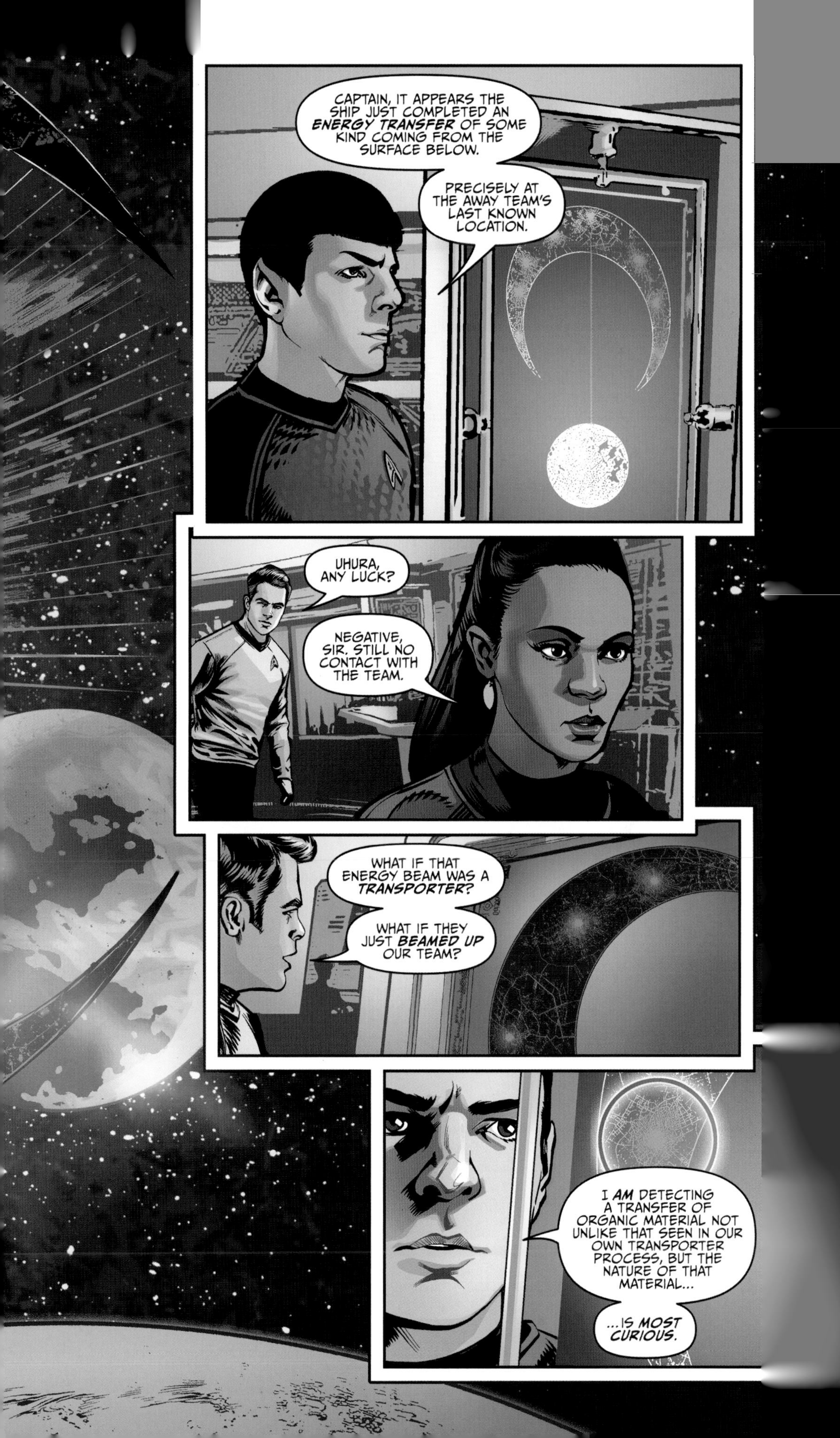
CAPTAIN, IT APPEARS THE SHIP JUST COMPLETED AN ENERGY TRANSFER OF SOME KIND COMING FROM THE SURFACE BELOW.
PRECISELY AT THE AWAY TEAM'S LAST KNOWN LOCATION.
UHURA, ANY LUCK?
NEGATIVE, SIR. STILL NO CONTACT WITH THE TEAM.
WHAT IF THAT ENERGY BEAM WAS A TRANSPORTER?
WHAT IF THEY JUST BEAMED UP OUR TEAM?
I AM DETECTING A TRANSFER OF ORGANIC MATERIAL NOT UNLIKE THAT SEEN IN OUR OWN TRANSPORTER PROCESS, BUT THE NATURE OF THAT MATERIAL...
...IS MOST CURIOUS.

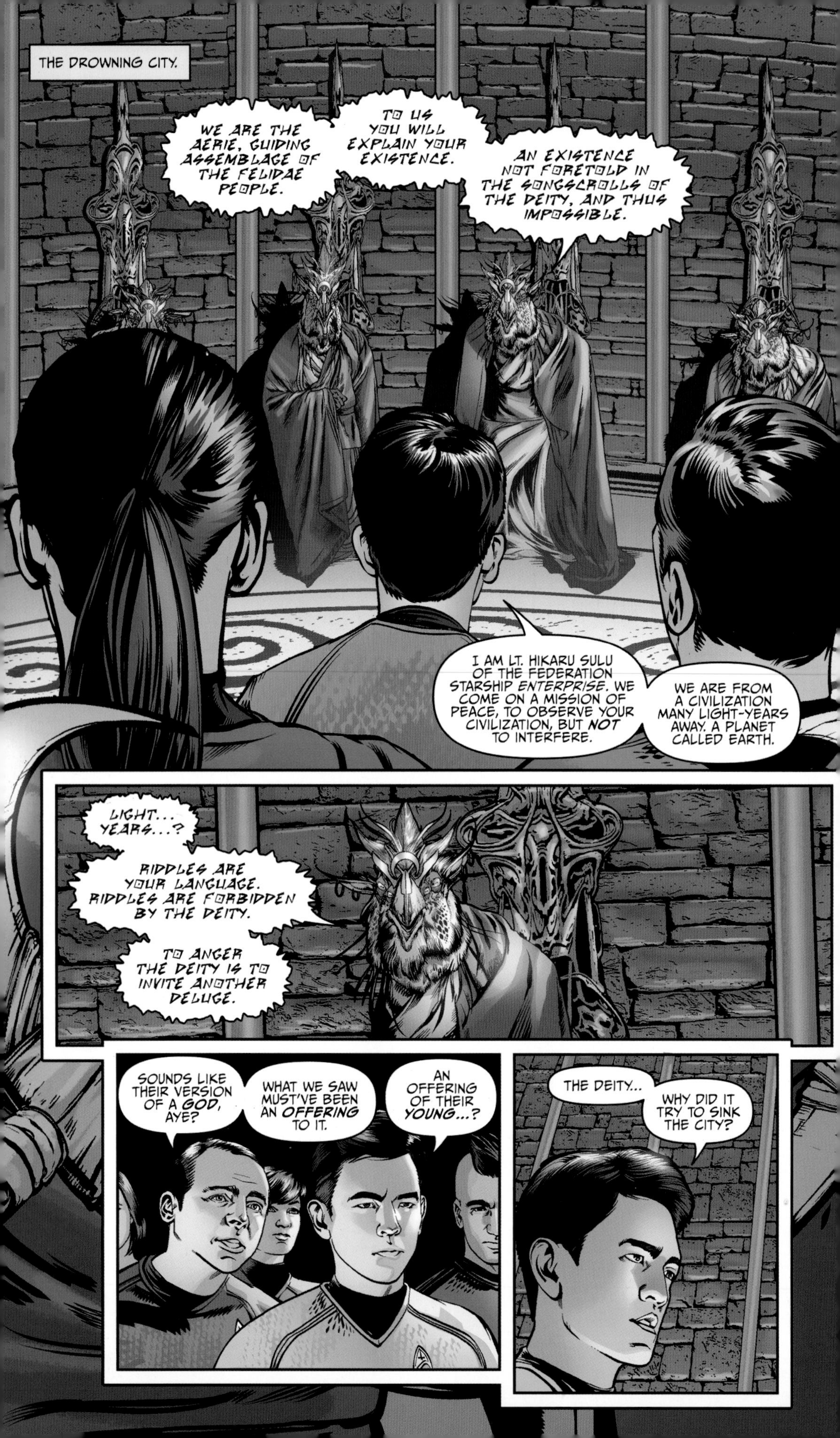

THE DROWNING CITY.
WE ARE THE AERIE, GUIDING ASSEMBLAGE OF THE FELIDAE PEOPLE.
TO US YOU WILL EXPLAIN YOUR EXISTENCE.
AN EXISTENCE NOT FORETOLD IN THE SONGSCROLLS OF THE DEITY, AND THUS IMPOSSIBLE.
I AM LT. HIKARU SULU OF THE FEDERATION STARSHIP *ENTERPRISE*. WE COME ON A MISSION OF PEACE, TO OBSERVE YOUR CIVILIZATION, BUT ***NOT*** TO INTERFERE.
WE ARE FROM A CIVILIZATION MANY LIGHT-YEARS AWAY. A PLANET CALLED EARTH.
LIGHT... YEARS...?
RIDDLES ARE YOUR LANGUAGE. RIDDLES ARE FORBIDDEN BY THE DEITY.
TO ANGER THE DEITY IS TO INVITE ANOTHER DELUGE.
SOUNDS LIKE THEIR VERSION OF A ***GOD***, AYE?
WHAT WE SAW MUST'VE BEEN AN ***OFFERING*** TO IT.
AN OFFERING OF THEIR ***YOUNG...?***
THE DEITY...
WHY DID IT TRY TO SINK THE CITY?

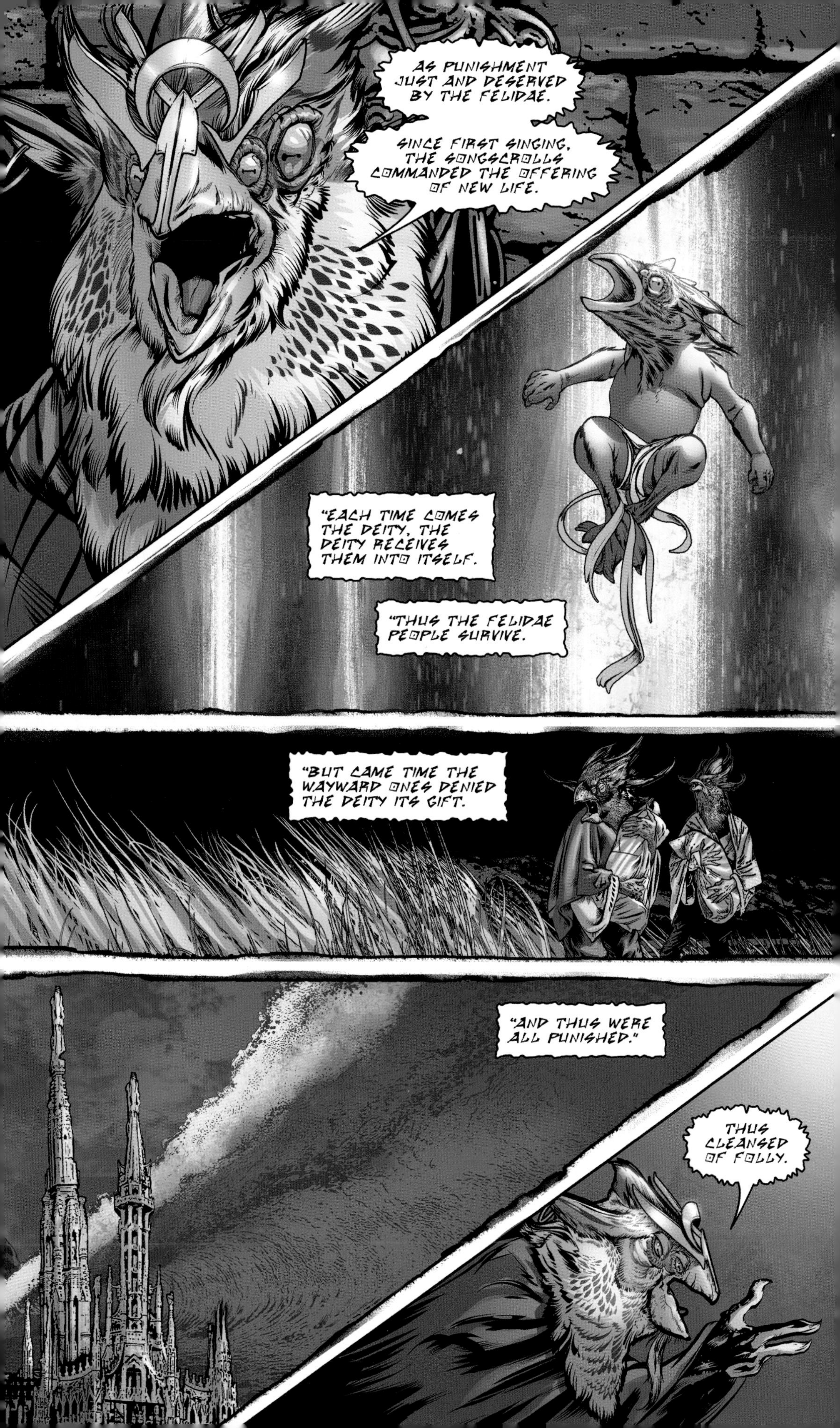
AS PUNISHMENT JUST AND DESERVED BY THE FELIDAE.
SINCE FIRST SINGING, THE SONGSCROLLS COMMANDED THE OFFERING OF NEW LIFE.
"EACH TIME COMES THE DEITY, THE DEITY RECEIVES THEM INTO ITSELF.
"THUS THE FELIDAE PEOPLE SURVIVE.
"BUT CAME TIME THE WAYWARD ONES DENIED THE DEITY ITS GIFT.
"AND THUS WERE ALL PUNISHED."
THUS CLEANSED OF FOLLY.

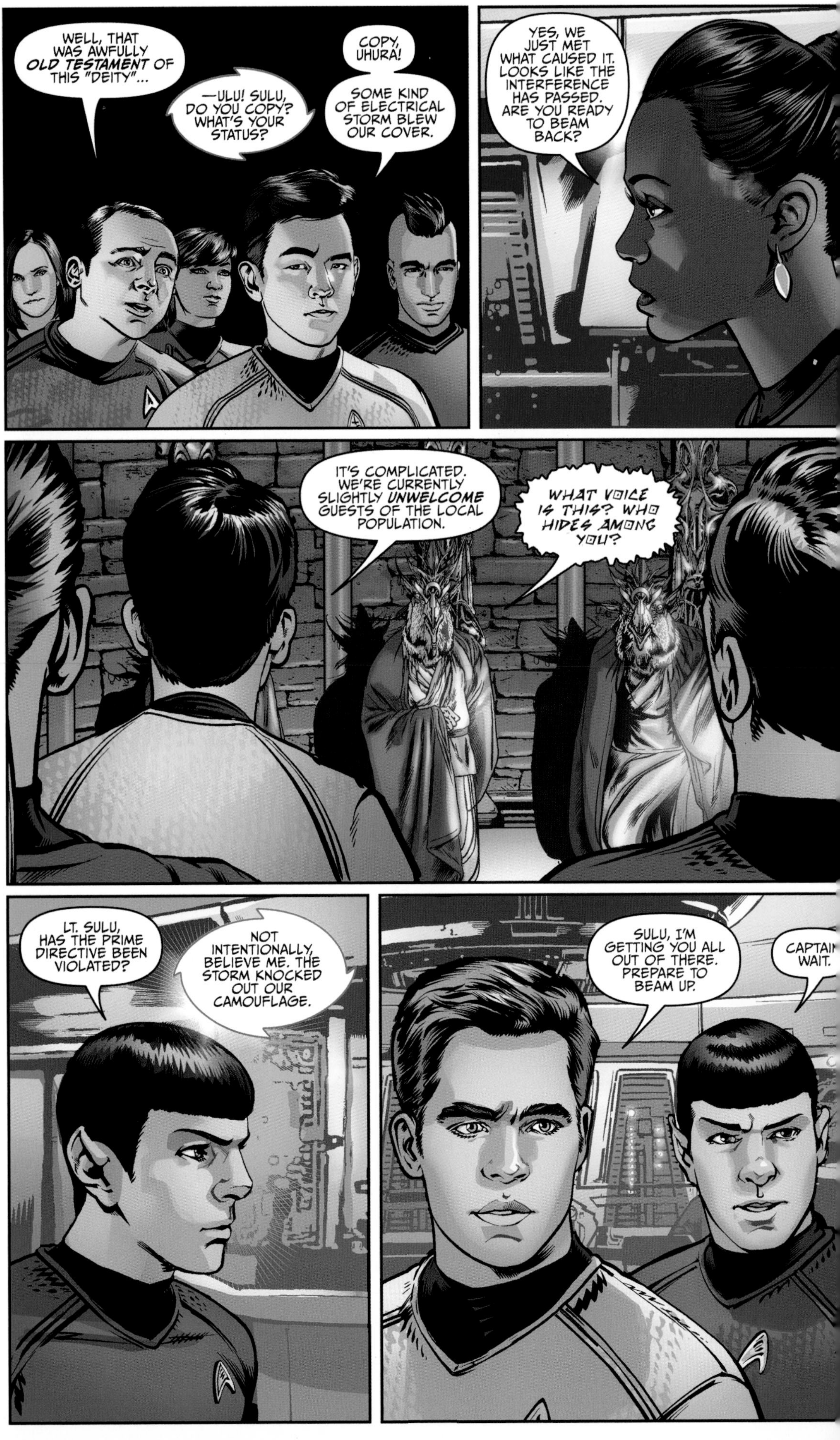
WELL, THAT WAS AWFULLY ***OLD TESTAMENT*** OF THIS "DEITY"...
—ULU! SULU, DO YOU COPY? WHAT'S YOUR STATUS?
COPY, UHURA!
SOME KIND OF ELECTRICAL STORM BLEW OUR COVER.
YES, WE JUST MET WHAT CAUSED IT. LOOKS LIKE THE INTERFERENCE HAS PASSED. ARE YOU READY TO BEAM BACK?
IT'S COMPLICATED. WE'RE CURRENTLY SLIGHTLY ***UNWELCOME*** GUESTS OF THE LOCAL POPULATION.
WHAT VOICE IS THIS? WHO HIDES AMONG YOU?
LT. SULU, HAS THE PRIME DIRECTIVE BEEN VIOLATED?
NOT INTENTIONALLY, BELIEVE ME. THE STORM KNOCKED OUT OUR CAMOUFLAGE.
SULU, I'M GETTING YOU ALL OUT OF THERE. PREPARE TO BEAM UP.
CAPTAI
WAIT.

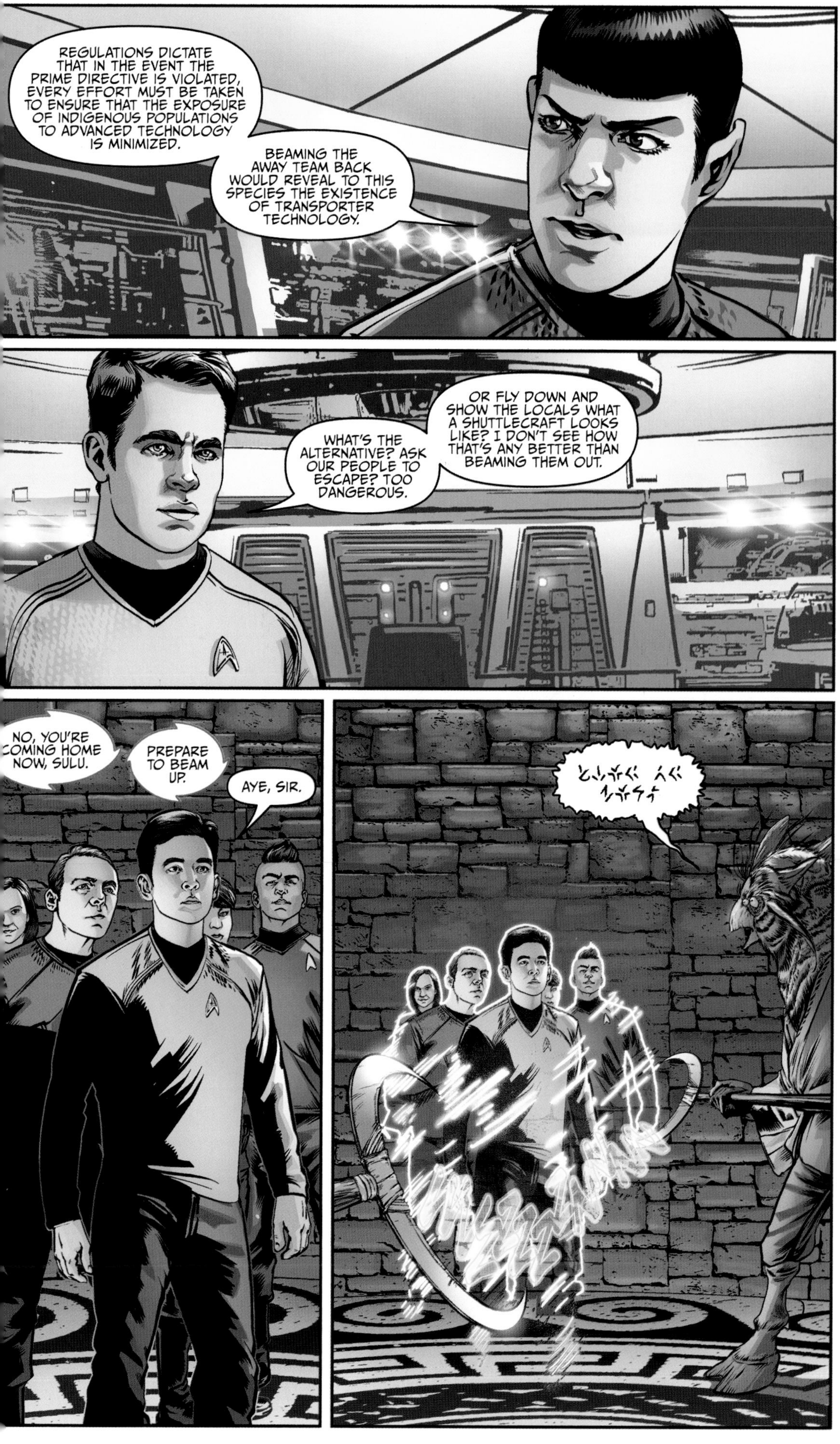
REGULATIONS DICTATE THAT IN THE EVENT THE PRIME DIRECTIVE IS VIOLATED, EVERY EFFORT MUST BE TAKEN TO ENSURE THAT THE EXPOSURE OF INDIGENOUS POPULATIONS TO ADVANCED TECHNOLOGY IS MINIMIZED.
BEAMING THE AWAY TEAM BACK WOULD REVEAL TO THIS SPECIES THE EXISTENCE OF TRANSPORTER TECHNOLOGY.
WHAT'S THE ALTERNATIVE? ASK OUR PEOPLE TO ESCAPE? TOO DANGEROUS.
OR FLY DOWN AND SHOW THE LOCALS WHAT A SHUTTLECRAFT LOOKS LIKE? I DON'T SEE HOW THAT'S ANY BETTER THAN BEAMING THEM OUT.
NO, YOU'RE COMING HOME NOW, SULU.
PREPARE TO BEAM UP.
AYE, SIR.

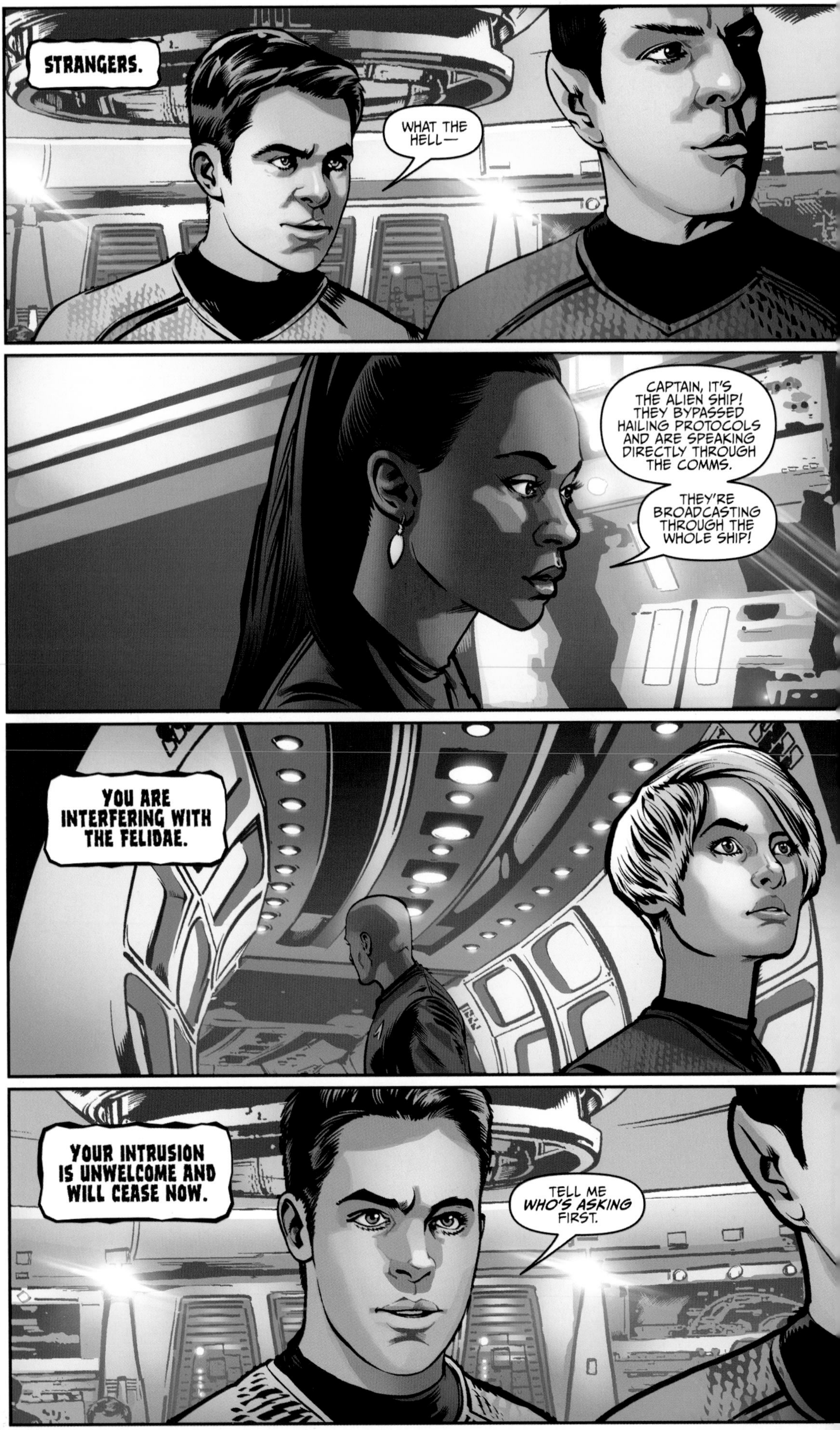
STRANGERS.
WHAT THE HELL—
CAPTAIN, IT'S THE ALIEN SHIP! THEY BYPASSED HAILING PROTOCOLS AND ARE SPEAKING DIRECTLY THROUGH THE COMMS.
THEY'RE BROADCASTING THROUGH THE WHOLE SHIP!
YOU ARE INTERFERING WITH THE FELIDAE.
YOUR INTRUSION IS UNWELCOME AND WILL CEASE NOW.
TELL ME WHO'S ASKING FIRST.

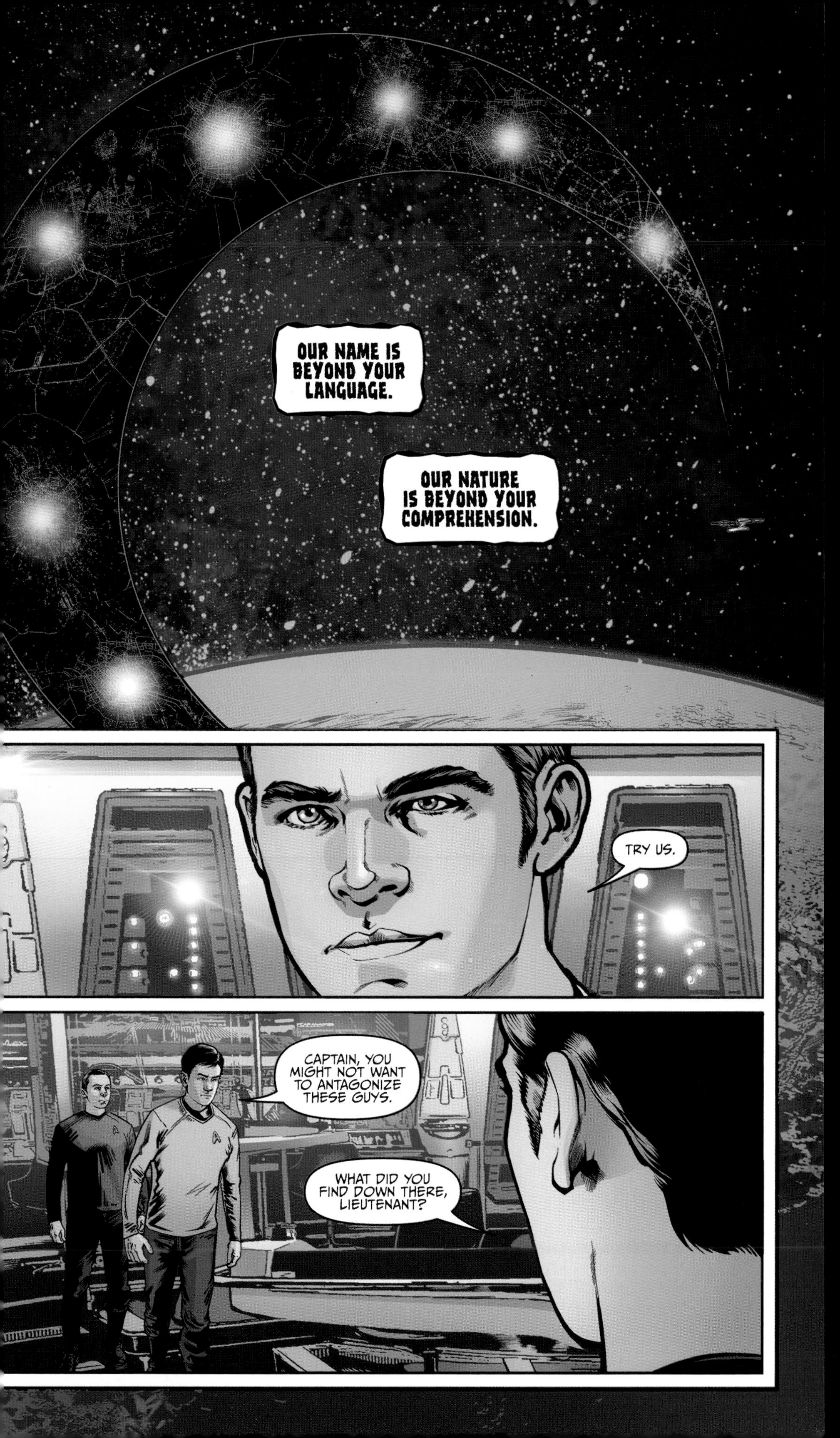
OUR NAME IS BEYOND YOUR LANGUAGE.
OUR NATURE IS BEYOND YOUR COMPREHENSION.
TRY US.
CAPTAIN, YOU MIGHT NOT WANT TO ANTAGONIZE THESE GUYS.
WHAT DID YOU FIND DOWN THERE, LIEUTENANT?

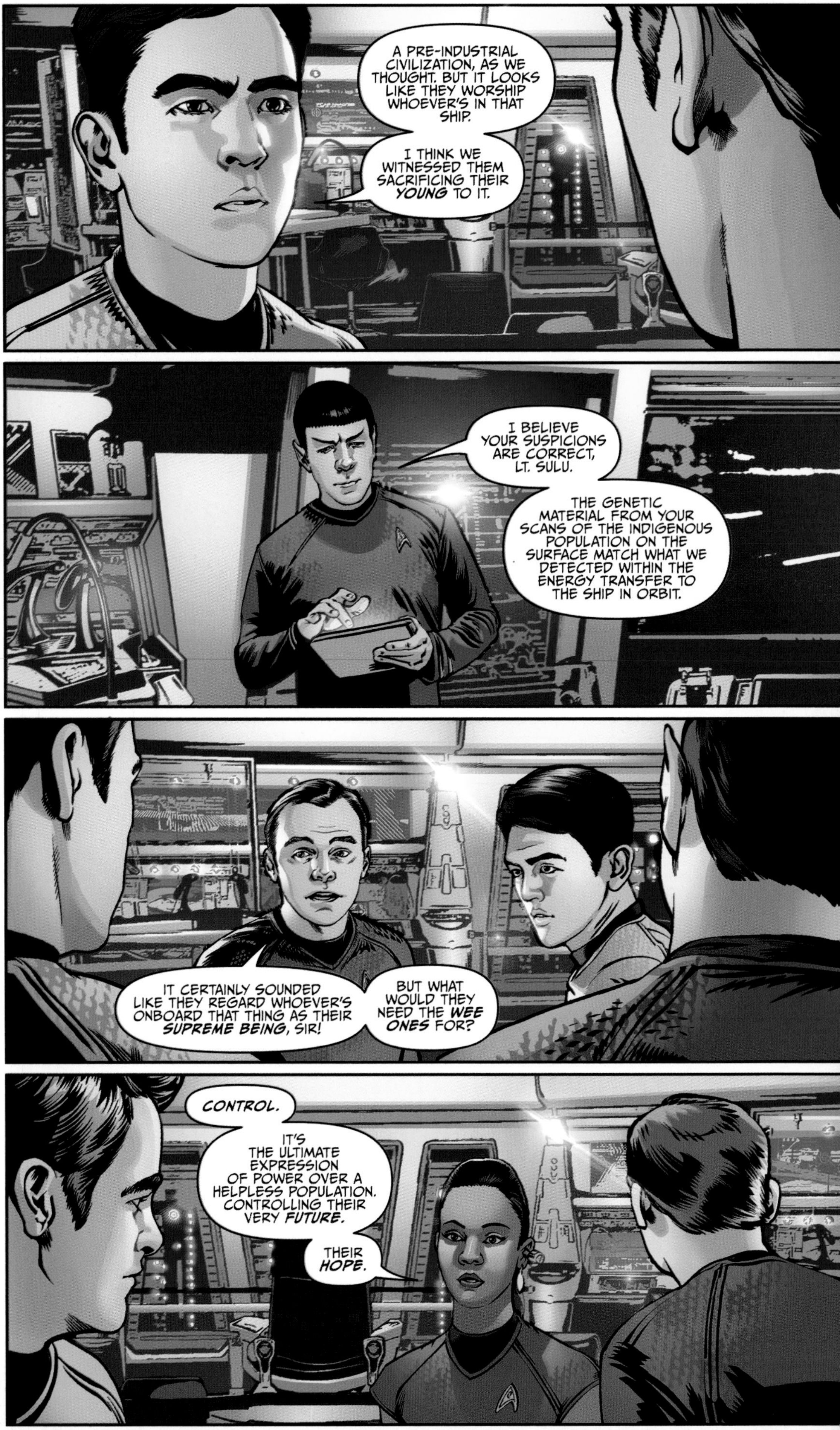
A PRE-INDUSTRIAL CIVILIZATION, AS WE THOUGHT. BUT IT LOOKS LIKE THEY WORSHIP WHOEVER'S IN THAT SHIP.
I THINK WE WITNESSED THEM SACRIFICING THEIR *YOUNG* TO IT.
I BELIEVE YOUR SUSPICIONS ARE CORRECT, LT. SULU.
THE GENETIC MATERIAL FROM YOUR SCANS OF THE INDIGENOUS POPULATION ON THE SURFACE MATCH WHAT WE DETECTED WITHIN THE ENERGY TRANSFER TO THE SHIP IN ORBIT.
IT CERTAINLY SOUNDED LIKE THEY REGARD WHOEVER'S ONBOARD THAT THING AS THEIR *SUPREME BEING*, SIR!
BUT WHAT WOULD THEY NEED THE *WEE ONES* FOR?
CONTROL.
IT'S THE ULTIMATE EXPRESSION OF POWER OVER A HELPLESS POPULATION. CONTROLLING THEIR VERY *FUTURE.*
THEIR *HOPE.*

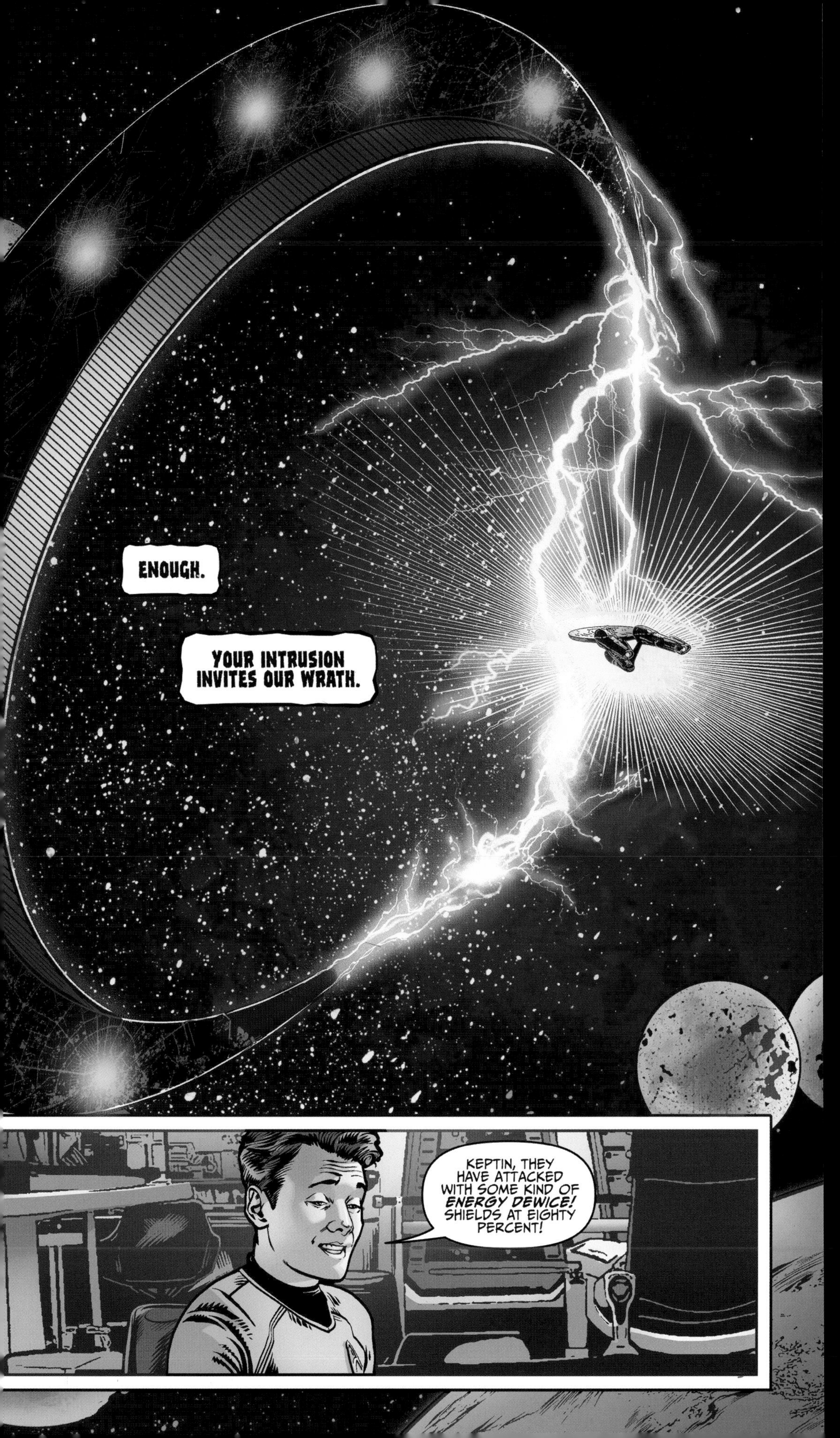
ENOUGH.
YOUR INTRUSION INVITES OUR WRATH.
KEPTIN, THEY HAVE ATTACKED WITH SOME KIND OF *ENERGY DEWICE!* SHIELDS AT EIGHTY PERCENT!

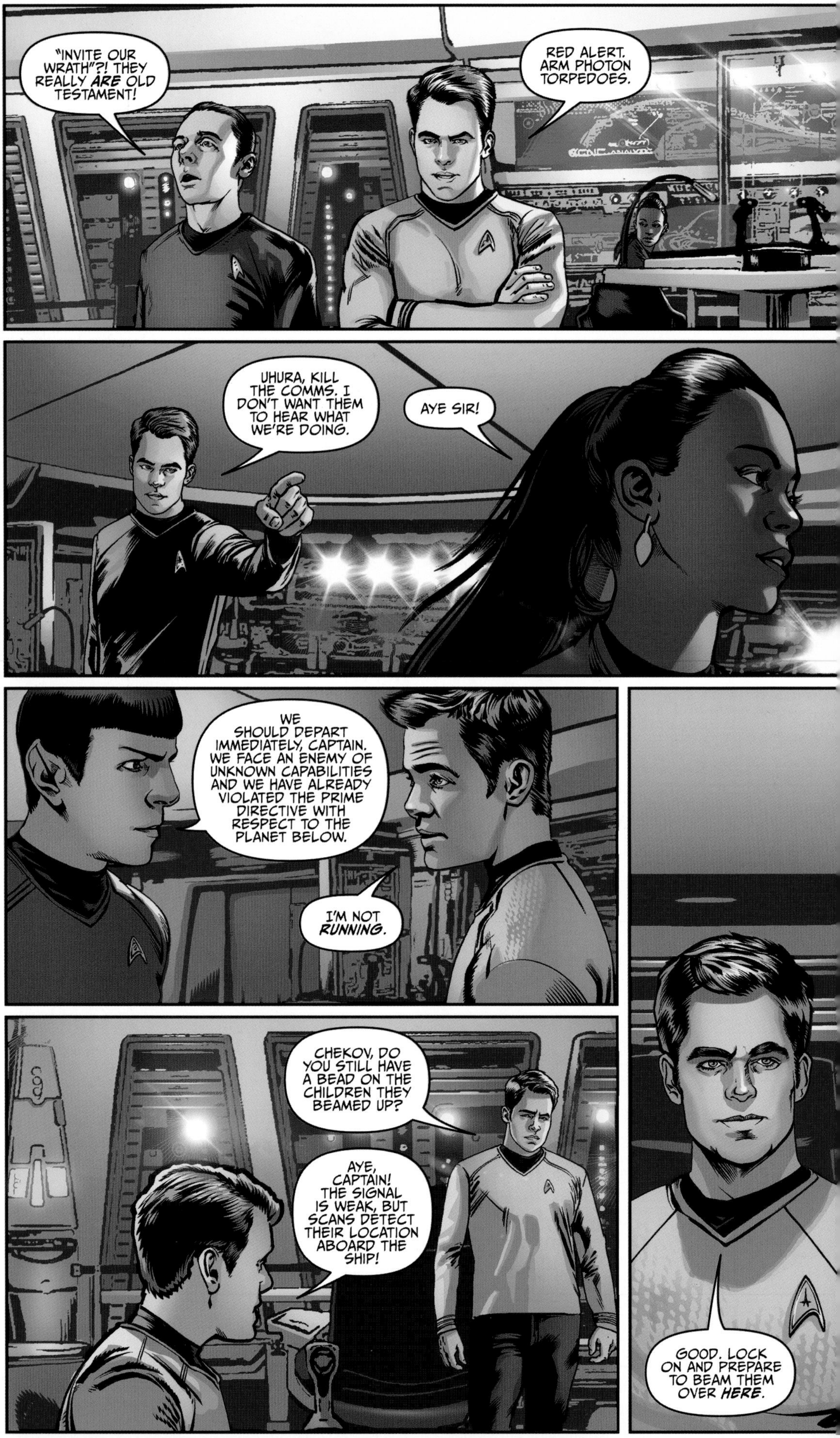
"INVITE OUR WRATH"?! THEY REALLY *ARE* OLD TESTAMENT!
RED ALERT. ARM PHOTON TORPEDOES.
UHURA, KILL THE COMMS. I DON'T WANT THEM TO HEAR WHAT WE'RE DOING.
AYE SIR!
WE SHOULD DEPART IMMEDIATELY, CAPTAIN. WE FACE AN ENEMY OF UNKNOWN CAPABILITIES AND WE HAVE ALREADY VIOLATED THE PRIME DIRECTIVE WITH RESPECT TO THE PLANET BELOW.
I'M NOT *RUNNING*.
CHEKOV, DO YOU STILL HAVE A BEAD ON THE CHILDREN THEY BEAMED UP?
AYE, CAPTAIN! THE SIGNAL IS WEAK, BUT SCANS DETECT THEIR LOCATION ABOARD THE SHIP!
GOOD. LOCK ON AND PREPARE TO BEAM THEM OVER *HERE*.

CAPTAIN, TO BRING THEM ABOARD WOULD FURTHER VIOLATE—

THE PRIME DIRECTIVE WAS ALREADY VIOLATED THE SECOND OUR FRIENDS IN THE SHIP STARTED PLAYING GOD WITH THE INDIGENOUS POPULATION.

BY ALL ACCOUNTS THEY'VE BEEN DOING IT FOR A LONG TIME. IT ENDS NOW.

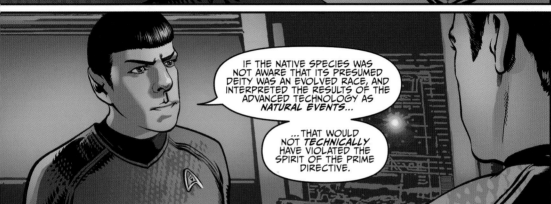

IF THE NATIVE SPECIES WAS NOT AWARE THAT ITS PRESUMED DEITY WAS AN EVOLVED RACE, AND INTERPRETED THE RESULTS OF THE ADVANCED TECHNOLOGY AS *NATURAL EVENTS*...

...THAT WOULD NOT *TECHNICALLY* HAVE VIOLATED THE SPIRIT OF THE PRIME DIRECTIVE.

NEVER THOUGHT I WOULD HEAR YOU INVOKE A "SPIRIT" IN THE NAME OF COLD HARD LOGIC, SPOCK.

AND THAT'S MY POINT. LOGIC DOESN'T APPLY ANYMORE. NOW IT'S ABOUT DOING WHAT'S *RIGHT*.

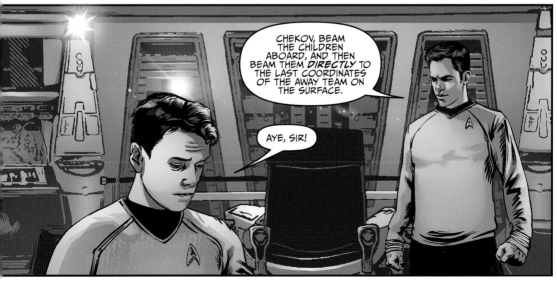

CHEKOV, BEAM THE CHILDREN ABOARD, AND THEN BEAM THEM *DIRECTLY* TO THE LAST COORDINATES OF THE AWAY TEAM ON THE SURFACE.

AYE, SIR!

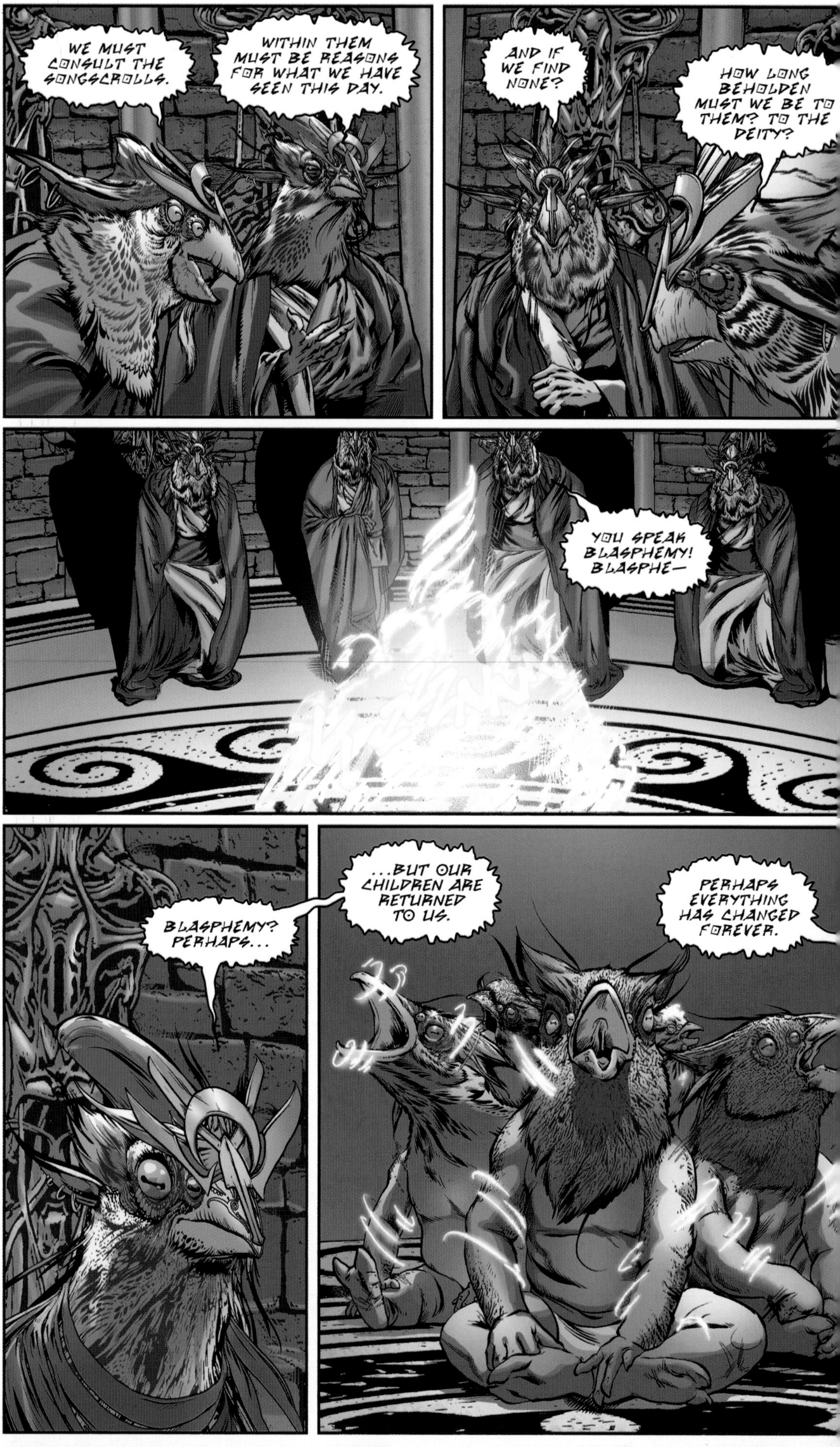
WE MUST CONSULT THE SONGSCROLLS.
WITHIN THEM MUST BE REASONS FOR WHAT WE HAVE SEEN THIS DAY.
AND IF WE FIND NONE?
HOW LONG BEHOLDEN MUST WE BE TO THEM? TO THE DEITY?
YOU SPEAK BLASPHEMY! BLASPHE—
BLASPHEMY? PERHAPS...
...BUT OUR CHILDREN ARE RETURNED TO US.
PERHAPS EVERYTHING HAS CHANGED FOREVER.

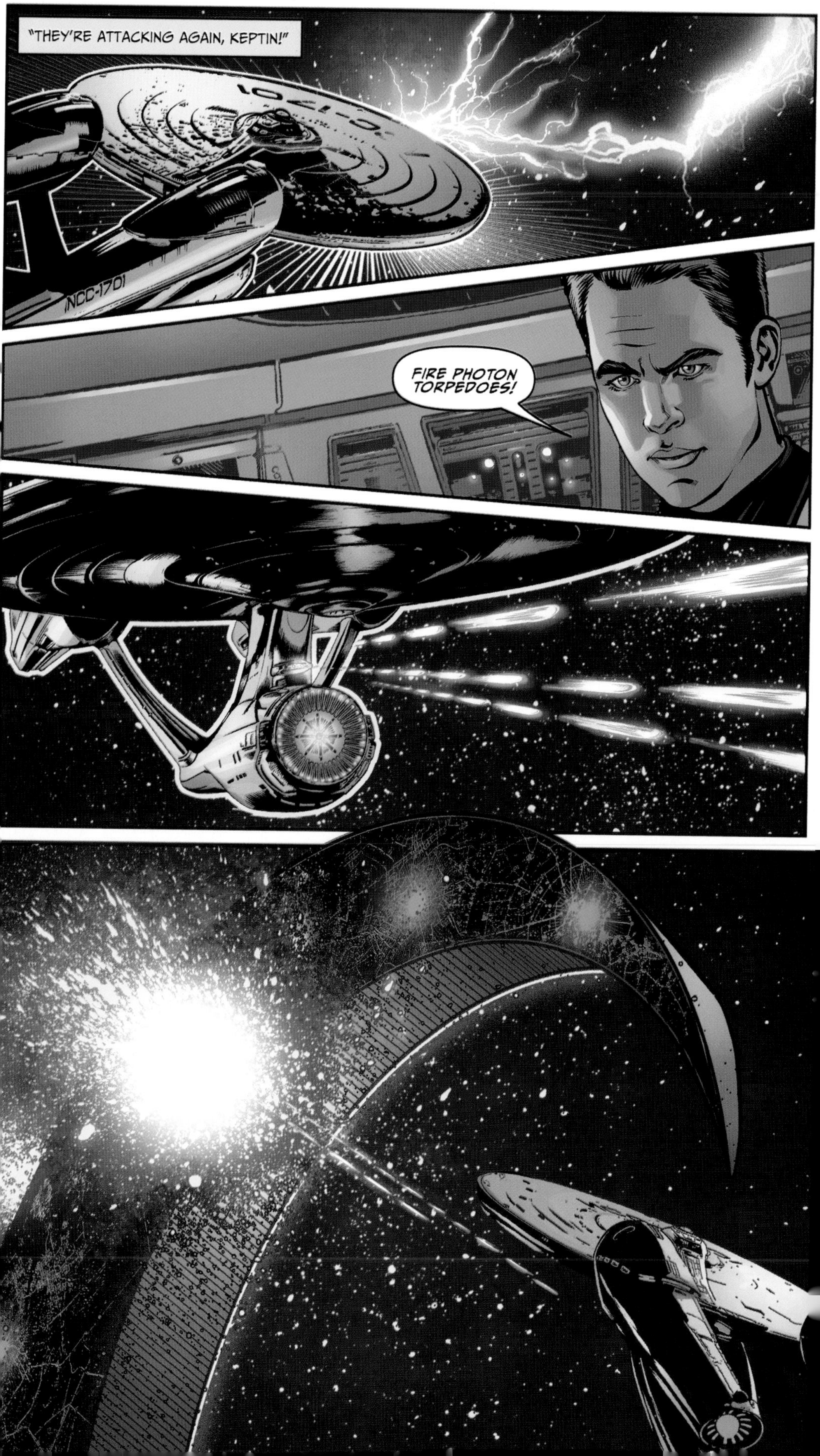
"THEY'RE ATTACKING AGAIN, KEPTIN!"
NCC-1701
FIRE PHOTON TORPEDOES!

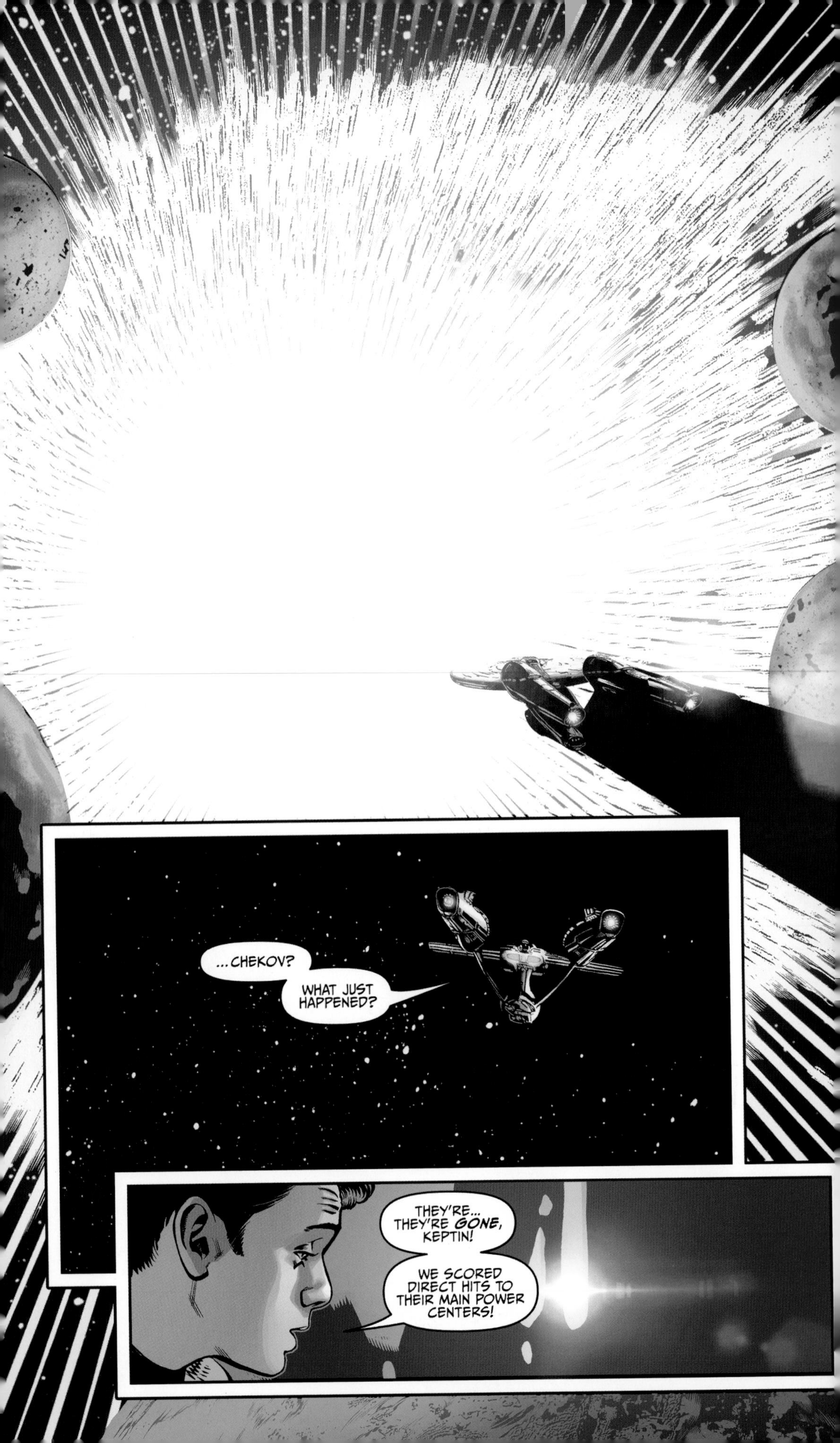
...CHEKOV?
WHAT JUST HAPPENED?
THEY'RE... THEY'RE GONE, KEPTIN!
WE SCORED DIRECT HITS TO THEIR MAIN POWER CENTERS!

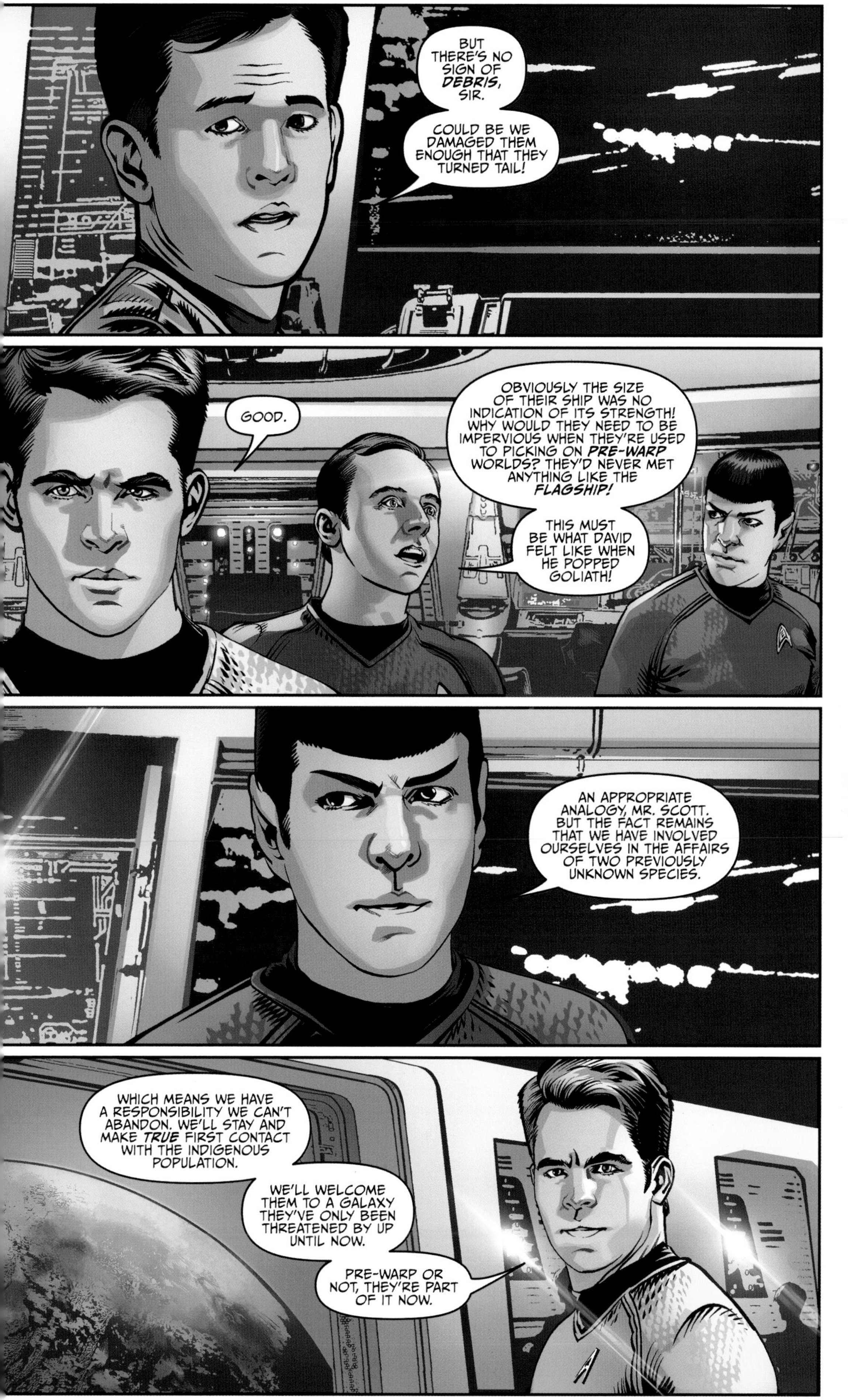

BUT THERE'S NO SIGN OF DEBRIS, SIR.
COULD BE WE DAMAGED THEM ENOUGH THAT THEY TURNED TAIL!
GOOD.
OBVIOUSLY THE SIZE OF THEIR SHIP WAS NO INDICATION OF ITS STRENGTH! WHY WOULD THEY NEED TO BE IMPERVIOUS WHEN THEY'RE USED TO PICKING ON PRE-WARP WORLDS? THEY'D NEVER MET ANYTHING LIKE THE FLAGSHIP!
THIS MUST BE WHAT DAVID FELT LIKE WHEN HE POPPED GOLIATH!
AN APPROPRIATE ANALOGY, MR. SCOTT. BUT THE FACT REMAINS THAT WE HAVE INVOLVED OURSELVES IN THE AFFAIRS OF TWO PREVIOUSLY UNKNOWN SPECIES.
WHICH MEANS WE HAVE A RESPONSIBILITY WE CAN'T ABANDON. WE'LL STAY AND MAKE TRUE FIRST CONTACT WITH THE INDIGENOUS POPULATION.
WE'LL WELCOME THEM TO A GALAXY THEY'VE ONLY BEEN THREATENED BY UP UNTIL NOW.
PRE-WARP OR NOT, THEY'RE PART OF IT NOW.

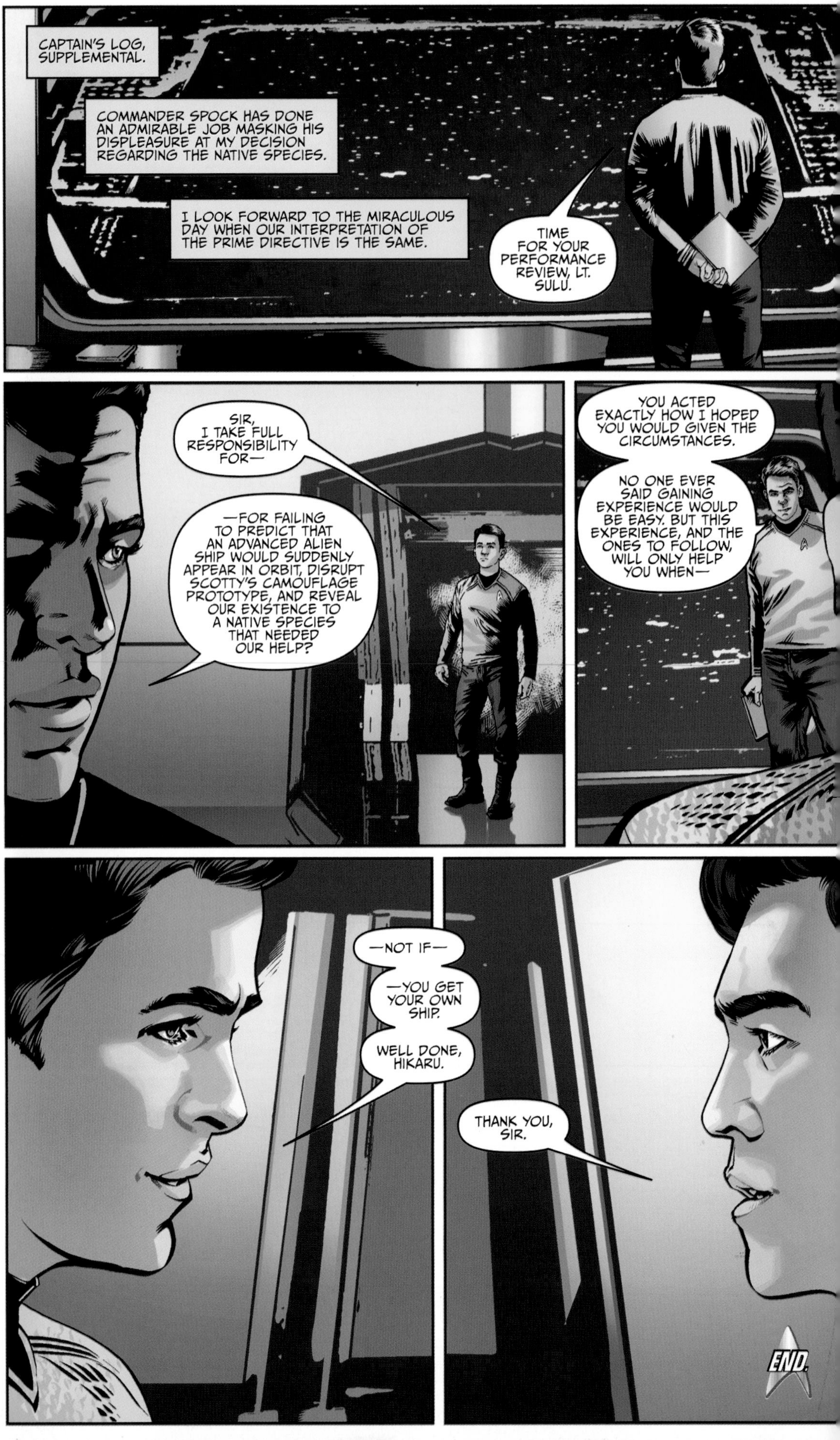
CAPTAIN'S LOG, SUPPLEMENTAL.
COMMANDER SPOCK HAS DONE AN ADMIRABLE JOB MASKING HIS DISPLEASURE AT MY DECISION REGARDING THE NATIVE SPECIES.
I LOOK FORWARD TO THE MIRACULOUS DAY WHEN OUR INTERPRETATION OF THE PRIME DIRECTIVE IS THE SAME.
TIME FOR YOUR PERFORMANCE REVIEW, LT. SULU.
SIR, I TAKE FULL RESPONSIBILITY FOR—
—FOR FAILING TO PREDICT THAT AN ADVANCED ALIEN SHIP WOULD SUDDENLY APPEAR IN ORBIT, DISRUPT SCOTTY'S CAMOUFLAGE PROTOTYPE, AND REVEAL OUR EXISTENCE TO A NATIVE SPECIES THAT NEEDED OUR HELP?
YOU ACTED EXACTLY HOW I HOPED YOU WOULD GIVEN THE CIRCUMSTANCES.
NO ONE EVER SAID GAINING EXPERIENCE WOULD BE EASY. BUT THIS EXPERIENCE, AND THE ONES TO FOLLOW, WILL ONLY HELP YOU WHEN—
—NOT IF—
—YOU GET YOUR OWN SHIP.
WELL DONE, HIKARU.
THANK YOU, SIR.
END.

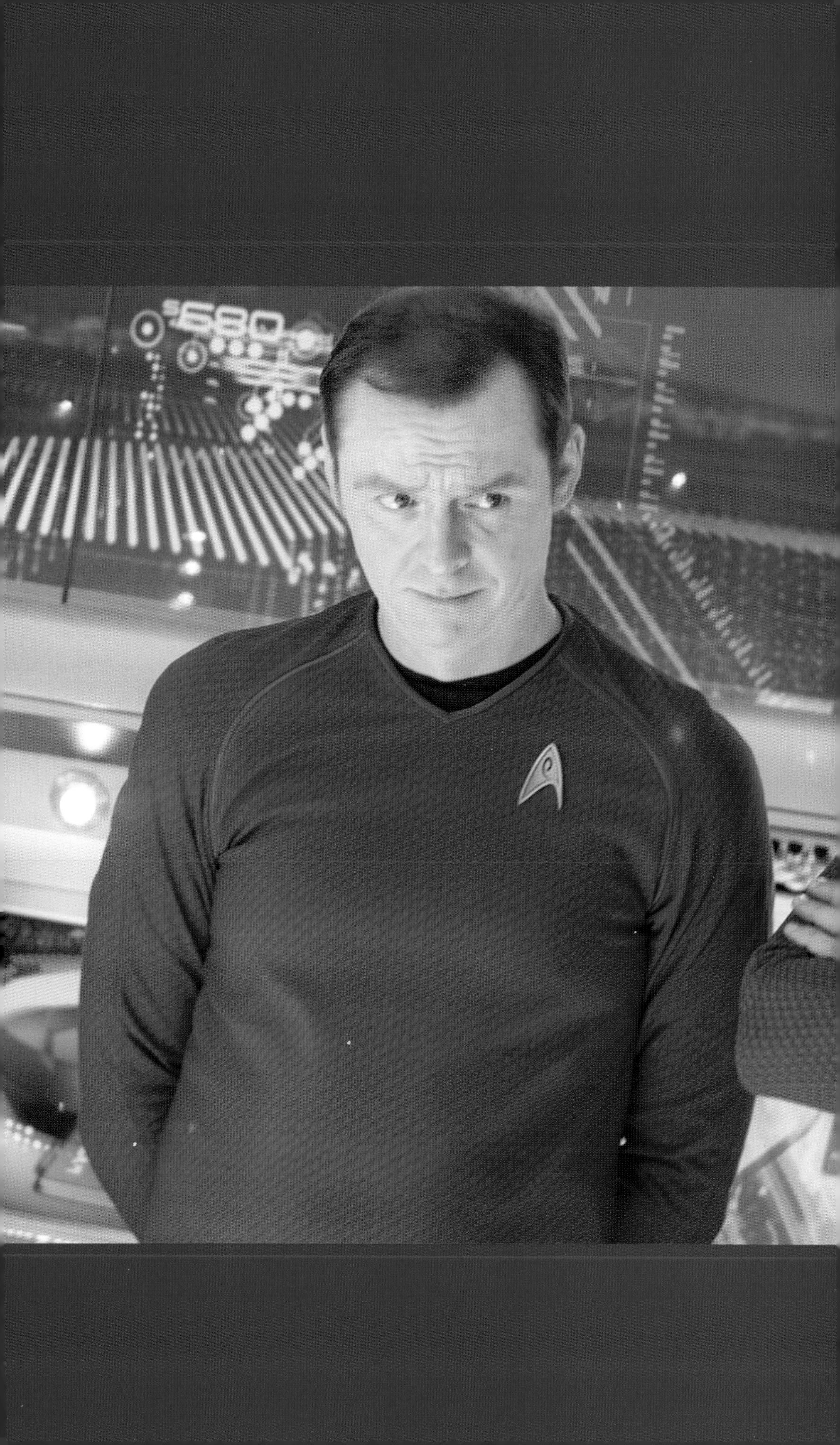

FLESH AND STONE

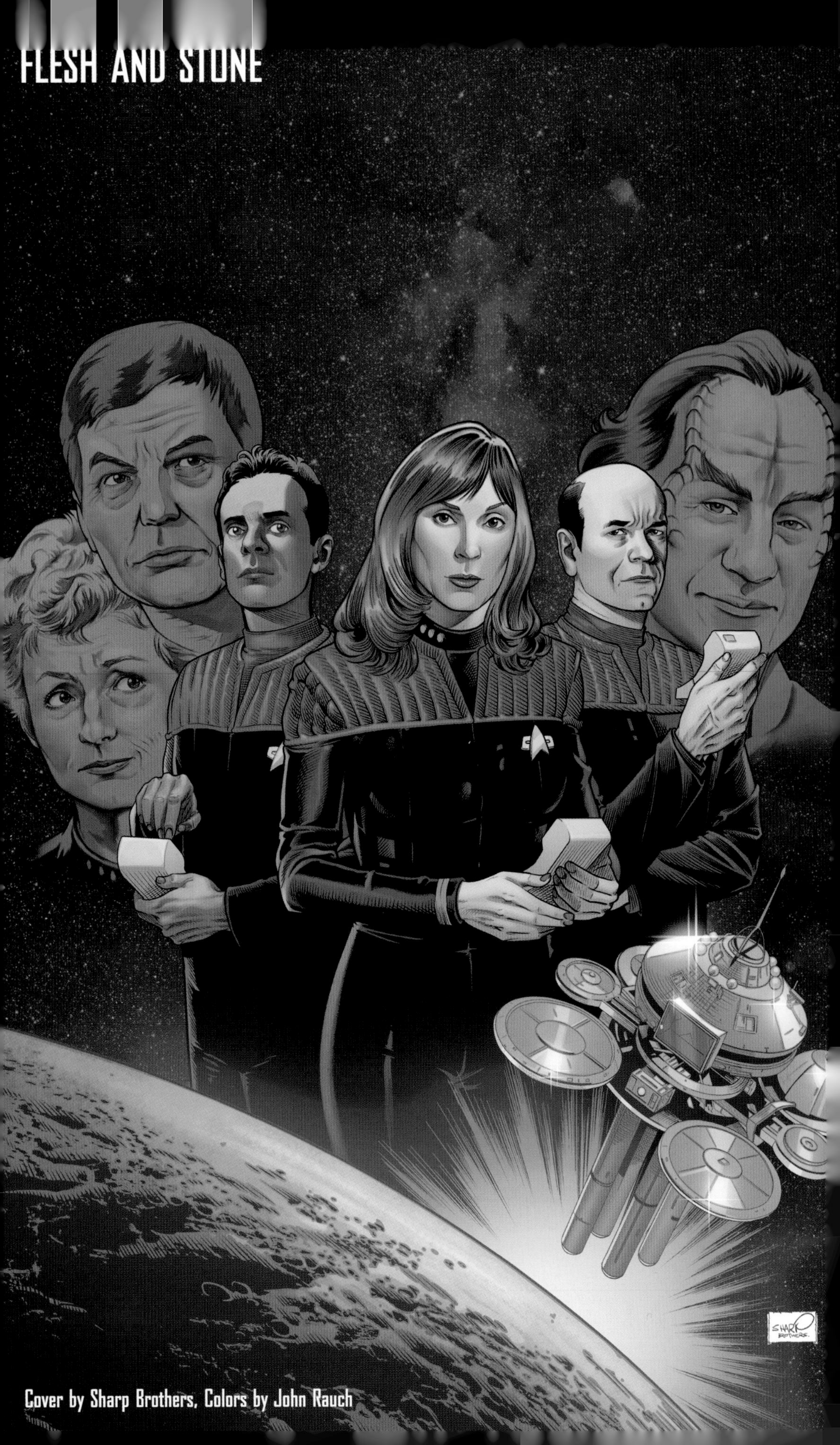
SHARP BROTHERS

Cover by Sharp Brothers, Colors by John Rauch

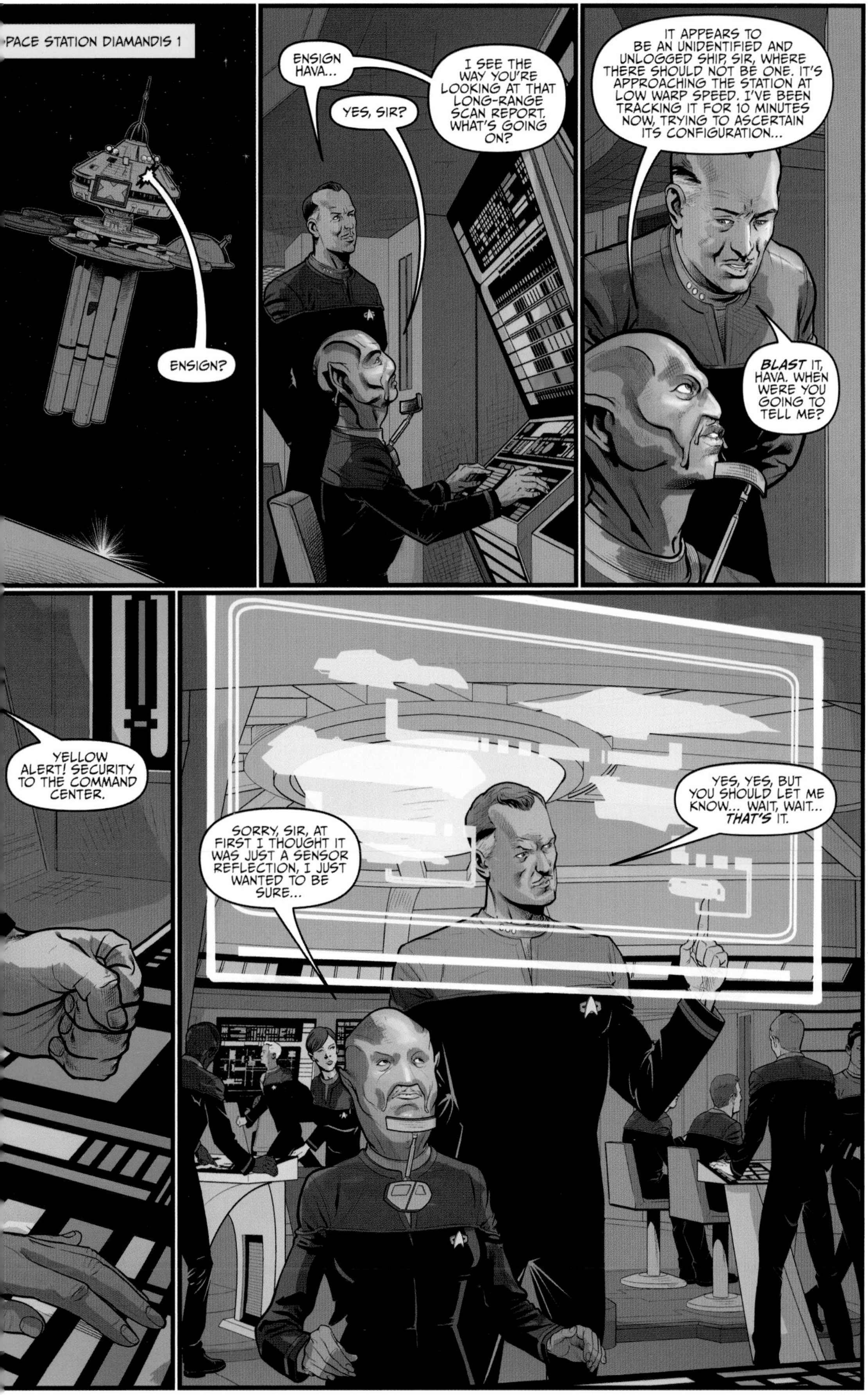
PACE STATION DIAMANDIS 1
ENSIGN?
ENSIGN HAVA...
YES, SIR?
I SEE THE WAY YOU'RE LOOKING AT THAT LONG-RANGE SCAN REPORT. WHAT'S GOING ON?
IT APPEARS TO BE AN UNIDENTIFIED AND UNLOGGED SHIP, SIR, WHERE THERE SHOULD NOT BE ONE. IT'S APPROACHING THE STATION AT LOW WARP SPEED. I'VE BEEN TRACKING IT FOR 10 MINUTES NOW, TRYING TO ASCERTAIN ITS CONFIGURATION...
BLAST IT, HAVA. WHEN WERE YOU GOING TO TELL ME?
YELLOW ALERT! SECURITY TO THE COMMAND CENTER.
SORRY, SIR, AT FIRST I THOUGHT IT WAS JUST A SENSOR REFLECTION, I JUST WANTED TO BE SURE...
YES, YES, BUT YOU SHOULD LET ME KNOW... WAIT, WAIT... *THAT'S* IT.

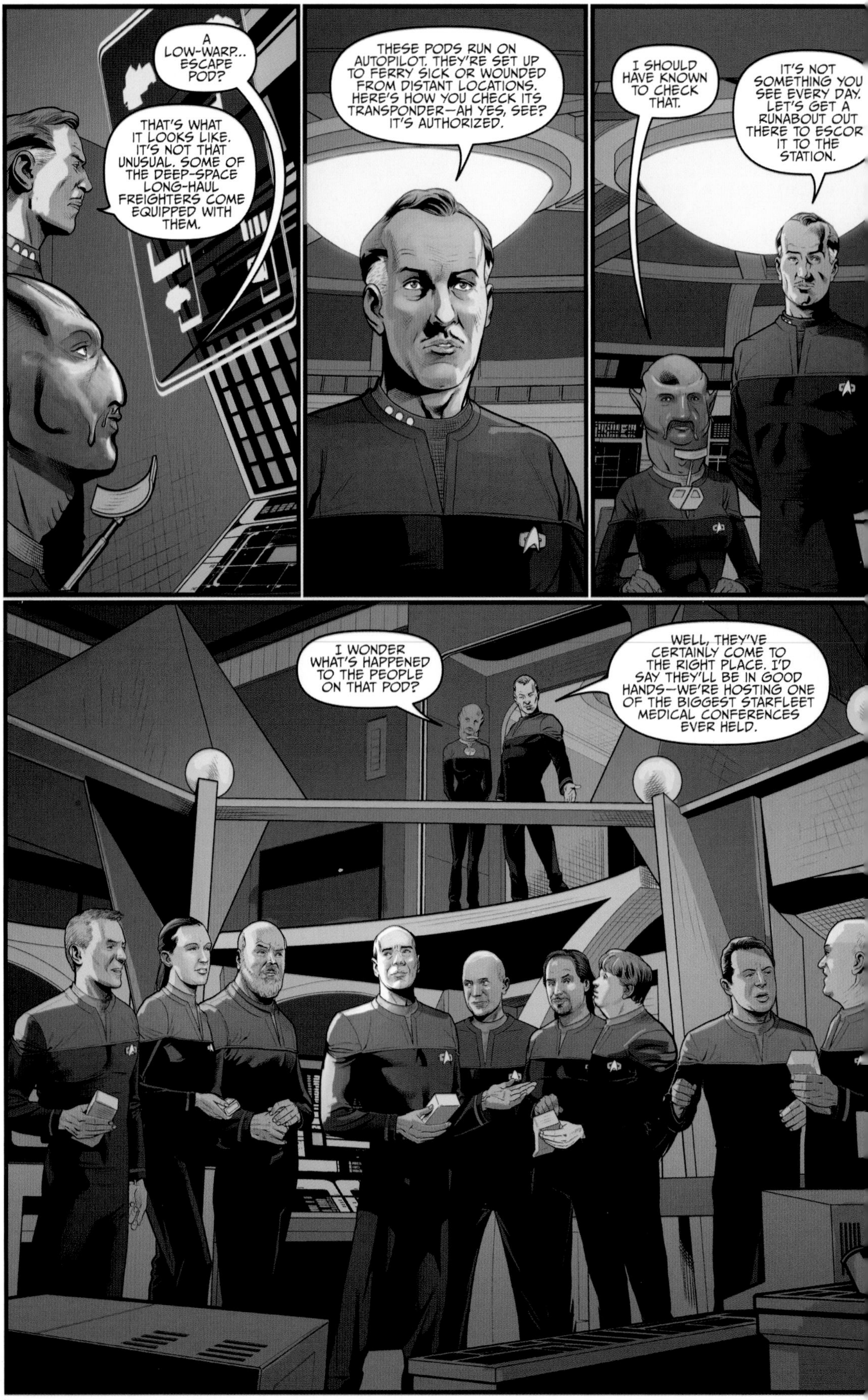
A LOW-WARP... ESCAPE POD?
THAT'S WHAT IT LOOKS LIKE. IT'S NOT THAT UNUSUAL. SOME OF THE DEEP-SPACE LONG-HAUL FREIGHTERS COME EQUIPPED WITH THEM.
THESE PODS RUN ON AUTOPILOT. THEY'RE SET UP TO FERRY SICK OR WOUNDED FROM DISTANT LOCATIONS. HERE'S HOW YOU CHECK ITS TRANSPONDER—AH YES, SEE? IT'S AUTHORIZED.
I SHOULD HAVE KNOWN TO CHECK THAT.
IT'S NOT SOMETHING YOU SEE EVERY DAY. LET'S GET A RUNABOUT OUT THERE TO ESCOR IT TO THE STATION.
I WONDER WHAT'S HAPPENED TO THE PEOPLE ON THAT POD?
WELL, THEY'VE CERTAINLY COME TO THE RIGHT PLACE. I'D SAY THEY'LL BE IN GOOD HANDS—WE'RE HOSTING ONE OF THE BIGGEST STARFLEET MEDICAL CONFERENCES EVER HELD.

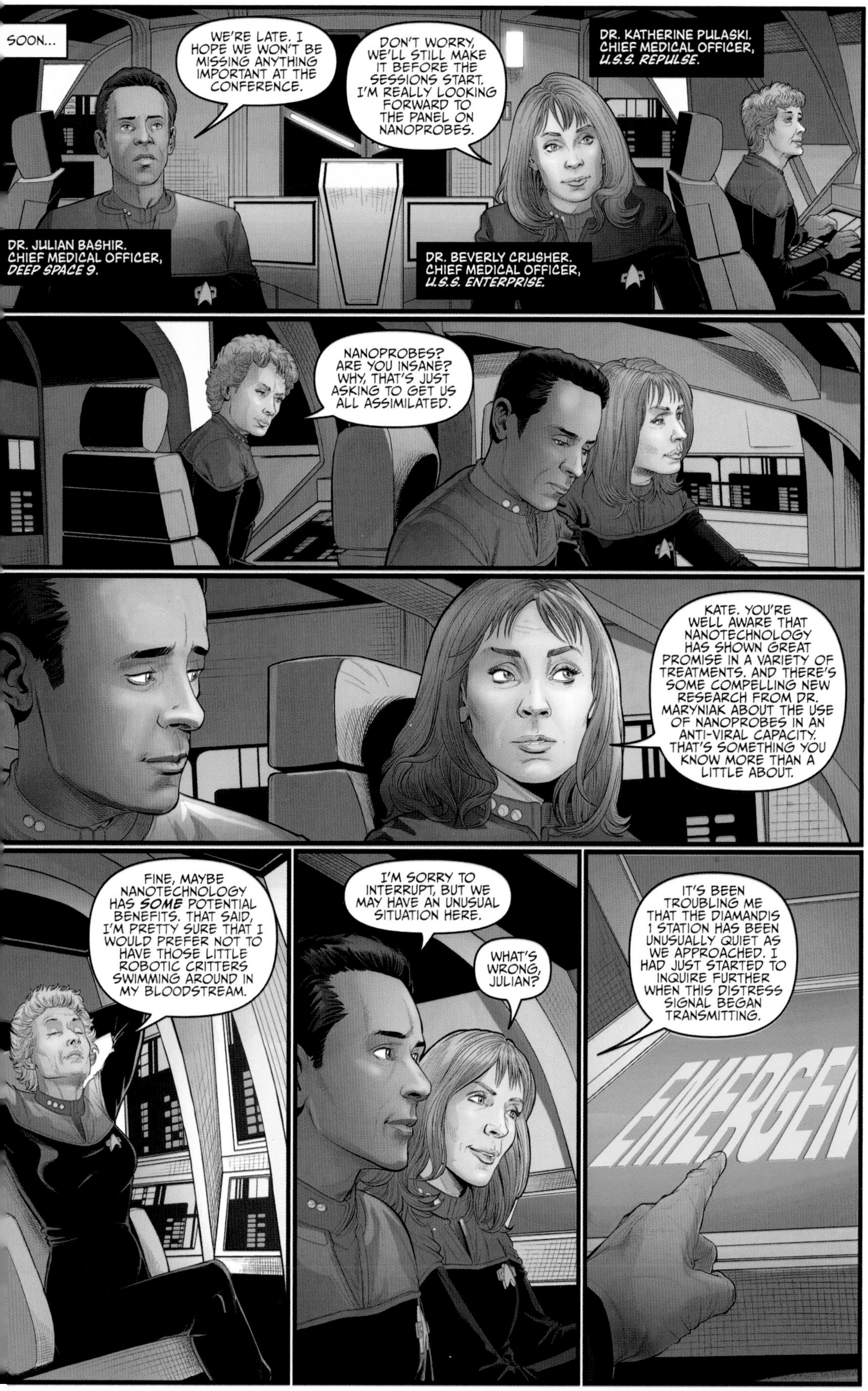
SOON...
WE'RE LATE. I HOPE WE WON'T BE MISSING ANYTHING IMPORTANT AT THE CONFERENCE.
DON'T WORRY, WE'LL STILL MAKE IT BEFORE THE SESSIONS START. I'M REALLY LOOKING FORWARD TO THE PANEL ON NANOPROBES.
DR. KATHERINE PULASKI. CHIEF MEDICAL OFFICER, U.S.S. REPULSE.
DR. JULIAN BASHIR. CHIEF MEDICAL OFFICER, DEEP SPACE 9.
DR. BEVERLY CRUSHER. CHIEF MEDICAL OFFICER, U.S.S. ENTERPRISE.
NANOPROBES? ARE YOU INSANE? WHY, THAT'S JUST ASKING TO GET US ALL ASSIMILATED.
KATE. YOU'RE WELL AWARE THAT NANOTECHNOLOGY HAS SHOWN GREAT PROMISE IN A VARIETY OF TREATMENTS. AND THERE'S SOME COMPELLING NEW RESEARCH FROM DR. MARYNIAK ABOUT THE USE OF NANOPROBES IN AN ANTI-VIRAL CAPACITY. THAT'S SOMETHING YOU KNOW MORE THAN A LITTLE ABOUT.
FINE, MAYBE NANOTECHNOLOGY HAS SOME POTENTIAL BENEFITS. THAT SAID, I'M PRETTY SURE THAT I WOULD PREFER NOT TO HAVE THOSE LITTLE ROBOTIC CRITTERS SWIMMING AROUND IN MY BLOODSTREAM.
I'M SORRY TO INTERRUPT, BUT WE MAY HAVE AN UNUSUAL SITUATION HERE.
WHAT'S WRONG, JULIAN?
IT'S BEEN TROUBLING ME THAT THE DIAMANDIS 1 STATION HAS BEEN UNUSUALLY QUIET AS WE APPROACHED. I HAD JUST STARTED TO INQUIRE FURTHER WHEN THIS DISTRESS SIGNAL BEGAN TRANSMITTING.

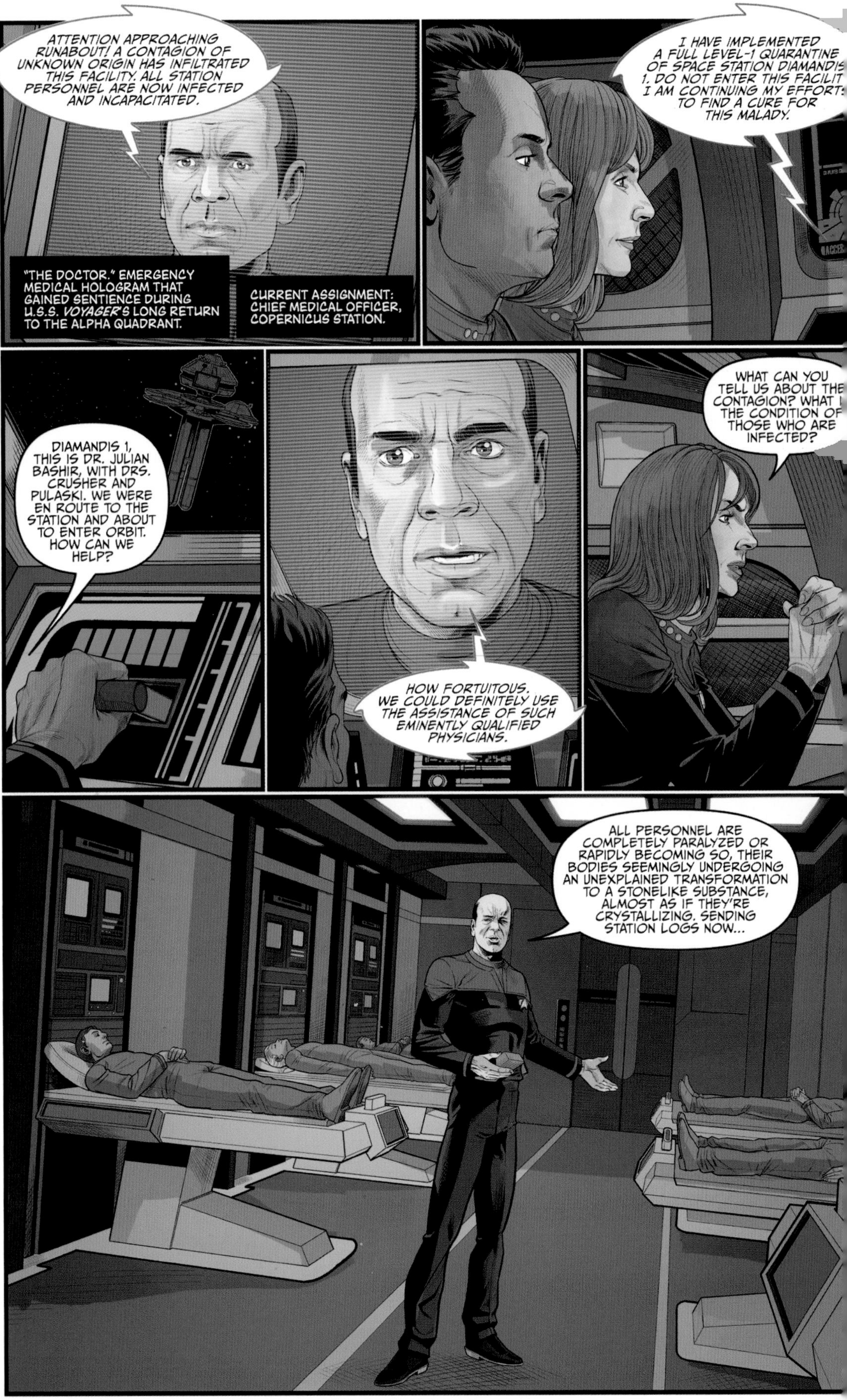

ATTENTION APPROACHING RUNABOUT! A CONTAGION OF UNKNOWN ORIGIN HAS INFILTRATED THIS FACILITY. ALL STATION PERSONNEL ARE NOW INFECTED AND INCAPACITATED.
"THE DOCTOR." EMERGENCY MEDICAL HOLOGRAM THAT GAINED SENTIENCE DURING U.S.S. VOYAGER'S LONG RETURN TO THE ALPHA QUADRANT.
CURRENT ASSIGNMENT: CHIEF MEDICAL OFFICER, COPERNICUS STATION.
I HAVE IMPLEMENTED A FULL LEVEL-1 QUARANTINE OF SPACE STATION DIAMANDIS 1. DO NOT ENTER THIS FACILIT I AM CONTINUING MY EFFORT TO FIND A CURE FOR THIS MALADY.
DIAMANDIS 1, THIS IS DR. JULIAN BASHIR, WITH DRS. CRUSHER AND PULASKI. WE WERE EN ROUTE TO THE STATION AND ABOUT TO ENTER ORBIT. HOW CAN WE HELP?
HOW FORTUITOUS. WE COULD DEFINITELY USE THE ASSISTANCE OF SUCH EMINENTLY QUALIFIED PHYSICIANS.
WHAT CAN YOU TELL US ABOUT THE CONTAGION? WHAT I THE CONDITION OF THOSE WHO ARE INFECTED?
ALL PERSONNEL ARE COMPLETELY PARALYZED OR RAPIDLY BECOMING SO, THEIR BODIES SEEMINGLY UNDERGOING AN UNEXPLAINED TRANSFORMATION TO A STONELIKE SUBSTANCE, ALMOST AS IF THEY'RE CRYSTALLIZING. SENDING STATION LOGS NOW...

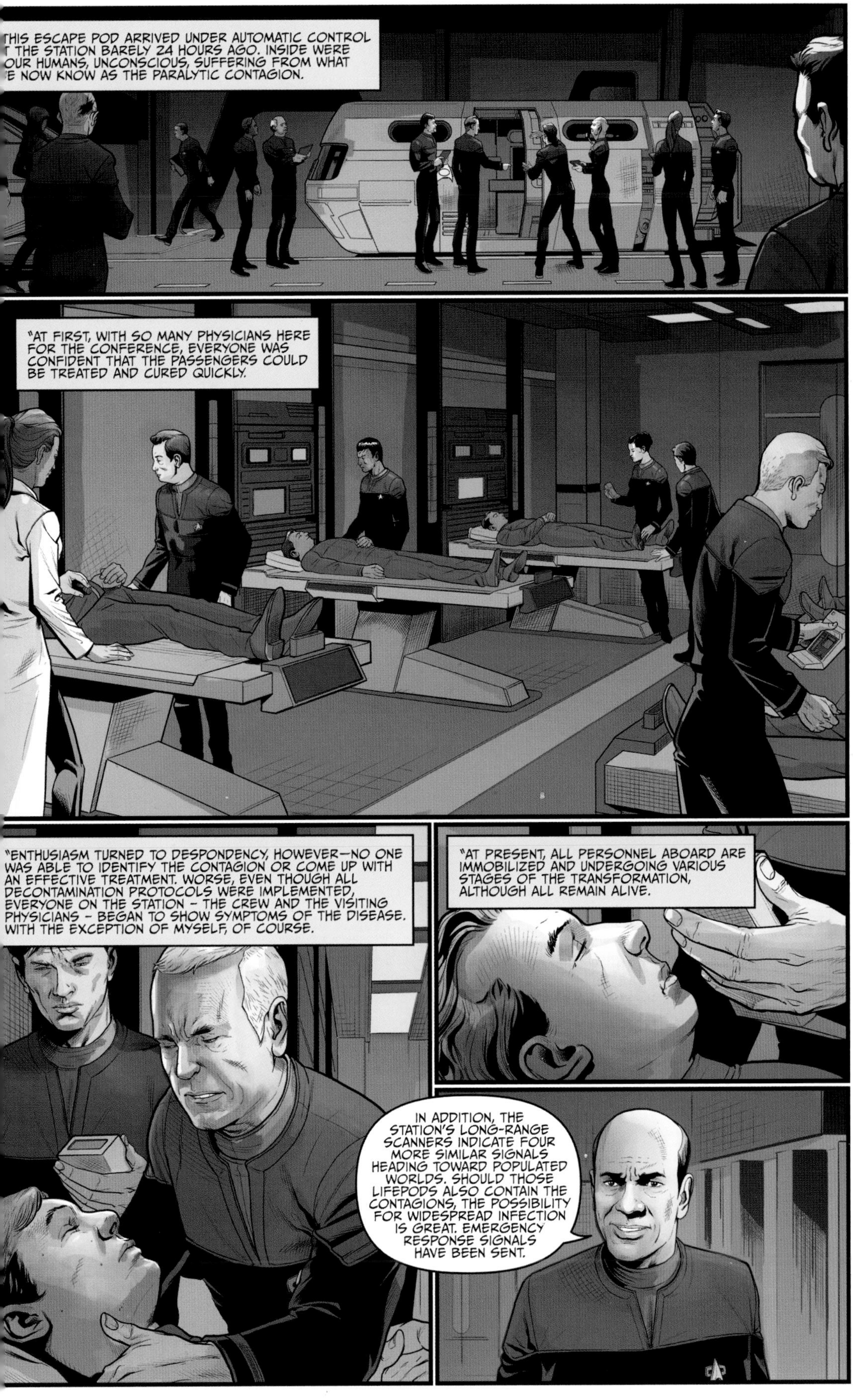
THIS ESCAPE POD ARRIVED UNDER AUTOMATIC CONTROL
T THE STATION BARELY 24 HOURS AGO. INSIDE WERE
OUR HUMANS, UNCONSCIOUS, SUFFERING FROM WHAT
E NOW KNOW AS THE PARALYTIC CONTAGION.
"AT FIRST, WITH SO MANY PHYSICIANS HERE FOR THE CONFERENCE, EVERYONE WAS CONFIDENT THAT THE PASSENGERS COULD BE TREATED AND CURED QUICKLY.
"ENTHUSIASM TURNED TO DESPONDENCY, HOWEVER—NO ONE WAS ABLE TO IDENTIFY THE CONTAGION OR COME UP WITH AN EFFECTIVE TREATMENT. WORSE, EVEN THOUGH ALL DECONTAMINATION PROTOCOLS WERE IMPLEMENTED, EVERYONE ON THE STATION - THE CREW AND THE VISITING PHYSICIANS - BEGAN TO SHOW SYMPTOMS OF THE DISEASE. WITH THE EXCEPTION OF MYSELF, OF COURSE.
"AT PRESENT, ALL PERSONNEL ABOARD ARE IMMOBILIZED AND UNDERGOING VARIOUS STAGES OF THE TRANSFORMATION, ALTHOUGH ALL REMAIN ALIVE.
IN ADDITION, THE STATION'S LONG-RANGE SCANNERS INDICATE FOUR MORE SIMILAR SIGNALS HEADING TOWARD POPULATED WORLDS. SHOULD THOSE LIFEPODS ALSO CONTAIN THE CONTAGIONS, THE POSSIBILITY FOR WIDESPREAD INFECTION IS GREAT. EMERGENCY RESPONSE SIGNALS HAVE BEEN SENT.

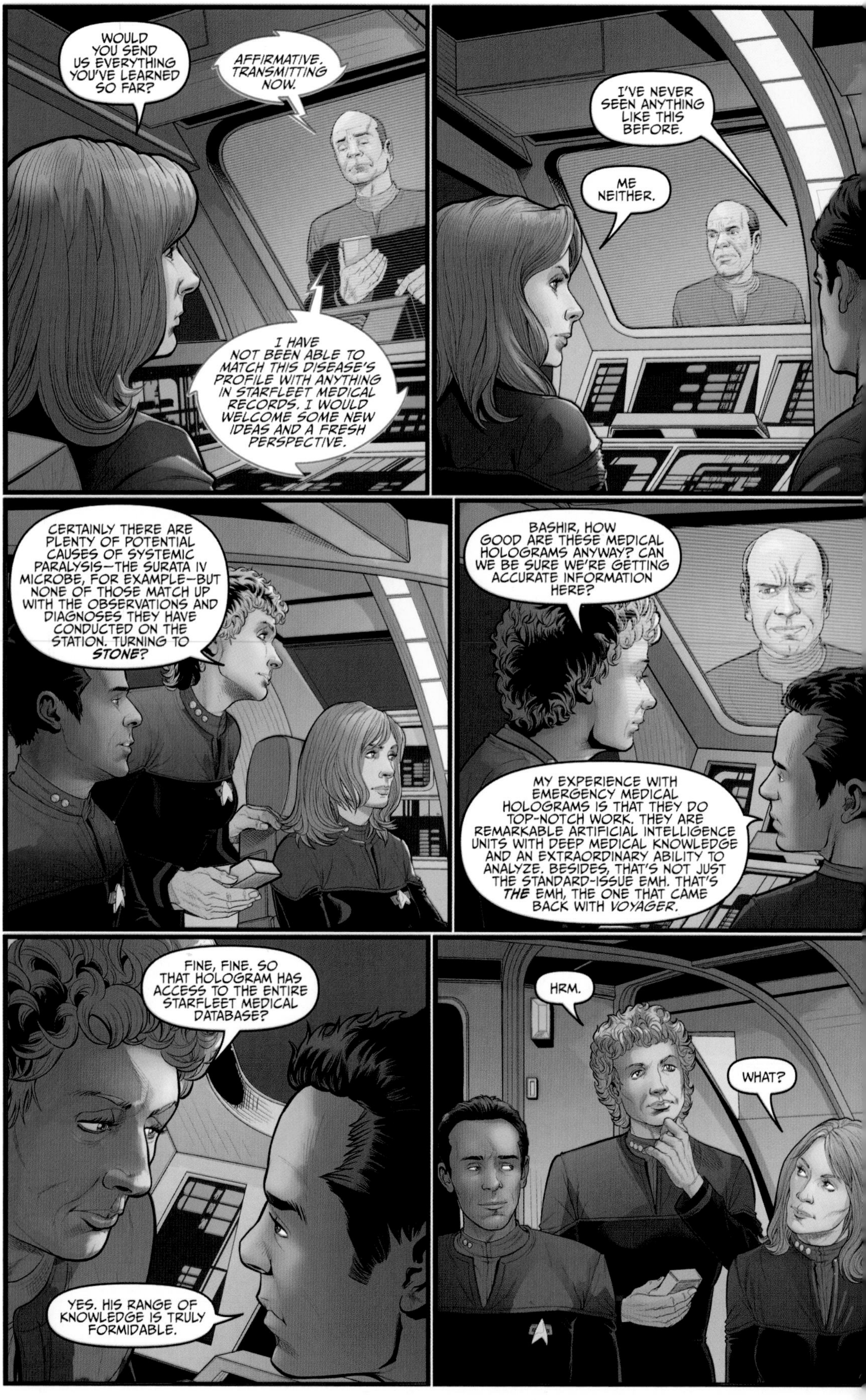
WOULD YOU SEND US EVERYTHING YOU'VE LEARNED SO FAR?
AFFIRMATIVE. TRANSMITTING NOW.
I HAVE NOT BEEN ABLE TO MATCH THIS DISEASE'S PROFILE WITH ANYTHING IN STARFLEET MEDICAL RECORDS. I WOULD WELCOME SOME NEW IDEAS AND A FRESH PERSPECTIVE.
I'VE NEVER SEEN ANYTHING LIKE THIS BEFORE.
ME NEITHER.
CERTAINLY THERE ARE PLENTY OF POTENTIAL CAUSES OF SYSTEMIC PARALYSIS—THE SURATA IV MICROBE, FOR EXAMPLE—BUT NONE OF THOSE MATCH UP WITH THE OBSERVATIONS AND DIAGNOSES THEY HAVE CONDUCTED ON THE STATION. TURNING TO *STONE*?
BASHIR, HOW GOOD ARE THESE MEDICAL HOLOGRAMS ANYWAY? CAN WE BE SURE WE'RE GETTING ACCURATE INFORMATION HERE?
MY EXPERIENCE WITH EMERGENCY MEDICAL HOLOGRAMS IS THAT THEY DO TOP-NOTCH WORK. THEY ARE REMARKABLE ARTIFICIAL INTELLIGENCE UNITS WITH DEEP MEDICAL KNOWLEDGE AND AN EXTRAORDINARY ABILITY TO ANALYZE. BESIDES, THAT'S NOT JUST THE STANDARD-ISSUE EMH. THAT'S *THE* EMH, THE ONE THAT CAME BACK WITH *VOYAGER*.
FINE, FINE. SO THAT HOLOGRAM HAS ACCESS TO THE ENTIRE STARFLEET MEDICAL DATABASE?
YES. HIS RANGE OF KNOWLEDGE IS TRULY FORMIDABLE.
HRM.
WHAT?

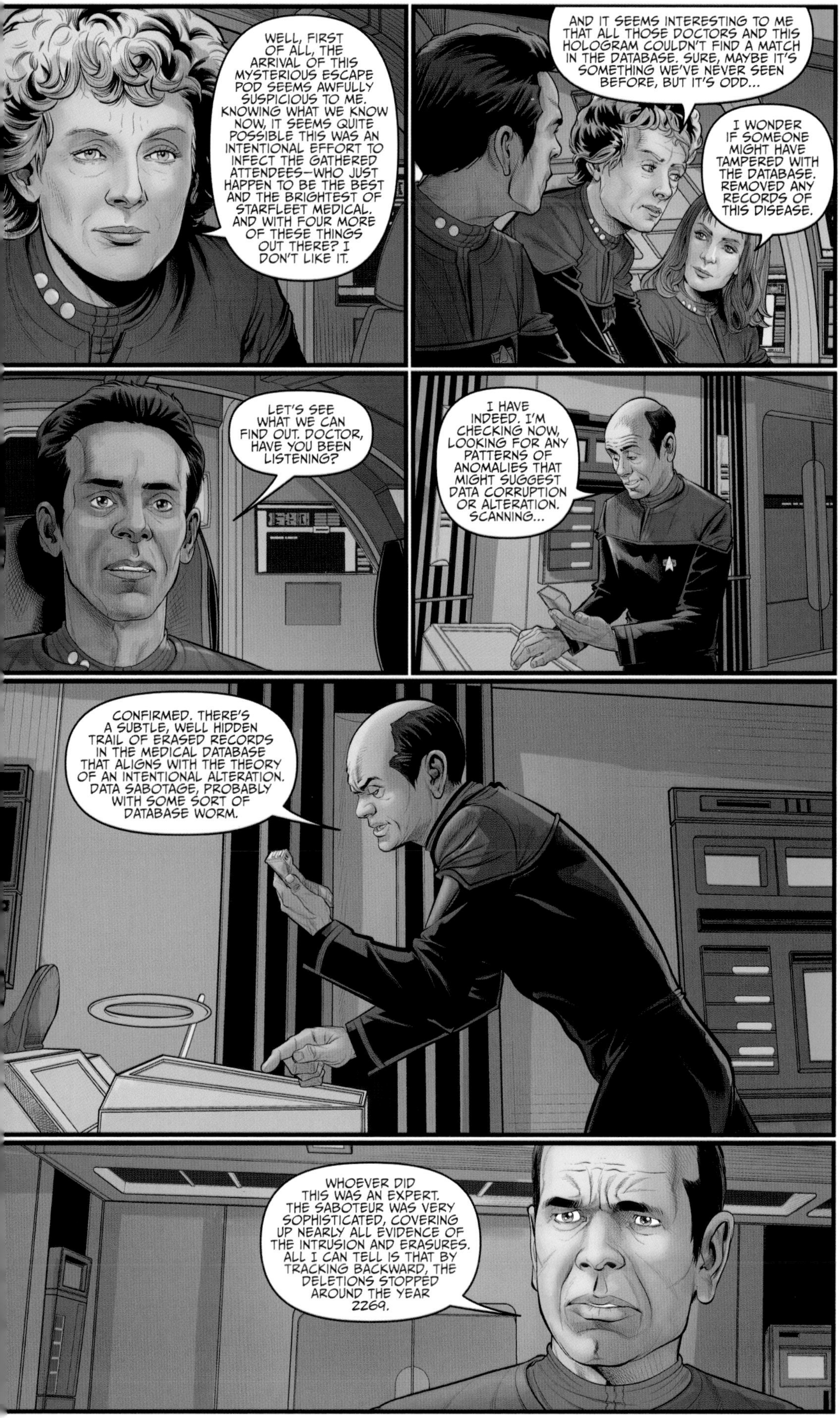
WELL, FIRST OF ALL, THE ARRIVAL OF THIS MYSTERIOUS ESCAPE POD SEEMS AWFULLY SUSPICIOUS TO ME. KNOWING WHAT WE KNOW NOW, IT SEEMS QUITE POSSIBLE THIS WAS AN INTENTIONAL EFFORT TO INFECT THE GATHERED ATTENDEES—WHO JUST HAPPEN TO BE THE BEST AND THE BRIGHTEST OF STARFLEET MEDICAL. AND WITH FOUR MORE OF THESE THINGS OUT THERE? I DON'T LIKE IT.
AND IT SEEMS INTERESTING TO ME THAT ALL THOSE DOCTORS AND THIS HOLOGRAM COULDN'T FIND A MATCH IN THE DATABASE. SURE, MAYBE IT'S SOMETHING WE'VE NEVER SEEN BEFORE, BUT IT'S ODD...
I WONDER IF SOMEONE MIGHT HAVE TAMPERED WITH THE DATABASE. REMOVED ANY RECORDS OF THIS DISEASE.
LET'S SEE WHAT WE CAN FIND OUT. DOCTOR, HAVE YOU BEEN LISTENING?
I HAVE INDEED. I'M CHECKING NOW, LOOKING FOR ANY PATTERNS OF ANOMALIES THAT MIGHT SUGGEST DATA CORRUPTION OR ALTERATION. SCANNING...
CONFIRMED. THERE'S A SUBTLE, WELL HIDDEN TRAIL OF ERASED RECORDS IN THE MEDICAL DATABASE THAT ALIGNS WITH THE THEORY OF AN INTENTIONAL ALTERATION. DATA SABOTAGE, PROBABLY WITH SOME SORT OF DATABASE WORM.
WHOEVER DID THIS WAS AN EXPERT. THE SABOTEUR WAS VERY SOPHISTICATED, COVERING UP NEARLY ALL EVIDENCE OF THE INTRUSION AND ERASURES. ALL I CAN TELL IS THAT BY TRACKING BACKWARD, THE DELETIONS STOPPED AROUND THE YEAR 2269.

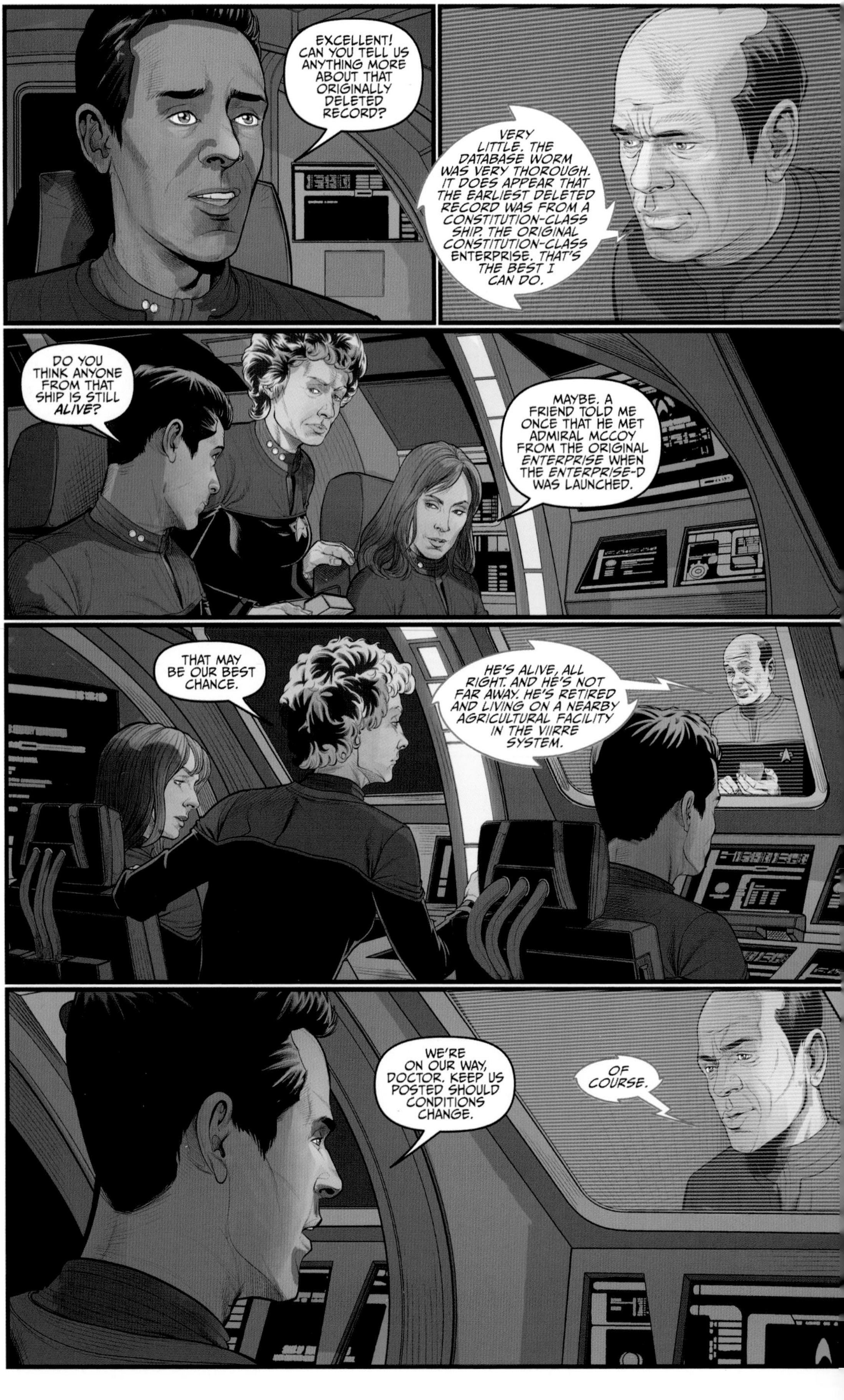
EXCELLENT! CAN YOU TELL US ANYTHING MORE ABOUT THAT ORIGINALLY DELETED RECORD?
VERY LITTLE. THE DATABASE WORM WAS VERY THOROUGH. IT DOES APPEAR THAT THE EARLIEST DELETED RECORD WAS FROM A CONSTITUTION-CLASS SHIP. THE ORIGINAL CONSTITUTION-CLASS ENTERPRISE. THAT'S THE BEST I CAN DO.
DO YOU THINK ANYONE FROM THAT SHIP IS STILL *ALIVE?*
MAYBE. A FRIEND TOLD ME ONCE THAT HE MET ADMIRAL MCCOY FROM THE ORIGINAL *ENTERPRISE* WHEN THE *ENTERPRISE-D* WAS LAUNCHED.
THAT MAY BE OUR BEST CHANCE.
HE'S ALIVE, ALL RIGHT. AND HE'S NOT FAR AWAY. HE'S RETIRED AND LIVING ON A NEARBY AGRICULTURAL FACILITY IN THE VIIRRE SYSTEM.
WE'RE ON OUR WAY, DOCTOR. KEEP US POSTED SHOULD CONDITIONS CHANGE.
OF COURSE.

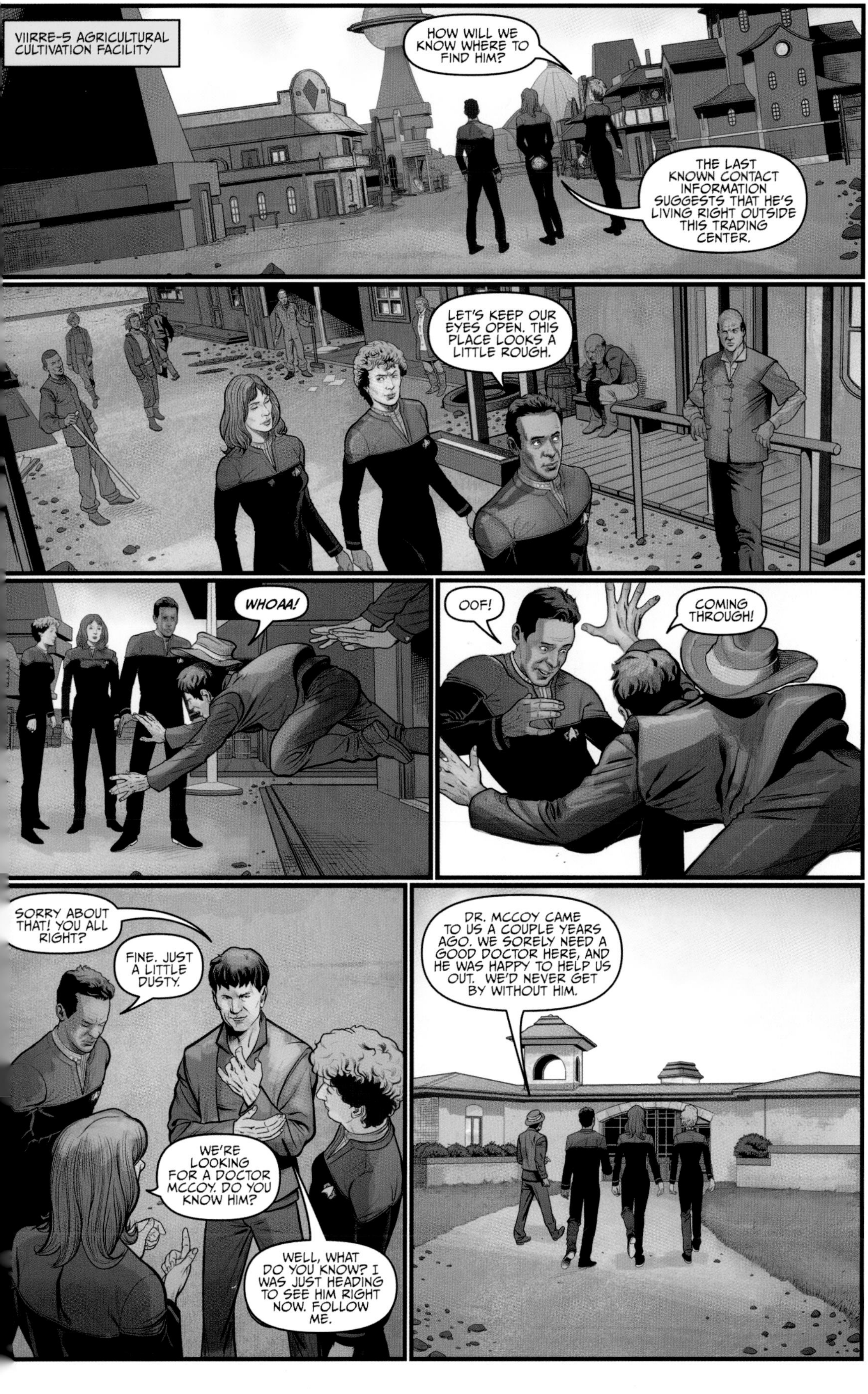
VIIRRE-5 AGRICULTURAL CULTIVATION FACILITY
HOW WILL WE KNOW WHERE TO FIND HIM?
THE LAST KNOWN CONTACT INFORMATION SUGGESTS THAT HE'S LIVING RIGHT OUTSIDE THIS TRADING CENTER.
LET'S KEEP OUR EYES OPEN. THIS PLACE LOOKS A LITTLE ROUGH.
WHOAA!
OOF!
COMING THROUGH!
SORRY ABOUT THAT! YOU ALL RIGHT?
FINE. JUST A LITTLE DUSTY.
WE'RE LOOKING FOR A DOCTOR MCCOY. DO YOU KNOW HIM?
WELL, WHAT DO YOU KNOW? I WAS JUST HEADING TO SEE HIM RIGHT NOW. FOLLOW ME.
DR. MCCOY CAME TO US A COUPLE YEARS AGO. WE SORELY NEED A GOOD DOCTOR HERE, AND HE WAS HAPPY TO HELP US OUT. WE'D NEVER GET BY WITHOUT HIM.

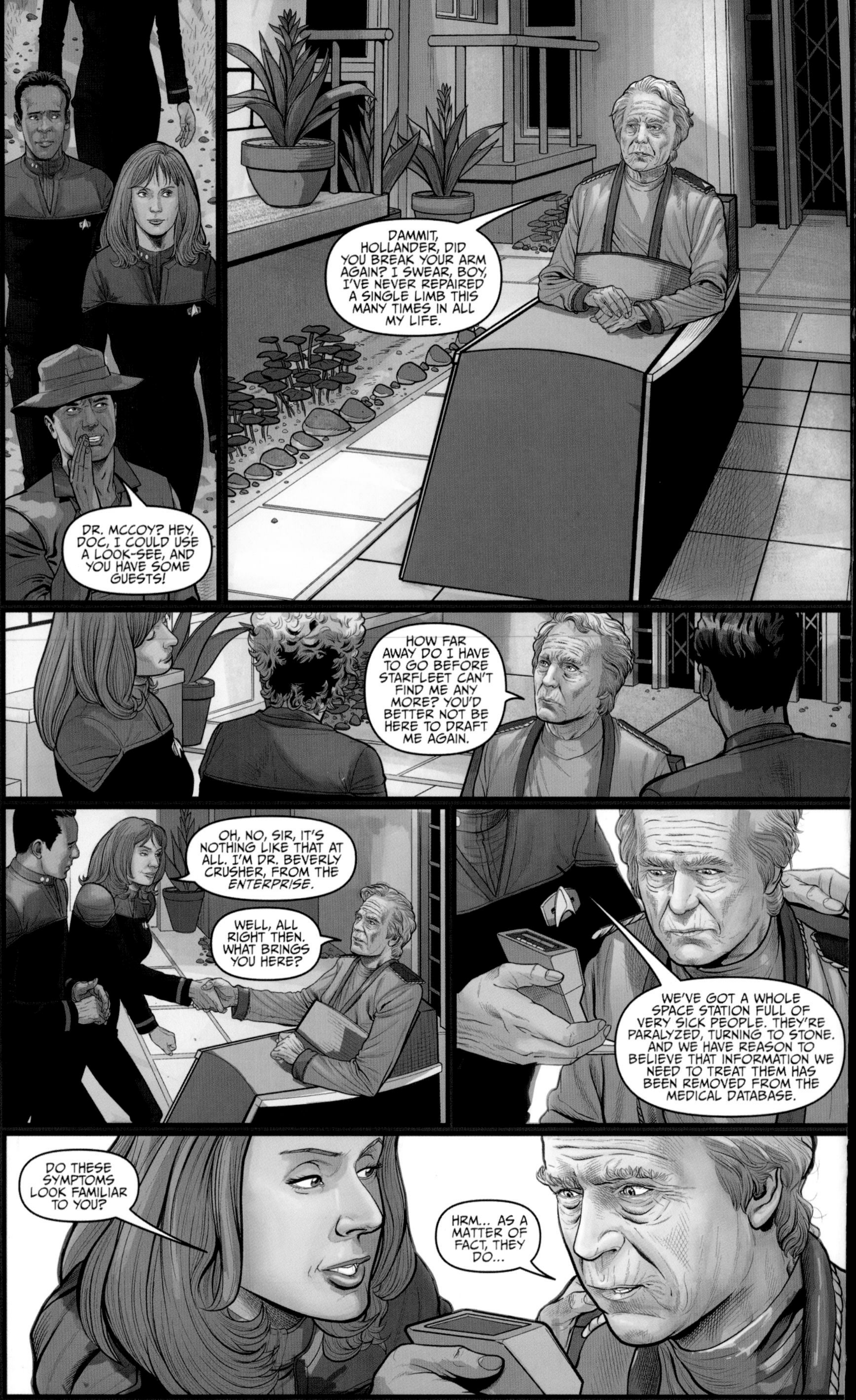
DAMMIT, HOLLANDER, DID YOU BREAK YOUR ARM AGAIN? I SWEAR, BOY, I'VE NEVER REPAIRED A SINGLE LIMB THIS MANY TIMES IN ALL MY LIFE.
DR. MCCOY? HEY, DOC, I COULD USE A LOOK-SEE, AND YOU HAVE SOME GUESTS!
HOW FAR AWAY DO I HAVE TO GO BEFORE STARFLEET CAN'T FIND ME ANY MORE? YOU'D BETTER NOT BE HERE TO DRAFT ME AGAIN.
OH, NO, SIR, IT'S NOTHING LIKE THAT AT ALL. I'M DR. BEVERLY CRUSHER, FROM THE *ENTERPRISE*.
WELL, ALL RIGHT THEN. WHAT BRINGS YOU HERE?
WE'VE GOT A WHOLE SPACE STATION FULL OF VERY SICK PEOPLE. THEY'RE PARALYZED, TURNING TO STONE. AND WE HAVE REASON TO BELIEVE THAT INFORMATION WE NEED TO TREAT THEM HAS BEEN REMOVED FROM THE MEDICAL DATABASE.
DO THESE SYMPTOMS LOOK FAMILIAR TO YOU?
HRM... AS A MATTER OF FACT, THEY DO...

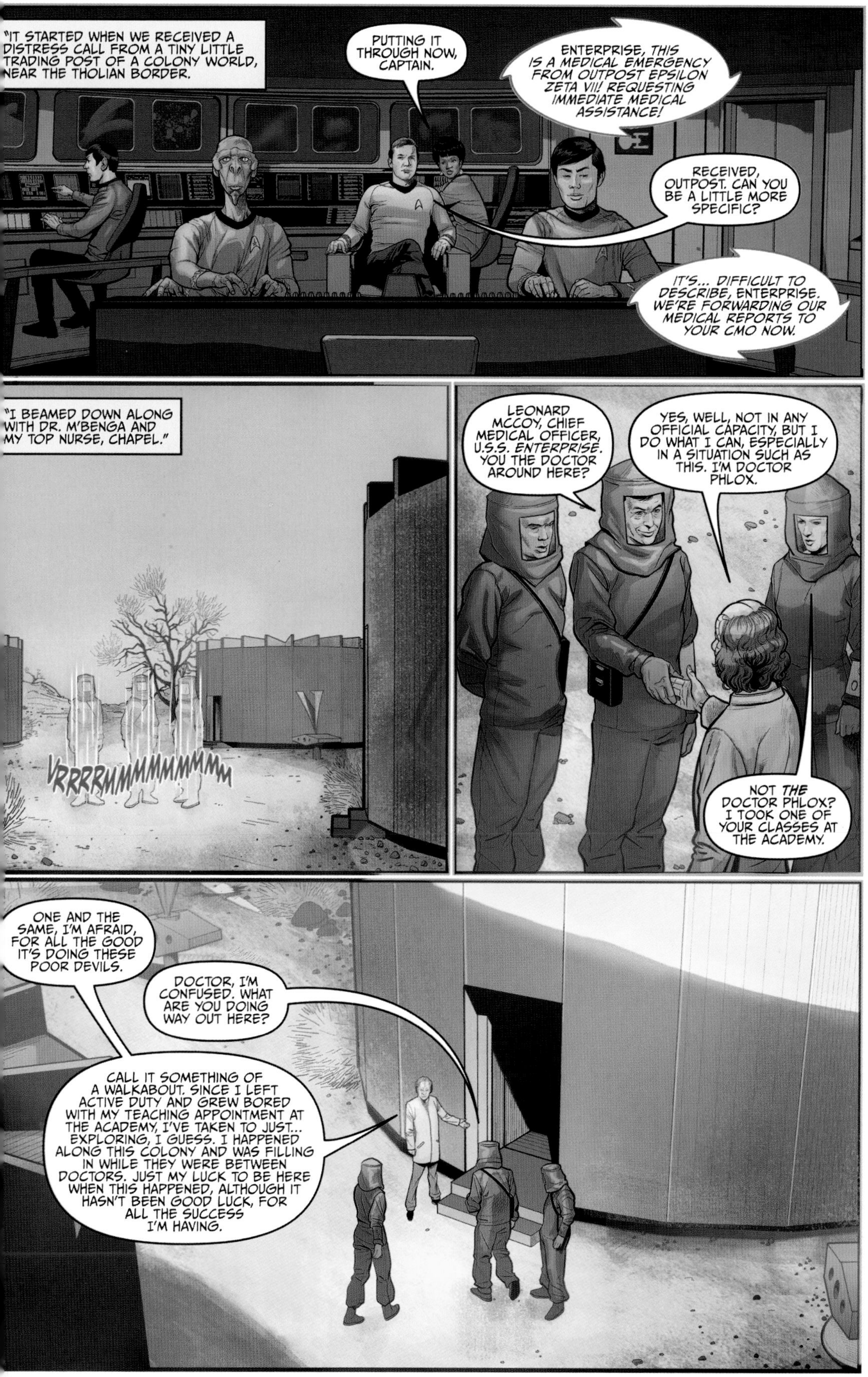
"IT STARTED WHEN WE RECEIVED A DISTRESS CALL FROM A TINY LITTLE TRADING POST OF A COLONY WORLD, NEAR THE THOLIAN BORDER.
PUTTING IT THROUGH NOW, CAPTAIN.
ENTERPRISE, *THIS IS A MEDICAL EMERGENCY FROM OUTPOST EPSILON ZETA VII! REQUESTING IMMEDIATE MEDICAL ASSISTANCE!*
RECEIVED, OUTPOST. CAN YOU BE A LITTLE MORE SPECIFIC?
IT'S... DIFFICULT TO DESCRIBE, ENTERPRISE. WE'RE FORWARDING OUR MEDICAL REPORTS TO YOUR CMO NOW.
"I BEAMED DOWN ALONG WITH DR. M'BENGA AND MY TOP NURSE, CHAPEL."
VRRRRMMMMMMMM
LEONARD MCCOY, CHIEF MEDICAL OFFICER, U.S.S. *ENTERPRISE.* YOU THE DOCTOR AROUND HERE?
YES, WELL, NOT IN ANY OFFICIAL CAPACITY, BUT I DO WHAT I CAN, ESPECIALLY IN A SITUATION SUCH AS THIS. I'M DOCTOR PHLOX.
NOT *THE* DOCTOR PHLOX? I TOOK ONE OF YOUR CLASSES AT THE ACADEMY.
ONE AND THE SAME, I'M AFRAID, FOR ALL THE GOOD IT'S DOING THESE POOR DEVILS.
DOCTOR, I'M CONFUSED. WHAT ARE YOU DOING WAY OUT HERE?
CALL IT SOMETHING OF A WALKABOUT. SINCE I LEFT ACTIVE DUTY AND GREW BORED WITH MY TEACHING APPOINTMENT AT THE ACADEMY, I'VE TAKEN TO JUST... EXPLORING, I GUESS. I HAPPENED ALONG THIS COLONY AND WAS FILLING IN WHILE THEY WERE BETWEEN DOCTORS. JUST MY LUCK TO BE HERE WHEN THIS HAPPENED, ALTHOUGH IT HASN'T BEEN GOOD LUCK, FOR ALL THE SUCCESS I'M HAVING.

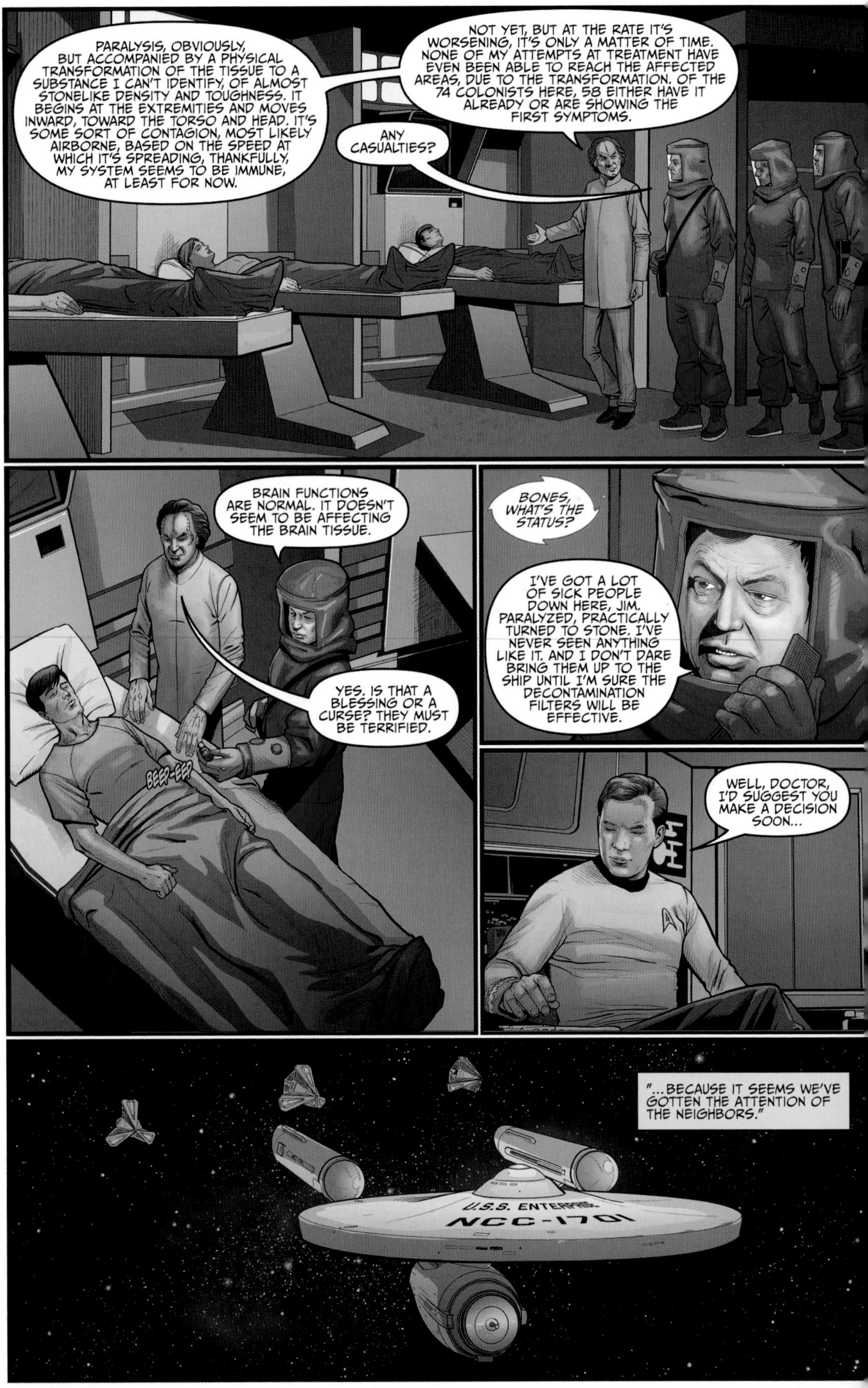
PARALYSIS, OBVIOUSLY, BUT ACCOMPANIED BY A PHYSICAL TRANSFORMATION OF THE TISSUE TO A SUBSTANCE I CAN'T IDENTIFY, OF ALMOST STONELIKE DENSITY AND TOUGHNESS. IT BEGINS AT THE EXTREMITIES AND MOVES INWARD, TOWARD THE TORSO AND HEAD. IT'S SOME SORT OF CONTAGION, MOST LIKELY AIRBORNE, BASED ON THE SPEED AT WHICH IT'S SPREADING, THANKFULLY, MY SYSTEM SEEMS TO BE IMMUNE, AT LEAST FOR NOW.
ANY CASUALTIES?
NOT YET, BUT AT THE RATE IT'S WORSENING, IT'S ONLY A MATTER OF TIME. NONE OF MY ATTEMPTS AT TREATMENT HAVE EVEN BEEN ABLE TO REACH THE AFFECTED AREAS, DUE TO THE TRANSFORMATION. OF THE 74 COLONISTS HERE, 58 EITHER HAVE IT ALREADY OR ARE SHOWING THE FIRST SYMPTOMS.
BRAIN FUNCTIONS ARE NORMAL. IT DOESN'T SEEM TO BE AFFECTING THE BRAIN TISSUE.
YES. IS THAT A BLESSING OR A CURSE? THEY MUST BE TERRIFIED.
BEEP-EEP
BONES, WHAT'S THE STATUS?
I'VE GOT A LOT OF SICK PEOPLE DOWN HERE, JIM. PARALYZED, PRACTICALLY TURNED TO STONE. I'VE NEVER SEEN ANYTHING LIKE IT. AND I DON'T DARE BRING THEM UP TO THE SHIP UNTIL I'M SURE THE DECONTAMINATION FILTERS WILL BE EFFECTIVE.
WELL, DOCTOR, I'D SUGGEST YOU MAKE A DECISION SOON...
"...BECAUSE IT SEEMS WE'VE GOTTEN THE ATTENTION OF THE NEIGHBORS."
NCC-1701

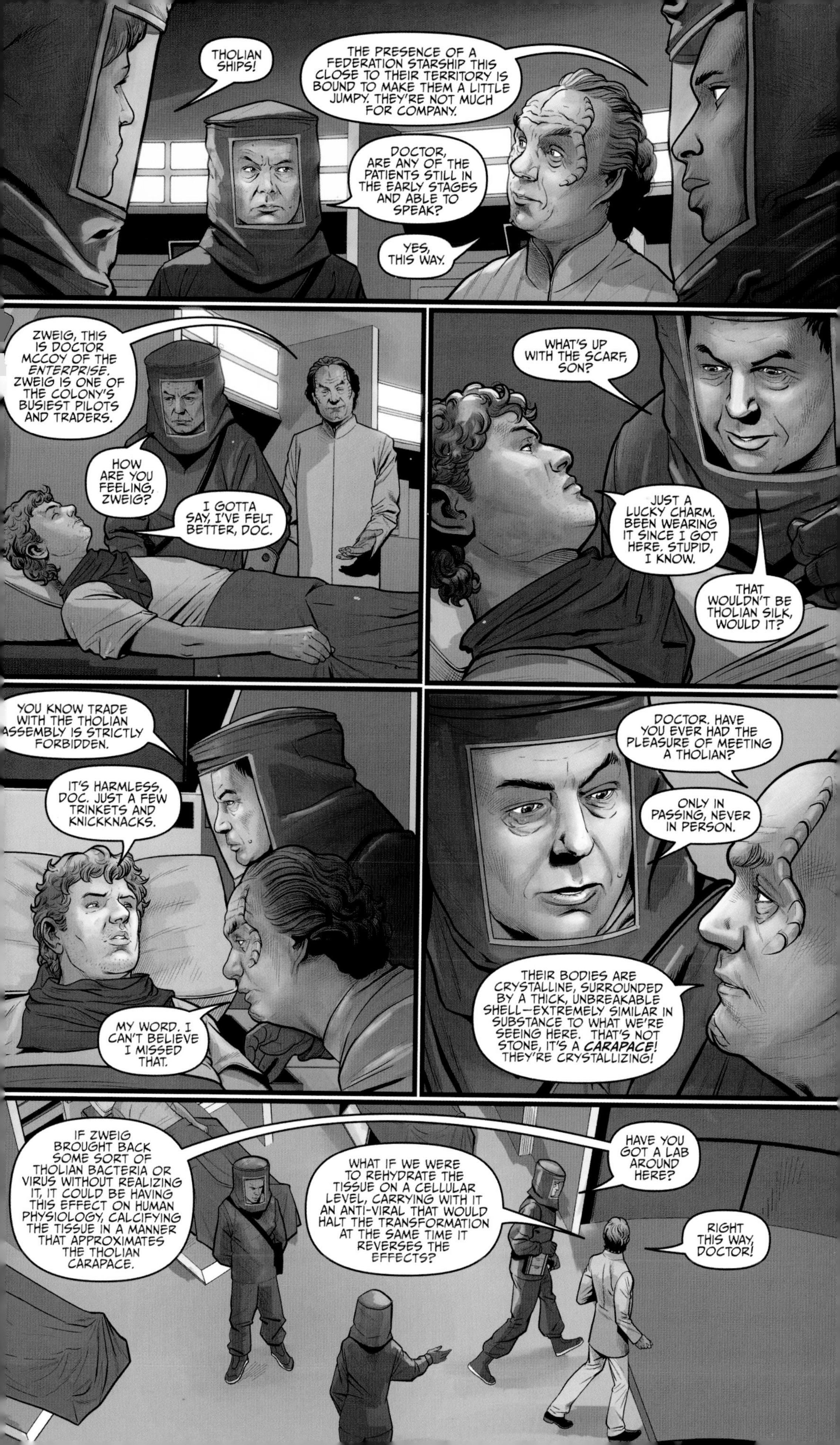
THOLIAN SHIPS!
THE PRESENCE OF A FEDERATION STARSHIP THIS CLOSE TO THEIR TERRITORY IS BOUND TO MAKE THEM A LITTLE JUMPY. THEY'RE NOT MUCH FOR COMPANY.
DOCTOR, ARE ANY OF THE PATIENTS STILL IN THE EARLY STAGES AND ABLE TO SPEAK?
YES, THIS WAY.
ZWEIG, THIS IS DOCTOR MCCOY OF THE *ENTERPRISE*. ZWEIG IS ONE OF THE COLONY'S BUSIEST PILOTS AND TRADERS.
HOW ARE YOU FEELING, ZWEIG?
I GOTTA SAY, I'VE FELT BETTER, DOC.
WHAT'S UP WITH THE SCARF, SON?
JUST A LUCKY CHARM. BEEN WEARING IT SINCE I GOT HERE. STUPID, I KNOW.
THAT WOULDN'T BE THOLIAN SILK, WOULD IT?
YOU KNOW TRADE WITH THE THOLIAN ASSEMBLY IS STRICTLY FORBIDDEN.
IT'S HARMLESS, DOC. JUST A FEW TRINKETS AND KNICKKNACKS.
MY WORD. I CAN'T BELIEVE I MISSED THAT.
DOCTOR. HAVE YOU EVER HAD THE PLEASURE OF MEETING A THOLIAN?
ONLY IN PASSING, NEVER IN PERSON.
THEIR BODIES ARE CRYSTALLINE, SURROUNDED BY A THICK, UNBREAKABLE SHELL—EXTREMELY SIMILAR IN SUBSTANCE TO WHAT WE'RE SEEING HERE. THAT'S NOT STONE, IT'S A **CARAPACE**! THEY'RE CRYSTALLIZING!
IF ZWEIG BROUGHT BACK SOME SORT OF THOLIAN BACTERIA OR VIRUS WITHOUT REALIZING IT, IT COULD BE HAVING THIS EFFECT ON HUMAN PHYSIOLOGY, CALCIFYING THE TISSUE IN A MANNER THAT APPROXIMATES THE THOLIAN CARAPACE.
WHAT IF WE WERE TO REHYDRATE THE TISSUE ON A CELLULAR LEVEL, CARRYING WITH IT AN ANTI-VIRAL THAT WOULD HALT THE TRANSFORMATION AT THE SAME TIME IT REVERSES THE EFFECTS?
HAVE YOU GOT A LAB AROUND HERE?
RIGHT THIS WAY, DOCTOR!

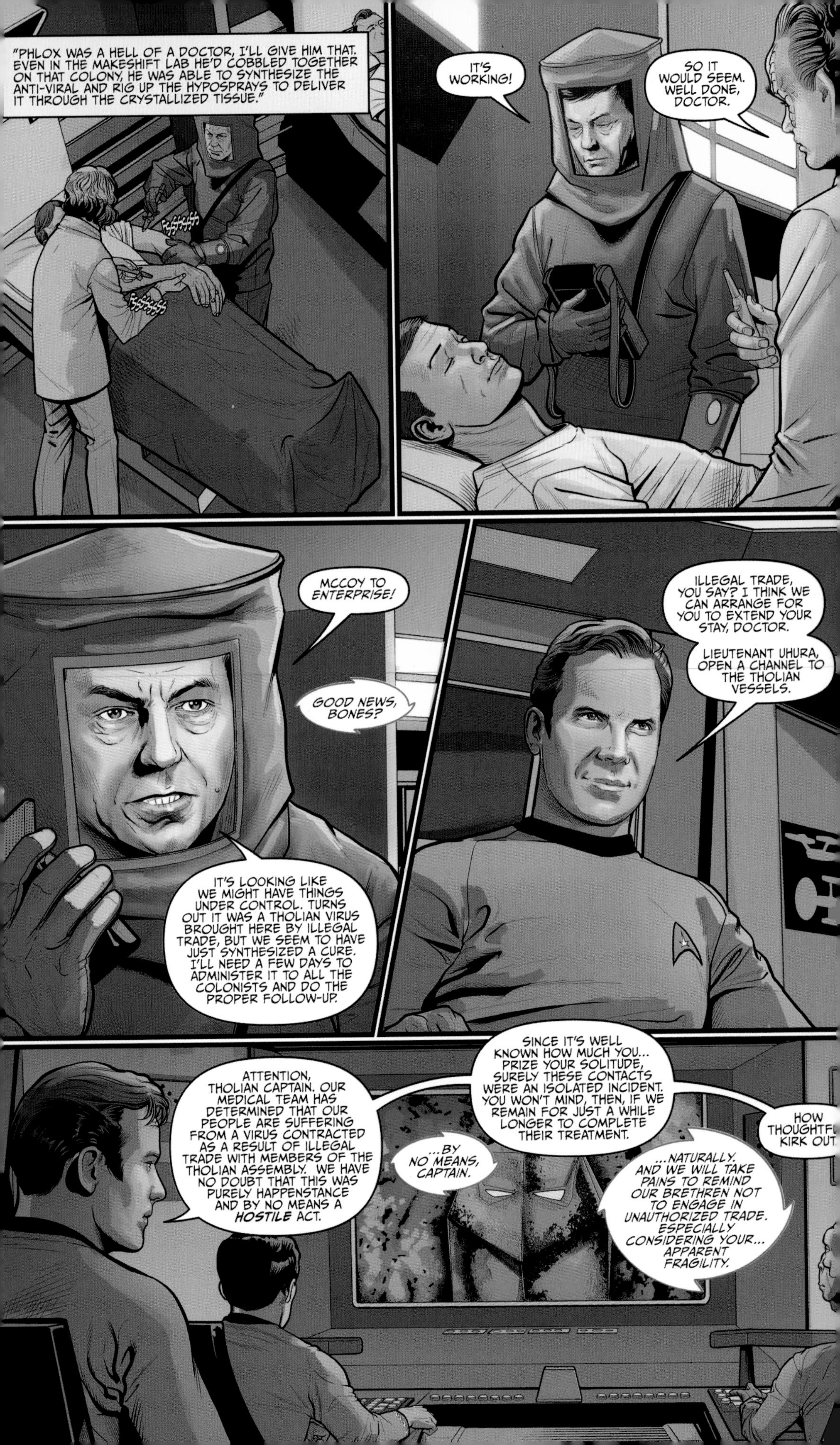
"PHLOX WAS A HELL OF A DOCTOR, I'LL GIVE HIM THAT. EVEN IN THE MAKESHIFT LAB HE'D COBBLED TOGETHER ON THAT COLONY, HE WAS ABLE TO SYNTHESIZE THE ANTI-VIRAL AND RIG UP THE HYPOSPRAYS TO DELIVER IT THROUGH THE CRYSTALLIZED TISSUE."
IT'S WORKING!
SO IT WOULD SEEM. WELL DONE, DOCTOR.
MCCOY TO *ENTERPRISE!*
GOOD NEWS, BONES?
IT'S LOOKING LIKE WE MIGHT HAVE THINGS UNDER CONTROL. TURNS OUT IT WAS A THOLIAN VIRUS BROUGHT HERE BY ILLEGAL TRADE, BUT WE SEEM TO HAVE JUST SYNTHESIZED A CURE. I'LL NEED A FEW DAYS TO ADMINISTER IT TO ALL THE COLONISTS AND DO THE PROPER FOLLOW-UP.
ILLEGAL TRADE, YOU SAY? I THINK WE CAN ARRANGE FOR YOU TO EXTEND YOUR STAY, DOCTOR.
LIEUTENANT UHURA, OPEN A CHANNEL TO THE THOLIAN VESSELS.
ATTENTION, THOLIAN CAPTAIN. OUR MEDICAL TEAM HAS DETERMINED THAT OUR PEOPLE ARE SUFFERING FROM A VIRUS CONTRACTED AS A RESULT OF ILLEGAL TRADE WITH MEMBERS OF THE THOLIAN ASSEMBLY. WE HAVE NO DOUBT THAT THIS WAS PURELY HAPPENSTANCE AND BY NO MEANS A **HOSTILE** ACT.
...BY NO MEANS, CAPTAIN.
SINCE IT'S WELL KNOWN HOW MUCH YOU... PRIZE YOUR SOLITUDE, SURELY THESE CONTACTS WERE AN ISOLATED INCIDENT. YOU WON'T MIND, THEN, IF WE REMAIN FOR JUST A WHILE LONGER TO COMPLETE THEIR TREATMENT.
...NATURALLY. AND WE WILL TAKE PAINS TO REMIND OUR BRETHREN NOT TO ENGAGE IN UNAUTHORIZED TRADE. ESPECIALLY CONSIDERING YOUR... APPARENT FRAGILITY.
HOW

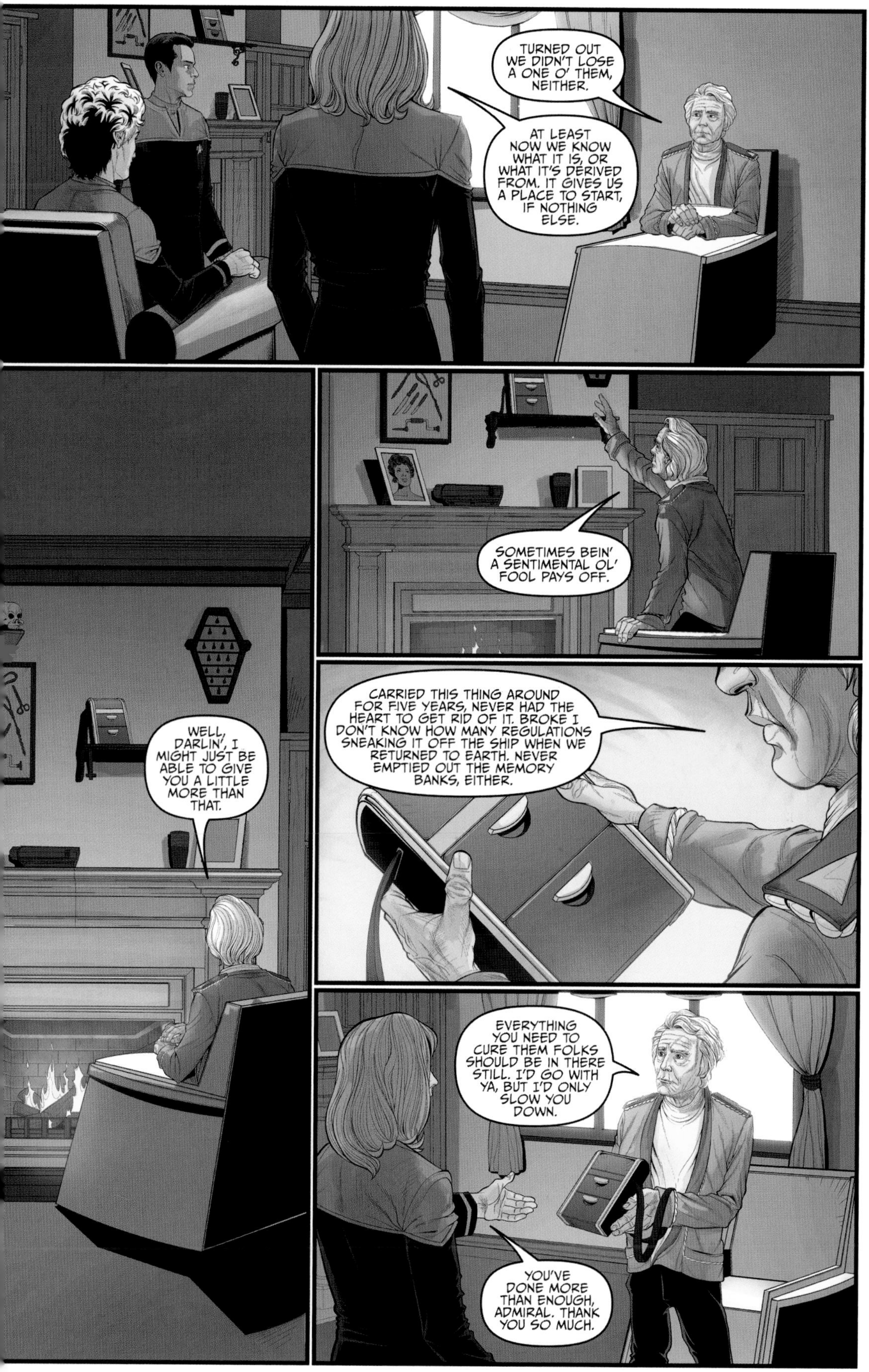
TURNED OUT WE DIDN'T LOSE A ONE O' THEM, NEITHER.
AT LEAST NOW WE KNOW WHAT IT IS, OR WHAT IT'S DERIVED FROM. IT GIVES US A PLACE TO START, IF NOTHING ELSE.
WELL, DARLIN', I MIGHT JUST BE ABLE TO GIVE YOU A LITTLE MORE THAN THAT.
SOMETIMES BEIN' A SENTIMENTAL OL' FOOL PAYS OFF.
CARRIED THIS THING AROUND FOR FIVE YEARS, NEVER HAD THE HEART TO GET RID OF IT. BROKE I DON'T KNOW HOW MANY REGULATIONS SNEAKING IT OFF THE SHIP WHEN WE RETURNED TO EARTH. NEVER EMPTIED OUT THE MEMORY BANKS, EITHER.
EVERYTHING YOU NEED TO CURE THEM FOLKS SHOULD BE IN THERE STILL. I'D GO WITH YA, BUT I'D ONLY SLOW YOU DOWN.
YOU'VE DONE MORE THAN ENOUGH, ADMIRAL. THANK YOU SO MUCH.

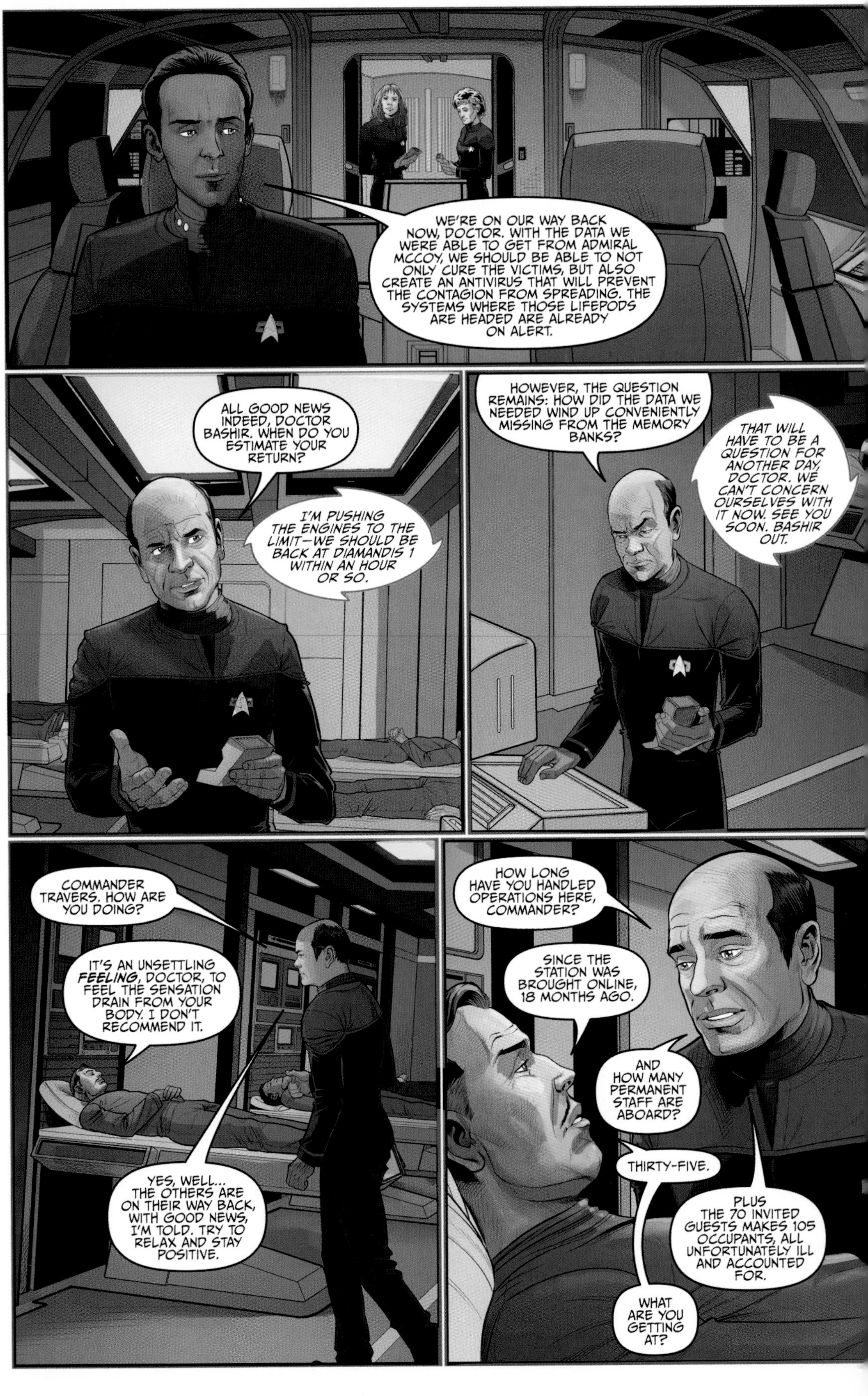

WE'RE ON OUR WAY BACK NOW, DOCTOR. WITH THE DATA WE WERE ABLE TO GET FROM ADMIRAL MCCOY, WE SHOULD BE ABLE TO NOT ONLY CURE THE VICTIMS, BUT ALSO CREATE AN ANTIVIRUS THAT WILL PREVENT THE CONTAGION FROM SPREADING. THE SYSTEMS WHERE THOSE LIFEPODS ARE HEADED ARE ALREADY ON ALERT.
ALL GOOD NEWS INDEED, DOCTOR BASHIR. WHEN DO YOU ESTIMATE YOUR RETURN?
I'M PUSHING THE ENGINES TO THE LIMIT—WE SHOULD BE BACK AT DIAMANDIS 1 WITHIN AN HOUR OR SO.
HOWEVER, THE QUESTION REMAINS: HOW DID THE DATA WE NEEDED WIND UP CONVENIENTLY MISSING FROM THE MEMORY BANKS?
THAT WILL HAVE TO BE A QUESTION FOR ANOTHER DAY, DOCTOR. WE CAN'T CONCERN OURSELVES WITH IT NOW. SEE YOU SOON. BASHIR OUT.
COMMANDER TRAVERS. HOW ARE YOU DOING?
IT'S AN UNSETTLING FEELING, DOCTOR, TO FEEL THE SENSATION DRAIN FROM YOUR BODY. I DON'T RECOMMEND IT.
YES, WELL... THE OTHERS ARE ON THEIR WAY BACK, WITH GOOD NEWS, I'M TOLD. TRY TO RELAX AND STAY POSITIVE.
HOW LONG HAVE YOU HANDLED OPERATIONS HERE, COMMANDER?
SINCE THE STATION WAS BROUGHT ONLINE, 18 MONTHS AGO.
AND HOW MANY PERMANENT STAFF ARE ABOARD?
THIRTY-FIVE.
PLUS THE 70 INVITED GUESTS MAKES 105 OCCUPANTS, ALL UNFORTUNATELY ILL AND ACCOUNTED FOR.
WHAT ARE YOU GETTING AT?

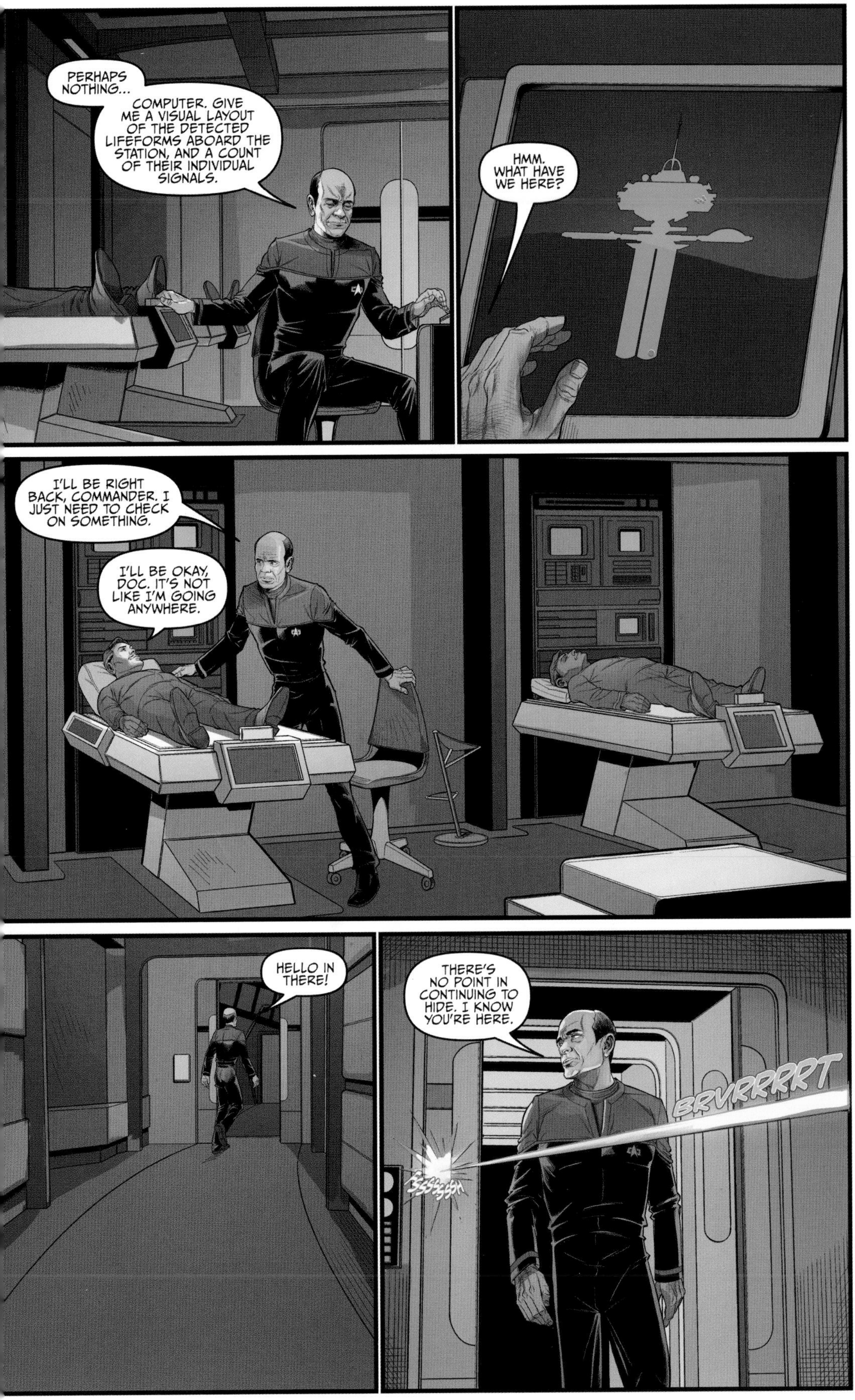
PERHAPS NOTHING...
COMPUTER. GIVE ME A VISUAL LAYOUT OF THE DETECTED LIFEFORMS ABOARD THE STATION, AND A COUNT OF THEIR INDIVIDUAL SIGNALS.
HMM. WHAT HAVE WE HERE?
I'LL BE RIGHT BACK, COMMANDER. I JUST NEED TO CHECK ON SOMETHING.
I'LL BE OKAY, DOC. IT'S NOT LIKE I'M GOING ANYWHERE.
HELLO IN THERE!
THERE'S NO POINT IN CONTINUING TO HIDE. I KNOW YOU'RE HERE.
BRVRRRRT
SSSSSSSH

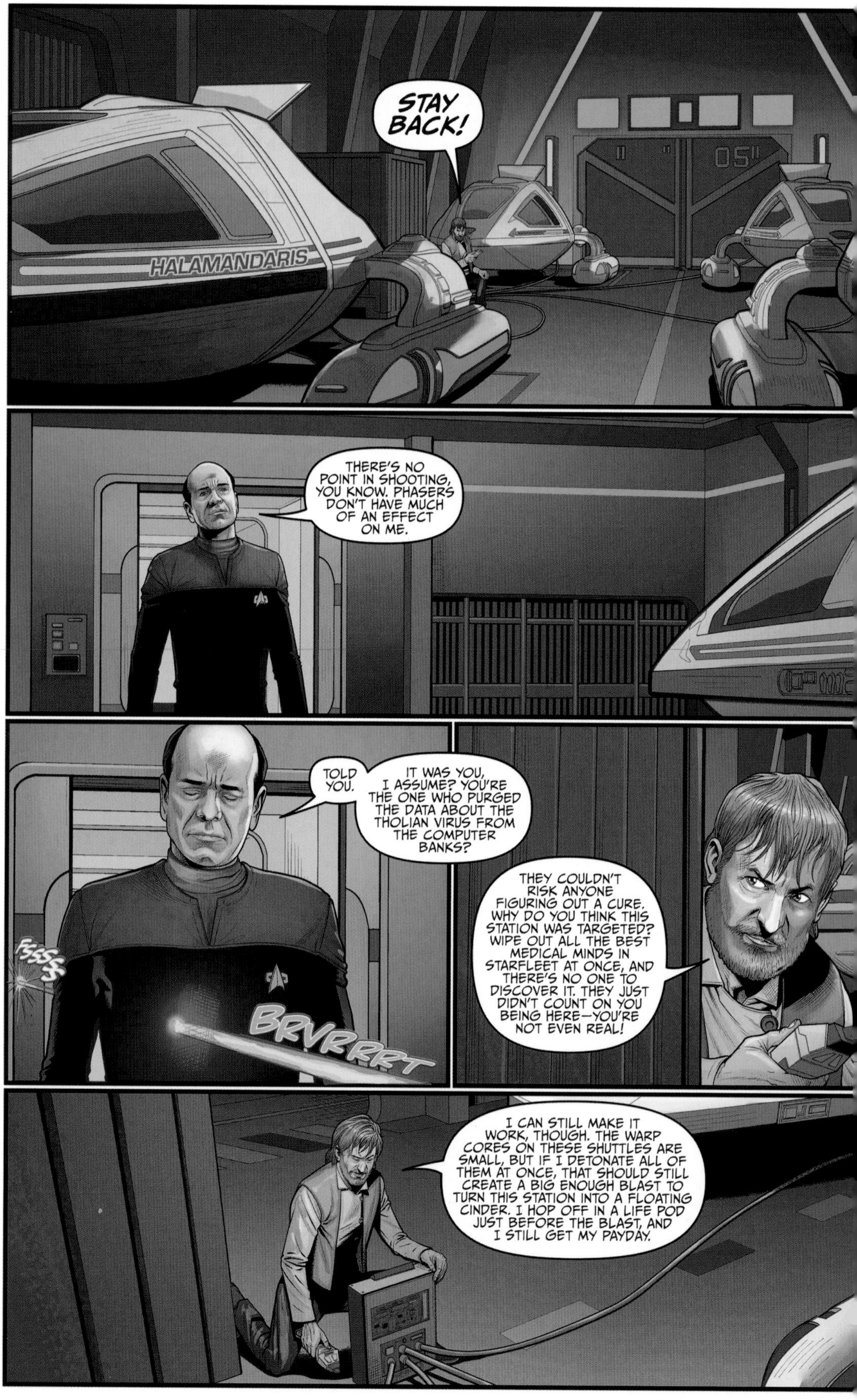
STAY BACK!
HALAMANDARIS
THERE'S NO POINT IN SHOOTING, YOU KNOW. PHASERS DON'T HAVE MUCH OF AN EFFECT ON ME.
FSSSS
BRVRRRT
TOLD YOU.
IT WAS YOU, I ASSUME? YOU'RE THE ONE WHO PURGED THE DATA ABOUT THE THOLIAN VIRUS FROM THE COMPUTER BANKS?
THEY COULDN'T RISK ANYONE FIGURING OUT A CURE. WHY DO YOU THINK THIS STATION WAS TARGETED? WIPE OUT ALL THE BEST MEDICAL MINDS IN STARFLEET AT ONCE, AND THERE'S NO ONE TO DISCOVER IT. THEY JUST DIDN'T COUNT ON YOU BEING HERE—YOU'RE NOT EVEN REAL!
I CAN STILL MAKE IT WORK, THOUGH. THE WARP CORES ON THESE SHUTTLES ARE SMALL, BUT IF I DETONATE ALL OF THEM AT ONCE, THAT SHOULD STILL CREATE A BIG ENOUGH BLAST TO TURN THIS STATION INTO A FLOATING CINDER. I HOP OFF IN A LIFE POD JUST BEFORE THE BLAST, AND I STILL GET MY PAYDAY.

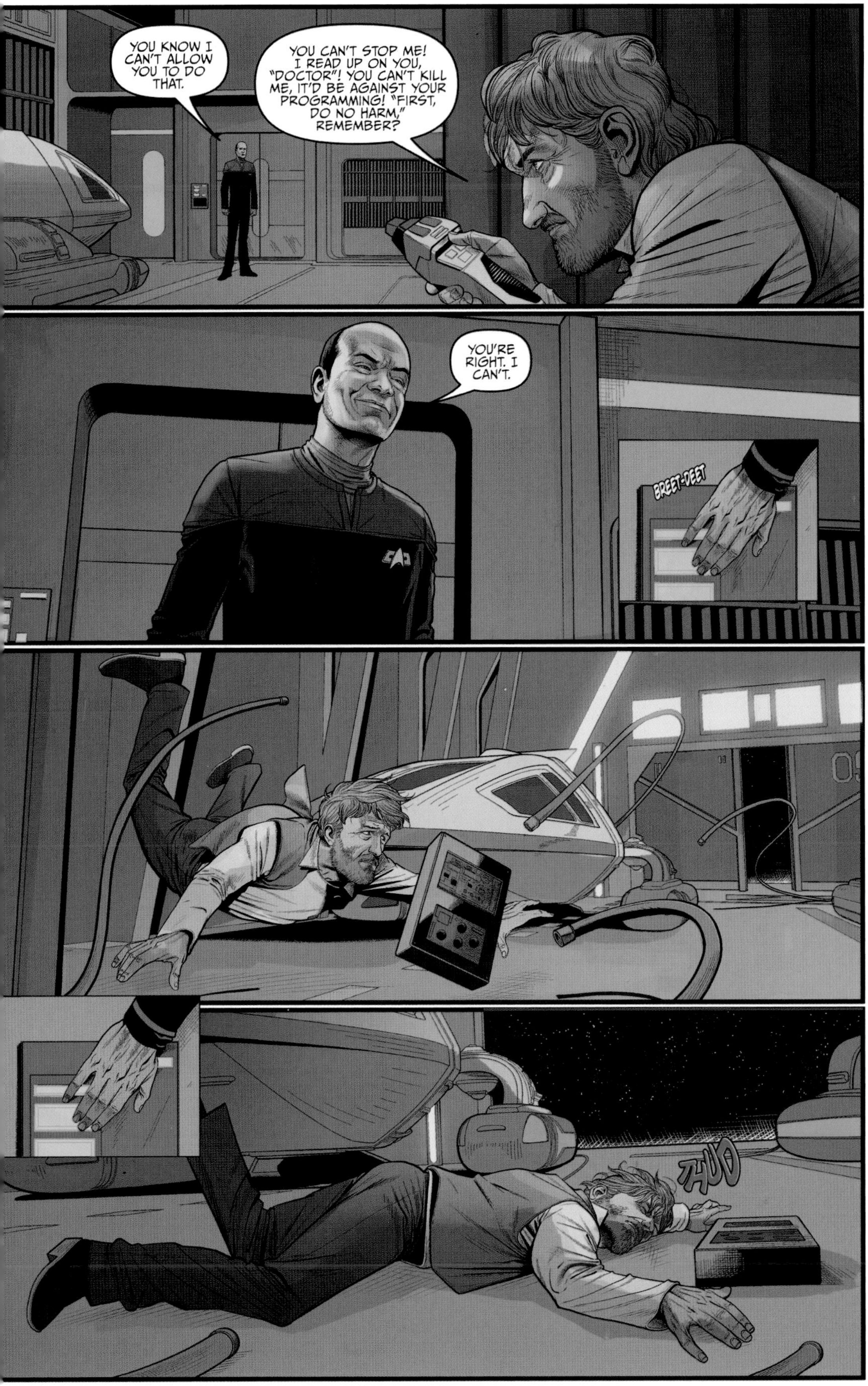
YOU KNOW I CAN'T ALLOW YOU TO DO THAT.
YOU CAN'T STOP ME! I READ UP ON YOU, "DOCTOR"! YOU CAN'T KILL ME, IT'D BE AGAINST YOUR PROGRAMMING! "FIRST, DO NO HARM," REMEMBER?
YOU'RE RIGHT. I CAN'T.
BREET-DEET
THUD

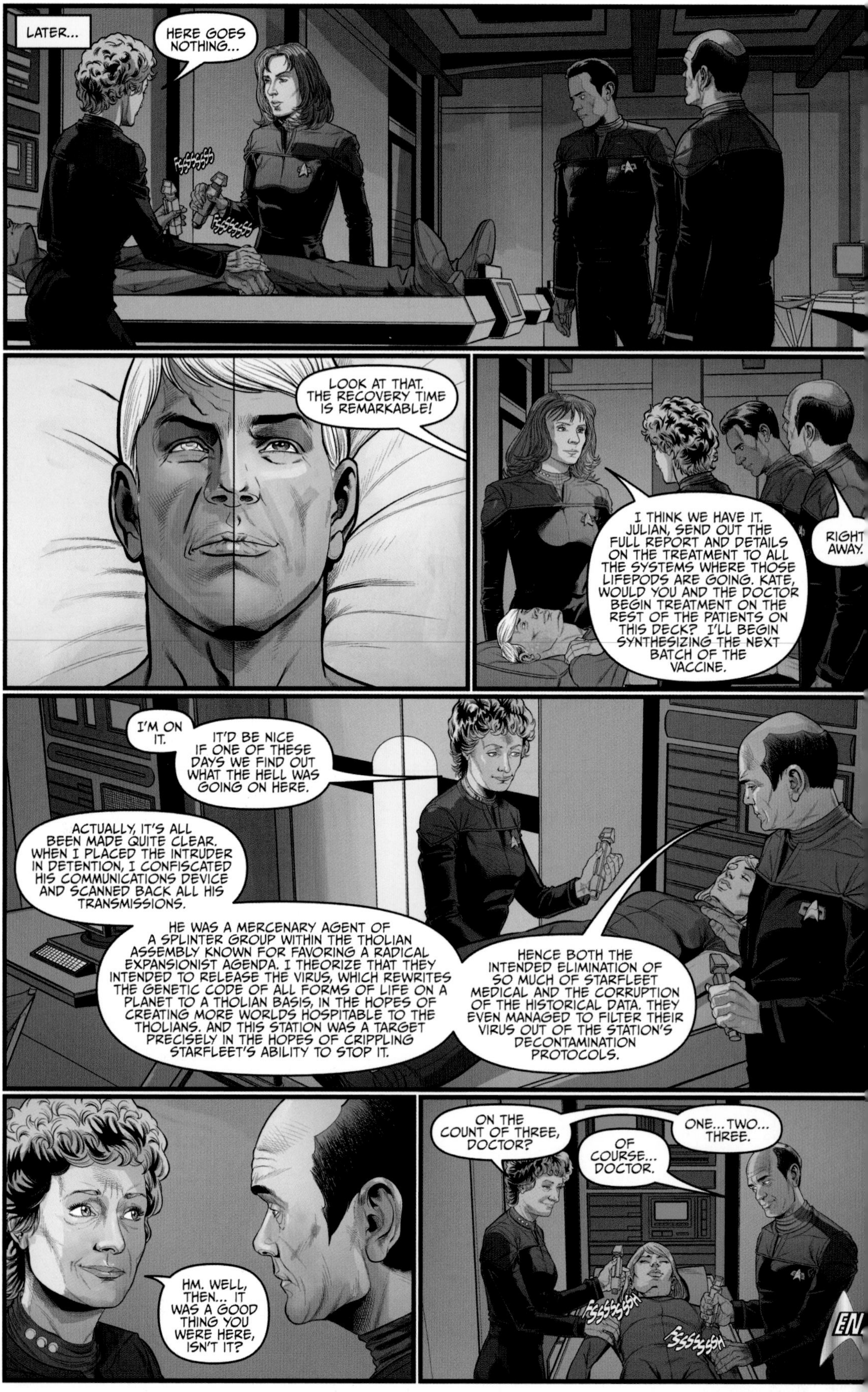
LATER...
HERE GOES NOTHING...
FSSSSSS
FSSSSSS
LOOK AT THAT. THE RECOVERY TIME IS REMARKABLE!
I THINK WE HAVE IT. JULIAN, SEND OUT THE FULL REPORT AND DETAILS ON THE TREATMENT TO ALL THE SYSTEMS WHERE THOSE LIFEPODS ARE GOING. KATE, WOULD YOU AND THE DOCTOR BEGIN TREATMENT ON THE REST OF THE PATIENTS ON THIS DECK? I'LL BEGIN SYNTHESIZING THE NEXT BATCH OF THE VACCINE.
RIGHT AWAY.
I'M ON IT.
IT'D BE NICE IF ONE OF THESE DAYS WE FIND OUT WHAT THE HELL WAS GOING ON HERE.
ACTUALLY, IT'S ALL BEEN MADE QUITE CLEAR. WHEN I PLACED THE INTRUDER IN DETENTION, I CONFISCATED HIS COMMUNICATIONS DEVICE AND SCANNED BACK ALL HIS TRANSMISSIONS.
HE WAS A MERCENARY AGENT OF A SPLINTER GROUP WITHIN THE THOLIAN ASSEMBLY KNOWN FOR FAVORING A RADICAL EXPANSIONIST AGENDA. I THEORIZE THAT THEY INTENDED TO RELEASE THE VIRUS, WHICH REWRITES THE GENETIC CODE OF ALL FORMS OF LIFE ON A PLANET TO A THOLIAN BASIS, IN THE HOPES OF CREATING MORE WORLDS HOSPITABLE TO THE THOLIANS. AND THIS STATION WAS A TARGET PRECISELY IN THE HOPES OF CRIPPLING STARFLEET'S ABILITY TO STOP IT.
HENCE BOTH THE INTENDED ELIMINATION OF SO MUCH OF STARFLEET MEDICAL AND THE CORRUPTION OF THE HISTORICAL DATA. THEY EVEN MANAGED TO FILTER THEIR VIRUS OUT OF THE STATION'S DECONTAMINATION PROTOCOLS.
HM. WELL, THEN... IT WAS A GOOD THING YOU WERE HERE, ISN'T IT?
ON THE COUNT OF THREE, DOCTOR?
OF COURSE... DOCTOR.
ONE... TWO... THREE.
FSSSSSSSH
FSSSSSSSH

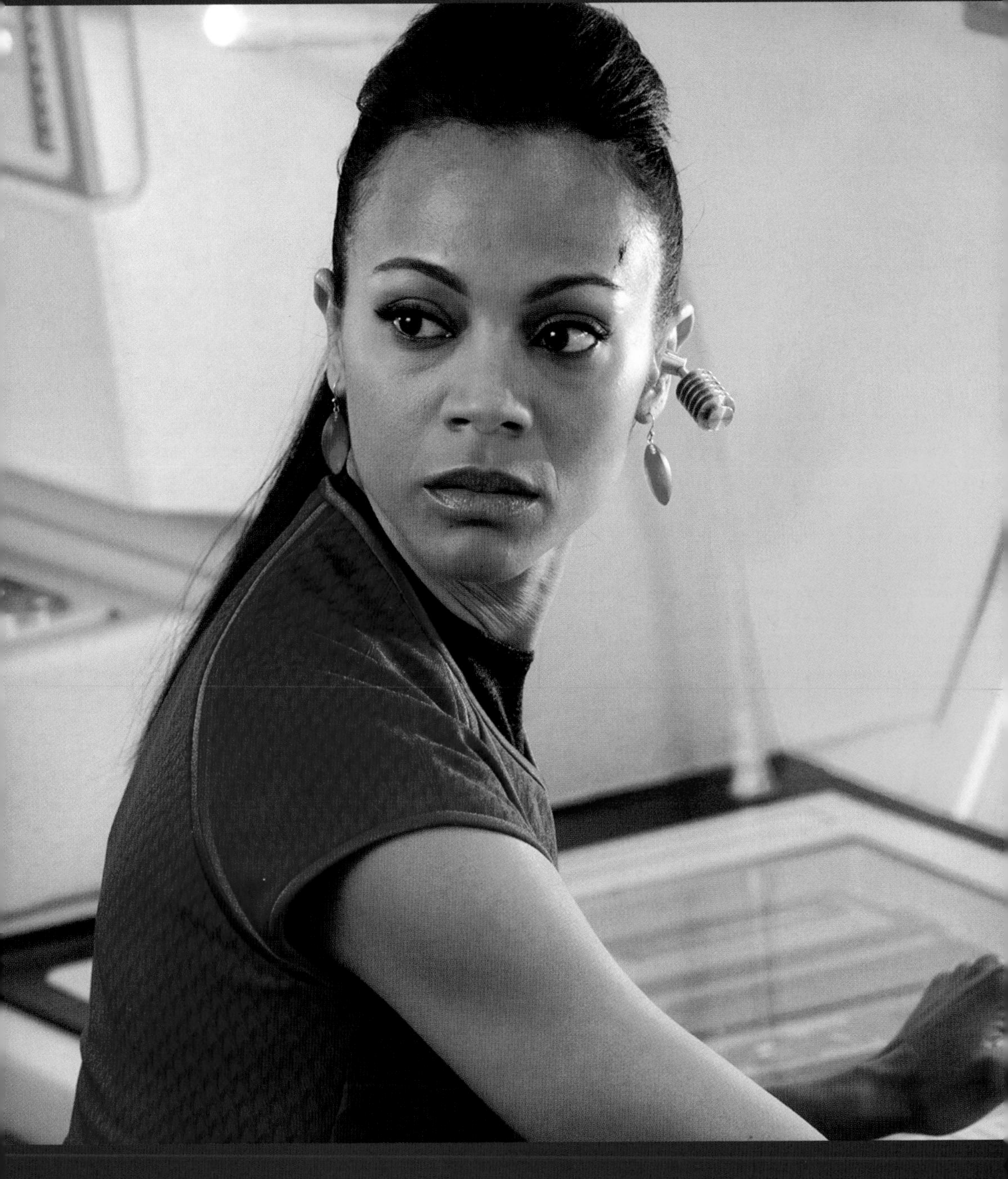

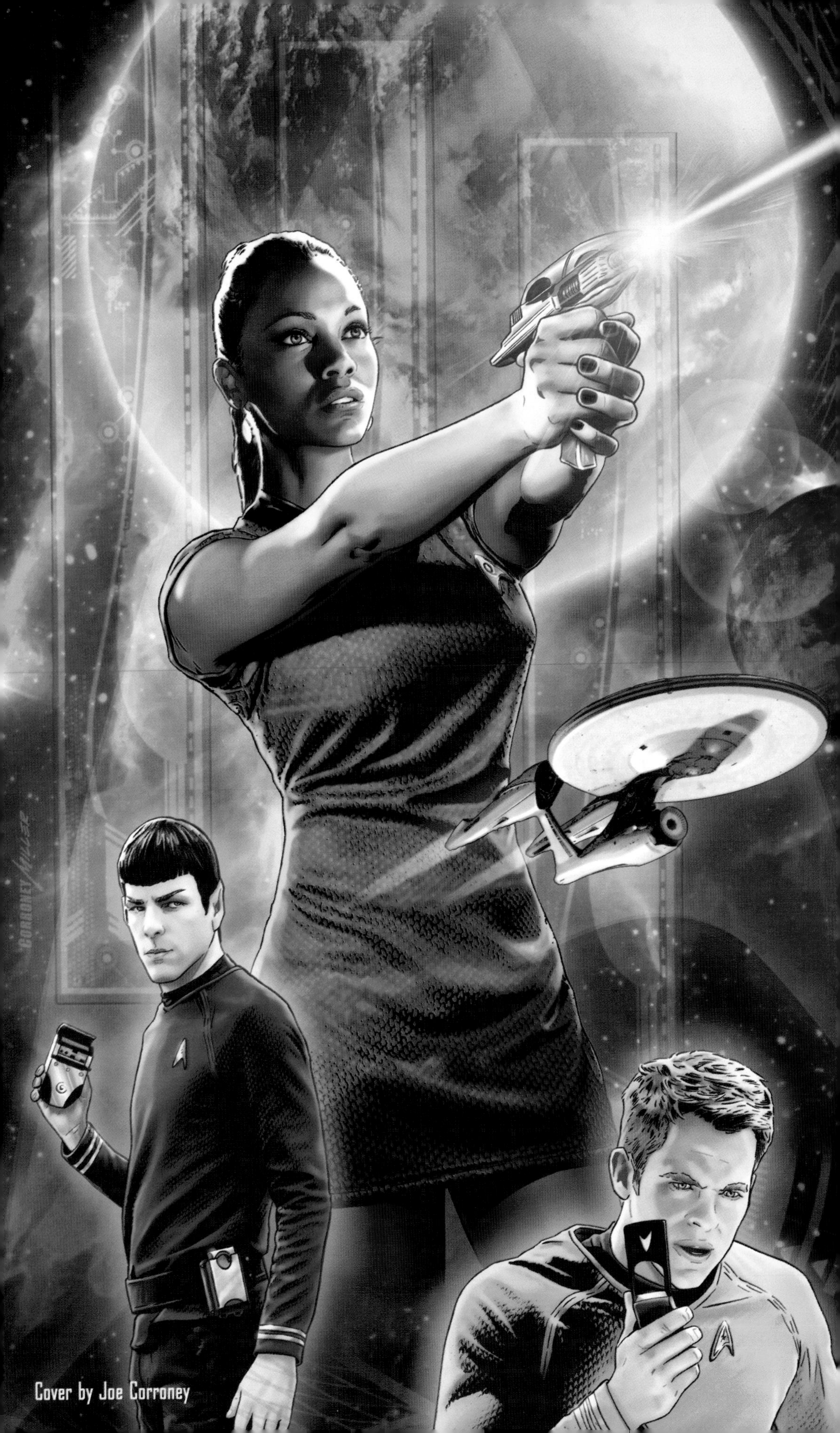

Cover by Joe Corroney

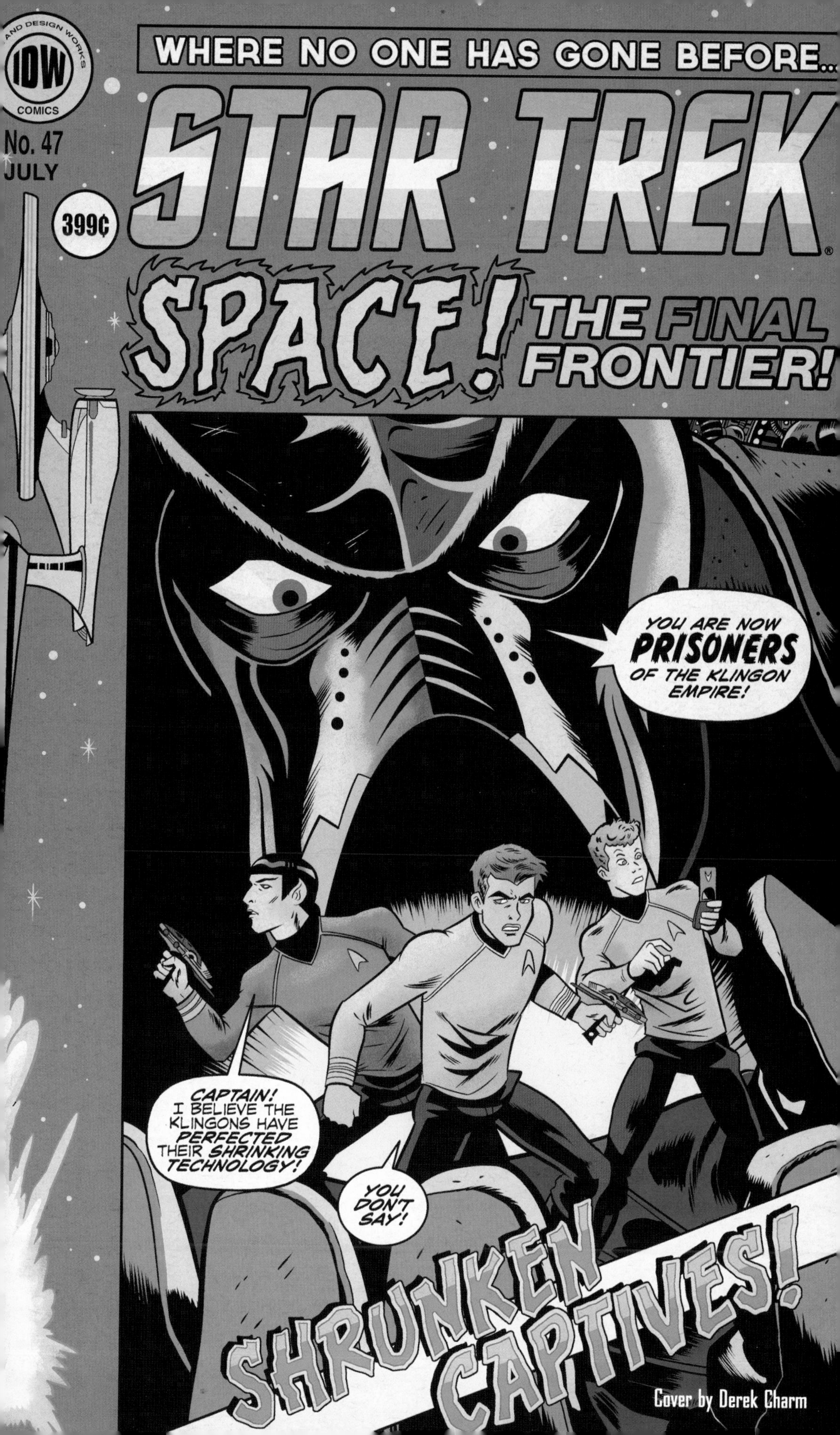
IDW
IDEA AND DESIGN WORKS
COMICS
No. 47
JULY
399¢
WHERE NO ONE HAS GONE BEFORE...
STAR TREK®
SPACE! THE FINAL FRONTIER!
YOU ARE NOW PRISONERS OF THE KLINGON EMPIRE!
CAPTAIN! I BELIEVE THE KLINGONS HAVE PERFECTED THEIR SHRINKING TECHNOLOGY!
YOU DON'T SAY!
SHRUNKEN CAPTIVES!
Cover by Derek Charm

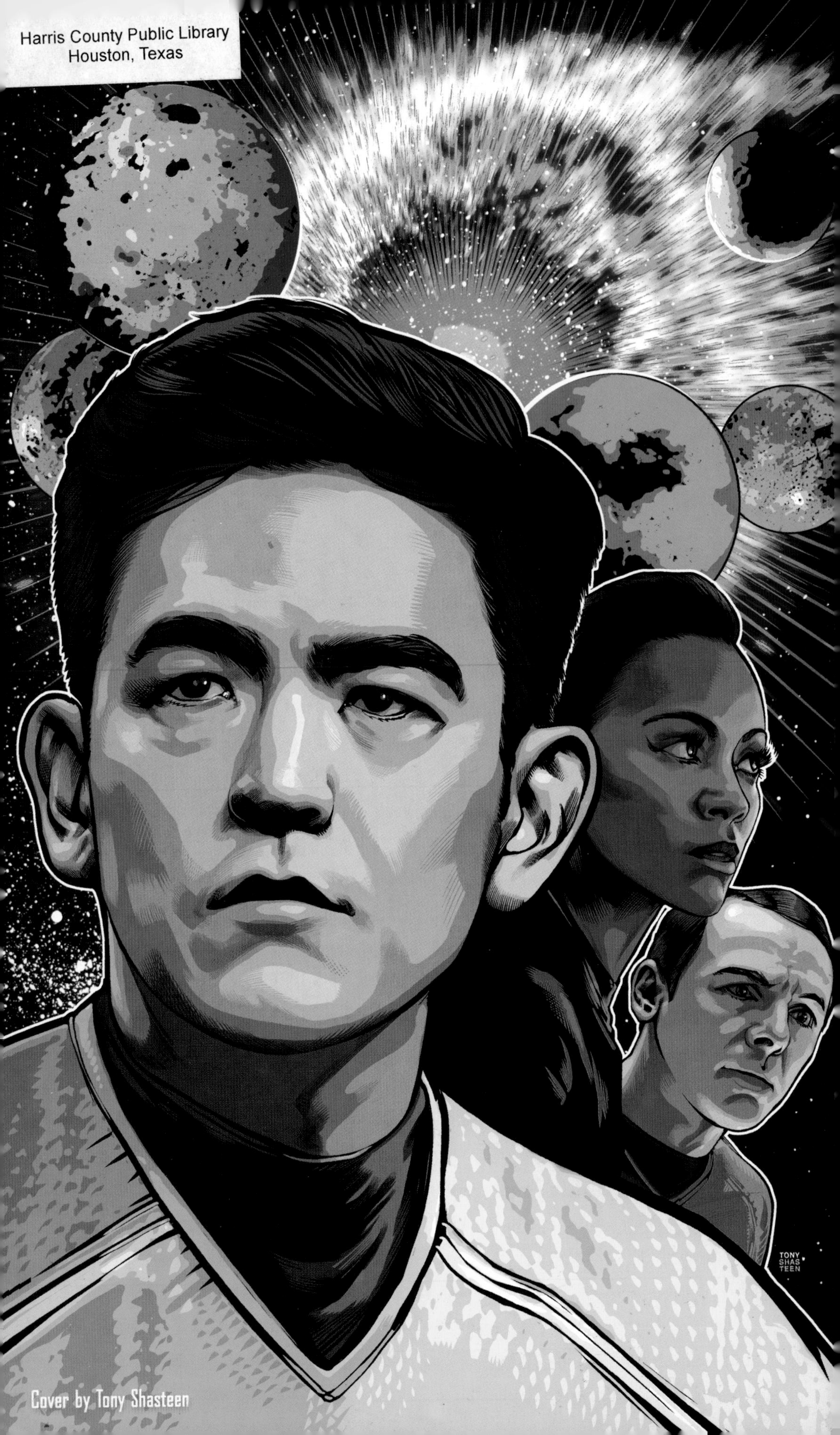
TONY
SHAS
TEEN

Cover by Tony Shasteen